OCT 2016

WINGS

of

FIRE

Also by Charles Todd

A Test of Wills

WINGS

of

FIRE

Charles Todd

St. Martin's Press · New York

A THOMAS DUNNE BOOK.
An imprint of St. Martin's Press.

Design by Nancy Resnick

Library of Congress Cataloging-in-Publication Data

Todd, Charles.
    Wings of fire : an Inspector Ian Rutledge mystery / Charles Todd.
       p. cm.
    "A Thomas Dunne book."
    ISBN 0-312-17064-5
    I. Title.
PS3570.O37W56   1998
813'.54—dc21

                                  97-39643
                                     CIP

First edition: March 1998

10 9 8 7 6 5 4 3 2

For D

You know why.

WINGS
of
FIRE

1

The bodies were discovered by Mrs. Trepol, widow, occupation housekeeper and cook to the deceased.

It was not a morning of swirling sea mists and gray drifting sheets of rain, although afterward Mrs. Trepol remembered it that way.

In fact, the clouds had lifted in the night. The sea was gleaming in patchy May sunlight down below the headland, the house cast long shadows across the wet grass, and an unseasonable warmth already touched the light breeze as she came out of the wood at the side of the big kitchen garden. Her eyes jealously studied the cabbages in their neat rows, measuring them against the size of her own, deciding that hers still had an edge. Well, of course they should! She'd always had the finest garden in the village, and hadn't she proved it with ribbons won at every Harvest Festival? The onions were taller—surely they hadn't been that high on Saturday? But anyone could grow onions. Her peas were already straggling up the sticks she'd set beside them, and growing peas was an art. No sticks stood beside these sad little stalks! She'd be cooking hers before these saw their first blossoms. Old Wilkins, who had kept the Hall's gardens and stables since the lads had all gone off to the war, knew more about horses than vegetables.

Not that he didn't crow over his work.

"Your carrots look a mite *small*, Mrs. Trepol," he'd say, hanging over the rock wall by her front walk. "Compared to mine, that is." Or, "Them beans is spindly. Put 'em in late, did ye?"

Nosy old fool!

Her complacency restored, she went up the three steps to the kitchen door and let herself in with her key as she always did. Not that this was her day to clean. Mondays normally were her day off. But tomorrow she wanted to visit her sister—Naomi's husband had offered to take them both to market in the morning—and Miss Livia never minded if occasionally she shifted her time.

The long stone passage was cool and quiet. At the end of it, she took off her coat, hung it on the peg as she always did, pulled her apron over her head, then stepped into the heart of her domain. And noticed at once that the breakfast dishes, usually neatly stacked on the drain board, hadn't been brought down. She looked around the kitchen, saw that it was much as she'd left it on Saturday evening, not even a crumb marring her scrubbed floor, saw too that no one had opened the curtains.

Oh, my dear! she thought, pityingly, Miss Livia must've had another bad night, and she's still asleep!

Going up to the back parlor, she found that those curtains were also closed. And for the first time she felt a tremor of alarm.

Mr. Nicholas always opened them at first light, to watch the sea. He'd said once that it made him feel alive to see the dawn come and touch the water . . .

Miss Livia must have had a *terrible* night, then, if he'd missed the dawn on her account! Mrs. Trepol had never known that to happen in all the years she'd worked in the house. Mr. Nicholas was always up at first light . . . always . . .

She went out into the hall and looked up the curving stairs.

"Mr. Nicholas?" she called softly. "I've come. Is there anything I can do? Would you care for a cup of tea?"

The silence around her echoed her words and she felt very uneasy now. Surely if he was sitting by Miss Livia's bed, he'd have heard her and come out to speak to her?

Unless something was wrong with *him*—

2

She hurried up the stairs and went down the passage to Mr. Nicholas' room, tapping lightly on the panel. No one answered. After a moment's uncertainty, she turned the knob and opened the door.

The bed was made. From the look of it, it had not been slept in. Mr. Nicholas could always make it neatly, but never as smoothly as she did. This was her work. *Saturday's* work . . .

She went back down the passage and knocked lightly at Miss Livia's door. Again there was no answer. She opened it gently, so as not to disturb Miss Livia, or Mr. Nicholas, if he'd fallen asleep in the chair by his sister's bed, and peered around the edge.

That bed too was untouched. The coverlet was as smooth as glass. Like Mr. Nicholas'. And there was no one in the chairs.

Suddenly very frightened, she listened to the house around her. Surely if Miss Livia had been taken down to the doctor's surgery in the night, there'd be a message left in the kitchen! But this wasn't her day; Mr. Nicholas wouldn't have known she was coming in. Well, then, someone would have mentioned it at services on Sunday morning. Eager to gossip—

Going to the long study at the end of the gallery, which Mr. Nicholas and Miss Livia shared, Mrs. Trepol knocked and waited, then reached for the knob as she had twice before.

And then fright turned suddenly to terror. She quickly drew her hand back, bringing it to her flat chest almost protectively, her heart thudding uncomfortably beneath her fingertips.

She stood there for several seconds, staring at the shut door, her voice refusing to call Mr. Nicholas' name, her hand refusing to reach again for the brass knob.

Whatever was behind that door, it was something she couldn't face, not alone, not with her heart hammering like it was going to jump out of her chest and run away.

She turned and fled down the stairs, stumbling on the old, worn treads, nearly falling headfirst in her haste, thinking only of the safety of the kitchen but not stopping there, rushing down the passage, on into the early sunlight and back the way she'd come, toward the village and Dr. Hawkins. Only then did she remember her coat, but nothing would have taken her back into that house. Shivering, on the verge of tears, driven by uncertainty, she ran heavily and awkwardly through the gardens, heedless of the cabbages, and towards the copse of trees where the path to the village began.

What was left of the family gathered in the drawing room for a drink when everyone else had finally gone home, but conversation was stilted, uneasy, as if they were strangers meeting for the first time and had yet to find common ground. The truth was, they *felt* like strangers. In the circumstances. Unsettled, uncomfortable. Isolated by their thoughts.

Then Stephen said abruptly, "Why do you suppose they did it?"

There was an odd silence. No one, thank God, had asked that all the long day! Not through the services nor the burials nor the reception at the Hall afterward, where friends and villagers had mingled, talking in subdued voices. Remembering Olivia and Nicholas, recalling some small incident or ordinary encounter, a conversation—all safely in the past. Avoiding the how and why of death, as if by tacit agreement. Avid curiosity dwelt in their eyes, but they were sensitive to the delicacy of the situation. *Suicides.*

No one had spoken of the poems, either.

Susannah said quickly, "What business is it of ours? They're dead. Let that be the end of it."

"Good God, Nicholas and Olivia were your brother and sister—"

"Half brother and sister!" she retorted, as if that might distance her from real pain.

"All right, then, *half* brother and sister! Haven't you even wondered about it? Don't you feel anything?"

"I feel grateful that they could be buried with Mother in the family vault," Susannah answered. "Thanks to the rector's kindness! In the old days, it wouldn't have been allowed, you know that. Suicides weren't buried in the *churchyard*, much less in the crypt! And we'd have been ostracized along with them. It's still bad enough, God knows. London will be an ordeal, facing all my friends, knowing pity's behind their sympathy—" She stopped, unwilling to lay her emotions out, raw and painful, for the others to paw over. "I don't want to talk about it! What we've got to face now is, what's to become of the house?"

4

Daniel said, "I'd always understood it was left to the survivors to sell." He glanced around the room. Susannah. Rachel. Stephen. Himself. He was Susannah's husband, but he'd always been treated as one of the family. That had been a source of great pride to him. With feelings running so high over the Troubles in Ireland, he might have been seen as less, well, *acceptable* socially, without the Trevelyan connection behind him. Not that the Trevelyans were so high and mighty, but they were *old* blood, respected. His eyes moved on. Cormac. Olivia and Nicholas'd left Cormac out of their wills. Daniel had found himself wondering, sometimes, who Cormac's Irish mother had been—if it had made a difference. Cormac was a FitzHugh, but not a Trevelyan. Not Rosamund's child. Nor wed to one of Rosamund's children. Nor, like Rachel, a cousin on the Marlowe side.

Rachel said, "Yes, that's what I'd been told. Unless they changed their minds. At the end." As they'd changed their minds about living . . . She took a deep breath and refused to think about it. And instead found herself listening again. To the sounds of the house. Since she'd walked through the door two days ago, she'd felt it. Swallowing her, drawing the very breath from her body. Frightening her with a stillness that wasn't stillness . . .

Stephen said, moving his cane along the pattern of the Persian carpet's intertwined medallions. "Well, I for one know what I think we *should* do. We should turn this place into a memorial. A museum in Livia's memory."

Susannah stared at him in surprise.

Cormac said, "Don't be ridiculous! It's the last thing she'd have wanted! Olivia spent her entire life hiding from people. Do you think she'd be pleased to have strangers wandering about in here *now*?" He moved gracefully around the room, tall and oddly beautiful in a very masculine way.

"It isn't up to you," Stephen retorted. He tried not to watch. He tried not to resent that grace. And couldn't help it. The war had left him with half a foot. And this damned cane. Trenchfoot and gangrene, for God's sake, not honorable wounds! No more long walks over the Downs, no more tennis, no more dancing, no more riding to hounds. He could still bowl at cricket, but awkwardly, terrified he'd lose his balance and fall flat on his face.

"All the same, Cormac's right," Rachel said. "I can't imagine this place a museum. Livia would feel it was a betrayal."

"Think of the cost," Daniel added. "You'd need money for upkeep, repairs, staff. A trust of some sort. Olivia may have been famous, but she wasn't *that* rich! In her own right, I mean."

"*We* could afford it," Stephen persisted. "Or perhaps the National Trust would be interested."

"Not without a handsome endowment," Cormac replied, stopping by the windows, his back to them. "It would take more than three quarters of your inheritance."

"What are you saying? That we divide up the furniture—the sideboard for me, the piano for you, and who's going to take the grandfather's clock?—then sell the house and grounds? Pretend Olivia and Nicholas never existed, that the family—what's left of it—doesn't *care*?" Stephen was steadily losing his temper.

"You want a museum to your own memory, not hers," Susannah said suddenly. "It's *your* immortality you're thinking about, don't pretend it isn't!"

"Mine?"

"Yes, yours! The war's changed you, Stephen—and not for the better. Oh, I've heard you at dinners since she was found out, simpering when someone asks who the love poems were written about. You think it's you, her darling, her favorite!" There was heavy sarcasm in her quiet voice. He'd been Mother's favorite too. He was Susannah's twin—and always so much more than her equal.

"Well, what if they were written about me? I've as much right as any of you to think what I please. You're greedy, that's what it is, wanting the money, wanting every penny you can squeeze. And that's why she left her literary estate to me. A pity she didn't include the house as well!"

"Who died last?" Rachel put in diffidently, not sure she wanted to know. "If it was Nicholas, then it's his will we're haggling over, not hers."

"They were the same. Everything to each other, and if that failed, the poems to Stephen, and the house to the four survivors, jointly,"

6

Cormac told her over his shoulder. There was no resentment in the level voice that he hadn't been included.

"I'd hate to see day-trippers wandering through here," Susannah said, "staring like spectators at a hanging, then eating their pasties and cider out on the lawns overlooking the sea." She shuddered. "It's horrid."

"More horrid if this place is lost," Stephen declared. "She's a major English poet, for God's sake!"

"When was the last time you were in Stratford? Or Wordworth's home in Grasmere?" Rachel asked. "Empty, musty, travesties of houses. Like mummified bodies, on view because of vulgar curiosity. I don't want to see this place kept like a waxwork long beyond its usefulness, genteelly crumbling at the edges. I want—to be finished with it."

"Or is it yourself you're thinking about?" Stephen demanded. "Is it your own secrets they might find, browsing around in here?"

Rachel looked at him coldly. "What's that supposed to mean?"

"That all of us have private lives, and one day biographers will be delving into them, laying them bare in the name of scholarship. To learn more about Olivia, how she lived, who her family was— that's the lot of us—how she came to be a poet in the first place."

"That's a dreadful thought!" Daniel exclaimed. There were skeletons in *his* family closet that he wouldn't care to see rattled. Name him an Irishman who didn't have them!

"The price of fame," Susannah said sourly, her fair, pretty face twisting into a grimace. "And an even more cogent reason for stopping them in their tracks. By selling the house. None of us ever expected to live here anyway. Olivia knew that, she could have arranged for her own museum if that was what she truly wanted. She didn't."

There was another silence. Then Cormac, used to board meetings and finding consensus, used to making choices, said, "Right, I take it you're three to one? For the sale of this property? Stephen can do as he pleases with Olivia's personal papers—manuscripts, letters, contracts, and so on. That ought to satisfy inquisitive scholars. Sad to say, I doubt there's much of a *literary* estate. She was young. And poets aren't . . . prolific."

7

No, Rachel thought, watching him. You've already gone through her papers, haven't you? You were here first. Did you take any of them, I wonder? Were you afraid for your reputation in the City? Or were you merely curious about your stepsister's secrets?

"Livia seldom wrote to any of us," she said aloud. "Or to anyone else, as far as I know. Perhaps Stephen might want whatever letters we've kept of hers? For the collection?" But not Nicholas' letters, not those.

"Did she keep a diary?" Daniel asked, and as every face swiveled to stare at him, he added, "Well, surprising numbers of people do! Lonely people, especially. Invalids—" He stopped.

"No," Stephen said shortly. "I'm sure she didn't."

"You didn't know her any better than the rest of us did," Susannah retorted. "Not after you were grown. She could have kept *twelve* diaries, and who would have guessed?"

"I came home more often than the rest of you put together!"

"What? Four times a year? At most five? It was uncomfortable here, you know that. She didn't *want* us to come. She'd made herself a recluse, yes, and Nicholas too, he was as set in his way as she was. And they were only in their middle thirties—it's unnatural!"

"I remember the last time I was here," Daniel said. "You could tell she couldn't wait until we were gone."

"We brought in the real world," Susannah agreed. "Life. She lived in that strange half-world of hers. I never understood why she wrote such bleak poetry. Well, not counting *Wings of Fire*, of course. *Scent of Violets* and *Lucifer* gave me the creeps, I can tell you! But then she was a cripple. They're often dreary people anyway, suffering and wretched. I suppose her mind dwelt on such things."

"*She* wasn't dreary," Rachel said suddenly. "And she wasn't truly crippled. I think we bored her."

"Don't be silly," Daniel said. "That's ridiculous. Her family?"

"It's true! For the past six or seven years I've had the feeling she didn't need us. That her life was full, that she had all she wanted right here."

"I don't know how Nicholas put up with it all these years," Susannah said, glaring at Rachel. "I'd have gone mad!"

"Livia told me once that he was paying a debt," Stephen remembered out of nowhere. "Odd thing to say, wasn't it? I asked what sort of debt, and she said a debt of blood." He got up and limped over to the drinks table and poured himself another whiskey.

Cormac said, "Oh, for God's sake!" And sat down again, impatient with the lot of them.

"I don't want to stay the night here," Susannah said, looking up at her husband as she changed the subject. "We'll find rooms at The Three Bells."

"Don't be morbid!" Daniel told her. "Mrs. Trepol has already made up our rooms here."

"I'm not morbid! This *place* is morbid! It's like a hothouse where something unhealthy thrived. And it was never that way while Mother was alive." She glanced up at the elegantly framed portrait over the hearth. Rosamund Beatrice Trevelyan, who'd had three husbands and children by each of them, loving them all with equal devotion, stared back at her with a half smile that captured both serenity and passion. The artist had found more than just beauty in the face he'd painted. "Mother had such *life*! Such warmth. There was always laughter, brightness, here. And that's all disappeared, it—it drained away without our knowing it, after she died. I've come to hate the Hall. I never actually realized that until now. And after dinner we're leaving."

"I'll go with you, if you don't mind. I'd—rather not stay, either," Rachel said, but for reasons of her own. There were ghosts here. She knew it now. She, who'd never believed in ghosts in her life, believed in them here. Not things in sheets that moaned and rattled chains. Those she could handle. These were . . . different.

"You haven't decided—" Cormac began.

"Sell," Susannah said, and Daniel nodded. After a moment, Rachel sighed and with a single movement of her head acknowledged her agreement.

"Over my dead body." Stephen promised. "In the courts if need be, but I'll fight you. *This house ought to be preserved!*"

"Selling is the soundest move you could make," Cormac said. "Put it off, and you'll find yourselves taking a loss. That's a majority, then? When the wills are read tomorrow, you should instruct

9

Chambers accordingly. As to the furniture, you might draw up lists of what you each want. And if there should be any conflict—"

"We're not touching a stick of furniture until this has been settled," Stephen said stubbornly, his jaw tight and his face flushed.

"Let Chambers work out a compromise. Agreed? What you don't want personally, you should put up for sale. With the house, I think. It'll bring far more that way. People with money enough to buy country houses these days don't have the proper furnishings to put in them." He looked around thoughtfully. "I've been considering a place in the country myself. I wonder . . ." With a shrug he let the thought die, then said, "I suppose it's nostalgia. I spent a good part of my own life here too."

"I want Mother's portrait," Susannah said immediately. "And there's the Wedgwood coffee service. I'd like to have that as well. It was Grandmother FitzHugh's."

Her husband added, "I'd like to have the trophies for the horse races Rosamund's stables won. Those ought to stay in the family anyway."

Cormac said, "I haven't any right to ask, but I'd like the guns. The ones that came from Ireland with my father. And his collection of walking sticks. They belonged to him before he married Rosamund, so in a sense I have some small claim on them."

Susannah turned to Rachel. "Is there anything you particularly fancy?" Rosamund had loved Rachel like one of her own. They all had. Nicholas had been deeply fond of her, you could tell that, and they always said Richard—Susannah shivered and refused to think of Richard.

Rachel looked down at her hands, and the glass of sherry they were holding. "I don't know. Yes, I do!" She lifted her eyes and regarded all of them. "I don't have any claim on the Cheney side of the family. But, I'd like Nicholas' collection of ships. The ones he carved. If no one else wishes for them?"

Her glance reached Stephen's furious face and then she realized how callous it must sound to him, four people coolly coming to terms over the household goods of the newly dead. Her face flushed.

"They haven't been decently buried for more than three hours!" Stephen said. "You're ghouls! It's revolting!"

"Practical, that's all," Daniel answered. "Just as well to have it all straight in our minds. What about you?"

"Nothing of mine is leaving here." He gripped his glass tightly."And nothing of Olivia's is to be touched. Do you hear me? Nothing!"

"Then that's settled," Susannah said with satisfaction. "And very amicably." She smiled up at Rosamund's image again. "Mother would be proud of us, not quarreling."

"Who's left to quarrel?" Rachel said pensively. Except for you and Stephen, she added to herself. The youngest, the FitzHughs. I barely remember Anne—only that she and Olivia were so much alike that the adults couldn't tell them apart. And I could. Now Olivia is dead as well. The end of the Marlowes. And both of the Cheneys are gone too, Richard . . . and Nicholas. Rachel threw off her deepening depression and pulled herself back to what Stephen was saying.

"Not yet, it isn't settled!" Stephen fumed. "If Chambers won't stop you, I'll find my own lawyers. Bennet will act for me—"

"Don't be an ass, Stephen," Cormac said without rancor. "You'll still lose. And more to the point, so will the family. The courts will agree with the majority—once the family's dirty wash has been thoroughly aired in all the newspapers. Do any of us want that?"

Mrs. Trepol came to the door to say that dinner was waiting. She looked tired and sad.

Stephen put down his drink and made to follow her.

"Will they? Agree with you?" he asked over his shoulder. "She's O. A. Manning, remember? That's bound to count for something. And the fact that none of us is going hungry. You don't destroy a national heritage as easily as you might a mere family estate."

Putting down her glass on the small walnut table beside her chair, Rachel watched them walk out the door of the drawing room and across the hall to the dining room. She'd never seen Stephen so angry. Or so determined. She had a very uneasy feeling that it just might come down to a court matter. And in the end, he'd win. Stephen.

Somehow Stephen always seemed to win. Even as a child, he'd been the luckiest of them all. Cornish luck, Rosamund called it. He'd survived four years of bloody war with half a dozen medals for bravery and a reputation for wildly daring heroics. Devil FitzHugh, they'd called him at the Front. Lucky.

Fey, the old woman in the woods would have said . . .

2

Jan Rutledge, returning to London in late June, found a mixed welcome at Scotland Yard. Warwickshire had not been a complete triumph—there were those who believed the outcome was more politically sound than judicially defensible, and others saw in his success a taste for notoriety. Chief Superintendent Bowles himself had set that rumor flying. "Not a *well-defined* closure, would you say? Field day for the press, of course, name in all the papers. I'd not care for that sort of thing, myself . . . but some do."

Rutledge himself, still mentally and physically drained by events in Upper Streetham, was glad enough to be relegated once more to the mundane while he tried to heal.

It didn't last as long as he'd anticipated. There had been a series of brutal knifings in the City and the newspapers were attempting to resurrect the old Ripper killings, making far-fetched comparisions in order to expand circulation. People had tired of the Peace, which had brought more misery to the country than any sense of enormous Victory. They were tired of grimness and stoicism, of poor food, no jobs, strikes, and unrest, and there was even a boredom with the struggle to revive the England they remembered before the Kaiser played for power in Europe. Any news that didn't have to do with the strife of ordinary life, that could be parlayed

13

into sensationalism, was followed with the frisson of fear that comes from knowing that you're safe even while the tigers noisily devour your neighbor.

Superintendent Bowles, on whose turf the knifings began, was already scenting a powerful public upsurge in attention, and never one to shirk the glow of reflected glory, he took over the cases himself.

And that soon meant allowing Rutledge into the investigation as well, because of the need for manpower.

It was not something Bowles relished, and he put off any briefings for three whole days.

Then fate stepped in—he had extraordinary good fortune, he told himself, it was a sign of his righteous nature—and offered a partial solution. He grabbed it with both fists, and had soon twisted it around to his own satisfaction. Then, with energy and a sense of mission, he went to find Inspector Rutledge.

It was a warm day in early July, the sun flooding the dusty windows and collecting in pools on the dusty floor of the small office Rutledge had been allotted.

"Beautiful day! Damned shame to be shut up inside. And I'm off to the City and conferences for the rest of the afternoon."

Rutledge, looking up from his paperwork, said, "The Ripper?" He'd been expecting Bowles to send for him.

"Yes, they've all but called him that, haven't they? Certainly drawn every parallel they can think of, although this fellow doesn't gut his victims, just all but flays them, there's so many cuts on the body. Still, it's bloody enough to make the innuendos successful. But that's not what I wanted to talk to you about. It's this."

He tossed a heavy sheet of paper on Rutledge's desk, and it settled upside down on the dark green blotter. Rutledge turned it over and saw the crest at the top. "Home Office."

"Yes, well, that's where it came from, but if you want my own interpretation, it originated in the War Office. Or the Foreign Ministry. Read it."

Rutledge scanned the typed lines.

It said, in the flowery phrases of a man asking a favor he didn't care to ask, that Scotland Yard was kindly requested to look into a trio of deaths in Cornwall that had been ruled a double suicide and an accidental death. The local people had not seen fit to pursue the cases further, but now information had come to hand that these were possibly not, in fact, what they appeared. If an officer could be spared from the Yard to travel to Cornwall and quietly go over the evidence, to be sure that all was as it should be, the undersigned would be very grateful.

Rutledge considered the letter again, then regarded Bowles. "What cases? And what new information?"

"It seems," Bowles said, availing himself of a chair, "that a certain Lady Ashford, who is somehow related to all three deceased parties, felt that there had been a hasty judgment, and insufficient consideration had been given to the likelihood of murder. Sounds like the old bitch got left out of the wills, and is now raising holy hell with some lord or other of her acquaintance, and he's palmed her off on another lord in the Home Office, who's now palming her off on *us*, worse luck!"

Suddenly realizing what he'd just been saying, Bowles' amber goat's eyes flickered. In his irritation, he'd lost sight of his goal. Rapidly mending fences, he added, "It means, of course, that whoever we send out has got to mind his manners with the local people and still satisfy this Lady Ashford that her fears are groundless. Or, if they *aren't*, reopen the cases as soon as possible and deal with them before we all get a black name for sheer incompetence." He gestured to the letter. "He's important, this Secretary. If we don't please *him*, we'll never hear the end of it from upstairs."

Rutledge read the letter again. "There's a Henry Ashford in the Foreign Office," he said thoughtfully. "Very highly placed." He had gone to school with Ashford's brother.

Trust Rutledge to know! Bowles scowled. "Yes, well, that's as may be."

"And you want me to go to Cornwall?"

"It's the kind of thing you can handle. Bennett, now, he's available, but he's as clumsy as hell when it comes to soothing ruffled feathers in little old ladies, however good he is in Whitechapel. And there's Harrison. I could spare him, but he's not got the patience to pussyfoot around anyone else's investigation. He'll go in with the notion they're in the wrong and before you know it, the Chief Constable will be demanding his recall! And the Home Office will be wanting to know what we thought we were about, choosing the likes of *him*." He sighed. "You're the best I've got. Simple as that."

"And what about those murders in the City?" Rutledge asked. He was beginning to know his man. Bowles wanted Rutledge out of the way . . .

"Well, I don't think we'll solve them overnight! And if you don't stay beyond a week, then I'll have you to fall back on when I need you."

A week. You didn't spend a week exploring the closed cases of the County constabularies. Did that mean that Bowles felt there *would* be a reopening of the investigation? Something to keep Rutledge out of London—more to the point, out of the City—until Bowles had caught his own man?

Suddenly Rutledge realized that he didn't care either way.

Going to Cornwall would be better than being cooped up at the Yard with time on his hands and Hamish growling from boredom at the back of his mind . . . He turned and looked out at the sunshine. "The report you asked me to do is finished. I can leave this afternoon, if it suits you."

Bowles stared at the other man. Was he too willing? Was he intending to be down in Cornwall and finished with this matter before the weekend? Or did Rutledge know something that he didn't about the London killings? And was all too pleased to be excluded from them? That would be a fine kettle of fish, sending Rutledge out of harm's way just as the roof started to fall in here! Suspicious, he said, "Well, I'd not rush the investigation if I were you. It'll all be to do over again if we don't satisfy this sod in the Home Office!"

"I won't rush it." Rutledge was still looking out the window, his mind already on the road west. Stirring to life, Hamish, a voice from the past, said, "It's a bonny day. I'm not the man for four walls and a door."

Which made them seem to shrink in upon him. Shivering, Rutledge turned back to Bowles. "What do you have on these cases?"

"Precious little. His lordship didn't deign to send us more than this."

He passed over several sheets. Copies of death certificates for Olivia Alison Marlowe, spinster. Nicholas Michael Cheney, bachelor. Both dead by their own hands. The dates were the same. This spring. And for Stephen Russell FitzHugh, bachelor, death by misadventure. A fall. Three weeks ago. While he, Rutledge, was still in Warwickshire.

"Seems ordinary enough. In both cases."

"It is. But as far as we're concerned, the Home Office, like God, is never wrong!"

It was four o'clock in the afternoon before Rutledge was ready to leave for Cornwall. But the days are still long in July, and the warmth of the sun was soothing. In the trenches during the Great War he'd hated the hot days of summer, when the smells of urine and corpses and unwashed bodies overwhelmed the senses and sickened the mind. You cursed the Germans for making you stand in your own stink, never mind that they were standing in the lines smelling their own. One sergeant, who swore he'd never bathed at home in Wales, laughed at the raw replacements who gagged and puked, calling them sodding poufs for their sensitive noses. Blankets, coats, shirts, trousers, socks, they all were unspeakable in summer, and worse in winter when the wool never dried.

Hamish chuckled. "Missing it, are ye?"

"No," Rutledge said tiredly, "unable to forget."

"Aye," Hamish answered with relish from the dark corners of his mind, "that's the game, man, you can't run from it."

The doctors at the clinic had told him that it was natural for him to hear the voice of Corporal MacLeod, shot by a firing squad just before the shelling that buried the salient, smothering men and mud and corpses alike with such force that that it had taken hours to dig out the barely living—Rutledge among them. He'd suffered several wounds, shell-shock, and severe claustrophobia, but the doctors at the aid station had pronounced it fatigue, given him twenty-four hours to sleep it off, patched him up, and sent him back to the lines. Experienced officers were in short supply. He couldn't remember much about the year after that, only Hamish's voice keeping him at his post—harrying, tormenting, haunting him until he was sure that others must have heard it too. He'd lived in agony at the thought of seeing the owner of that voice in the dark of the night or a star shell burst or among the rotting corpses that sometimes twitched from the maggots inside them. Somehow he must have carried out his duties well enough—no one reported him, and his men left him alone, too exhausted and worried and frightened themselves to care about anything except survival, and the dreaded next offensive. A long war...

The road to Salisbury was not busy. And in the air flowing through the motorcar, sweet scents of wildflowers and ripening corn and the early haying followed him through the countryside. It would have been faster by train but he hated the small compartments, crammed cheek by jowl with other people while his heart pounded with fear and the palms of his hands were damp with the sweat of being hemmed in and unable to fight his way out.

Finding an inn twenty miles beyond Salisbury, he stopped for the night, ate a dinner of baked mutton and potatoes, with green beans on the side, and slept ill in the small, airless, low-ceilinged room he'd been given. The next day he picked up a line of squalls along the Devon border, riding the winds over the coast and disputing with the sunshine for dominance. Twice he nearly missed his turning as the rains poured down, and half an hour later the roadsides steamed as the sun broke through again. Hamish kept up a running commentary as they drove through villages that brimmed with life, waysides still thick with late wildflowers, and tiny, isolated cottages with thatched roofs or rampantly blooming gardens. So different, so different from the devastation in France. Sometimes small herds of dairy cows being driven down the road from one field to another blocked his path, or fat gray geese waddling between rain puddles and village ponds, or carts pulled by patient horses, in no hurry to be anywhere, the drivers turning to stare with intent interest at his motorcar. Between the deep hedgerows he was often the only human being in sight, although birds darted in and out and butterflies danced across the bonnet. The peace spread through him, soothing.

It was late in the evening when he reached Borcombe, tucked into a deep valley that ran down to the sea below a long headland. The rain had stopped, but heavy clouds still obscured the sky, and lights from houses and a busy pub already glistened across the wet pavements though the time was only a little after nine. It was a smallish village, and he quickly found the house he was looking for on the corner of Butcher's Lane, home of Constable Dawlish. Pulling up before the white picket gate, he opened the door and got out stiffly, taking a moment to stretch his tired legs and massage aching shoulders. Then the door was opening at the top of the stone steps and a man in shirtsleeves was staring out.

"Inspector Rutledge?"

"Yes." He opened the gate and went up the short, flagstone walk. "Constable Dawlish?"

They shook hands on the threshold and Dawlish ushered him into a small, warm room off the entry hall. "Let me take your coat, sir. A bit cool for July, isn't it? It's the rain, I expect. Have you had any dinner?"

"Yes, thank you. But I could do with some tea."

"Kettle's on the boil now, sir." Dawlish gestured to the dark red horsehair sofa. "You'll be comfortable over there. And I've got all the papers about the case in the folder on the table beside you. Inspector Harvey is sorry he can't be here, but he had to go along to Plymouth. There's a man there, fits the description of one we've been looking for. Talked three widows out of their savings."

"We'll manage well enough without Harvey at this stage," Rutledge replied, taking Dawlish's measure. He was tall and thin, a young man with old eyes. "On the Somme, were you?" he asked, hazarding a guess.

"Part of the time. I was over there three years. Felt like thirty."

"Yes. It did."

Mrs. Dawlish, small and plump, came in with a tray of tea, thick sandwiches, and dainty cakes. She smiled shyly at Rutledge as she set the tray on a second table by the hearth but well within reach of the sofa, and said, "Help yourself, Inspector. There's plenty more in the kitchen." And then she whisked herself out of the room, the perfect policeman's wife.

"I'll read these reports tonight," Rutledge said as he took the cup Dawlish poured. "First, I'd rather hear your own point of view."

Dawlish sat down and frowned earnestly at the cup in his hands. "Well, to tell the truth, I don't see murder anywhere in this affair. Two suicides and an accident. That's how it seemed to me. And to Inspector Harvey as well. There was no note with the suicides, but I was there, I saw the bodies, and you'd have a hard time, Inspector, setting up a murder to appear a suicide so fine as that. The bodies, the room, their faces. We don't know why they decided to kill themselves, that's right enough. But Miss Olivia Marlowe, she'd been a cripple and must have suffered something fierce from it. The housekeeper said she had many a bad night. And Mr. Nicholas Cheney, he'd done naught else but care for her all his life. Except for the war, of course—he was gassed at Ypres, and sent home. I suppose he felt there was nothing left to him if she went first. Too late, to his way of thinking, to start again. With his damaged lungs. Or maybe he wouldn't have wanted to. Some people are like that, they're content with what they know, however bad it is, and fear what they don't know, however good it might turn out. He was young, younger than she was by four years, he could have married, had a family of his own. But I'm wandering from the facts—"

Rutledge shook his head. "No, no, I want to hear. You knew these people, after all. And you saw the bodies."

Relieved that the gaunt man from London wasn't pushing to have his own way, willy-nilly, Dawlish nodded. "Well, then, I accepted what I saw for what it seemed. There was no reason to do other-wise, and you can't make up a case for murder when there's no cause, no evidence to base it on. So the family was notified, they came and buried their brother and sister. It was as simple as that. But then they were clearing out the house to ready it for the mar-ket—and it's a handsome house, they'll sell it easy, even out here in the middle of nowhere. There was money made on the war, and a lot of it wants to be *respectable* money now." There was no bit-terness in the quiet voice, and only a hint of irony that those who had done the fighting weren't the ones who had made their fortunes from it.

"The house might bring in enough to kill for?"

"Possibly, though it'll require a good deal of work to bring it up to being a showplace again. They'll have to consider that in setting the price. And whatever they do get, it has to be split among the surviving family. It took more than a fortnight to clear out the house—just of personal belongings and the like. They'd all stayed to do that, except Mr. Cormac, who'd had to return to the City part of the time but was back that last weekend. At any rate, that last day when they were leaving, Mr. Stephen, the youngest, went head over heels down the stairs and broke his neck. But there was no one who could have been responsible for that, as far as we can tell. They were all outside at the time; he called out the window and said he was on his way down. And the next thing you knew, he'd fallen. Mr. Cormac went in to see what was keeping him, and set up a shout at once. No time to push him, no time to do more than find him, from what the others said. It's a long sweep of stairs, the treads worn, and he went down with enough force to bruise the body. So he wasn't dead to begin with and then just tossed over a banister. Besides, he'd called down, every one of them heard him." He finished his first sandwich and reached for another. "Dr. Hawkins said he may have been hurrying, and with his bad foot— from the war—just missed his step. The others were that upset they'd been so impatient with him."

"And they are? These others?"

"It's a complicated family, sir. There's Cormac FitzHugh, now, he's very well thought of in the City. He was there. He's Mr. Brian FitzHugh's son, born in Ireland before Mr. Brian married Miss Rosamund. Miss Susannah was there, she's twin sister to the man who fell. Miss Susannah and Mr. Stephen were Mr. Brian's children by Miss Rosamund, you see. And Miss Susannah's husband, Daniel Hargrove, was there. And of course Miss Rachel, she's a cousin on the Marlowe side of the family. Miss Olivia's cousin, to be exact. Miss Olivia's father was a Marlowe. Miss Rosamund, Miss Olivia's mother, was married three times, and had two children by each of her husbands. But they're all gone now except for Miss Susannah. She's the last of the lot. Marlowe, Cheney, or FitzHugh."

"This Rosamund, the mother—and stepmother—of all these children—"

"Rosamund Trevelyan, sir, whose family has owned the Hall since time out of mind. Her father's only child. A lovely lady, sir, quite a beauty in her day. There's a fine portrait of her up at the house, if they haven't taken it away yet. If ever a woman deserved to be happy, it was that one. But sorrow seemed to be her lot. Still, to her dying day, nobody ever heard a harsh word from her. At her services, the rector spoke of the 'light within', and she had that." He smiled wistfully. "So few people do."

"She's—in one way or another—the key to this family, then. And to the house."

"Aye, that's true enough. Miss Rachel, now, she was Miss Rosamund's first husband's niece. Captain Marlowe, that was, Olivia's father. Miss Rachel has been in and out of the house all her life. Mr. Hargrove, Miss Susannah's husband, first came here when he was going on twelve, I'd say. Miss Rosamund had a string of race horses, most of them Irish bred, and more than a few bought from the Hargrove stables. Fine animals, they were, won dozens of prizes. As a lad I won more than a bob or two betting on them myself."

"Who inherited the house when Rosamund died?"

"The house belonged to old Adrian Trevelyan, like I said. Miss Olivia's grandfather. He left it to her, not her mother—no reflection on Miss Rosamund, you understand, but he wasn't best pleased with her choice of third husband, and there're some who say he left the house to Miss Olivia to keep it out of FitzHugh hands. Not to speak of the fact that Miss Olivia was a cripple and it was more likely that she'd have need of a home, unmarried and not apt to be. I doubt anyone in the family—and certainly no one in the village—knew she was to become a famous poet."

"Poet? Olivia Marlowe?"

"Aye. O. A. Manning, she was known as. I've never read any of her poems. Well, not much in my line, poetry. But the wife has, and she tells me it was very pretty."

Pretty, thought Rutledge, was an understatement for O. A. Manning's work. Haunting, lyrical, with undercurrents of dark humor at times, and subtle contrasts that caught people and emotions with such precision that lines stayed with you long afterward, like personal memories. She'd written about the war too, and he'd read some of those poems in the trenches, marveling that anyone could have captured so clearly what men felt out there in the bloody shambles of France. Could have found the courage to put it into words. He hadn't known then that O. A. Manning was a woman.

But of course the *Wings of Fire* poems were different, and perhaps it was those that Dawlish's wife knew. Love poems, and unlike the poems Shakespeare had written to his dark lady, these were light and warmth and beauty intermingled with such passion that they sang in the heart as you read them. *Wings of Fire* had touched him in a way that few things had.

Hamish growled, his voice a low rumble in the back of Rutledge's mind. "Thought of your Jean, did you, as you read those lines? She's no' worthy of that kind of love! My Fiona was. She gave me the book before I took the troop train to London. They found it in my pocket, wet with my blood, when they dug out my corpse."

Nearly choking on his tea, Rutledge coughed and said, "Leaving the suicides for the moment, none of the four at the house that last day had anything to gain from killing Stephen FitzHugh?"

"As to Mr. Cormac FitzHugh, nothing. He has no rights in the house. Miss Rachel and Mr. and Mrs. Hargrove will receive a larger share of the sale now, but we looked into that. Their finances are in order, and there's no reason to think they needed the extra money."

"Where money's concerned, people will do strange things. All right, I think you've told me all I need to hear for the moment. Where am I staying?"

"I've put you at The Three Bells, sir. Not far from the church. You can't miss it."

"Thank Mrs. Dawlish for the tea." Rutledge collected the papers on the table and added a good night. It was raining again, and he dashed to his car, reaching it and climbing inside just as a wind-driven downpour swept over the headland and rattled against the picket fence like distant machine gun fire.

"Do ye think it was witchcraft that made yon woman write as she did?" Hamish asked, still intrigued with Olivia Marlowe. "She knew the war too well, man! It's unnatural!"

"It wasn't witchcraft, it was genius," he answered before he could stop himself. It was a habit too hard to break, responding to Hamish.

Rutledge got out as the squall passed, started the engine, and drove too fast though the slanting rain. The inn came up before he expected it, and he nearly skidded as he came to a splashing stop in front of it. Beyond it he could see the spire of the church rising like a spear against the backdrop of storm clouds and wind-tossed trees.

"With your luck, you'd survive the car crash. And live in a chair for the rest of your days, with no one but me for company," Hamish pointed out, and Rutledge swore.

The inn was small, sway-backed gray stone under a dark slate roof that seemed to be slowly pushing the whole building deeper into the earth from sheer weight. He was expected, and the landlord gave him a room overlooking a small cultivated enclosure in the back, more a tangle of overgrown roses and rhododendron than anything that could be dignified by the name of "garden." He unpacked with swift efficiency and in ten minutes was abed and asleep.

He was never afraid to sleep. Hamish couldn't follow him there.

But Jean could.

In the darkness, hours later, the wind shifted, and the sea's breath drifted in the half-open window, bringing with it the softness of summer. Rutledge stirred, turned over, and began to dream of the woman he'd loved—and who'd wanted no part of the shattered remnants of the man she'd promised to marry. Jean, who in her own way haunted him too.

She touched his arm, and led him down a path he remembered, and for a time he thought it was real, that she was there beside him, her hand warm in his, her laughter silvery in the stillness, her skirts brushing lightly against him, and nothing had changed . . .

3

Breakfast was hearty the next morning, the innkeeper inquisitive. Rutledge parried his questions and left after his second cup of coffee. Out on the street, he turned and looked at the sky, a habit drilled into him by war, when the direction of the wind could mean the difference between a gas attack and none. He thought it was going to be a fair, warmish day, in spite of the mists that twisted like wraiths around chimney tops and trees, and he decided to walk. There had been a set of keys in the folder Constable Dawlish had given him, and a sketchy map. It gave no indication of distances. A countryman's map.

It was very early, and although a few people were already in their gardens getting a jump on the day, the streets were still quiet. A smallish village with only one main road coming in, passing the church, and running downhill between the shops to catch up again with the tiny River Bor close to where it met the sea. Houses jostled each other as they spilled down the valley, sometimes roof to porch or separated by lanes and rock gardens. A glimmer of water at the bottom of the road marked the sea, he thought, though it was just as likely to be the little river.

The ironmonger was busy setting out barrels and a plow or two, the sounds of children's laughter floated from somewhere, and there was an elderly woman limping down the other side of the street. He crossed over and stopped her.

Closer to, she was truly a crone, bent with age, gray hair bundled into an untidy bun at the back of her neck, a black shawl that was so old it was nearly gray over her shoulders, and a gnarled cane that seemed to be no more than an extention of the gnarled hand that held it.

"Please—" he began, not wanting to startle her.

But she looked at him with sharp, watery eyes that seemed to see him—and through him.

"Stranger in Borcombe, are ye?" she demanded, looking him up and down. "If you're wanting the constable, he'll not be about for another twenty minutes at best."

Startled, Rutledge said, "Actually—"

"You want directions, then?"

"To the Trevelyan house. Can you tell me how to find it?"

"Are ye a walker, lad?"

It had been years since anyone had called him *lad*. "Yes."

"Ye'll need to be. Follow this road for a mile, more or less. Ye'll soon come to a parting of the way, and ye'll take the right fork. Follow *that* as far as it goes, and ye'll see a pair of gates and a drive leading uphill. When you come to the top, ye'll have the way fine from there."

As directions went—if they were correct—they were as clear as any he'd ever been given. The crone chuckled hoarsely. "I've lived here eighty year and more."

It was as if she'd read his mind. Hamish stirred uneasily, and the woman's glance seemed to sharpen. But she said nothing, limping on her way as if the conversation had come to a satisfactory conclusion. He watched her, and she seemed to know it. Old as she was, he thought, a woman feels a man's eyes.

Hamish laughed. "You've no' spent any time in the Highlands, man!" was all he said to that.

Rutledge set out, following the woman's directions, along the narrow, hilly road he'd traveled the night before. Finding the fork between curving fields of late hay, he walked on past a cottage or two and small patches of farmed land, and beside a long sweep of

26

rough pasture. Within half an hour, he had reached the gates, dark with age and damp, leading through tall, wet stands of rhododendron backed by taller trees, into what seemed to be a sea of mist. But as he followed the rutted drive curling uphill, he came out into sunlight and brightness. And there at the end of a graceful sweep of lawn stood a house set in formal gardens, protected by the slope of the headland beyond.

It was an old house, the architectural history of four centuries locked in its embrace. Rutledge could trace a Tudor core, with Restoration, Georgian, and Victorian additions, but there was also an older, battlemented gateway near the stables that came from a dimmer past. The great palaces of the English nobility, Blenheim and Hatfield, Longleat and Chatsworth, spoke of power and money. This house whispered of longevity and old bloodlines. Of timelessness and pride and peace.

He stood there, looking across at it, imagining its past, and searching for a key to its owners. What he felt was . . . sadness? No, that wasn't it, it was a stronger emotion, something about the place that tugged at him.

Hamish, on the other hand, didn't find it to his liking. "There's too many dead here," he said uneasily. "And they don't lie quietly in their graves!"

Rutledge chuckled. "I'd haunt the estate too, if it'd been mine. I wouldn't go peacefully to the churchyard in the town. Not with that view."

For beyond the headland he could see the sea, already in the clear and gleaming in the morning light, whitecaps dancing in the sun. There seemed to be a small strand where the land ran down to the sea. Then, turning to his right, he could see the distant roofs of Borcombe.

Damned if the old crone hadn't sent him the longest way around! You could walk from the last house he could see in the village into a copse of trees, and out of them into Trevelyan land, in what? Ten minutes? Say, fifteen all the way to the house.

He unlocked the door with the key that Dawlish had given him and stepped into the wide front hall, where the curving staircase swept down from a gallery above. The hall itself was old, with a

27

massive stone hearth at one side, and great oak beams that were black with age and smoke encompassing the hall and the long gallery that ran at the top of the stairs.

It was here then that Stephen FitzHugh must have fallen to his death. Rutledge walked to the stairs and began to examine them carefully, the uneven treads, the dark oak of the banisters, the ornately carved balustrade. If you fell to the left from the top, he thought, considering the possibilities, you'd come straight down, avoiding the curve. If you slipped on the right, you'd glance off the curve, slowing your momentum certainly, but with force enough to do damage anyway. But no one had said in the Inquest which direction Stephen had been coming from, his left or his right along the gallery.

The report Rutledge had read over breakfast indicated that Stephen FitzHugh hit the balustrade somewhere at the curve, broke his neck, and rolled the rest of the way to the hall, either dead already or nearly so. The doctor had noted the imprint of the carving on the back of Stephen FitzHugh's neck, just below the cracked vertebrae that had killed him. Hawkins had also included a description of the amputation of the foot that had made the dead man's balance uncertain at best, and possibly in this situation, prevented him from recovering it quickly enough to save himself from a nasty fall. The man's cane had been found at the curve, jammed into the balustrade on the opposite side of the stairs. An accident . . . it would be hard to quarrel with the Inquest's results.

The house was cold, no fires lit with no one living here, and he kept his coat on as he walked through it slowly, carefully. A handsome home, not a baronial palace. The formal rooms—dining room, drawing room, a large library—were well furnished with heirlooms but looked as if they had not seen company for some time. Everything stood in its proper place, no magazines strewn about, no flowers in their tall vases, no sunlight pouring through open drapes, no dogs lolled on the hearth rugs. He remembered as a child being taken to a stately home, and a woman's shrill echoing voice declaiming, "Here the family entertained three prime ministers, six members of the royal family, and the Queen, who was particularly fond of that blue silk chair."

And he had twisted about, seaching in vain for them, until his father had told him to stand still and pay attention.

A back parlor, overlooking the gardens and the sea, and the kitchen quarters below, were more ordinary, as if people actually lived there, mussing up the carpet with their shoes, wearing out the upholstery with their bodies, reading the books on the low shelves. Or cooking at the big stove, washing up at the stone sink, sitting down to peel potatoes in one of the old brown wooden chairs.

He returned to the staircase. Generations had come down them, gone up them, and no one had worried about them. Until now. Hamish, stirring restlessly in the back of his mind, whispered, "I didna' like this business. Leave the dead in their graves, man!"

Upstairs were the bedrooms. They were beautifully proportioned, with tall windows and handsome fireplaces. But old-fashioned now, as if no one had worried about the faded hangings and the worn carpets, preferring the familiar to the new.

He found the upstairs study where the suicides had occurred, thanks to the floor plan that Dawlish had sketched for him. It was a long room, windows looking out over the sea and over the gardens. A room of light and the warmth of the sun, neither a man's nor a woman's, but used, comfortable, ordinary. Nothing here to tell anyone where a famous poet worked, except perhaps for the typewriter sitting covered on a table by the seaward window. A guide would have to make do with the collection of books on either side of the table, set neatly on their shelves. "Here the poet found her inspiration among the works of . . ."

But did she? Who could know?

Nearby was another table, where someone had been carving. The hull of a great ship lay, white and unfinished, among the scraps and curls of wood. It was a scale model of an ocean liner, Rutledge thought, looking at it. And there were others in a long case beneath the garden windows, intricately fashioned miniatures. He recognized several of them—the *Olympia*, the *Sirius*, the *Lusitania*. Whose work were these? Nicholas Cheney's? Had they been a hobby for its own sake or did they represent a love of the sea that had been repressed to this room?

He crossed the room to the couch against the wall, where the

29

bodies of brother and sister had lain side by side in death, their hands touching as if for comfort as the darkness closed in. Why had they died?

"I don't like it here, man," Hamish said. "If you're going to investigate a murder, get about it."

"Murder sometimes has its roots in other places than the few feet of space where it happened. Still, why here? Why on that night?"

"*Hello?*"

A voice calling from the hall below startled him badly.

He walked out to the gallery at the top of the stairs and looked down. There was a woman at the foot of the stairs, the front door open behind her, and she was looking up anxiously, as if almost afraid of what might walk out of one of the rooms there to confront her.

"Inspector Rutledge," he said, moving towards the steps. "I arrived last night and came to have a look around. Constable Dawlish provided me with keys."

"Oh!" she said, smiling up at him with relief on her face. "I thought I heard voices when I walked in. I didn't know who might have found their way in. The press has been very troublesome."

She was slim, perhaps in her thirties—it was hard to tell—her oval face pink from walking, her light brown hair curling ridiculously around it, escaping from the knot at the back of her neck. Not pretty, yet very attractive. She waited until he had reached the hall and said, "I'm so glad they've finally sent someone from Scotland Yard. I'm Rachel Ashford. The one who's been fighting to get these ... deaths ... reopened."

"Lady Ashford?"

Her smile changed. "My husband is dead. His brother has the title now. Sir Henry. Did *he* tell you that Lady Ashford wanted to reopen the investigation? How very like him!"

"You're Peter Ashford's widow?" Rutledge asked, surprised. "I was in school with him."

"Peter died in the war. Trying to take Mount Kilimanjaro, out in Kenya."

"I'm sorry. I hadn't heard." So much for Bowles' "titled old bitch." But it was a shock, Peter's death. Another name added to the long list of friends gone. More than once he'd felt the guilt of surviving. As if it was somehow obscenely selfish, when so many had died. After a moment, he made himself go on. "And you believe the investigations done by Inspector Harvey and Constable Dawlish were mishandled?"

"Yes."

"Why?"

"Because—oh, because of intuition, I suppose." She made a wry face at him. "And I can't help but feel that coincidence can only be stretched so far. Three deaths in the same family in little more than a month? I—I *knew* Livia and Nicholas, they weren't at all what the papers say, an invalid and her devoted keeper. It's wrong, the notion that they could have killed themselves because of ill health!"

"I understood that Olivia Man—Marlowe—was crippled. And that Nicholas Cheney had been gassed in the war."

"Well, yes," she said defensively, "certainly that's true, since you put it so baldly. Olivia lost the strength of one leg in childhood, from the crippling disease. She used a chair for a long time, then Nicholas carved a brace for her, and after that, she could move about as she pleased. It was wonderful! I can still hear her laughter when she first tried it—we were all outside her bedroom door, while Nanny put it on—and she began to laugh, and Nicholas was jumping up and down beside me, shouting encouragement, and Rosamund was crying, and Richard was pounding on the door, he was so beside himself with excitement . . ." Her voice faded and she looked up the stairs defensively, as if afraid she'd hear the children's voices again. "If she killed herself," Rachel continued after a moment, "it wasn't because of her leg! She accepted it, she lived with it, she'd come to terms with the pain—it wasn't something that drove her to despair and suicide."

The sunlight pouring through the open door failed to reach them or warm the vastness of the hall. But he could hear birds somewhere, singing.

"If she had wanted to kill herself—for whatever reason—" Rutledge said, "why would she allow Nicholas to join her in death? Why not see that he survived, and got on with life. However hard it might seem to be at first? Why not kill herself in her bedroom, with no one to see?"

She pressed her fingers to her eyes, as if they still hurt from crying. Or to hide them from him. "I've asked myself that a hundred—a thousand—times since then. They were very close, Olivia and Nicholas. I'd have said, if anyone had ever thought to ask me, that she would have jumped into the sea in the night, rather that let him die with her. It doesn't mean that perhaps in the first shock he might not have *wished* to follow, but Nicholas had a cool head, a clear mind, he wasn't the dramatic, overly emotional sort of man who could leap into the sea himself the next morning. When she was already dead." Dropping her hands, she said painfully, "If you understand what I'm saying?"

He did, though Hamish was grumbling that it made no sense. "Yet they died together."

"Yes, and that's what put me off in the very beginning. I didn't say much to the others; they wouldn't have wanted to hear me worrying over what couldn't be changed. Or making it worse by starting a fuss over it. But the more I thought about the circumstances, the more I was convinced that something was very wrong, very—unusual."

"Do you think one of your cousins—including Stephen—could be capable of murdering Olivia and Nicholas? For whatever reasons?"

She stared at him, stunned. "Oh, God, no! Susannah and Stephen couldn't have killed either of them. And Daniel, what on earth for?"

Rutledge smiled. "Where there's murder, there's usually a murderer."

"But not one of us!" she cried, alarmed.

How often had he heard the same cry when he'd begun an investigation into suspicious death. Murder, possibly. *But not one of us*. A stranger. A madman. An envious neighbor or colleague. The woman down the road. But not one of us. Then the finger-pointing began, as suspicion and fear and uncertainty and old memories came to the surface.

"Who, then?" he asked gently.

"That's why I called Henry and begged him to ask the Yard to come down here and look into the deaths. Someone who could be objective, someone with the experience to judge what had really happened. Not a village policeman who preferred the safest answer to embarrassing the family any more than it already was. I mean, suicide is unacceptable enough—murder would be, well, a family calamity." She looked at him, seeing him for the first time. The thin face. The haunted eyes. Intelligence, too, but something more. She couldn't quite put her finger on it.

"There were no photographs upstairs. Do you have any of the family that I could borrow for a time?" He was mainly interested in Olivia Marlowe, the woman behind the poems. But it helped, often, to see the faces of the dead if you were late at the murder scene.

"We'd taken them all. The house will be put up for sale soon, and we didn't want to leave—I've just come to fetch the ships," she said, flustered. "I—I haven't had the courage yet to go in there. Where they—where it happened. There are photographs in my things, I'll find them. Where are you staying?"

"The Three Bells," he said, curious about her reaction. "What can you tell me about Stephen FitzHugh's death?"

She shivered, not looking over his shoulder at the stairs, though her head had turned that way. "It was awful. He was lying at the foot of the steps, his eyes wide, a little blood—I couldn't tell if it was from his ear or his mouth—smeared across his cheek. Cormac said he died as we watched, but I saw nothing change, didn't hear a sigh or—or anything. And I was kneeling there, beside him, my hand on his chest, calling his name. It was—I've seen men die before. I was in London when the Zeppelins came over, I was there when they pulled people out of one of the buildings. But this was *Stephen*." She collected herself with an effort and turned towards the open door. "I'd better leave now," she said ruefully. "Men don't like it when women start to cry, and I've found it hard sometimes . . ."

He let her go, watching her slim figure hurry down the drive and turn towards the sea.

So that was Lady Ashford, born Rachel Marlowe, and cousin to the people who lived here. Peter's wife. Widow. He remembered Peter, tall and fast at games, level-headed and very good at whatever he did. He'd had a gift for languages, he could pick them up with apparently no effort, and speak them like a native. All that wasted in an obscure action on the flanks of a mountain whose one claim to fame was that Queen Victoria had had two mountains in East Africa, and had given Kilimanjaro to the Kaiser, next door in Tanganyika, who'd had none. Bloody silly thing to do in the first place. And Englishmen had died trying to retake it from the Germans under that master strategist, Von Lettow-Vorbeck, who knew how to pin down men who would otherwise have been fighting in France.

Rutledge turned and went back up the stairs to the sitting room, standing there with his eyes roving the furnishings, the books, the wooden ships that Nicholas Cheney carved. *He* had left more of himself here than the poet, after all . . .

Two people who died together for no apparent reason. No expression of regret, no apologies to the living. No explanation of the deed, no excuses, no last confessions, no lines of bitterness meant to hurt the survivors. Just . . . silence.

Hamish, uneasy and sensitive to the unsettled atmosphere of Rutledge's mind, called to him to leave, to wash his hands of this case and go back to London.

Rutledge gave up trying to hear the stillness, and walked out into the gallery again on his way to Olivia's bedroom.

A voice down in the hall said harshly, "What the hell—*who* the hell are you?"

Rutledge looked down, not seeing anyone at first, then finding the tall man who stood just in the shadows of a doorway.

"Inspector Rutledge, Scotland Yard," he said. "I've a key from Constable Dawlish, and I'm here on official business. Who are you?"

"Official—what's happened?" the other man demanded sharply.

"The inquiry into the deaths of Miss Marlowe, Mr. Cheney, and Mr. FitzHugh is being reconsidered by the Yard," Rutledge said, and started down the stairs.

The man in the doorway was handsome in a way that few men

are, reminding Rutledge of Greek statues, that same mix of perfect body and face and mind that the Golden Age admired most. And yet there was something about him that was pure Irish. Was this Daniel Hargrove, the husband of Susannah FitzHugh?

Before he could test that, the man said, "I'm Cormac FitzHugh. A member of the family. No one has told me of any renewed inquiry! Neither the local police nor the family's solicitors. What are you doing here?"

"Surveying the scenes of death," Rutledge responded, coming to the last step and staying where he was. He'd dealt with officers of this man's ilk, accustomed to giving orders and expecting instant, unquestioning obedience to them. He'd never liked such men.

Hamish growled, "Bloody, arrogant bastards, the lot!"

"I'm putting a stop to this right now! You'll hand over your keys, if you please, and leave the grounds at once. There will be no reopening of any affairs to do with my family."

"I'm afraid, Mr. FitzHugh, that you have no say in this business. It's a police matter, at the request of the Home Office. You have no option but to cooperate." He paused. "Unless, of course, you have something to hide in any of these three deaths?"

FitzHugh looked as if Rutledge had struck him. "I wield considerable power in the City—"

"That's as may be," Rutledge answered him. "It doesn't count here, I'm afraid."

"Yes, I've something to hide," FitzHugh said shortly, changing directions so quickly that Rutledge was nearly caught off guard. "My stepbrother and my stepsister killed themselves. It isn't something I'm happy about, but it was a choice they both made. The reasons behind their deaths were extremely personal, and since there's no question that suicide was the cause of death, laudanum to be precise, self-administered, I see no reason on earth why their unhappiness must be dragged through the newspapers. It serves no purpose, and it will hurt my cousin, my half sister, her husband, and me. For the delectation of a public who couldn't care less about my family but who thrive on titillation. My God, look at what they're already doing with these knifings, raising the spectre of the

35

Ripper as if it was something to be proud of, not buried and forgotten!"

Rutledge agreed with him there, but said nothing.

After a moment, Cormac FitzHugh sighed and then added more reasonably, "There's no hope of deflecting you from this investigation?"

"Sorry. None." He made no mention of the fact that the conclusions might well be the same as those the Inquest had reached. Or that so far he'd seen no evidence, heard no new information, to do more than he was already doing, asking general questions. Rutledge was more interested in where the other man's mood was taking them.

Cormac seemed to argue something with himself and, reluctantly, to come to a decision. "All right, then, come in here; we needn't stand in the hall like unwelcomed guests." He led the way into the drawing room, looking with distaste at the closed curtains and the empty space over the mantel where a large portrait had hung. "I'm not used to the house like this. It was never empty in my childhood. Nor dark and dreary and full of sadness. But then my childhood has vanished, taking the memories with it, I suppose. Sit down, man."

Rutledge took the chair across from his and wondered what this polished denizen of the City was about to tell him in such confidence.

It wasn't what he expected.

"I've never told anyone of this. If you speak of it, I'll deny I said it now. I'll claim that you made it up in a desperate need for promotion or to build your reputation, whatever fits. Do you understand me? I can do you considerable harm, professionally."

Rutledge got to his feet. "The Yard doesn't respond to threats."

"This isn't a threat, God damn it! I'm trying to protect my family, and I have every right to do that. What I'm about to tell you is disturbing, unproved, and frighteningly true. But the murderer is already dead, and there's no use in punishing the living, is there?"

"What are you talking about?" Rutledge asked, as Hamish growled a warning.

36

Cormac FitzHugh took a deep breath. He'd judged his man, he knew he was right, and he got on with it. "Olivia Marlowe— O. A. Manning—was a brilliant poet and a woman to whom life was a thing to be possessed, to be lived and worshipped and enjoyed. She was also a cold-blooded murderer."

4

Rutledge stared at the man's face, at the conviction and the pain there. He himself felt the shock, the onslaught of an unexpected grief. He hadn't known the woman at all, but he'd known her poems. *How could a soul that produced* Wings of Fire *be capable of wanton killing?*

"*Because,*" Hamish shouted at him, "*she knew the depths as well as the heights a man can reach! And it's uncanny—I want no part of her!*"

FitzHugh was watching him, acknowledging his reaction. His eyes were a very fine gray-blue in this light, clear and straightforward.

"Now you know why I'd stoop to any threat to protect what I've told you."

"You've told me, but you haven't convinced me," Rutledge heard himself saying.

FitzHugh got up and went to the lacquered cabinet against the wall that led to the hall, and opened it. Rummaging around inside, he found two glasses and a cut-glass decanter of whiskey. "I don't know about you, but I need this." He held up the second glass, raising his eyebrows.

Rutledge nodded. Talking as he poured the whiskey and added

soda, FitzHugh said, "I think she killed Nicholas. That it was a murder and suicide, not a double suicide. I don't see Nicholas cravenly taking the easy way out. She must have tricked him. Although, to be truthful, the gassing left him with a cough and rawness in his lungs. He may, for the first time, have really understood the pain that Olivia felt all those years. I don't know. It's hard to fathom. I have to believe it was suicide, but I can't help but feel, when I'm honest about it, that she planned his dying. Whatever he himself decided in the end, she was prepared to take him with her. She'd never been alone. It may be that she couldn't bear to be alone in death. Who knows what was in her mind."

He brought the whiskey and soda to Rutledge and sat down with his own, taking a long draught as if to dull the pain. Rutledge drank a little of his, waiting, looking at the room again, this time seeing the Chinese silk on the walls, the lovely proportions of the fireplace, the molded medallions on the ceiling. The polished wood of the floors, dark now and lifeless. As Olivia was lifeless. None of this could touch her. But there was still her *reputation* . . .

"I do know for a fact—for a *fact*, mind you, although there's no proof whatsoever—that Olivia killed her twin sister Anne. Anne died at eight, fell from an apple tree where we were all playing. I wasn't part of the family then, my father had come here with horses he'd sold to Rosamund. Rosamund Cheney, she was, her second marriage. Her first husband, Captain Marlowe, died out in India. Cholera, when he went back to wind up his affairs out there. She married a close friend of his, James Cheney. At any rate, Nicholas was a child at the time I'm talking about, his brother Richard still in leading strings. We'd all gone out to the orchard to play, and I started climbing trees, throwing down apples. They don't grow very well here, small and sour, but as children we didn't care. Olivia said she'd climb as well, and found a tree of her own."

He swirled the whiskey in his glass, staring at it as if it might have more answers than he did. "I was still in the other tree when Anne climbed up after Olivia. Nicholas was just under their tree, holding on to the trunk and looking up at them—probably wishing he could do the same, but his legs were too short to reach the first branch. Anne was—sometimes stubborn. Spoiled a little, I think.

40

She reached the branch where Olivia was sitting and said, "These are my apples now, you must find another tree."

Looking at Rutledge again, he said, "Olivia refused. She was never one to give way when it was wrong. 'That's not fair,' she'd say, and stick to her guns through whatever battle followed. I admired her for that . . ."

"What happened?" Rutledge asked, as he stopped again. "Get on with it, man!"

"They argued, Anne insisted. And Olivia shoved her out of the tree. She hit a branch coming down, that's what saved Nicholas. But it tipped her on her head, and when she struck the tree trunk's main root, which was just showing above the grass, it fractured her skull." He shivered. "God! When I saw Stephen lying at the foot of the stairs, I thought he'd done the same thing!" He drank more of his whiskey, then said, "I was out of the tree I'd climbed in an instant, skinning both knees as I came down, though I didn't remember that until much later. And I got to Anne first. She was dead. I looked up at Olivia, and she stared back down at me. There was nothing in her face. I was the hireling's son then, the horse trainer's brat. I played with them, I ate with them sometimes, but I wasn't one of them. So I ran for help and never told what I'd seen. Just that Anne had fallen while we were climbing."

"You never spoke of it to your father?"

"He was already besotted with Rosamund Cheney. He wouldn't have believed me—that one of her precious daughters could have killed the other one? He'd have called me a troublemaker and boxed my ears, instead. The lucky thing is, Anne didn't fall on Nicholas. There might have been two deaths that day, instead of one. They were both some distance up, she and Olivia. It was a long way to fall."

"I thought Olivia was crippled. How is it that she could climb so high?"

"She was. But the bad leg followed her, braced her, as her arms pulled her higher into the tree. Coming down again was more of a problem. But Olivia wasn't one to—to be denied a normal life. We pushed her chair everywhere, to the water's edge, to the orchard, to the cliff. Down to the village, sometimes."

"An interesting story. But as you said, there's no proof."

"No. It could still do a great deal of harm, all the same. And there's Richard."

"The one in leading strings?"

"Yes, that's right. He was lost on the moors when he was five. There was a family picnic, and he and Olivia went for a walk. She came back without him, and although we searched until dark and again through the night, with lamps brought from the nearest houses, we never found him. Or his body. He had simply disappeared."

"And you think Olivia killed him, somehow hiding the body?"

"God knows. Speculation was rampant. Some said the gypsies had taken him. He was a handsome child, very fair and more like Rosamund than Nicholas, who was dark. Others believed he'd fallen down one of the old mine shafts. The point is, Olivia had walked away with him and Olivia came back without him. He may have wandered into one of those bottomless pools on the moors. Or he may have been thrown in. The pool nearest the picnic was dragged, with no luck. I wouldn't have thought about Olivia killing him—if I hadn't been a witness to Anne's death. And that left only the two, you see, Olivia Marlowe and Nicholas Cheney. James Cheney died soon afterward. Cleaning his guns. That was the verdict at the inquest. I often wondered if it was grief over Richard that made him careless. He was distraught—they had to lash him to a horse to get him off the moors. Rosamund, Rosamund was always a pillar of strength. I'll never forget her tramping through the darkness, lamp in hand, determined, silent, tears on her face, but not a single word did she speak. I went with her. I thought if anyone could find the boy, she might. She had this streak of—I don't know—intuition. She hadn't wanted to go on the picnic, but there were guests from Wells, and James thought it would please them. That haunted him to the end."

"There's still no proof," Rutledge said, as Hamish took up the theme of intuition. Rutledge had nearly lost his own in the aftermath of war and in the struggle to regain his balance. Now he fought against the deep voice in his head, reminding him of the last time he'd used that intuition. Warwickshire. Not a time he wanted to dwell on. Instead, he said to FitzHugh, "You tell me these things, but they could all be lies. Someone else could have done the killings. Or they could have been accidents, misfortunes, not murder."

FitzHugh drained his glass, then rose to set it on the mantelpiece. "As you say. But for God's sake, man, bear it in mind, what I've told you. And don't be the hero, don't drag Olivia Marlowe or O. A. Manning or any of the rest of us through the tribulations of exposure. If I'm right, and Nicholas died at Olivia's hand, let it go down as suicide. Can you do that much for us?"

"And Stephen FitzHugh? Your half brother?"

"He lost half of his foot in the war. He fell down worn stairs. But it was my fault, if you want the truth. When he stuck his head out the window to say that he would be no more than five minutes, I was impatient, I had a train to catch, and I told him that he'd damned well better make haste or we were leaving without him. And he did make haste. And he died. I'm still waking up at night in a cold sweat, trying to call back those words."

"But he was the only family member who was against selling the house, as I understand it. Now it can be sold without any problems."

"And I'm very likely to buy it," Cormac FitzHugh said, reaching for Rutledge's empty glass and setting it beside his own. "That's what brought me down this morning. I'd toyed with the idea. I'm looking for a house in the country, but I was thinking of something closer to town than this. Now I feel guilty about the house as well. Letting it go out of the family. I can't follow Stephen's plan, I can't turn it into a museum for O. A. Manning—God, the scholars would have a field day if they stumbled over what I've just told you! Olivia would not only be famous, she'd be notorious."

Rutledge stood up. "Which window did your brother call from, before he fell?"

FitzHugh stared at him blankly. "Which window? It was from the room that had been Father's. To the right of the stairs. Do you want to see it?"

"No, that's not necessary. Not this morning. I've taken enough of your time. I've work to do in the village. Will you be staying here? In the house?"

"If I can find Mrs. Trepol and persuade her to make up my room." He grinned. "I'm not useful in that regard. Horses I know, and contracts, and how to handle stockholders at a meeting. Sheets and towels are beyond me."

"What do you do for a living?"

"I have a business in the City. FitzHugh Enterprises. Made my fortune in iron and steel, branched out into other interests. Oil. The Navy's looking into that." He smiled, immense charm, Irish charm, changing his face. "They call me a war profiteer in some quarters. Because I made money on the killing. But the men in the trenches, when the first tanks came over the barbed wire, didn't worry about their cost, only about what they could do to the Germans. I saved lives, if you come right down to it."

"Were you in the war as well as profiting from it?"

The grin faded. "Oh, yes, Inspector, I was. That surprises most people. I was one of the code breakers. I have a skill at mathematics that certain people at Cambridge remembered quite well. I don't think I *could* have gotten into the real fighting—I was more useful where I was. Boring work. You never knew whether what you'd just decoded was the most important secret of the campaign or the least important. You just did your best. Like everyone else."

Rutledge closed the front door behind him and stepped out into the drive. The sunlight now was brilliant, the mists gone, the sea such a deep blue it hurt the eyes to look at it. He walked down the drive and took the path towards what turned out to be a shingle strand, long and narrow and swept by the tides in every gale, but this morning busy with gulls and choughs and a pair of ravens that were squabbling over something the water had brought in. It appeared to be what was left of a fish. The headland shut out the wind, and there was unseasonable warmth by the water, and a stillness of the air that reminded him of France, just before the artillery barrages began. He stood there, looking out to sea, watching a wisp of steam that came out of Wales and sailed, below the horizon, to faraway ports. It was peaceful here, but there were straggles of rocks again to his right, jutting out where the land began to rise once more, tumbled and rough and water-sprayed. He wondered if in the past wreckers had stood here with their lanterns and lured ships onto a stormy shore. Cornwall had always lived from the sea, one way or another.

Shadowed, the headland on his left was massive and dark, white water creaming at its base. And the house was invisible from here, only the line of the roof and the clipped lawns foretelling its presence.

There was the sound of footsteps on the shingle behind him, and he turned to see Rachel Ashford coming towards him. He waited for her, and she said, "Has he gone yet?"

"Cormac FitzHugh? No, I left him in the house."

Chewing her lip for a moment, she thought about it. "Well, I'll just have to wait until tomorrow, won't I? For the ships." Then she looked up at him, shading her eyes with her hand. "I know," she said, answering what she read in his face. "I wasn't actually ready to fetch them anyway. It's just—" After a moment, she went on in different voice, "You've been in there. What did you feel?"

She meant the study upstairs. And he couldn't pretend to misunderstand.

He said, looking out to sea, "I don't know."

But Hamish said, very clearly, "The lassie didn't ask for lies!"

Startled, Rutledge turned back to her and said, "What makes you think there's anything to feel?"

It was her turn to be evasive. "I—you don't make decisions like that, and expect no trace of them to survive. I'm not fanciful, you know. But when I go inside that house, I hear the silence. And I can't tell what it's whispering to me. But I'm frightened."

"Would you like me to fetch the ships for you? Put them out in the gallery, where you could box them up without going inside the study?" He couldn't have said, afterward, why he'd volunteered to do it. Except that he could sense her pain. And pain he understood.

Surprised, she said, "Would you? I couldn't impose on Mrs. Trepol. Or ask the others, they'd have laughed at me. But if you could—when Cormac has gone? It—it would be very kind of you."

He couldn't stop the next question. It came out more bluntly than he'd intended. Because, he knew, it disturbed him deeply. "Do

45

you think Olivia Marlowe could have murdered her half brother, then killed herself?"

For an instant he thought she was going to faint, her face turned so white, and she took several gasping breaths, as if to steady herself. He reached out to catch her arm, but she shook him off.

"You—is that what you feel in that room?"

"No, it's a policeman's curiosity exploring the possibilities. After all, you sent for me to do that."

Color flooded back into her face, and she swallowed hard. "That was very cruel," she said, voice low and husky. "I can't picture, *in my wildest fancies*, any reason why Olivia would harm Nicholas. Or why he would harm her!"

And yet the very question had struck a chord in her, one she'd shut out of her mind with all the strength of her will. Until he'd put it into words.

5

They walked back to the village together, in a silence that brooded between them like a summer's storm, building and darkening, but not breaking. The shortcut through the copse was cool and dim after the sunlight.

Hamish was rattling on about women, about the moodiness this one evoked, about his relief at leaving the house and grounds of Trevelyan Hall. Rutledge ignored him. He was still trying to deal with the concept of Olivia Marlowe as a killer, and damning Cormac FitzHugh for putting it into his head.

No, it wasn't Olivia Marlowe that disturbed him. He, Rutledge, knew very little about Olivia Marlowe. It was O. A. Manning he knew, and the poetry had touched his own spirit in the darkness of war. Standing before God, Rutledge would have sworn that O. A. Manning was not a murderer. *Could not have been.* And yet, Cormac FitzHugh had no reason to lie, no reason to twist the truth, no reason to know that Rutledge the man, not the police officer, had seen something fragile shatter as he spoke.

As if she'd sensed something of the turmoil in Rutledge's mind, Rachel touched his arm and stopped. "What is it? What's bothering you?"

"I don't know," he told her truthfully. "I think I've come to

Cornwall on a useless errand." Better London, and boredom, than this!

"You've only been here one day," she said gravely. "How can you know that? Or did the Yard send you here just to please Henry Ashford, a gesture that was never intended to dig very deeply into these deaths?"

The old proverb—to let sleeping dogs lie—flitted through his mind. Instead, he said to her, out of nowhere, except that they were taking the shorter path to Borcombe, "Who is the old crone I met in the village this morning? She must be eighty, by the look of her. Stooped. But with extraordinarily clear eyes." And a perverted sense of humor, if he was any judge.

Rachel frowned. "Ah. You must mean Sadie. I'm not really sure what her last name is. She's been here for so long that she's just—Sadie. The old rector, Mr. Nelson, who's gone now, said he thought she'd been a nurse in the Crimea, and it turned her mind. But she has a healer's touch, it might be true enough. Midwife, confessor, horse doctor, comforter, prescriber of herbs. The villagers may go to her more often than to Dr. Hawkins."

"Witch?"

She chuckled, a low husky laugh that was at odds with her personality as he'd come to know it. Sensual, almost, and yet full of an appreciation of the ridiculous. "I suppose she's been called that too! No, if she's a witch, it's a white witch, not a black one. I've never heard of spells put on anyone or people dying under her care. Well, they die, yes, but of their ailments."

"No love potions?"

"No, sadly not," she said, a twist of pain in her voice that came out of nowhere. As if she sensed he'd heard it, she said, smiling, "I went to her once, begging a potion. I was madly in love, and I didn't know how to handle it. I thought she might give me something to put in his soup or his breakfast porridge—we were too young for goblets of wine, but I grew up on the stories of Tristan and Isolde. I knew—thought I knew—that such potions worked. She was very gentle, but she told me that love couldn't be bought."

He thought she was belittling herself and what had actually happened, but said nothing. It occurred to him to ask her about Anne, but it was not the time. Then she mentioned the name herself.

"It was Anne who'd read the old Cornish legends to me. Her grandfather Trevelyan—Rosamund's father—had compiled a collection of them, it was famous in its day, and there's a letter in the house from Tennyson, telling him how much the book stirred his imagination while he was writing *Idylls of the King*. I could quote long passages from it by heart. Well, we all could. Nicholas, especially. You'd have thought, watching our theatricals, that *he* was the poet. He read so beautifully."

"Tell me about Anne."

"Anne? My goodness, there's nothing to tell. Anne died when she was eight or nine. She was Olivia's twin, and they were so much alike, to look at them, that you couldn't believe it. But oddly enough they were quite different in natures. Anne was the sort of child who'd never met a stranger—she could cajole anyone into doing anything. Except Livia, of course! Stephen reminds—reminded—me of Anne, the same golden charm. Livia was, I don't know, one of those people who lived in her imagination, and found it rich enough that she didn't need other stimulation. She was quiet and thoughtful and very much her own woman, even in childhood."

"How did Anne die?"

"She fell out of an apple tree in the old orchard. It isn't there now, Rosamund had the orchard cut down, but it was beyond the back garden, sheltered by brick walls. We were all playing there, Nicholas and Olivia and Anne and I. And she reached too far for an apple, lost her balance, and came down on a root. I'd never seen a dead person before. I was terrified, out of my wits. I thought she was teasing, playing games with us."

"Was Cormac there?"

Rachel frowned. "I don't remember. He may have been. It was Nicholas I remember most, kneeling beside Anne, taking her hand, calling to her, crying because she wouldn't answer him. And Olivia having trouble coming down from the tree. Because of her leg. This was before Nicholas had carved a brace, of course."

"Anne fell? No one pushed her?"

She looked at him, surprised. "No, why should anyone push her? She was up in the tree, picking apples, and then she reached too far. We were all *children*, we would never have dreamed of such a thing!"

But children killed. It was something that he'd learned in London, his first year at the Yard.

They came out of the woods into a lane that joined the main street of the village, where houses clustered together under slate roofs that looked like quicksilver in the sun, lead in the rain. There were gardens behind every gate, crowded with vegetables and flaming with color.

Rachel stopped. "I go this way—I'm staying with a friend on the outskirts." She shaded her eyes again with her hand, and said, "You didn't mean that—about going back to London? You'll stay and see what you can find? I'll never persuade Henry to appeal for help again."

He laughed. "Probably not." Remembering the heat in London, the cramped little office, Bowles' pretensions, and the squalid knifings that had somehow captured the imagination of the city, he found himself saying, "No, I'm not going back yet. I'll be here for several more days."

She left, reassured, and he turned towards The Three Bells. But noticing the shingle on the front of the doctor's surgery, he opened the garden gate and went through to knock at the door.

A young woman with pretty strawberry blond hair opened the door and said, "Ah, you're just in time, if you want to see the doctor. Five more minutes, and he'd have gone through to his luncheon."

"Mrs. Hawkins?" he asked, guessing.

"Yes, and if you'll just wait here a moment," she answered, leading him into a small sitting room fitted out with bits and pieces of worn furnishings that had been relegated here from the rest of the house, "I'll tell him you're here. The name, please?"

Rutledge gave it to her, and she disappeared through the door beside him. A moment later she whisked back into the waiting room. "Dr. Hawkins will see you now." She held the door wide, ready to shut it behind him.

Rutledge went through into the tidy, surprisingly bright surgery. "Dr. Hawkins?" he said to the short, thickset man behind the desk. He was not as young as his wife, but not much beyond thirty-five, he thought.

"Indeed, and what can I do for you this morning?" His eyes raked Rutledge, from crown to toe. Seeing more than Rutledge cared to have him see. "Having trouble sleeping, are you?"

"No, I'm having no trouble at all, as it happens," Rutledge said stiffly. "I'm Inspector Rutledge, from Scotland Yard—"

"Oh, Lord, and what's happened *now*!"

"It isn't what is happening now that concerns me. I've been asked to look into the deaths of three of your patients, Stephen FitzHugh, Olivia Marlowe, and Nicholas Cheney."

Hawkins stared at him, then threw his pen on the desk with such force that it bounced and nearly rolled off the edge. "Those deaths are history. Closed. The Inquest agreed with my first impressions and my considered opinion. An accident and a double suicide. Surely you've read the medical report?"

"I have, and it's very thorough. All the same, there are questions I must ask. And that you are required to answer."

"I know damned well what I'm *required* to do," Hawkins said irritably. "And I've done it." His eyes narrowed and he looked at Rutledge with sudden suspicion. "You aren't planning to dig up the bodies, are you? That's all I need right now!"

"In what way?"

"Look, I've been a good doctor here. I took over from my wife's father, who's nearly gaga now, war finished him, too much to do, too little energy to do it. I've built a decent practice, and I'm being considered for a partnership in Plymouth. I learned my craft in the war, doing things I'd never thought in school I'd be expected to do. Sew up the dying, send the living back to the Front, find a way to keep the shell-shock cases from being shot for cowardice—" he saw Rutledge flinch, and added with relish "—and even deliver forty-seven babies to refugees who had no place to sleep them- selves, much less with infants to nurse! I've paid my dues, I've earned the right to move on to better things, and if my future part- ners get wind of the fact that three—*three*—of my cases are being exhumed, under Scotland Yard's eager eye, I'll be dead, stuck here forever. No chance at Plymouth, no hope of London in the end."

"The fact that Scotland Yard has an interest in these deaths in no way is a reflection on you—"

"The hell it isn't! For God's sake, man, I filled out the death certificates! It has everything to do with me!"

"Then you're convinced that there's nothing in either of the suicides or in the accident that could warrant further police interest?"

"That's exactly what I am! Convinced beyond any shadow of a doubt!"

"It hasn't occurred to you that something in the pasts of these three people might change the circumstances enough that what appeared to be suicide was actually murder and suicide? To use an instance I came across recently."

Hawkins threw up his hands. "*Murder* and suicide? You've been drinking, I can smell it on your breath. Enough to be having delusions?"

"No, I'm as sober as you are," Rutledge said, reining his temper in hard.

"Not bloody likely, when you suggest such things as you did just now! I walked into that study and found two people on the couch. A man and a woman. Their hands were touching, his left and her right. In the other hand, each held a glass. There had been laudanum in the glasses, and it was on their lips and in their mouths and in their guts. Enough to kill both quickly, and several times over. Miss Marlowe had had poliomyelitis, and contrary to what people tell you, paralysis is not painless. She had been given laudanum by my father-in-law and by me, as needed. Until this spring she'd used it responsibly, no indications of addictions or abuse. But it's as painless a death as you could wish for, if you have to go out. I can't blame her for choosing it, and I saw no evidence that either one had forced drinking it on the other. No bruises about the mouth or tongue, none on the lips. Nothing else in their stomachs to arouse suspicion. Double suicide. That's precisely what it was. No more, no less."

"Nothing in their stomachs to suggest that one might have secretly given an overdose to the other, before swallowing his or her own draught?"

"It's hard to introduce laudanum secretly into clear soup, spring lamb, roasted, vegetables and potatoes."

"People of their sort usually drank wine with meals, and coffee afterward."

"The state of digestion tells me that they lived for enough hours after their meal that it couldn't have been in their wine or their coffee. I'd say they swallowed the laudanum some time after midnight. As if they'd sat up talking about it, and then decided to do it. Or possibly around dawn. They'd been dead for some time when Mrs. Trepol discovered them on Monday morning. Over twenty-four hours. Now my own meal is waiting, and if you'll excuse me, I'll go and eat it. My advice to you is to return to London and do something useful there. There's very little crime in a place like Borcombe. We haven't needed the services of Scotland Yard in living memory, and I doubt if we will in the next twenty years!"

Rutledge left the doctor's office, thinking over what he'd been told that morning.

Damn all, if you came right down to it!

No crimes, no murderers, no reason for a seasoned Scotland Yard inspector to waste his time here.

"But just what ye're good for—nithing," Hamish declared. "What if Warwickshire was only a bit of luck, and none of *your* doing? What if you failed there, and haven't had the sense yet to see it? What if ye're failing now, because you haven't got the skills to tell whether there's murder here or no? That house is haunted, man, and if you don't find out why, ye'll be defeated by your own fears!"

After lunch at The Three Bells, Rutledge felt restless and uncertain. He told himself it had nothing to do with Hamish's remarks, or the frustration he felt over where to turn next. Cormac FitzHugh had seemed to be so certain of his facts. Rachel Ashford was unsettled by the notion of murder being done, even though she'd called in the Yard herself. Hawkins was not cooperative, and the police in Borcombe had no reason to stir up the pot for murder, when their investigation had ended so creditably.

He thought about it for several minutes, staring out his window towards the sea, then picked up his coat and went in search of the rectory. It stood four-square beside the church, gray stone with white trim at the windows and doors, but built more for long service than for beauty.

The rector wasn't in his office, but the housekeeper sent Rutledge around the back to where he was pottering about in his garden. It was a big garden, green and prosperous, with roses by the house and the scent of wall flowers coming from somewhere, sweet and elusive.

The rector was middle-aged, a man more accustomed—from the look of him—to working in the ground than preaching from a pulpit. He straightened up when he saw Rutledge coming across the strip of lawn between the vegetables and the flowers. "Good afternoon," he said, neither effusively nor coolly, but with the manner of a man who'd rather be about his own business just now than God's.

"Inspector Rutledge, from London," he replied. "Mr. Smedley?"

"Aye, that's right," the rector said with a sigh and put down his hoe.

"No, keep working, if you like. I'd prefer to stay out here and talk than go inside." The housekeeper, if he was any judge, had long ears. "It isn't a matter for a priest so much as a question of information that I need."

"Well, then, if you don't mind?" He picked up his hoe and began to chip at the weeds between rows of what appeared to be marigolds and asters next to a line of sweet peas.

"I'm here because London has a few remaining questions about several deaths in May. At Trevelyan Hall."

The rector glanced at him with a smile. "So gossip was right this morning. And you'd hardly set foot in the place."

"Yes, but the questions I'm about to ask you aren't for the ears of gossips. Good intentioned or ill. I want to know about the people who died. The woman and the two men. What they were like, how they lived, why they should die, so close together."

The rector's back was to Rutledge now, as he turned to come down the other row. "Ah. Well, that's a long story. Do you know much about the family?"

"About the grandfather who owned the Hall. About the daughter who had three husbands and six children, only one of whom is still living. About the cousin. And about the stepson who lives in London and made his fortune. I could have learned all this from the shopkeepers and the housewives on their way to market. I need more. To satisfy London that all's well."

"And why should London doubt that?"

"The Home Office has been going through reports. They like to be thorough. Three deaths in one family in such a short time raises . . . doubts?"

"None of those here, I can tell you that much! I don't know of any questions raised when Olivia and Nicholas were discovered, nor any gossip that's flown about since. And in a village like this, it's your surest sign that all's well. As for the death of Stephen FitzHugh, the man fell in an empty house, all the members of his party outside and accounted for. Unless you believe in ghosts, I don't suppose there's much to be suspicious of in that."

"Strange that you should mention ghosts," Rutledge said idly. "I'm told the Hall is haunted. And not by anything that can be exorcised by the church."

The rector straightened again and looked at him. "Who has told you these tales?"

"A Scotsman, for one," Rutledge answered.

The rector smiled. "They're great ones for the Sight, the Scots. Has he also told you whether murder has been done?"

Touché.

"Has murder been done? Now—or in the far past?"

"Not to my knowledge," the rector said. "And I include the confessional in that answer. No one has confessed to me, and no gossip has reached me. The house has seen a good deal of sorrow in its time. But show me a house that hasn't been touched by grief. Especially not with the war and the influenza epidemic. You'll see the wounded for yourself. We were spared the sickness here—the

55

worst of it, anyway. We lost only three souls to it. But even three is too many in a village this size."

"Tell me if you will how a woman like Olivia Marlowe, who was reclusive and knew very little of the outside world, could write such poetry?"

He went back to his hoeing. "There's a question only God can answer. But who says she knew very little of the world? I've read the poems. They speak to me of a frightening knowledge of the human condition. Of the human soul. And yet she never spoke of her writing to me. And I never asked her questions about it. Come to that, we only knew at the very end that she was O. A. Manning. It'd been kept a dark secret, even from her family. I'd say Nicholas knew, and that was it."

"But if she had such understanding and such spirit, why keep it secret?"

"Well, Inspector, I take it you have no secrets—painful or otherwise—that you prefer to hide from the world? Not immoral secrets, not terrible secrets, perhaps, but those that wound your spirit?"

Which was too damned close for comfort. Rutledge began to reassess his earlier opinion of the priest. Hamish was murmuring viciously, rubbing salt into the fresh wound. But then it was always fresh . . .

"Her paralysis, then?'

"She found it confining," Smedley said pensively. "But never a cross to bear. What she feared most, I think, was to be judged on that account, and not on her work. You've read the literary magazines since the news broke, I suppose? Everyone scrambling to understand the woman, and not the verse. Delving into her life as if it held answers. Making an issue of her condition."

"Was she ugly? Misshapen? Did she not know how to dress well? To do her hair? Talk to people? Is that what she ran away from, and buried in her genius?"

Mr. Smedley began to laugh before Rutledge finished his catalog. "I have a very poor opinion of the women you've known, Inspector, if that's how you judge the fair sex! Even as a churchman I know better than that!"

"Then describe her to me," Rutledge said irritably.

Smedley leaned on his hoe and looked up at the dormers of his house. "For one thing, her mother was beautiful. Rosamund. In Olivia, it came out in other ways. You found you couldn't forget her, yet you couldn't say why that was. She had lovely eyes, inherited from her father. I suppose her strength may have come from him as well, although Rosamund had great strength too. Transport Olivia to London, and except for the useless limb, she'd not be that much different from any young woman you found there. She'd have had more than her share of beaus, if the men in the city had half the sense they were born with! No, Olivia wasn't ugly or misshapen. She dressed like any other countrywoman. No floating scarves, none of those shiny black gowns or exotic feathers. No literary pretensions at all. A warm manner, a pleasant nature, but never serene. Serenity had not been granted to her." He shrugged. "Her hair, always one of her glories, was darker than Rosamund's, that shade of brown that turns to gold in the sunlight. More like her father's. George Marlowe was a very fine man. Rosamund adored him, and she was bereft when he died in India. She told me herself that they feared for her health, and sanity, for a time. Her courage saw her through. And her faith."

Rutledge felt his confusion deepen. Did everyone see Olivia in a different light? And if they did, *where was the real woman?*

"I was surprised when she took her life," Smedley said after a moment. "Olivia. I wouldn't have expected it of her. For Nicholas to follow her seemed—oddly—reasonable enough, I can't tell you why, it just did. But for Olivia to die by her own hand—it shook me deeply. It was as if a bedrock from which I drew my own strength had suddenly been shaken to its roots and crumbled. I wept," he said, as if that still surprised him and left him uncertain of himself. "I wept not only for myself and for her, but for what was lost, with her going. She was the most remarkable woman I've ever known. Or ever hope to know."

"And Nicholas?"

"He was an enigma," Smedley replied slowly. "In all the years I'd known him, I never really *knew* the man. He had great depths, great passion. A wonderful mind. We played chess and argued over the war and discussed politics. And I was never allowed behind the wall of his patience."

When Rutledge didn't respond, Smedley added almost to himself, "I don't know that Nicholas wasn't my greatest failure . . ."

6

When Rutledge walked into the dark, narrow lobby of The Three Bells, the innkeeper handed him a small package that had been delivered earlier.

Rutledge took it through to the public bar, where he ordered a pint and when it came, sat staring at the package for another several minutes before opening it. Faces somehow lent reality to facts . . .

There were photographs inside, as he'd expected. With a note: "Please, I'd like to have these back when you've finished with them."

There was no signature, but he knew they'd come from Rachel Ashford. He tried to see Rachel and Peter together, to imagine Peter marrying her, and failed. Not because she wasn't the sort of woman Peter could have loved, but because Peter as he remembered him in school must have been very different from the man who'd died on Kilimanjaro. Just as he, Rutledge, had changed out of all recognition from the boy who'd had so many fine dreams and plans for his future.

Taking the photographs out of their wrapping and spreading them out on his table, he looked at them, not sure what he was going to see, not certain he wanted to see them now.

There were several older ones. Rosamund Trevelyan at twenty—

there were names and dates on the back—shining with youth and beauty and some inner peace. He looked at her more closely. Yes, there was strength as well, and a sense of laughter in her eyes. Anne and Olivia standing amid the roses in the back garden, so alike that there was a question mark on the reverse by their names. Two girls in lace-edged white dresses with long sashes and ribbons in their hair, smiling shyly for the camera. Pretty girls, with tumbling curls and the shape of Rosamund's face if not her beauty. The same girls again, this time a little older, with a small boy and another child in a long dress. Nicholas and Richard. Nicholas was already tall for his age, dark unruly hair and dark eyes, although in the photograph you couldn't tell if they were brown or dark blue. Another one, when Richard was five and Nicholas was seven or eight, on the moors with their family. Richard was now a boy with a wide, mischievous grin and gleeful eyes. A born troublemaker, some would say, ready for any game. Was that how he'd been lured away?

Nicholas, frowning at the camera, was intense, chin up, eyes defiant. But he was smiling in another photograph, with Olivia now—Anne would have been dead several years—and Rosamund, holding a pair of twins in her arms, all but invisible in swathes of christening robes. Susannah and Stephen. But Rosamund still seemed no more than a few months older than the girl she'd been at twenty, with a tilt of her head and a smile in her eyes that any man might respond to. Lovely, vivid with spirit. Olivia, on the other hand, was nearly in her shadow, a slim girl with long hair that curled around her face, Nicholas beside her with his arm protectively around her. Rutledge looked again at Olivia. This was the budding poet, this was the woman who had left her mark in words, and yet there was something about her, something in the shadows, that drew him back to her face, wishing it was larger, clearer. Unforgettable, the rector had said. But what?

A man with Cormac on one side, and the twins, now walking, at his boots, holding on to his legs and grinning shyly at the camera. Brian FitzHugh, his elder son, and his children by Rosamund. Brian wasn't handsome, and yet he had an attractiveness that came from his smile. Cormac, on the other hand, was remarkably handsome already, a slim boy with grace in the set of his shoulders, and strength in his eyes. Who knew himself, and felt no doubts about where he might be going. The twins were as fair and pretty as cherubs, with Rosamund's beauty and only a faint shadow of their father, more in their sturdy build than in their features. Her liveliness in their faces.

The last two were of men. An older, bearded man, straight and broad-shouldered, beside a younger man in uniform. Captain Marlowe, Rosamund's first husband, with her father, Adrian Trevelyan. Trevelyan wasn't smiling, as most of his generation seldom smiled for the camera, but Marlowe had been laughing when this photograph was taken, catching him with its reflection in his eyes, and giving remarkable spirit to his face. Rutledge could understand why Rosamund had fallen in love with him. They must have been a handsome pair. The other man, tall, standing alone beside a horse, was James Cheney, Nicholas' father, and Rutledge didn't have to glance at the back of the photograph to identify him. His son was his image, darkly attractive and yet a quiet, introspective man.

Rutledge looked at the collection again, and thought of the faces. All dead now but two. Cormac and Susannah. One who belonged, and one who didn't.

The elderly barkeep came over to ask if he'd like a refill for his glass, and looked down at the photographs. "The Trevelyans," he said. "Aye, it were a grand family, that one. I remember the old master, not one to trifle with, but the fairest man I ever came across. Doted on his daughter—well, she were a beauty, and no question there, but a *lady*, and you recollected your manners around her! But one to say thank you and please, as if you'd done her a favor, not a service. Now that one—" a gnarled finger pointed to the Captain "—he died out in India of the cholera, and Mr. Trevelyan, he claimed he'd lost a son. And Miss Rosamund was so ill of grief, the doctor feared for her life. There were some saying she married Mr. Cheney hoping to forget, but there was love there as well. I saw them together, often, and there was love. But Mr. FitzHugh surprised us all, marrying Miss Rosamund. He wasn't—he wasn't Quality, like her. Irish gentry, *he* said, but who's to know?

61

Still, she was happy enough. And she doted on the twins. A good mother."

"Two of her children died young."

"Aye, they never found the little one. There was a tramp through here not many years back that reminded me of Richard Cheney. Same devil's look in his eyes. That boy was afraid of naught, and tempted God and Satan with his antics. Ran away from home twice, nearly set the Hall on fire one Guy Fawkes Night, with a bonfire in the nursery. I was a groom at the Hall then, when they kept so many horses, and he'd beg to ride anything with four legs!"

Another customer walked into the bar, crutches still awkward under his armpits. A leg missing. The barkeep heard the uneven *thump-thump*, looked over his shoulder, and said, "Right with you, Will." He turned back to Rutledge. "They say Miss Olivia wrote poetry, but I don't know. Not in a woman's line, is it? How'd she know about the war, then, and the suffering? Somebody's got it all wrong."

He went away to serve the other man, and then to speak to a pair of fishermen slumped in the corner benches, arguing dispiritedly over what had become of the pilchard runs that had once been Cornwall's fishing wealth, and what to do about the outlanders from as far away as Yarmouth, their big boats overfishing Cornish seas. Rutledge was left looking down at the faces that stared unseeingly back at him. Remembering what the barman had said.

Was that the key? Was that why Nicholas had had to die too? Because he wrote the poetry that had made O. A. Manning famous?

Rutledge shook his head. It wasn't what he wanted to believe.

The next morning, Rutledge kept his promise to Rachel Ashford and accompanied her back to the Hall. The sun was brilliant, blindingly bright at sea, and touching the land with colors that vibrated against the eye.

They walked through the copse again, coming out to stand for a moment looking up at the house. It was shimmering, like some mythical castle on a mythical hill, and Rachel said, "Odd, isn't it? How very impressive the house is? And yet if you look at it architecturally, there must be a hundred homes in Cornwall alone that are as fine. Finer, even. This one is old and rambling and very small by most standards. But I love it with all my heart. Peter said—" she stopped, cleared her throat, and went on, "Peter said that it was in the stone, that sparkling quality. And the angle of the sun caught it sometimes."

"Yes, that could be true," Rutledge said. He'd thanked her for the photographs when she came to the inn, and promised to return them before he left Cornwall. But he hadn't told her any of the thoughts that had rampaged through his head most of the night, until Hamish had clamored for peace. After that, he'd slept, but fitfully. It had seemed that he could hear the sea from his room, and the wash of the waves kept time with his heartbeats.

She looked at him. "You'll be leaving soon. I can feel it. With nothing done about my problem."

"I can't find anything to keep me here," he said. "Look, Rachel—" he realized he was using her given name, but somehow Mrs. Ashford was not how he thought of her "—there's neither proof nor evidence to show that something's wrong. I'm wasting the Yard's time if I pretend there is."

Rachel sighed. "Yes, I know."

"Would you be happier if I did find something? That Olivia was a murderer? That Nicholas was? And as for Stephen, I can't see that there's anyone to kill him. If everyone is telling the truth and you were all outside at the time he fell."

"You talk about Nicholas and Olivia," she said harshly, walking on, "but not about the living. About me. About Susannah and Daniel. About Cormac."

"You told me yourself that you couldn't accept the possibility that they were murderers. Are you saying that *you* might have been the killer?"

"No, of course not! I—all right, if you want to know, Cormac came to see me last evening. He wants to buy the house. Out of guilt, he says. Because he can't do what Stephen wanted and make it a museum, but in a way it stays in the family. A compromise. *We* get our money and *he* has a country home and Stephen is somehow pacified."

"Pacified?" It was an odd choice of word.

"Yes, apparently Stephen had this silly the notion that he'd been the inspiration for the *Wings of Fire* poems—the love poems—and Susannah said the museum was really to his glory, not Olivia's. It was cruel, but she was furious with him for making such a silly fuss when everyone else had agreed on selling. That's the point, you see, we'd always more or less expected the house would be sold when Olivia and Nicholas died. But Adrian Trevelyan had made certain, in his will, that Cormac couldn't inherit the house. He left the house to Olivia, not Rosamund, to prevent it!"

"You know that for a fact?"

"Well, I was a child, Inspector, but a child hears things, a child is sometimes very quiet in a corner, and the adults forget he—or she—is there. And they talk. And that child listens. Sometimes it doesn't mean anything, sometimes it does. But I have a clear memory of Adrian speaking to Rosamund when James Cheney died. We'd just had the reading of his will, and so I knew what a will *was*. And Adrian said, 'I won't be here to see you wed again.' And she said, 'I don't think it's likely that I shall—I'll never find another man like George Marlowe, and I won't be as lucky as I was with James.' And Adrian replied, 'You're young. You have a zest for living. You'll take another husband, and I won't be here. So I'm changing my will, my love, and taking the house from you. Do you mind if I give it to Olivia? I've loved her, and her father in her, since she was put into my arms as a newborn. I'd like to think of her here, moving through my house, loving it, after I'm gone. You've got the house George left you, and Nicholas will have James'. Olivia has no other home, may never have one.' To my disappointment, eavesdropping, Rosamund asked for several days to think about it, and I never heard the outcome, until Adrian died and his will was read. I knew then what they'd decided, between them. That's why Cormac's suggestion . . . upset me. I couldn't tell him what Adrian had said, could I? That house has always been a haven of warmth and love, and now we're all quarrelling over what becomes of it, *spoiling* it! Every time I'm reminded of Stephen's death, I remember that he died still angry with us for not doing what he'd asked of us."

"Rosamund had another home?"

"Yes, in Winchester, in the Close, actually. It was George Marlowe's—he bought it himself. My own father inherited the family home, where he and George had grown up. George was the younger son, and chose the army."

"And Nicholas had a house?"

"In Norfolk. I've been there, a very pretty place."

"And so he could have left Trevelyan Hall, if he'd been unhappy here, and gone elsewhere to live. Or, assuming he married and didn't want to bring his bride to the Hall, he could take her to his own home?"

They had reached the drive now, and Rachel turned away, looking towards the headland. "I don't think Nicholas would have married and left here."

"But if in fact he wished it, he could have."

After a moment she said quietly, "Yes."

Which might have given Olivia a motive for killing Nicholas?

He looked at Rachel, suddenly aware of something that he hadn't felt in her before. "You were in love with Nicholas, weren't you? Most of your life."

"No! I was fond of him, but love . . ." Her voice died away, and the lie with it.

"Did you ever love Peter?" Rutledge asked harshly, feeling the pain of a man he'd known, somehow mixed with his own. Peter deserved better!

She whirled on him. "What do you know about love! Yes, I loved Peter, he was wonderful, gentle and kind and I've missed him every day since he sailed for Africa!"

"But loving him isn't the same as being in love with Nicholas, is it?"

"Don't!" she cried, and ran up the steps to the door, fumbling to unlock it through her tears. "I won't listen to this! Go away, I'll take care of the ships myself! I don't need you or anyone else!"

He came up behind her and quietly took the key from her. "I'm sorry," he said gently. "I shouldn't have said any of that to you."

"But I brought you here, didn't I?" she said as the door swung wide and the house seemed to be waiting for them. "It was a mistake, I see that now. Just go back to London and leave me alone!"

If Cormac had spent the night here, there was no sign of it.

Rutledge made tea in the kitchen and brought it to Rachel in the small parlor that overlooked the sea. He had opened the drapes when he took her there, to alleviate some of the air of grief that the darkened rooms seemed to evoke. She was not crying now, but there was a bleakness in her face that made him feel guilty as hell. She took the cup with a nod, then began to sip it as if she needed it badly. He walked to the windows, his back to her, and looked out at the sea. As Nicholas had done every dawn since childhood, although Rutledge wasn't aware of that. But Rachel was. She concentrated on the tea with fierce attention, but the tall figure of the man before her, no more than a silhouette, was like a knife in her heart.

Afterward they went up to the gallery. There were boxes she'd left in one of the bedrooms, and she fetched those while he went into the study, opened the cases, and brought out the finely wrought ship's models. They were of such perfection that he could see the tiniest detail clearly, and he marveled at the patience and workmanship that had gone into them. But then the rector had spoken of Nicholas' patience.

He gave her the first one, the *Queen of the Sea*, at the door of the room, and she took it the way a priest takes the host, with trembling fingers. He made a point not to look at her face, her eyes. She knelt and began to wrap it carefully in cotton batting, then just as carefully lowered it into a box filled with torn strips of newspaper. He went back for the next, and brought that to her as well. The *Olympic*. He remembered when she was launched, 1910. The sister ship of the ill-fortuned *Titanic*. There was also the German *Deutschland* and her sister, the *Kaiser Wilhelm der Grosse*. And the earliest of the great liners, the *Sirius*, handsomely afloat on a beautifully carved sea with dolphins at her bows. And the *Acquitaine*, launched in time to become a hospital ship in the Dardanelles. He wondered how many ghosts had followed *her* home to England. The *Mauritania* had served off Gallipoli, the sister ship of the *Lusitania* sunk by a German U-boat in 1915.

"Was it the ships or the sea that intrigued Nicholas Cheney?" he asked as the last of the liners went into her paper and batting slip. He hadn't told Rachel how empty the cabinet looked without them, as if something that was alive in the room had been taken away.

"Both, I think. He told me once—when we were children—that he'd grow up to be a great sea captain. One of his ancestors was an admiral, on his mother's side, and had fought at Trafalgar. I suppose that was what put the idea into his head. There was a small boat down on the strand that he used from time to time. Sometimes Olivia went out with him. Sometimes I did. He was a different man on the water. I—I don't exactly how, but it was there."

She closed the last box, and with his help taped the tops of the others as well, then together they carried them down to the hall. But at the stairs she stopped and looked back over her shoulder with such haunted eyes that he turned away and made a show of shifting the boxes in his arms. Hamish, in the back of his mind, stirred restlessly and ominously. He was sensitive to lost love— he'd died before returning to his own.

Rachel left before Rutledge did, and when he came out, shutting the door behind him, he found himself face to face with the old crone who'd given him the longer directions to the house on his first morning. She stared up at him and grinned. What had Rachel called her? He couldn't remember.

"Ye found your way, I take it?"

"Both ways, actually."

She cackled. "Is Miss Rachel still here?"

"No, she left some time ago."

"And you'd not be knowing, would ye, of any old rags Miss Olivia was leaving for me? They'd not be in those boxes yonder in the hall?"

"No, Mrs. Ashford packed those this morning. She's coming to fetch them in a cart later."

"And none in the kitchen by the back door?"

"Not that I recall."

She sighed. "I saw the devil yesterday, and wasn't asking the likes of *him* for rags. But Miss Rachel's a lady, she'd not turn me off."

Rutledge smiled. She might seem sharp as a tack, but her mind wandered. "I'll ask her when I see her next."

The old woman leaned back and looked up at the house. "I was here the day Mr. Stephen fell."

"You were what?"

"I was here," she said irritably. "I'd helped Mrs. Trepol with the clothes she was taking for the church bazaar—bags of them, there were, and Miss Susannah asked if I'd like the rags. For my rugs."

He looked at the gnarled hands. "You make rugs?"

"Are ye deaf, then, young as ye are?" she retorted tartly.

"Tell me about Mr. Stephen," he suggested hastily.

"He was in the house, looking for something. Searching high and low. I don't know what it twas, but he was in a taking over it. Said he'd find it or know the reason why. He shouted at Mrs. Trepol, asking her if she'd moved it. And she were near to crying, telling him she'd never touch his things. And then she was going out the back door, and I heard Mr. Stephen on the stairs, a racket, and him yelling 'Damned foot!' And I knew the Gabriel hounds were here again, riding high through the passages and down the stairs like the demons they are. I turned away, afeerd of 'em"

"What you heard was his fall, then? And he was alone?"

"Except for the hounds. They were baying at him, sharp and shrill and angry."

"Did you say anything to Mrs. Trepol? Or anyone else?"

"There was naught to say! Outside Mrs. Trepol was marching along the path with her back stiff with hurt, and inside the family was crying out and making fuss enough without me. Mr. Cormac caught up with us, going for the doctor, but didn't say what was amiss. I didn't like the look on his face, I can tell you, cold and dark."

"But you're a healer," he said. "Or so I've been told in the village. Didn't you go to see if you could help Stephen FitzHugh?"

She gave him a look of disgust. "I heal, God willing, but I don't raise the dead from their sleep!"

"But you couldn't be sure—"

"I told ye, Londoner, that I'd heard the Gabriel hounds. That's all I needed to know. They're never wrong. I've heard 'em afore, when there was death walking the land. In this house. In the woods. Wherever evil strays."

She turned and walked off, hobbling on her stick, leaving him to Hamish, who was trying to force words into his mind. But what the hell were the Gabriel hounds she'd talked of, some family banshee?

"I've been trying to warn you," Hamish said grimly, "what they were. The souls of unchristened children. A child who dies before he's blessed by the church. Unshriven. Not wanted by God—nor by the devil."

"I don't believe a word of it—that's Highland nonsense!" he said aloud before he could stop himself.

The old woman turned and looked at him. And silently crossed herself.

He felt his face flush.

In the bar after lunch was an elderly man in an old but fine suit and collars and cuffs that gleamed whitely in the dimness. Several people had clustered around his bench, talking quietly and nodding at whatever he said in response. A half dozen men stood around outside in the sunshine, playing keels, their shadows flicking across the dusty glass of the windows. Four other men sat around the hearth reliving the war. Two had lost limbs—an arm, a foot. Another wore an eye patch. Except for the women speaking with the doctor, it was a male enclave.

The barkeep said, "That's the old doctor. The father-in-law of Dr. Hawkins. Penrith's his name. Those that don't hold with the new ways of Dr. Hawkins still come to speak to him. But his mind's going these days. Shame, but there it is. Age catches us all, in the end." The barkeep must have been as old if not older than Penrith.

Rutledge, looking across at the bearded doctor, smiled to himself at the comment, then went up the stairs two at a time to his room, to get the photographs Rachel had sent him. When the doctor was finally sitting there alone, Rutledge joined him and bought him beer before opening the subject of the Trevelyan family.

"Sorrowful history, the Trevelyans had," Penrith said, tired old eyes looking up at Rutledge. "I saw them through most of it. And held their hands when they mourned. Old Adrian died in his bed, as he should, but not the others. Sad, sad, it was. I did what I could. Young Hawkins doesn't understand about that, he's not a village man. I was."

Rutledge used his handkerchief to clear off a space, then took out the photographs and made a fan of them on the table. "What can you tell me about these people?" What light there was from the narrow windows fell across them, gently touching their faces.

"Ah—more secrets than I want to remember. That's the gift of old age, Inspector. You begin to forget. And in forgetfulness is peace."

"But I'd like to know their secrets. To satisfy myself that all's well. That there was nothing done—now or before—that should have roused suspicion."

The old man chuckled. "Suspicions? A doctor always has suspicions, he's worse than the police. But sometimes there's more compassion in silence than in words. When you can't undo the harm that's been done, sometimes you bury it with the dead. James Cheney killed himself, and I said it was an accident cleaning his guns. Why burden Rosamund with more grief than she already had? The boy was lost, there was no bringing either of them back. Father or son. And Olivia was in such a state that I thought she'd lose her reason, swearing she'd never let Richard out of her sight, except to look at a plover's nest she'd found. And Nicholas saying that it was his fault, he hadn't watched out for either of them when he'd known he ought to. And the servants crying, and no man about the place but Brian FitzHugh, to see to the burying."

"FitzHugh was there when Cheney died?"

"Oh, aye, he was, he'd come and go—about the horses they raced, Miss Rosamund and her father. Winners, the lot of them. Good bloodlines. Like the Trevelyans. And now only Miss Susannah is left. And she's more Irish than Cornish, if you don't mind my saying it!"

"What do you know about Cormac FitzHugh?"

"Nothing," the old man said, finishing his beer. "He never

needed me for any doctoring, not a splinter in the foot nor fall from a horse. When they sent him away to earn his own living, I was glad. Miss Olivia said one day she'd write some poems about him. I paid no heed to it then, I thought it was girlish foolishness, romantic nonsense."

Rutledge stared at the watery eyes in the bearded face. Was the doctor trying to say that the love poems were written by Olivia to Cormac FitzHugh? That they had nothing to do with her half brother Stephen, whatever he'd tried to believe?

Tired from a restless night, Rutledge sat in a chair by his window and let himself drowse. He was just into that soft, floating ease between sleeping and waking when he heard sharp taps, a woman's high heels, coming briskly up the stairs. And then sharper taps as she rapped on his door.

Jerked into wakefulness, he straightened his tie, ran a hand over his hair, and went to open the door. Rachel, he thought hazily, come to fetch her photographs.

But it was a tall, slim blond woman with angry eyes who stared up at him when the door swung wide.

"Inspector Rutledge?" she said crisply, looking him up and down.

"Yes," he said. "I'm Rutledge."

"I'd like to speak to you. In your room, if I may. The parlor is not private, this time of day."

When he hesitated, she said, "I'm Susannah Hargrove. Stephen FitzHugh's sister."

He stood aside and let her come in, gesturing to the chair he'd drawn up to the window. He stayed where he was by the door, on his feet.

She ignored the chair. Instead she rounded on him like a battleship bringing her heavy guns to bear.

"My brother Cormac telephoned to my husband's office in London and left a message that you're here to reopen the matter of my family's recent losses. His secretary passed it along. Is that true? Or did she get it wrong?"

"I'm afraid it is true," he said gravely. "Which is not to say that

71

Scotland Yard won't come to the same conclusions in all three deaths."

"Yes, I'm sure it will—too late. Too late for *us*! The family, I mean. We'll be dragged through the newspapers, our dirty linen hung out for all to goggle at, and then, when you are *quite* satisfied, you'll beg our pardon and take the train back to London as if nothing had happened! It's bad enough, Inspector, to have to smile at people who know very well two members of your family killed themselves. If the police start whispers of murder, we'll all be disgraced. I'm expecting a child in the late autumn. I won't have it brought into the world in the midst of a nasty police matter!"

He fought back a smile at her vehemence, and said only, "I've said nothing about murder. To you or to your half brother."

"Why else would Scotland Yard give a-a *damn* about some obscure village matters, if there weren't suspicions on somebody's part? Is it because Olivia was famous? Is that why you're here to bedevil us?" Tears overlaid the anger in her eyes, but she held them back, fighting hard.

When he didn't immediately answer, she turned her back on him and stared out the window. "I knew that was what it must be. I told Daniel it could be nothing else! Why did Olivia have to do something so—so selfish! If she wanted to end it all, why did she have to leave shadows on the house—on us! I grew up there too, I don't deserve to have my memories, my very *childhood*, turned into something hostile and empty and grotesque! And if you have your way, we won't even be able to sell the house and be rid of it!" She whirled around and stared at him. "I hate that house now! I want it sold and all of the past ripped out of it by new owners who don't know—don't care—who we were!" She swallowed hard, then the tears came. "Who will buy it," she demanded huskily, "if there was murder as well as suicide there. We'll have it hung around our necks, like our sins, for the rest of our lives."

He pulled out his handkerchief and held it out to her, but she ignored it, fumbling in her handbag for one of her own. "I've just lost my brother," she said brokenly. "And now this! And the doctor said I wasn't to be *upset*."

"If you don't believe murder has been done, why should you

hate the house so much?" he asked, in an attempt to distract her. "What has it done—what has been done there—to distress you?"

She made a dismissive gesture with her hand. "It isn't what was done, it's what's been lost. Rosamund—my mother—held such light in her hands, and the house—all of us—were touched by it. And then she died, and it was all changed, all different, all—I don't know! Dark and dreary and full of Olivia's obsessions!"

"Obsessions about what?"

"How should I know? Olivia was a woman who lived in her thoughts, in her feelings. I'm not like that, I feel, I cry, I laugh. She was silent. I didn't—I couldn't understand her. It's—unnatural—in a woman to write as she did. I still don't think of her as that poet. I think somehow they must have got it all wrong!"

"Do you believe Nicholas Cheney could have written those poems?"

She stared at him, tears drying on her lashes. "*Nicholas*? I—it hadn't occurred to me—to any of us! Do you think it *was* Nicholas? Truly?"

He said carefully, "I don't know enough about your family to offer that as a possibility. I'm just answering your question about Olivia Marlowe."

Her face fell. "Oh."

"Do you know why Nicholas and Olivia killed themselves?"

Susannah shook her head. "I've lain awake at night, wondering why anyone could do such a thing. I was her sister—half sister—but she never said a word to me about her feelings—about despair, desperation. You'd have thought . . . but she didn't! And Nicholas—it's like a betrayal—to go off like that and leave me alone just before Stephen died! Mother betrayed me too—I've always suspected, feared, down deep inside that she killed herself too!"

Pain welled in her eyes, deep and terrifying. "What's wrong with my family? I'm the only one left now—not counting Cormac. One day will something awful happen to me, will I leave this child without a mother, and without anyone of its own to love? Cormac was that way—alone. He never had any one else. However beautiful he is, Cormac is terribly alone, and I don't want my child to grow up in that kind of world!"

7

Rutledge calmed her down as best he could, asking her if she'd like him to summon Dr. Hawkins.

But Susannah shook her head. "No. I don't need a doctor, I need a little peace, and if you'd only go back to London and leave us as we were, I'd be able to forget."

"You said that Rosamund might have killed herself. Did you mean that metaphorically, in the sense that she killed herself with worry or ignored her own health, didn't take proper care, that sort of thing? Or that she took her own life, deliberately and knowingly?"

"She died of an overdose of laudanum. Dr. Penrith said it was a mistake, that in the night she'd accidently miscounted the drops she was supposed to take. But I was afraid her strength had run out. Her laughter. I was afraid that she was tired of facing the next morning, and the next night. She was afraid to marry again, even though there were any number of men who would have been glad to have her. She said she'd buried the last man she loved, she would never do it again, that there wasn't enough left of her heart to put into another grave. Her solicitor, Mr. Chambers, was rather like James Cheney, strong, steady, a good man. I thought she was fond of him, and most certainly he cared for her. But it wasn't enough. *She wasn't . . .*"

Susannah took a deep breath. "I can't talk about it any more! Daniel is downstairs, he'll have fits if he sees me so upset. Daniel would do anything to make me happy. It isn't fair to worry him like this." She asked to use the water and his basin to wash her face, and he went to find the linen cupboard in the passage outside his room, to bring towels for her. She thanked him, looked searchingly in the mirror when she'd finished, and said, "Will you give me your arm down the stairs? I don't mind going up them, but since Stephen's—since then, I've had a thing about coming down them. About falling. I dream about it, sometimes. My foot slipping, the weight of the baby . . ." She shivered.

"You were all outside when he fell?"

"Yes, impatient, in a hurry, not thinking about his foot. I remember saying to Rachel that Stephen could be so tiresome at times. All this bother just for some old books he wanted to find. As if he couldn't come back anytime for them! And then Cormac went inside, shouted to us to come at once, and it was already too late. I felt so ill I thought I might miscarry!"

He took her down the stairs, and she leaned heavily on his arm, as if clinging to life itself. But once in the passage outside the bar, she smoothed her skirts, gave him a relieved smile, and walked with absolute assurance through the door to where her husband was waiting.

Daniel had some remarks of his own to make about Rutledge's presence in Borcombe, hinting darkly at the Government having ignored Olivia until it was too late, and now wanting to seem efficient and solicitous.

"It's a nasty business, Inspector, to destroy a family for political gain!"

Rutledge let him have his say, and finally they left in a new motorcar, murmuring something about friends in the next town who would be waiting upon them for dinner. Over her shoulder, Susannah gave him a last pleading glance before turning to answer some question her husband had put to her.

It was very late, and Rutledge, unable to sleep, finally got up and dressed and let himself out of the inn in the darkness of a fading moon, his pockets filled with candles and matches from his room.

He tramped through the silent streets, where not even a dog roused up to bark at him, but there was an owl in the darker woods who spoke softly as he passed. Death omens, owls had been called, but he'd always found a strange comfort in their lonely sounds.

There was no light in the house, no indication that Cormac was in residence. Deep in his own thoughts and problems, Rutledge hadn't considered that impediment. But somehow he knew that the house was empty the instant he put his hand on the latch and turned the key. Stepping inside and closing the door behind him, he fumbled for a candle and the matches. It flared brightly, startling him— in the trenches it could bring a sniper's bullet in its wake—but he managed not to drop it. Hamish, grumbling with dislike, waited until he'd lighted the candle and said, "Try the library first. Not the study. She'd not keep them *there*."

But Rutledge knew that the study was where he was heading, and he climbed the stairs slowly, quietly, to walk along the gallery and stop for a moment to listen to whispers that seemed to follow him. It was only the sea, and he recognized it at once, but a shiver passed through him all the same. He thought of Rachel and her ghosts. *What was there in this house that had marked it so strongly?*

He opened the study door and was surprised that the moonlight poured so intently through the room's windows. No one had closed the curtains here, and he stopped to count back. Yes, there must have been a full moon on that Saturday night. Olivia and Nicholas could well have died in its light, for it would have poured through these windows like a silver sea.

Hamish, unsettled and arguing fiercely with Rutledge, blotted out the sounds of the waves coming in against the headland. But they were there, an undercurrent that somehow soothed. As if the vastness of the sea dwarfed human griefs and sorrows and pain.

Who had been the first to die? he wondered again, looking at the couch in the candle's faint glow. The man or the woman? The killer or the victim? Or were they both—somehow—victims?

After a time he went over to the bookshelves by the typewriter and looked through the volumes there. Surely the others had had their own copies, they wouldn't have needed to take *hers*?

The candle's light moved along the shelves, stirred by his breath. And there on the spine of a slim dark blue book were letters that gleamed like molten gold: *Wings of Fire*. He pulled it out, then began his search again. A wine-dark volume, like blood in this shadowy corner, and written in silver: *Lucifer*. The one his sister Frances had said set London on its ear. Trust her to know what Society felt about the new, the different, the timely.

Soon afterward he found *Light and Dark*, then *The Scent of Violets*. And when he'd nearly given up, *Shadows*.

The candle was dripping hot wax on his fingers. He swore, collected his booty, and stood up. Something seemed to move in the darkness, and in its wake stirred a faint scent of sandalwood and roses. He froze, but it was only the silk shawl over Olivia Marlowe's typewriter, disturbed by his movements, slipping softly off the cold metal and brushing his arm.

Laughing to himself at his own susceptibility, he who had lived among the dead in France, he pulled the shawl gently back into place and went out of the room, closing its door behind him.

The gallery was quiet and empty, the hall as well. There were no ghosts here. And yet—there was something that stirred Hamish into Scottish complaint again.

Ignoring him, Rutledge went down the stairs, blew out his candle, and opened the door into the soft darkness beyond.

Where something stood in the drive like a being out of hell and regarded him with a stillness that made Hamish yell out a warning.

Rutledge, accustomed to night forays into no man's land where the danger was much more real and often silently swift, held his ground and said, "What is it you want?" But he could feel his heart thudding from the surprise.

The rector said, "It's you, then, Inspector?"

"What the hell?"

Mr. Smedley lowered the blanket he'd thrown over his nightclothes and head and said, "I saw lights moving about in the Hall. I didn't stop to dress, I came at once. I wanted to know who or what was walking about here! Was it you? Or are you here on the same errand? I'd been told that Mr. FitzHugh had decided not to stay at the Hall after all. I thought it was still quite empty!"

"I came for some books," Rutledge said, hearing the defensive note in his own voice. "I thought they might help me in my understanding of the poet."

"Ah, yes. The poems." He sighed. "Come back to the rectory with me, man, and we'll sit down like decent Christian folk, in good light."

Rutledge chuckled, locked the door, and followed him down the drive. "You're a brave man to come looking for intruders in an empty house," he said, catching up.

"Pshaw!" Smedley answered. "I'm not afraid of anything the human mind can conceive! One recognizes the face of evil in my profession, just as you do in yours. But you'll notice that I did not walk into the house, and I came armed." From the folds of his blanket he produced a very businesslike heavy iron poker that gleamed darkly in the pale light of the moon.

"What happened to turning the other cheek?" Rutledge asked, amused.

Smedley laughed. The shadows of the copse fell over them. "It's all very well in its place, you understand, but I don't believe our Lord intended for us to turn the other cheek to criminals. After all, he threw the moneylenders out of the temple."

"And you believed that there was a criminal in the Hall tonight?"

"I most certainly didn't expect to find Scotland Yard creeping about the premises. But the house has much that's valuable in it, and we have our share of tramps and good-for-naughts coming around. The saddest are the men who can't find work and have too much pride to beg. We've done what we could as a parish, but I don't think I could fault a man who was desperate enough to steal for his family's table. Not to condone it, you perceive, but to understand what needs drive him."

"You have an unusual Christian charity."

"Well, I didn't enter the Church for sake of my pocket, but because I have a hunger in my own soul."

"And has it been satisfied?"

"Ah, yes. It has. Though I must admit that the perplexities have multiplied more than I'd expected. Find one answer, and open the door to a hundred more questions. Now, if you please, we'll walk silently here. Old Mrs. Treleth has a small dog that takes great pleasure in keeping her neighbors awake, if he can pounce on the smallest noise as an excuse."

They walked quietly out of the wood, down the lane to the main road, and then turned towards the church. Mrs. Treleth's dog continued to slumber.

By the rectory gate, Rutledge said, "I've disturbed your sleep enough for one night, I'll go along to the inn."

"Indeed, I'm wide awake, and you'll pay for it with your company!" Smedley said lightly. "Come along quietly, you'd not be any happier than I if we wake my housekeeper. She's worse than the little dog, God forgive me!"

They made their way to his study with a minimum of noise, and the rector said, pulling his blanket more closely around him, "As I'm not dressed for the church, I feel no qualms about a wee dram of something—shall we say—strengthening? As a Devon man, may I offer you a cup of our finest cider?" There was a gleam in his eye.

Rutledge said, straight-faced, "I'd be delighted."

Devon cider could kick like a team of army mules, deceptively smooth on its way down, and building a fire in the belly that was unexpectedly hard on the head. He'd had Calvados in Normandy that did the same, and wondered if the two had common roots.

Smedley returned with two tall cups and a cold jug. He set them on the table between his chair and Rutledge's, and said, "You can put those books down, I'm not here to wrestle your soul for them. As a matter of fact, I have copies of my own. Your midnight foray was unnecessary."

"Ah, but I would have had to ask for them," Rutledge said with an answering grin. "And I preferred not to do that. To draw more attention to this investigation than it's already created."

"So it's an investigation now?"

"No," Rutledge said shortly. "I'm still . . . considering the options."

Smedley quietly chuckled, acknowledging that he'd touched Rutledge on the raw, and handed him his cup. Then his face changed, and as he pulled the blanket around him more comfortably, he said, "Well, I don't know any answers. It's between you and your conscience, when you find yours."

"What do you mean by that?"

Smedley shrugged. "We must all decide how to use the knowledge we collect in life. In my work and in yours as well, I'm sure, there are painful decisions to be made. And painful choices. They're never really the same, are they? Decisions and choices. Why did you suddenly want the books?"

"Because when I came down to Cornwall, I didn't know that one of the victims was O. A. Manning. Only that a woman named Olivia Marlowe was dead. Now I think the poems must have some bearing on her life, if not her death. I'd like to—understand—both women, if I can."

"Have you read them before? The poems?"

"Oh, yes. I read *Scent of Violets* at the Front. My sister sent me a copy. It frightened me, in a way. That someone else saw and felt the things that haunted me and I never had the courage to write about even in letters home." He couldn't have said to Jean or to his sister for that matter, worldly as Frances was, what it was like to live in the nightmare of war. His letters had been light, giving a superficial account of suffering, and not the bedrock. He thought Frances had guessed.

But Jean had preferred the lies . . .

Hamish stirred but said nothing about Fiona.

"And *Wings of Fire*? Have you read that?"

"They're extraordinarily moving, those poems. Where did Olivia Marlowe, spinster of this parish, learn so much about love?"

"A question I've asked myself over and over again. Cormac was the only man she saw much of who wasn't a part of the family. I know, Stephen claimed that she'd taken her fondness for him and extended it to the experience between a man and a woman. It may be true—she was capable of that leap of understanding, if anyone was. And Stephen was the kind of child—the kind of *man*—who endeared himself to everyone. I've forgiven him sins that I'd have turned another lad over my knee for committing. Told myself he was fatherless, and young, and meant no harm. But I loved the boy as I'd have loved my own son, for the goodness in him, and the

81

light. He was very like Rosamund, and I know my own weakness in that direction too." He frowned. "Perhaps that's what Olivia saw in him. Rosamund."

He sat in silence, drinking from his cup, and letting the sounds of the house creak and breathe and whisper around them. Comforting sounds. Then he said, "And the last collection, the *Lucifer* poems? Have you read those?"

"Not yet." He'd been in hospital when they came out last year.

"It's a very interesting study of the face of evil. Olivia understood that, just as well as she understood love and war and the warmth of life. As a priest I found it . . . disturbing. That she should know the dark side of man so much better than I. That she should believe that God tolerated evil because it has its place in His scheme. That there are some who are not capable of goodness in any sense. The lost, the damned, the sons of Satan, whatever you choose to call them, exist among us, and cannot be saved because they don't have the capacity for recognizing the purpose of good. As if it had been left out of the clay from which they were formed."

Rutledge thought about a number of the cases he'd worked on before the war. And some of the acts of sheer wanton viciousness that he'd witnessed in France. He believed in evil, and in the capacity of man to be evil. In a sense, evil paid his wages. He wasn't as sure as Smedley was that everyone had a capacity for good.

Smedley drained his cup. "I'd not like to think that Olivia Marlowe knew such a being as she describes. Actually *knew* him. I'd not like to think that I'd met him, on the streets of Borcombe or along the farm lanes or in one of the towns on market day. I would have trouble with that."

Rutledge finished his cup as well, and felt his head beginning to spin. He had a hard head for liquor, but cider could leap out of the jug at you, when you were tired and unsettled and had an empty stomach. "You don't think Olivia herself was capable of such evil?"

Smedley stared at him. "You must lead a drearier, more despairing life in London than most of us can comprehend," he said, "to ask me that! But I won't answer you directly, I'll tell you to read the poems yourself. And then decide."

82

He stood up, gathering the blanket about his burly shoulders. "I think I can sleep, now," he added, "and I'll be surprised if you don't as well. Leave the books until morning. You'll be glad of that advice, believe me."

Rutledge took the advice along with the books, went home to bed and fell asleep almost at once. He wondered, on the brink of sliding into the depths, if he'd have one hell of a headache tomorrow . . .

He did. But whether it was cider or lack of sleep that pounded through his skull, he wasn't sure. Breakfast and several cups of the inn's violent black coffee seemed to help. He realized that it was Sunday morning, and that the village of Borcombe was on its way to church services or a day of leisure.

Suddenly Rutledge didn't care about murder or the poems or about the job he'd been sent to do.

He sent a note by the boot boy to Rachel Ashford. Although he himself had no idea where she was staying, he trusted to the village intelligence system that worked more swiftly and more thoroughly than anything the Allies had devised during the war. The boy said instantly he knew where she could be found, and pocketing the coin Rutledge had given him, he set off at a trot.

Ten minutes later he was back with a reply, and had pocketed his third coin of the morning. Two from the London gentleman and one from the lady.

Rutledge opened the envelope and read the brief lines at the bottom of his own scrawled request.

"I'd love to sail. I'll join you in twenty minutes. Ask the innkeeper if we might use his boat. I know where it's kept."

So he went in search of the innkeeper, and received permission to take out the *Saucy Belle* with Mrs. Ashford. Although he hadn't sailed since before the war, Rutledge had some experience and thought—correctly—that Rachel might have more.

She came to the inn wearing sensible shoes and a pair of what looked like men's tousers, cinched tightly at the waist with an oversized belt. Her eyes smiled as he looked at her, but she made no explanation, whether these were Peter's clothes or borrowed from someone else. They walked together down the road towards the sea and the small assortment of boats there. Rutledge had a basket over his arm, courtesy of The Three Bells and a generous bribe to the cook. Rachel said after a moment, "You've more foresight than I have. I was so glad of the invitation to sail, I didn't think of food. Or is that a man's thing? Peter was remarkably good at foraging; he said he'd learned it young."

Rutledge laughed. "He was always hungry at school. I never knew anyone so good at scrounging. His mother sent him generous boxes—tins of canned goods and packages of cakes and biscuits. The Scottish shortbreads usually lasted the longest. I remember they sometimes took the taste of the woolens in his trunk, but we never minded that. When they were finished, we were desolate, until he'd convinced some other boy to share hidden rations."

They had reached the overturned boats on a small shingle strand that was just above the reach of the tides. "That's the *Belle*," she said, pointing to a red dinghy that looked as if it could use a fresh coat of paint and perhaps more than a little caulking.

Rutledge considered it dubiously. "Are you sure it won't sink beneath us?"

"Oh, no," she assured him. "It's quite sound. He just hasn't had it out much this summer. His son Fred didn't come back from the Navy. Torpedoed in the North Atlantic. Fishing hasn't been all that good, anyway. Cornwall's going to have a bleak future, economically. Trade gone and the pilchards as well. Everyone is complaining."

So were the hopeful gulls, wheeling overhead. Between them, Rachel and Rutledge dragged the *Belle* down to the water and clambered in. Rachel watched him critically.

He grinned at her. "You don't trust me. I see that."

"It isn't a matter of trust but of self-preservation. I've still time to leap overboard if you're a rank amateur, likely to do us a mischief."

But he knew what he was about, and soon had the little boat out of the shelter of the river's mouth and into open water. The sea was smooth this morning, wind ruffling it much farther out, where whitecaps danced lightly, but in the lee of the land, it was easy to row as far as the small strand below the Hall, beyond to round the headland, and then back to the strand again, where they pulled the boat up and splashed ashore.

Rachel turned to him, her face aglow with something he couldn't read, until she said, "I haven't done that in ages! It's wonderful to be on the water again. Peter was a landsman, he didn't know stem from stern, but Nicholas loved to sail, to be out in all weathers, to feel the tug of the sea under the hull and the fierce pull of the wind. When he went off to war, he had his heart set on the Navy, but they wouldn't have him—no experience, they said! And so he wound up in Flanders, in the mud and the horror and the killing— and the gas." The glow faded, and she turned to reach for the basket as Rutledge made the boat fast to some rocks.

"Tell me about your cousin Susannah, Mrs. Hargrove."

She straightened up and stared at him, the basket in her arms.

"Is that why you brought me here?" she asked quietly. "To pick over my memories and then make your decision about returning tomorrow to London?"

"No," he said curtly. "You mentioned the family, not I. She came to see me yesterday. That's why I asked."

She looked away from him, then set down the basket and began to climb the slight rise that led from the strand to the lawns. He followed her. At the top she stood looking across at the garden front of the house. "She's very much like Stephen, but a paler version—not quite as handsome, not quite as charming, not quite as lively, not quite as . . . loved. I think Rosamund somehow loved him best, because she saw in him her own immortality. Herself, young again and ready to go on with life. Or perhaps he reminded her of Richard. I thought about that sometimes myself. She loved Olivia because she saw George in her, and Nicholas because he was so—so very like his father. In his appearance, I mean. Inside, Nicholas had Rosamund's strength. Rosamund never showed favorites, at least not openly, but in her heart of hearts, who knows?"

"Tell me about her husbands."

"George was a wonderful man, exciting and very masculine. James was a fine man, with depths and intelligence and a sense of humor. And Brian FitzHugh loved her so much she couldn't help but love him back, but he was a weaker man." She turned to look at him, strain in her face. "Does that answer you?"

"Susannah said something about a Mr. Chambers who was in love with Rosamund and would have married her."

"Oh, yes, Tom Chambers was a very near thing. And I think he could have brought her out of her loneliness and depression. She was beginning to feel that too many of the people she loved had died. That it was somehow because of her. Her *fault*. I don't mean she told us that in so many words—we sort of pieced it together, among us. Which is why Mr. Chambers mattered. A new love, a new lease on life—soon she'd be happy again! And then one night she took a little too much laudanum to help her sleep, and died before morning."

"Susannah is afraid that her mother deliberately killed herself. But she won't accept that, she turns away from it in fear."

Rachel stared at him in surprise. "Does she? Susannah's never spoken of that to me! Or to anyone else, as far as I know. Are you sure? I mean, could it simply be the strange fancies of a woman expecting a child?"

"She was quite upset. If it's a fancy, she'll make herself ill before she delivers. I think, judging by what little I saw, that she'd terrified it might be true. Why?"

Rachel shook her head. "Rosamund took too much joy in life to kill herself. I find it hard to believe such a thing myself."

"You said just now that she was depressed—"

"Yes, but we're all depressed at some time or another! We all go through dark periods when living seems to be harder than giving up. Have *you* never felt that death seemed a friend you could turn to gladly?"

Hamish answered her first, bitterly. "Not for me did it come in friendship! I'd have lived if I could!"

Rutledge turned away, afraid she might read Hamish's response in his own eyes. "We're talking about Rosamund—" he answered lamely.

"No," Rachel said firmly. "Rosamund couldn't have killed herself! Nicholas would have known! *Nicholas would have told me!*"

86

8

$\mathcal{W}$ithout waiting for Rutledge to respond, Rachel added with false briskness, "Do you mind? While I'm here, I ought to see if Wilkins kept his promise to water the urns on the terrace. He sometimes forgets ..." She set off towards the house, a deprecating glance apologizing to him for not suggesting that he come with her. But she needed time on her own, to try to recover some of the promise of the morning.

She'd already dealt with—or tried to deal with—enough grief as it was. She couldn't bear to think of Rosamund as a suicide. Not the woman who'd been the very symbol of serenity, of brightness and vitality. Not the woman who'd been such a strong influence in her own childhood. It was impossible—a contradiction! But she hadn't been able to comprehend Nicholas choosing his own way out of whatever it was haunting him, either. She'd finally asked for Scotland Yard's help because she couldn't tolerate the uncertainty, the doubt. And now this man from London was making things *worse*, not better. Talking about murder. Questioning the very bedrock of the Hall, the woman who'd been its soul, its center ...

She'd approached Henry Ashford out of personal desperation. And they'd sent her a man who didn't care about Nicholas—who felt nothing for Rosamund, or even Olivia. He was dredging up more pain, more hurt, more doubt—dredging up all the things she'd much rather forget forever. He wasn't here to answer her need, he was too busy with his own, London's, and she'd never expected that to happen. While she still walked in the terrible darkness of Nicholas's death . . .

She could feel herself hating Rutledge, blaming *him*. It was wrong, of course, and she could tell herself that as many times as she liked, but deep inside, she found herself wanting to lash out, to hurt him, as he'd hurt her. *For planting seeds that might grow.*

Hamish was scolding him for upsetting Rachel, but Rutledge himself was glad enough for a brief space to think. He turned and walked up the lawns towards the headland, mind busy with the complexities of this case that wasn't a case. And with Rachel, who had loved Nicholas Cheney, whether she believed that or not.

The wind came bounding over the cliff face, ruffling his hair and tugging at his trouser legs as he moved higher along the grassy edge that rose at a fairly steep angle the closer he came to the top. Below him, the sea rhythmically threw itself at the rocky face, whispered softly, and then came back for another try. Farther out, there was a fishing boat moving slowly across the water, trailed by a half a dozen gulls. He could hear their cries echoing against the headland.

Turning, he looked back at the house. It rose above the colorful gardens with comfortable grace, first to a lawn that was reached by a broad flight of Italianate stone steps, and then by way of another flight, to the terrace enfolded by the two short wings that looked down on it. Rachel was moving about there now, where great stone urns spilled over with flowers, trailing blossoms and vines like bridal bouquets. It was a peaceful setting, not grand, but beautiful.

He turned again, this time to look towards the village, half hidden behind the copse that separated it from the grounds of the Hall. Past the church tower, he could just see the upper floor of the rectory, its windows dark blue squares in the sun.

Why had the rector been stirring at such a late hour of the night, much less looking out his windows? And could he see the Hall from there, could he have caught the movement of a candle in the study on the upper floor?

An interesting pair of questions . . .

Something had brought the man out of his bed and into the dark woods in such haste that he'd not stopped to pull on his trousers or a coat, he'd simply thrown a blanket around his nightclothes and taken a poker from the hearth. A poker for a living threat, not a dead one.

Rutledge crested the headland and moved a few yards down the far side, looking towards a meadow that he thought might well have been a walled orchard once, the land still rough and hummocky where the trees had been cut down but the roots and stumps left for the grass to swallow with time. Yes, now he could see the faint line of foundation that marked where a wall had run. It was here, then, that Olivia's twin sister had died. Out of sight of the house, the stables, and the gardens, behind a wall of brick and leaves.

Hamish was insistently calling his attention to something, and he glanced down at his feet. There was what looked like a large, scorched patch of earth, as if someone had burned something here. Not recently, not within the past few weeks—the grass was already growing greenly through the blackened stubs, and the fine ash was like a film on the ground, evenly spread about, no chunks, no remnants of anything identifiable. Scuffing the surface with his shoe, Rutledge thought it might have been paper rather than wood or rags that had fueled the fire, it had burned so thoroughly. Or else whatever was not consumed had been taken away.

He knelt, looking more closely, his fingers probing, and found something caught in one of the clumps of grass just outside the circle. It looked like a bit of faded ribbon, blue perhaps, or pale green, it was hard to say after days of wind and sun and rain draining it of most of its color. And closer in there was a thick edge of harder stuff, that might once have been heavy leather, like the end of a belt. Casting around for anything else, he discovered a small decorative silver corner, thin and blackened but still possessing a fine tracery of Celtic design. From a picture frame? A book? A locket?

Odd things to have cast into a fire!

Still squatting in the grass, he realized that he was just able to see the roof of the Hall, but there was not even a glimpse of the village, except for the battlemented top of the church tower. In the other direction, fields and woods. At his back, the sea.

Whoever had worked here knew he—or she—was out of sight of watchful eyes.

If you lived at the Hall and wanted to burn something, he thought to himself, why not in the grate? Or the stove in the kitchen? Or in the basket in the kitchen garden where trash was usually sent to be incinerated?

To come out here on the headland and build a fire with the wind clawing up over the cliff must have been a damned nuisance, trying to keep the flames from leaping out of control, to keep bits of paper or cloth from blowing every which way in a flurry of sparks, trying to prevent your eyebrows and fingers from being scorched as you worked over the blaze, feeding it. Then pouring water over the lot, to make sure it was dead before leaving it.

Unless ... unless you had something to burn that you didn't want anyone else to see. Or find the remnants of, in the ashes of the hearth. Or smell in the passages of the house, smoke hanging heavily, like a confession.

To come out here, in the daylight or the darkness, where the smoke and the smell and any remnants that the fire might accidentally leave wouldn't be noticed or rouse suspicion, indicated a need for privacy—or secretiveness.

He stood up, wondering who had used this patch of ground.

Rachel was coming towards him, just closing the last garden gate, and he hurried to meet her, not wanting her to see the burned spot. "Hungry?" he called, when she stopped to wait for him.

"Starved!" she answered, fetching up a smile. It was almost natural. "What were you looking at so intently? I called, and you didn't hear me."

"Did you? It was lost in the wind. I was wondering if that meadow over there might have been an old orchard."

"Yes, actually it was." She didn't pursue that train of thought, but said instead, "It's sad to think of the Hall being sold. Of strangers living here."

"I thought you were in agreement about selling the house? That only Stephen held out against it."

90

"Oh, I think it should be sold. There's nothing left here now of what we loved as children, and trying to keep it alive artificially, as a museum, would be much worse than strangers moving in. I mourn the past, that's all." She looked over her shoulder as they walked down the headland towards the beach again, as if hoping the house itself would tell her she was wrong. After a moment she added more to herself than to him, "I expect the best course after all is for Cormac to buy it. Which keeps the Hall in the family in a roundabout way, and we'll none of us feel guilty about choosing strangers over Olivia. Although it seems selfish to make poor Cormac the family's sacrificial lamb!" She smiled ruefully. "Have you ever noticed how many times feeling guilty shapes human decisions? Rather than love or pity or avarice or whatever else one might have felt instead? A wretched way of getting through life, isn't it?"

He grinned down at her. "In my work, feelings of guilt can be useful—sometimes even solve the crime for me." But there had been other times, he could have told her, when remorse and guilt never entered into the picture. A killer caught by some tiny mistake he made, not because of any human emotion driving him. Careful, elusive, cold. Rutledge found himself thinking that this new Ripper wouldn't be such a man. He was lashed by such savage desires he could tear flesh like paper. And he'd grow more and more careless as the fires consumed him as well as his victims.

The picnic basket was bountiful, pasties wrapped in napkins, beer for him, a thermos of tea for Rachel, an assortment of biscuits in a small tin, and a packet of cheese with a fresh loaf of bread. There were plums in the bottom in another napkin.

They did it justice, although Rutledge was preoccupied and Rachel found herself making self-conscious small talk, sticking with topics that couldn't lead her—and the Inspector—back to the Hall or its inhabitants.

Discussing her interest in Roman ruins in England was easier, then she found herself wondering aloud why he'd chosen police work when he might have gone into the law, like his father.

"I remember my father talking about briefs. A barrister defended the accused, he said, and a KC defended the law, and if the victim was alive, he might present his evidence about the robbery, the assault, the trespass. But if he was dead, he was the primary cause of the case, and had no role in it, except as proof that a crime had been committed." He grinned at her. "That seemed very unjust to a small boy burning with a sense of right and wrong that was entirely his own. I felt the victim should be heard, that his voice as well as his life'd been taken from him. I believed that the truth mattered. That protecting the innocent mattered. It seemed to me the police must be concerned about that if the courts were not. But that wasn't true, either."

"Why not?"

"Because," he said, looking away, "as I learned soon enough, the primary task of the police isn't to prove innocence, it's to prove guilt."

Something in his voice at the end warned her not to pursue the subject. She glanced up, and saw Cormac FitzHugh coming towards them across the lawns.

She said quickly, beginning to gather up the lunch things and put them back into the basket, "Are you leaving for London in the morning?"

"No," he answered, "not yet. I've a few more loose ends to clear up before I'm satisfied. But I promise I'll tell you when I'm finished here."

"That's fair enough," she answered, and stood up, brushing the sand from her trousers. By the time Cormac had reached them, she was already walking away along the strand, towards the headland.

Cormac called a greeting, and looking at the boat on the shingle said as he reached Rutledge, "I see you talked the landlord out of his boat for the day. I wish I'd thought about that myself." Then, his eyes following Rachel, where she was already out of earshot, he added, "I've been worried about her. She took Nicholas' death hard. Following on the heels of Peter's. Rachel is too level-headed to deny they're gone, but there's an emptiness she doesn't quite know how to fill. Lately she's even avoided me, and Susannah. As if the living remind her too much of the dead." He shook his head.

"I know how that is. I bury myself in my work and let the days run into each other."

"You aren't staying at the Hall?"

"I'd asked Mrs. Trepol to make up a bed," he said wryly, "then couldn't face the silence. Friends at Pervelly are putting me up."

"Is that where Mrs. Hargrove and her husband are visiting?"

Cormac turned back to Rutledge, surprise in his face. "Is Susannah down here? Daniel swore he wasn't letting her leave London again until she delivered. But she's always been more strong-minded than she looks. If she wants something, he can't stand in her way for very long. She's probably staying with the Beatons. She was in school with Jenny Beaton. Jenny Throckmorton, she was then."

"Your sister didn't want to hear of the investigations being reopened, either. She said there was enough disgrace in a double suicide, she didn't want her child born into a family where murder was suspected."

Cormac grinned. "Pregnant women are often edgy, I'm told."

"You've never married?"

He walked away, his back to Rutledge, and picked up a stone to skip over the incoming waves. "No," he said finally, "I haven't married. Like Rachel, I have scars that haven't healed."

Hamish rumbled uneasily, and Rutledge tried to ignore him. He said, "I haven't found any evidence of a crime being committed here. But I'd like to know why Nicholas Cheney died. To *understand* why," he amended. "I can't quite accept your suggestion, that Olivia didn't want to die alone."

Cormac came back to where Rutledge was standing. The whisper of the water running in was louder as the tide turned. "God knows," he said tiredly. "It might have had something to do with her poetry. Or what Nicholas knew about her, about her life. Or what she thought he might do afterward—after she'd gone. Or it might have been sheer bloody-mindedness."

"If she wanted her secrets kept, why leave her literary papers to Stephen? And surely you knew nearly as much about her history as Nicholas did. Possibly more. Killing *him* didn't seal her secrets in the grave."

"Ah, but she knew I was making a name for myself in London. That I'd go to any lengths to avoid scandal that might hurt my reputation in the City. It wasn't very likely, was it, that I'd be eager to rattle any family skeletons? There's a passage in one of her poems about 'secret histories, kept to the grave, last defense of master and slave 'gainst the final onslaught of heaven and hell, a Resurrection where the soul will tell what the tongue and the mind, in dreadful fear, had hoped against hope that none might hear.' " He shrugged. "The transfer of thousands of pounds is made on my handshake, the agreement to contracts and the trust of banks and investors. I'm as good as my word, and people depend on that. I had more to lose in telling than she did. She could have ruined me more easily than I could ever have ruined her."

"But you might have ruined O. A. Manning."

"Did she really care about O. A. Manning? She cut that part of her life short as well."

"Unless she'd said what it was she wanted to say, and knew it was safe forever, printed into lines on paper. That no one could take it from her."

Cormac studied Rutledge's face. "Do you mean a confession of sorts? I don't know the poems that well. I couldn't begin to guess what she intended, in writing them. I really don't believe that she herself knew what they were—only a force that had to find expression, regardless of the hand and mind that created it. Olivia was the most complex person I've ever known."

Rachel had reached the headland, where rocky outcrops blocked her way and the sea sent spray flying in the sunlight. She stopped, hesitating, looking back at them, a small, frail figure against the massive land mass and the vastness of the sea. After a moment, she turned and started towards them again. She moved with grace, her hair flying in the wind, her strides long and sure.

"From here, she might be Jean . . ." Hamish said softly.

Watching her, Rutledge said, "I still think Nicholas' death is the key. I could believe the rest of what you've told me, if I was satisfied there."

Cormac said, "Then you'll have to go to the grave for your answers. I don't have any to give you."

"Could it be connected with the house? In some way? If she'd died and Nicholas Cheney had lived, he would have inherited the Hall. And I don't believe, from what little I know of him, that he'd have sold it."

Surprised, Cormac's fair brows snapped together. He said slowly, "Then why not simply change her will—cut him out of it? The Hall was hers, to do with as she pleased. Why not leave it to Stephen? He claimed to be her favorite, and I think there might be some truth to that."

"Stephen would have kept the Hall, too."

"As a memorial, not as his home. There's a difference, I suppose."

Rutledge shook his head. "Whatever it is, I'll get to the bottom of it."

"Well, do me the courtesy of telling me what to expect," Cormac said, "when you've made up your mind. I don't want scandalous headlines in the morning paper staring back at me over my breakfast!"

"If I can," Rutledge said, but it wasn't the same promise he'd given Rachel.

After a moment Cormac said, "I've got to be on my way. Tell Rachel I'm sorry I missed her." His eyes crinkled at the corners in a smile. "But warn her I'm not ready to leave Cornwall yet." He walked off, moving swiftly and gracefully towards the house. Rutledge wondered whether he would buy it, as he'd thought about doing—or if the bitter memories here outweighed the sweet, even for him.

Cormac, whether he liked it or not, was still under Olivia Marlowe's spell. Just as Rachel was under Nicholas Cheney's—

She reached him, looking after Cormac and saying, "He doesn't look very happy. What surprises did you spring on *him*?"

"I didn't know that there were any surprises," he countered.

Rachel turned her attention back to Rutledge. "Does it ever bother you—as a man, I mean—when the policeman in you has to break into a person's peace and destroy it? Do you ever have qualms of conscience—nightmares—"

Hamish, answering for him, said, "Aye, there's nightmares! But no' the kind the lassie could bear!"

Seeing Rutledge's face respond to what she thought was her own challenge, she didn't wait for him to answer, and said instead, "Well, I suppose a conscience can grow accustomed to many things, when it has to!"

When he'd seen Rachel back to Borcombe, settled the boat where he'd found it, and returned the picnic basket to the inn, Rutledge went in search of Mrs. Trepol, housekeeper and cook. She was working in her garden, her hair tied up in a kerchief and an apron over her dress. As he paused at the gate that separated her walk from the road, she looked up, her eyebrows twitched, and she said, "I knew you'd come here before very long. When I saw you with Miss Rachel awhile ago."

"Inspector Rutledge. I'd like to talk to you about the deaths at the Hall." He opened the small iron gate set into the stone wall.

"It's my Christian duty to answer you, but thinking about it bothers my sleep. I try not to." She set the small trowel in the trug beside her and pulled off the old pair of men's gloves she wore to protect her hands. "Would you care for a cup of tea, then?"

Following her into the dimness of the house, he saw that there was a cat in the chair he'd chosen to sit in, and moved instead to the long window overlooking the front garden. She unceremoniously dumped the tom out of the chair and dusted it with her apron. "He knows better," she said, "but it's his favorite place. I'll be just a minute. Sit down, please, sir."

He did, and the tom stared balefully at him from sleep-narrowed eyes. The room was small, with more furniture than it could comfortably hold, but clean of dust. Silverplate picture frames of people he didn't recognize covered one table, beside small seaside souvenirs from Truro and Penzance. A plate holding pride of place commemorated the coronation of Edward VII, and a smaller one marked that of George V and Queen Mary. A cutting from a magazine, a photograph of the Prince of Wales in his Garter robes, had been framed and hung over the couch. This could be the parlor of any cottage in the west of England, Rutledge thought, feeling the quiet peace of it.

"Or in Scotland," Hamish said with a sense of loss in his voice. "There was my sister's wedding flowers under a glass bell, and the souvenirs were from Bannockburn and Edinburgh, not the seaside. A photograph of me in my uniform, with Fiona at my side . . ."

Mrs. Trepol came in with a tray bearing cups and a teapot, a small dish of cakes to one side. She set it on the tea table in front of the cold hearth, and poured a cup for him. That done, she sighed, as if she'd put off interrogation as long as good manners allowed. Straightening her back, she turned, handed him the cup, and said, "I told the police when it happened—"

"Yes, I know, and your statement was very clear," he assured her. "But I'm here merely to satisfy the Yard that the deaths were investigated—er—properly."

Nodding, she said, "Aye, well, the family was well thought of. I'm sure everything that could be done was. It was a shock to me, I can tell you! Walking into that house on my day off, and not finding Mr. Nicholas about—but sometimes Miss Olivia had a bad night, and he'd sit with her until the worst passed. After Miss Rosamund died, Mrs. FitzHugh she was then, and the staff was reduced, he was the one Dr. Penrith showed how to rub Miss Olivia's limbs and her back, to help the pain. Well, there was no entertaining, only the family coming there from time to time, and a full staff was wasteful! But to end their lives like that . . . I can't say how long it took me to get over my grief. I felt—I felt I should have been there, somehow." She brought him milk and the small bowl of sugar, then the cakes.

"That you could have prevented it? That you'd have guessed what was in their minds?"

"There was no *warning*, sir, none, just life going on in its ordinary way!" she told him earnestly. "But I thought if I hadn't been in such a hurry on the Saturday to leave, to run some errands I'd put off, I might have noticed some little difference, and Mr. Smedley could have come out to the Hall and spoken with them. Restored the balance of their minds!" There was pain in her voice, a heavy sense of guilt as she quoted unconsciously from the inquest verdict.

Suicide was still viewed as a crime against God. Mrs. Trepol sincerely felt a responsibility to save her employers' souls if she could—as well as their earthly lives. Not out of zealousness but from affection. She cared deeply.

"But if you didn't notice anything—if their behavior was normal—then whatever caused them to take their lives must have occurred after you left."

"What *could* have happened? There were no visitors expected that I knew of, and the post had come already, I'd have heard if it brought bad news. And look back on the day as I will, there was nothing that changed in that house! Nothing to cause such anguish that they'd want to die!"

"People don't kill themselves without a reason," he said, preparing to ask the question he knew very well would hurt her more. "Unless you think that Miss Marlowe was in such terrible pain that Mr. Cheney gave her too much laudanum, saw what he'd done, and then killed himself in grief."

She put her own cup down and stared at him. "Mr. Nicholas would never have done such a terrible thing as give her too much! Oh, no, sir, he was not the kind of man to make a mistake like that!"

Without answering her directly, he shifted tactics. "There has been a good deal of sadness in the Hall. Two children dying young. Miss Rosamund losing her husbands before their time. Then Mr. Cheney and Miss Marlowe. And finally, Stephen FitzHugh."

"As to that, sir, we all have our crosses to bear," she said stiffly.

"But sometimes there's a history of violence in a family. And sometimes one person is at the root of it."

"And who do you think stands at the root of this family's tragedies, sir?" she asked, bristling. "Mr. Cormac, who lives in London? Or Miss Susannah, who's the last of the Trevelyans? They're all that's left to do anybody a harm!"

"Miss Marlowe was an unusual woman. She wrote poetry of a kind that few men can produce. Where did she learn so much of life?"

"I never asked her, sir! Come to that, I never knew until she'd died that she was a writer of poems or anything else. Mr. Nicholas must have known, he sat working on his ships in her study, or went to find books she wanted in the library, or talked to her long hours of the day and night. I'd hear their voices, quiet and steady, as I moved about doing my cleaning. I think she'd have told *him*, she told him most everything important to her."

"Except the name of the man she was in love with?"

Her mouth fell open. "And who was that likely to be, I ask you! She never had suitors coming to the Hall, and she went out so little. No man was likely to stumble over *her* in Plymouth or London and sweep her off her feet! Mr. Nicholas and Mr. Stephen, they were her brothers. And old Wilkins couldn't light a fire in a grate!"

"Cormac FitzHugh wasn't her brother. He wasn't related to her or to her mother. A stepbrother by courtesy alone."

Mrs. Trepol gave Rutledge an odd look. "What makes you think Miss Marlowe was fond of Mr. Cormac? Or he of her?"

"Because she wrote of love in one of her books of poetry, and no woman—no man for that matter—could have written of love with such emotion if he or she had no knowledge of it."

Mrs. Trepol laughed. "Oh, there was love enough in that house to write a dozen books of poetry! Miss Rosamund loved her husbands and her children and her father with a deep and abiding feeling. Just living there, as I did as a young housemaid, you could wrap yourself in it. And Miss Olivia, she was very fond of Mr. Stephen; he could brighten her day just like his mother did. Mr. Nicholas used to tease her that she'd spoil him—Mr. Stephen—and Miss Olivia would say, 'He was born to spoil and love. Some people are.'"

Which told Rutledge that Mrs. Trepol had never read the *Wings of Fire* poems . . .

"Mr. Cormac FitzHugh used to live in the household. Miss Marlowe might have loved him once."

"But he never loved her, sir! I'd swear to that on a Bible, if I had to. He was close to her, in an odd way, Mr. Cormac was, like he knew her better even than Mr. Nicholas did. But it wasn't love between them. At least not on his part."

Because Cormac FitzHugh had recognized Olivia Marlowe for what she was, a murderer?

"Do you think that Miss Marlowe was capable of killing anyone? Besides herself?"

"Killing anyone? Miss *Marlowe*? I'd sooner believe my own husband, God rest his soul, could do such a thing! Whatever put such a nasty idea into your head? Not anyone in Borcombe, I'd trust my life to that!" The indignation in her voice was very real.

"And you'd be willing to swear, in a court of law, that no one in the Hall—none of Miss Rosamund's family—was capable of murder?"

She regarded him severely. "I don't know what they are getting up to in London," she said tersely, "to send you down here with such questions as that to ask decent, law-abiding folk, but I'll tell you straight out, that if there was murder done in the Hall on the night that Miss Olivia and Mr. Nicholas died, it was a cruel and godless person that did it and he's nobody we've ever seen in Borcombe or want to see. Now if there're no more you want to ask me, I've plants in my garden that still need to be watered!"

Back in his room at The Three Bells, Rutledge sat in the chair by the window with the books of O. A. Manning's poetry in front of him. But looking at the slim volumes, he found himself thinking instead about the poet. About the woman who had found such resources of understanding within her. And yet who had killed herself because her strength somehow came to an end.

Could a man or woman be so deeply aware of the mysteries of the human soul and yet be capable of such terrible crimes as the murder of children? Could she live with that knowledge of herself, and still create such beauty? Was that, finally, why she had killed herself? Assuming that Cormac FitzHugh had told Rutledge the truth . . .

How did you write poetry? How many words did you put on paper, and how often did you throw them away because they didn't say what you heard in your spirit? How many poems went wrong, how many lines were flat and soulless, how many were trite and tired and empty? How many pages were crumpled up and tossed aside before a few unexpected words sang in your head, while you responded with blood and bone? How easy had it been—or how painfully arduous? How tiring or overwhelming?

He thought about the opening lines to one of the love poems.

> *Love*
> *Comes on wings of fire*
> *That sear the heart with longing*
> *And a white-hot heat.*
> *In its wake, no peace remains,*
> *Only the scars of a terrible loss*
> *That mark the end of innocence.*

How many times had she revised that until she was satisfied?

He'd been inside the study where she had worked and died.

It was amazingly tidy.

Where Nicholas had been carving his fleet of ocean liners, there were scraps and curls of wood, the fineness of sawdust from sanding, the small splashes of paint from finishing touches put to bow and portholes and the funnels. He hadn't put them away, swept and dusted, before swallowing the laudanum. It was as if he'd expected to come back to them tomorrow.

But where the poet worked there was only the shawl-covered typewriter. No balled up sheets of paper, no pen or pencil lying where she'd scribbled a line to think about it, or tried a rhyme and found it weak. She had known she wasn't going to sit there ever again and write. She'd prepared for her death.

His hand came down hard on the embossed leather cover, hard enough to sting the flesh as he swore aloud. Inventively.

Olivia Marlowe had bequeathed O. A. *Manning*—all her papers and letters and contracts—to her half brother Stephen. And Stephen was dead.

Where were these papers now? And what was in them?

9

But neither Rachel nor the rector could tell Rutledge what had become of Olivia Marlowe's papers.

"I—I think Olivia's will is still in probate. And Stephen's as well," Rachel said. "I really wasn't interested in the papers. I mean, I *was*, in the sense that they were important for a study of Livia's poems, but not in any personal sense. If you're asking me if there was box sitting in the middle of a room, marked Papers for Stephen, or something, there wasn't. I just assumed—well, if she'd left them to him, he must have known where to look for them."

She was standing in the doorway of the cottage where she was staying, and Rutledge could hear someone moving about inside, and then a bird singing from a cage. It was a pretty place, with vines swallowing the narrow little porch and hollyhocks leaning against the walls between the windows.

"Which firm is handling the wills?"

"Chambers and Westcott for Olivia and for Nicholas. I don't know about Stephen. He had a friend in the City who was a solicitor."

It would be easy enough to find that out in London.

He thanked her and walked on to the rectory, expecting Smedley to be tending his garden, but the grim-faced housekeeper announced that he was having a nap and she wasn't about to disturb him.

Rutledge was just turning away when Smedley came down the stairs into the hall, his hair standing up in the back and his shirttail on one side hanging out of his trousers.

"Good afternoon, Inspector," he said, voice still thick with sleep. "Give me two minutes, and I'll walk in the garden with you."

Rutledge went around the back, walked along the tidy rows of vegetables and flowers, and was nearly to the small, scummy pond that had once held fish before Smedley stepped out the back door and came to join him. His hair was combed and his shirt neatly tucked into his trousers, his braces in place.

He cast a look at the sky, and said, "It has been a beautiful day. I hear you and Rachel took a boat out."

Rutledge smiled. "We did. And lived to tell the tale, though she had some doubts in the beginning. Who was the gossip?"

"It came by way of Mrs. Hinson, who had seen Mr. Trask outside the inn on her way to morning service. She then stopped to offer my housekeeper a small pot of the jam she made yesterday. And I was given the news with my tea, along with the jam."

"What do the gossips of Borcombe have to say about three deaths at the Hall, all in a matter of months?"

"Much as you'd expect. The women felt that Olivia's writing must have turned her mind. We aren't used to famous poets in Borcombe. I think they believed somehow it was a proper judgment on her, for writing about things best left unsaid and probably best left unfelt in a woman."

"And the men?"

Smedley frowned as he stooped to pull a yellowed leaf off the nearest carrot. "The men are of two minds about Olivia Marlowe. She was of course a Trevelyan, and they're above the common lot, in most eyes. You forgive a Trevelyan much that you might hold against the greengrocer or your neighbor across the road. At the same time, dying by her own hand was an admission that she'd overstepped the bounds, in a manner of speaking, and finally became aware of it. The universe, you might say, is now back in its stable orbit."

"What about Stephen FitzHugh? And Nicholas?"

"Stephen was a sore loss. Half the village adored him—every female under sixty, and more than a few over that! The other half, the men, admired him. A good man to have on your side, sense of humor, knew how to lose as well as to win. Quite a reputation for courage in the war, was wounded, decorated. Sportsman. Successful in his business, which was banking. Popular with the ladies. Yes, he was admired—and sometimes envied. That's natural. Nicholas was respected—Rosamund's son, the natural leader in village affairs, the man you turned to when there was trouble. Pillar of strength. Not the sort you'd expect to choose suicide. The general belief was that he found Olivia dead or dying, and in the first shock of grief, took his own life. That's romantic nonsense, but they're more comfortable with it than with the truth—that he might have wanted to die. But this isn't why you came to see me, I think?"

"I wanted to know what became of Olivia's papers. The ones she left to Stephen as her literary executor."

"They're probably still at the house. Stephen didn't want to sell, he wanted to keep the Hall as a memorial to his sister. The others took a few personal things, but he was dead set against removing much else. And was prepared to fight a bitter battle to have his way. Have you looked in Olivia's room? Or her desk?" He read the expression on Rutledge's face. "No, of course not. Well, I'd start there. It's not likely, is it, that Olivia sent them off to her solicitor? He'd have guessed something was wrong, and she didn't want that. Besides, we aren't sure just how soon after she decided to put an end to her life she acted on that decision. A day? A month? Five years? A few hours?"

"She had straightened up her desk. Nicholas hadn't cleared away his ships."

Smedley looked at him. "That's proof of nothing."

"Of, perhaps, a state of mind?"

"You're saying that she knew where she was going, what she was planning to do, and Nicholas didn't?"

Rutledge watched the light and shadows play on the upper windows of the rectory, a bird's flight reflected in them, and the movement of the apple tree's higher branches. "I'm saying that she was prepared. He wasn't."

"Or it might be that her poetry was terribly important. And his ships weren't. He could leave those, in safety."

Which brought Rutledge back again to those literary papers.

He walked to the Hall after dinner and stood looking up at the house in the golden shadows of the westering sun. He could hear sea birds calling, and somewhere a jackdaw singing lyrically. In his mind's eye, ghosts of the people who'd made the Hall a home stirred and moved about the lawns, laughing and talking and bringing life to the scene. To the emptiness.

Someone said, behind him, "They've not left—"

He turned to find the old woman, and remembered her name this time. Rachel had called her Sadie.

"No," he said. Then, playing her game, he asked, "Which ones do you see? Is Anne there?"

"Anne was willful, she must have her way or she'd set the nursery on its ear. They said it was a child's tantrums, but the tree grows as the twig is bent, and if her father had lived, that would have been different. Instead, the women spoiled her and let her do as she pleased, and she wanted to hold tight to everyone's affection, even the old master's—Mr. Trevelyan. Miss Rosamund's father, that was. Sometimes she'd put off her stormy ways, and sit quiet with a book in her lap, and he'd come into the room and mistake her for her sister. There was no telling them apart, unless Miss Anne was being her naughty self. Or she'd tell tales on the others, and once got Master Cormac a hiding for beating a horse, and him never one to abuse the animals. Master Nicholas, now, he stood up to her once, and refused to let her have the little soldiers he'd been given for his birthday. But she found them later and buried them out in the garden, and he never did discover where they were. She died soon after."

Her words made Rutledge's blood run cold. Here was a reason for Olivia to have killed her sister. A child's excuse for murder. He found he didn't want to know about Anne.

"Why did Richard die out on the moors?"

"There's none sure he did. 'Twas no body ever found. Miss Olivia said they fell asleep in the sunshine, and he was gone when she opened her eyes. She thought mayhap he'd wandered off to find the moor ponies. He were a restless child, with the energy of two and a devil in his eyes. Miss Rosamund called him her little soldier, and said he was born to wear a uniform. Like her first husband."

"And Nicholas?"

"Ah, he was one who always knew more than he said. Kept himself to himself, and you never guessed at what rivers ran inside him, or how deep. Bookish, some thought, but if you want to know my mind on that, he was waiting with a dreadful patience to grow up. As if there was something waiting for him. If there was, *we* never knew of it. He was content to stay by Miss Olivia and keep her spirits high when the pain was hard. But if you looked into his eyes when he stared out at the sea, you knew there was a roamer inside him. Not like Master Richard, but a man who saw distant places in his soul."

"How did you come to know the Trevelyan family so intimately?"

There was roguish laughter in her eyes as she stared back at him, giving a bawdy twist to his words. "Even the mighty use bedpans, like ordinary mortals," she told him. "I nursed the living when needful, and laid out the dead. Dr. Penrith sent for me when Miss Olivia had the crippling disease and was like to die. He didn't trust the London nurses they wanted."

She seemed today to be clear-minded and aware of what she was saying. Testing it, he repeated, "You laid out the dead?"

A wariness moved behind her eyes, though her expression didn't change. He took a chance and asked her, "Was there a killer in that house?"

But her eyes clouded as he watched her lined face, and she said, "I told you there were a Gabriel Hound in that house, and you'd hear him running some nights, before something bad happened. Running through the rooms, in the dark, looking for his soul. On those nights, the wind howled in the trees and rattled the windows, and I kept the coverlet over my head. Miss Olivia warned me once, when I spoke to her of it, and I knew to heed her. I'd die too if I told what I heard or saw. Which is why I've outlived them all but two, and Miss Susannah's safe enough in London."

"What about Cormac FitzHugh?"

"He's not a Trevelyan, is he?" she asked. "There's no Gabriel hound wants anything *he* has."

She walked off before he could ask her what had brought her to the Hall on this particular evening. Or what she knew of a fire built out on the headland. But her mind was already slipping away again, and he wasn't sure he'd have gotten a straight answer anyway.

Still, he listened again to what she'd said. "Miss Olivia warned me once, when I spoke to her of it, and I knew to heed her. I'd die too if I told what I heard or saw."

Miss Olivia.

He went on his way, taking his time and approaching the house as if he'd come as a guest and not an intruder.

Where would Olivia have left her papers? Not in the hallway where anyone might stumble over them, that was true enough. But would she have hidden them, or simply put them where Stephen would think to look?

He unlocked the door and went inside. Someone had left the drapes open. Cormac? The sun's warmth had flooded the hall along with its light, and there was a brightness here that somehow made him think of Rosamund.

"There doesna' need to be anything howling from the attics to haunt a house," Hamish reminded him suddenly.

"No," Rutledge answered aloud, agreeing with him. "But this brightness will fade with the dusk. What else is here?"

He went up the stairs to the study and stood in its doorway again, eyes roving the walls and furnishings. There was no place of easy concealment here. Not without moving rows of books—or Nicholas' ships—and then shifting heavy shelves. And Nicholas shared this room, after all.

He shut the door and made his way down the gallery to Olivia's bedroom, glancing briefly at the plan Constable Dawlish had drawn up for him, although he knew very well which door to open.

He stood on the threshold for a moment, then crossed to open the drapes, allowing the setting sun to wash into the dimness. As he did, he caught again that elusive perfume that he'd smelled when the shawl slipped off the typewriter. And it was stronger when he opened Olivia's closet door and looked at the clothing hanging on both sides of the deep recess. Skirts, dresses, dinner gowns, robes, coats, shawls, in neat and orderly rows, coats first, night robes last. Hatboxes stood in the back on shelves, next to half a dozen hand-bags. Several umbrellas hung on hooks to one side, and a cane with a heavily wrought silver head. Beneath the clothing were two rows of shoes, the right of each pair with a small metal tab like a stirrup under the instep, and straps at each end. For the brace she wore.

Without touching them he surveyed the clothes. She liked colors, rose and a particular shade of dark blue and a deep forest green, as well as crimson and winter black, summer white and pastels. Tailored clothes, evening dresses very stylish but never fussy. His sister, Frances, would have approved of them, would have pronounced Olivia Marlowe a woman of quiet good taste. Just as the rector had said. But was there another side of her? And where did it reside?

The closet had been built into what had in the past been a small dressing room. He walked into it, towards the shelves at the back, brushing against the clothing, and that perfume whirled out around him, almost in angry protest at his invasion of her privacy. Where had she found such an expressive scent? It touched the senses, lingered in the memory, confused the image he tried over and over again to draw. Elusive as she was—and more alive.

He began methodically to open each hatbox, starting at the top, and from some of them, the heavy odor of cedar shavings wafted up to him, displacing Olivia's perfume. Sweaters in a range of colors. Woolen stockings and scarves and gloves. Leather belts and leather gloves, Italian made and very supple. A fur hat, with up-swept brim and a dashing style. Frances would have adored it— and looked stunning in it.

Nothing else.

He had carefully stacked the boxes on the floor. Now he pulled out the thick wooden shelves, beginning with the top shelf, looking to see if any of the panels in the wall behind it were loose or even hinged. If Olivia had kept her writing a secret for so many years, it meant she knew how to guard her privacy. From servants as well as family. If there was no space for storing personal papers in the study where she worked, she would most certainly have considered her bedroom next as a repository, and this wide closet, which no one but a maid had any excuse to enter, was Rutledge's first choice.

The closet was too dark for him to be sure that the end panels couldn't be opened somehow, and he had to remove the middle and then the bottom shelf to run his hands over the wall.

Nothing.

He retrieved the bottom shelf to settle it back on the brackets that held it, and instead clipped the edge on the left-hand bracket. Part of the shelf broke off, and then something else tumbled down, ringing merrily as it bounced twice on the hard wood of the floor. A key? He got down on one knee to search for it, running his hand back and forth across the wood, and there was nothing. Frustrated, he moved back to the front of the closet and started again. It took him nearly five minutes to find it, where it had landed in a shoe.

A small locket, gold, the sort of thing little girls often wore. He took it over to the window, where the light was better. There were entwined initials on the outer face of the locket, and he made them out—MAM. Margaret Anne Marlowe? His fingers found the delicate catch and he opened the frame to two tiny portraits inside. They were in oil, lovely little miniatures of a man and a woman. After a moment he recognized them. Rosamund and her first husband, Captain George Marlowe. Anne's parents. An exquisite gift to a child on her birthday or at Christmas, to be worn when she was dressed up, with special care.

How had it come to be hidden among Olivia's things? Or had Olivia simply inherited it when her sister died, and lost track of it over the years?

Rutledge went back to the closet and brought the shelves out again, then the boxes and the shoes. On hands and knees, then standing, he searched every inch of the walls and the floor.

Nothing. Except for the half inch sliver of wood that had been knocked off the bottom shelf by his clumsiness.

He picked up the shelf, looking to see where the chip had come from, and if he could put it back where it belonged.

It was the end of a longer strip of wood that had been set very carefully into the back edge of the heavy shelf. With his penknife he gently pried that out of its slot, and when he did, another object tumbled out of the space hollowed out behind.

He picked up that and the shelf, and carried them both to the windows.

The second object was a man's gold pipe cleaner, smooth from long use, but the initials engraved in it were still legible. JSC. James Cheney, Nicholas's father? He set that on the sill beside the locket.

Holding the shelf up to the light, he looked into the carved-out hollow. Someone had stuffed cotton deep inside it, and embedded within the soft fibers he could see bits and pieces of other articles. The sun caught them in its brightness, as if pointing to them. He winkled them out, slowly and gently.

First came a small boy's cuff buttons, heavy gold and again with initials engraved on them. RHC. Richard Cheney? Behind them was a lovely little signet ring, that looked as if it had been crafted for a child. And carved deeply into the face of the ring was a coat of arms. Inside, engraved in the band itself, were the initials REMT. Rosamund Trevelyan. A gold crucifix came out easily, finely wrought, with the figure a little worn. From the letters on the reverse, it had belonged to Brian FitzHugh. Finally, at the very back, a watch fob in the shape of a small boat, with the initials NMC. Nicholas.

The sunlight flashed across the raised sail as Rutledge laid it with the others he had spread out on the wooden windowsill, and in spite of the warmth that poured through the glass panes, he felt cold.

He knew exactly what these were.

He had seen dozens of collections like them, in the trenches in France. A button from the greatcoat of a German officer, goggles from a downed airman, stripes from the sleeves of corporals and sergeants, collar tabs from officers, a battered Prussian helmet, a pistol taken from a corpse, an empty ammo belt from a machine gunner's nest, whatever a man fancied . . .

When his mind stubbornly refused to frame the words, Hamish did it for him.

"Trophies of the dead," he said softly.

Small golden treasures, very personal and surely very precious, that marked each of Olivia Marlowe's unwitting victims.

10

$\mathcal{R}$utledge forced himself to walk away from the things he'd found, and instead to go through the motions required of him.

He began with the olive wood desk on its graceful, delicate legs. In the several drawers he found stationery in various sizes, engraved, and matching envelopes, bottles of ink, scissors, a box of visiting cards with Rosamund's name on them, a book of accounts for shops in London and in Borcombe, a leather notebook with stamps and addresses—none of them of special interest—and the usual clutter of pens and pencils. The only truly personal item was a wooden pen holder, hand carved, in the shape of a monster fish, the kind drawn on ancient maps at the edge of the known world, where they waited to swallow unwary ships. On the bottom, following the curve of a tiny scale, he found the initials NMC/OAM. From Nicholas to Olivia. Or to O. A. Manning?

The bottom drawer on the left side was empty.

The dressing table, the tall chest, the bureau, and the bedside table yielded more personal things, perfume and cosmetics, combs and brushes, odds and ends of jewelry, filmy lingerie, silk scarves and stockings, lacy handkerchiefs, and a prayer book, candles, and matches. Nothing out of the ordinary in any way, though sometimes intimate and daunting.

He knew, from what Rachel had told him, that the family had already taken away the things that made a room personal and individual—pictures and photographs and possessions with a particular value that wouldn't be put up for sale with the house. But perhaps out of respect for Stephen's insistence, much of Olivia's life still survived in this room.

Yet Olivia had been careful to leave nothing behind for either the police or her biographers that could be construed—or misconstrued—into the woman who'd lived in this room.

The items buried deep in the closet must have been there a very long time, and if no one had found them before now, the chances were that no one might have discovered them for years to come. When they would have no meaning to strangers living here . . .

He went back to the window and picked up each article, one at a time.

Six victims, if these were indeed trophies. Olivia's sister, Anne. Her stepfather James Cheney. Her half brother Richard Cheney. Her stepfather Brian FitzHugh.

Her own mother, Rosamund Trevelyan.

And the man who'd spent his life in her service. Nicholas Cheney.

She'd been so sure of him, then, so sure that he would die with her. Or that she could send him into the darkness before her.

"Gentle God," Rutledge whispered softly.

And after a moment, he found himself silently cursing Chief Superintendent Bowles for sending him here.

Drawing the drapes again and closing the door firmly behind him, Rutledge went down the passage, his mind still working with a policeman's precision, his thoughts far from where his feet carried him. The tiny, betraying trophies had been safely returned to their hiding place, out of sight. But not out of his thoughts, burned with molten brightness into his very brain.

In Stephen's room was the comfortable chaos of living. There was a cricket bat in the corner, a pair of riding boots by the closet door, suits and shirts and jackets hung haphazardly on the rod inside, books on the table under the window—they were mostly about golf and tennis, Ireland and horses—and ivory inlaid cuff links in the dish on the dressing table, with a fish hook and a length of gut from a tennis racket beside them. But no boxes. No folders of personal papers, no literary failures or private letters or contracts. What Stephen kept here was the detritus of boyhood and the things one left in a country house visited fairly often.

In the interim between her death and his, Stephen might well have taken Olivia's papers to his bank for safekeeping. But Rutledge went through the drawers again, found a routine letter from Stephen's bank manager, and copied the address in his notebook.

As he was about to close the curtains, Hamish said, "When I was a laddie, Ma was a fierce one with broom and rag, nothing safe from her eyes when the fit to clean was on her. I'd hide what I cherished in the shed behind the straw, or above the rafters in the loft, after Pa died. She wasna' as tall as my pa."

Rutledge stopped, listening to what Hamish said. Stephen was a child from a large family. Nosy sisters and prying brothers. He might well have had a secret place of his own. But not in this room. He, Rutledge, had been damned thorough . . .

Or had he?

He glanced around the room again. He'd even had up the carpet, looked inside the grate, under the bed—

He knelt again by the bed. Nothing, only a thin coating of dust, sifting down gently since Mrs. Trepol's last visit.

The frame. The slats that held the springs. Above that the mattress, sagging a little in the center. The bedclothes—

The slats? What could you hide on a slat? A key, perhaps . . .

He went under the bed, on his back, mindful of his coat and careful not to scrape his head on the springs as he used his arms on the side boards to propel himself. Claustrophobia caught at him, and he had to shut his eyes against the wave of terror that ran through him. He coughed hard, the dry dust sucked into his drier throat. The springs were all but pressing into his face, not as high as he'd first thought!

With eyes still shut tight, he forced his breathing back to a normal rhythm. What you don't see can't fall in on you! he told himself sternly.

After a moment, searching with his memory rather than his eyes, he ran shaking fingers over the nearest slat, between the springs and the wood, barking his knuckles and collecting fine splinters. Nothing but more dust. There were five slats in all. He felt for the others, and began again, moving his shoulders and hips across the floor until he could reach each slat. Nothing. It was useless, he might as well give up. The last slat now—

Only the slight rustle of sound warned him in time, but the object still clipped his ear, falling, and he banged his head as he recoiled.

Slithering swiftly out from under the frame again, he turned and looked back. The springs were a good fifteen inches above the floor, not face high.

And a small book was lying, spine upward, in an inverted V on the floor. He reached for it, and managed to fish it out without going back under the bed again.

A prayer book, pages thin as rice paper, the tiny print old and ornately lettered, the cover worn black leather, the edges of the pages once gilded.

There was on the front cover an outline in raised leather, and Rutledge recognized it as the figure of St. Patrick, staff lifted to cast out the snakes.

On the flyleaf inside, in a spidery scrawl in fading ink, he read, "Presented to Patrick Samuel FitzHugh, on his first Communion, June, 1803. From his loving Sister Mary Joseph Claire."

FitzHugh, not Trevelyan or Marlowe or Cheney. The FitzHughs had been Irish Catholic, the Trevelyans and Marlowes and Cheneys Church of England. This had been hidden, but not for reasons that had anything to do with murder. As a boy, had Stephen had Catholic leanings his family didn't know about?

Rutledge thumbed through the fragile pages, eyes scanning the printed lines. In the back, where the pages were blank, someone had written out a family genealogy beginning with the parents of Patrick Samuel, then his marriage and offspring. The ink and writing changed over the next generations, which followed in sad order. So many of them died in the Potato Famine and the nightmare years afterward that it was more a litany of death than of life. At the top of the last page Rutledge found Brian FitzHugh's name, and Cormac's, but neither Stephen nor Susannah were recorded here. Nor, apparently, any other secrets that mattered to an investigation into murder.

After a moment, Rutledge dropped the prayer book into the drawer of the table by the bed, unwilling to go back under it. Then he changed his mind, and put the book back where it had come from. Putting it back took less time than finding it in the first place, and he did it holding his breath this time.

Afterward he dusted off his trousers and jacket, then closed the curtains at the windows.

The house was already too dark to do more than a cursory search elsewhere. Most of the other bedrooms had already been stripped of clothing, closets and desks and chests empty, drawers already smelling musty. But Rutledge, mindful of the hollowed out shelf in Olivia's room, checked each closet with infinite care.

There was nothing more to find, nothing that told him where Olivia had left her papers—not even whether they were still in the house. Susannah and her husband, Rachel and Stephen, with the help of Cormac, Mrs. Trepol, and the old woman Sadie, had spent days going through the house and cleaning room after room. He wasn't surprised to find nothing out of the ordinary where they had worked.

He went back to study. But the desk by the window was as sterile as the one in Olivia's bedroom. It was a wild goose chase—Stephen must have removed any papers left to him. Yet Rutledge had the feeling that a man hell-bent and determined to preserve his half sister's fame as a poet would stubbornly resist taking them too far, just as he'd fought to keep Olivia's room inviolate.

To which Hamish riposted, "What do you need the papers for, when you've found yon golden trophies? Or are ye shutting out what they say?"

The sun was a red ball on the horizon when Rutledge walked out to the headland, its warmth lingering in the light wind that preceded the stillness of sunset. Behind him the windows of the Hall were ablaze, and the weather vane on the church tower as well. *Red sky at night . . .*

117

He should have listened to Hamish and gone back to London on Saturday morning. He should have told Rachel this morning that there was no need to reopen the three deaths. Let sleeping murderers lie.

Now—now he was committed, the truth was something he had to uncover, for his own peace of mind. For the policeman in him who had to look at the good *and* the evil in human nature and live with its impact in his own soul.

What right had O. A. Manning to survive unscathed the nightmares of Olivia Marlowe? What right had she to be praised and revered as a creator of beauty, if she had been a woman without mercy or compassion?

Stephen FitzHugh had been left as Olivia's literary executor. To decide which of her papers and her worksheets biographers and critics and readers might see. And now, through no fault of his own, he was dead, and neither Rachel nor Susannah seemed to be particularly interested in shouldering the responsibility. Cormac, by his own admission, was more likely to destroy any family skeletons than allow them to rattle. The O. A. Manning he might choose to show to the public would be Olivia Marlowe's own public face, a quiet recluse who knew very little about the real world and yet had a wondrous insight into the human heart, a gift from God.

Or the devil. Depending on your knowledge of her.

Even if he, Rutledge, drove back to London in the morning, he would be the only person living who had proof that what Cormac suspected could be true. *His* burden to learn to live with. Not Cormac's. Not Susannah's. Not Rachel's.

Damn Stephen FitzHugh for falling down those blasted stairs!

If he stayed in Cornwall, he'd have to find a way to get to the bottom of a string of murders committed by a woman already dead.

But that was just the problem.

Olivia Marlowe had been buried. It was O. A. Manning who was still alive—and possibly had no right to be.

And when he, Rutledge, found out the whole truth, what in hell would he do about it? Deliberately destroy the author of *Wings of*

Fire? Bring down the beauty and the genius along with the cruelty and the lies?

"You've been executioner once," Hamish warned him. "And you no' have forgotten it. Will ye choose to do it again, then?"

Rutledge turned and walked back towards the house and the path to the village.

"If I have to," he said bitterly.

11

$\mathcal{T}$he next morning Rutledge sent a carefully worded message to London.

"Background material sparse but enlightening. No determination of crime possible at this time. Will take several more days, if presence not required in City."

Nothing to alarm Bowles, nothing to prevent Rutledge from coming to any conclusion he chose. And he had a feeling his superior would not be anxious to see him in London straight away.

The Monday papers had been awash with news of another killing in the City. Bowles had been interviewed in depth about the Yard's pursuit of the murderer, and talked fulsomely of modern forensic science and its role in tracking down the guilty party. Bowles leaned towards cold fact rather than intuition and a careful analysis of the killer's reasons for acting *now*, against this *particular* victim, and in this *particular* place. Rutledge had found that scientists were not always the best witnesses in the box, and as often as not a good man for the defense could walk rings around them.

He looked at his own cold facts. That Cormac had seen Olivia shove her sister out of an apple tree. That Olivia hadn't had the heart to dispose of her trophies of the dead, even in the face of her own death. That they were an admission of guilt in *six* possible murders, not just the two that Cormac laid at Olivia's door—indicating, perhaps, a cooler, more cunning skill as the child grew older.

But these facts, alone or together, were not sufficient proof of guilt in a courtroom. Cormac was young at the time, his own memory might have been at fault. A good barrister might point out that Olivia could have had those small articles in her possession for any number of reasons: she'd been given them, she'd taken them as a childhood prank, she'd won them in a wager. In themselves, without more evidence to lay out beside them, they couldn't be viewed as the fruits of sin.

Her papers might hold a confession. However convoluted or concealed in verse. But poets and writers were allowed literary license. That too could prove to be more circumstantial than conclusive.

Who then among the living might give him the proof he needed? Who would make a dependable, incontrovertible witness in the box?

He set out to look for one.

Constable Dawlish, finishing his breakfast in his wife's sunny kitchen, came out to the parlor to listen and found Rutledge's line of questioning hard to follow.

So did Hamish, who was still contending that they'd both live to regret staying on in Cornwall, and was muttering ominously about Rutledge's own stubbornness.

"You're asking about Mr. *Nicholas'* father?" Dawlish asked. "And Mr. Stephen's father? That was well before my time in uniform, sir! But James Cheney shot himself in his own gun room, and everyone knew he'd been blaming himself for what happened to his son. He took it hard, and who's to say whether the revolver went off by accident or of a purpose? Death by misadventure was the coroner's verdict, and Mrs. Cheney, sick with grief, thanked him for it. Are you thinking that she or one of the children might have shot him?" Dawlish shook his head. "I'd as soon believe my own wife would take a gun to *my* head, as Mrs. Cheney! You didn't know her, sir! And as for the children, they weren't old enough, any of them, to do such mischief. Besides, no man in his right mind

122

would have let a child so young handle a gun, much less play about with a loaded one."

"And Brian FitzHugh's death?"

"His horse threw him down by the sea, and he hit his head, drowned in the surf before anyone back at the house knew what had happened. They had to put the horse down as well, caught his leg in the rocks and damaged it badly. Mr. Cormac cried over it like a baby, holding it in his arms until Wilkins could fetch a pistol and do the job. Miss Olivia stood there watching, staring at Mr. Cormac as if he'd run mad. But Mr. Cormac, he'd trained that horse himself, and it was the best three-year-old the stables had had in twelve years."

"How do you know what Cormac and Olivia were doing?"

The constable's eyebrows rose in surprise. "Why, my father was a carpenter, sir, he was working in the stables at the time, rebuilding the stalls where they kept the mares waiting to foal. Mrs. Cheney had another wing put on for that."

"Is your father still alive?"

"No, sir, he died in the first year of the war."

A dead end. "Well, then, what was the story behind young Richard's disappearance?"

"There's a dozen ways a boy could die out on the moors. He wouldn't be the first lad to come to grief there. Nor the last."

"If he died on the moors, why was there no body found?"

"They looked, sir. They combed the rocks and the pools and the old mine shafts, they probed the quicksand, they put up flyers in all the towns around, they talked to the folk who live by the moors and to the gypsies who'd been camping near there in the month before. My father was in one of the search parties, and I went along with him. It was thorough."

"I want you to send men out again. To search the same ground, to draw me a map of where you've looked and what you've seen. Anything—a button, a scrap of cloth, a bone. I want it all brought in, and the spot marked on the map. Then I'll check it again myself."

"Sir!" Dawlish protested, aghast. "These are farmers and fishermen hereabouts, with a livelihood to earn! Have you any idea

123

how many men it'll take? And what a waste of time and energy that'll be?"

"Time and energy don't matter. Finding that boy's body does."

"And if after all our work, there's none found?"

"Then I'll know for a certainty that it can't be found."

Dawlish stared at the gaunt face, the intelligent, angry eyes. Humor the man from Scotland Yard, he'd been told. What he wants, let him have. As long as he returns to London as soon as possible, and with no cause to give a black eye to the local police in the matter of doing their duty.

With a sigh, he glanced at the napkin in his hand, then back to Rutledge. "I'll see that it's done, sir. You can leave it to me." But privately he was thinking that Scotland Yard would have been better served by putting their man onto finding that bloody killer in London, instead of raising a stir in far off Cornwall, where there was no connection to any murders.

The morning sun quickly gave way to clouds and rain, slow and steady, that drove the inn's keel players indoors to pass their time with skittles and long, rambling stories that seemed to lead nowhere except to wrangling over trifling details. For half an hour, Rutledge listened to them argue about which horse won the Derby in 1874 because someone swore old Mickelson had named his favorite dog after it. Even the innkeeper, Mr. Trask, couldn't tell Rutledge who Mickelson was.

"Could be he were that actor. A troop played in Truro one winter, and my father spoke highly of them. One had a little dog'd do tricks. I doubt half of *them* remember, either, who Mickelson might be, though you could hang and quarter them before they'd admit to it. Waiting for someone, are you, sir?"

In fact he was waiting for Dr. Penrith, though he didn't say so. Several women came in, asking for him too, but the retired doctor was not in his usual corner and it appeared he wouldn't be.

In the end, Rutledge walked down to Dr. Hawkins' surgery. When Mrs. Hawkins stuck her head out the door, trying to keep the rain out of her hallway, Rutledge asked for her father instead of her husband. Surprised, she said, "He's through by the fire, sir.

His joints are bothering him fiercely in this wet. Will you come this way, please?"

She took him into the part of the house where the family lived, and down a passage to a small room at the back. The fire burned high, a rush of warmth suffocating Rutledge after his brisk walk through the rain. The wool in his coat began to steam gently, giving off a distinct odor of Harris sheep.

Mrs. Hawkins promised them tea shortly, and left them. Dr. Penrith, pleased to see anyone to fill his empty hours, profusely welcomed Rutledge and insisted that he take a chair close by the hearth. A small spaniel, resting her nose on her master's foot, stared at him myopically as he came across the room, and thumped a tail on the hearth rug. Rutledge, feeling like a man unfairly condemned to walk in flames for a time, like the ghost of Hamlet's father, commiserated with his host on the afflictions of age, and then gently turned the conversation to the Trevelyan family.

Smiling, Dr. Penrith began to reminisce about Adrian Trevelyan, with whom he'd had a running battle over ancient Cornish legends as well as the Arthurian romances. With a chuckle he added, "Half the parish histories in England've been written by parish priests and doctors, but that old fool studied at Winchester and Cambridge, and thought himself a scholar. Pshaw! He wanted to track Arthur back to the Romans, but he's a *West Country* hero, and nothing to do with the Romans!"

Rutledge could hear the fondness in his voice, and pictured the two men arguing over their port for the sheer joy of contradiction and controversy. In lonely lives, even the smallest battles gave great satisfaction.

"Lancelot came from France," he pointed out, shifting in his chair as his knees turned to burned toast. Hamish, as always sensitive to Rutledge's moods, grumbled about hellfire and damnation in the back of his mind.

"Aye, and wasn't it just like a Frenchman to get around Guinevere! There'd been no whispers of such goings-on until Frogs took up the tales!"

Rutledge stifled a laugh and used the opening to change the direction of the conversation. "What were the whispers about the Hall, and Adrian Trevelyan's beautiful daughter?"

"None!" the doctor turned to retort angrily. "Like Caesar's wife, Rosamund was always above reproach!"

"What happened to Richard Trevelyan?"

The old eyes clouded with pain. "Who can say? If the gypsies had taken him, you'd think he'd have come home when he could get away. But there's been no boy ringing the doorbell to claim he's Richard. And no man either."

"Would Rosamund have believed them if they had come?"

"She was an intelligent woman. She tried to believe he'd been taken away—or run away and been lost, then found and not returned. It kept hope alive in her heart, and she told James the boy would turn up, wait and see! That he'd gone off to join the army, and some farmer or carter would be bringing him back soon enough, tired and hungry."

"And Miss Olivia?"

Dr. Penrith frowned. "Now there was an odd thing, you know. Miss Olivia never cried. She went out with the searchers, riding a pony because of her bad leg, and was gone all that day and the next, until I met her on one of the roads and sent her home. I've never seen a child look so tired; I thought she'd made herself ill again. But she stared at me, then said, 'Richard wanted a tombstone with an angel on it. He told me so. I want to buy one, just a small one, to remember him by. Can you tell me how much it will cost?' "

"How did you answer her?" Rutledge asked, intrigued.

"That they don't put up tombstones until they have the body, and she said, quite seriously, 'But that's not true. There are markers in the churchyard for any man lost at sea.' She had a raging fever by the time they got her home, and I heard no more about angels and tombstones."

Rutledge found himself thinking of a poem in one of the earlier volumes. It began,

They stood an angel in the churchyard for the man they lost at sea,
But for him I loved so dearly, there was never place for me

126

To come and mourn his passing, touch the earth beneath
*   my hand,*
Or bring him blood-red roses . . .

He tried to recall the last lines and failed.

But Hamish, the soft Scottish burr clear in his voice, provided them for him.

Alas, a frailer angel watches where you sleep
With pansies—for remembrance—lying at your feet.

Olivia herself had known where Richard lay—find him there, and the case was made!

When tea was brought, Rutledge asked about James Cheney's death, and Dr. Penrith shook his head sadly. "I couldn't tell Rosamund how he died. And at least he'd had sense enough to put the barrel to his temple and not in his mouth, for all the world to know what he'd been about! But who can say whether it was accidental or not, whether the thought came to him suddenly and he hadn't the will to turn it aside. One round was all he had put in the cylinder, and he used it. To end the pain. That was my guess."

"Who was in the house that day?"

"They all were. Olivia. Nicholas. Rosamund. And Adrian, of course. FitzHugh was there, he'd brought over the new brood mares. It was Cormac came for me, pleading for me to make haste, to do something. But it was useless. I knew that as soon as I saw James' body."

"And you never thought of murder?"

"Good God! Self-murder is terrible enough! And who would want to kill James? He was a *kind* man, a good man. The house had seen enough grief already, who could possibly want to add to Rosamund's burdens? There's no one alive that cruel!"

Agitated, he spilled his tea, and Rutledge knelt to mop it up with his napkin, his back to the scorching fire.

"What did Olivia have to say when she was told of James' death?"

"I don't remember," Penrith said testily. "It was a long time ago, and I was not concerned with Olivia, I was worried about Rosamund, and her father. He never recovered his spirits after that, you could see it clear."

The old eyes, fading into a milky gray, looked back into a past he didn't want to remember. "I walked behind their coffins," he said sadly. "Not because they'd been in my care. Not for Adrian's sake. But because in that house I found something I've never felt since under any roof, not even my own. Laughter was there, and happiness. And most of all, a glory. Brian FitzHugh told me once that it was in the very stones of the Hall, that it had been handed down with the Trevelyan blood and the Trevelyan land. That's romantic nonsense, an Irishman's blarney. But I knew what it was, I knew from the very first day I set eyes on her. It was Rosamund . . ."

Emotion had drained him. He began to nod over his tea cup, head sinking slowly until his chin rested on his cravat, and Rutledge gently removed the saucer from the gnarled fingers. Then, with the wet napkin and the tray, he slipped quietly out of the room and into the—by comparison—frigid passage.

Mrs. Hawkins, taking the tray from him, said apologetically, "He slips off to sleep easier every day. I wonder sometimes . . ." But she left the sentence unfinished, and instead showed him to the door. "Thank you for coming to cheer him a little," she said. "I don't expect you'll be in Borcombe much longer, but I know he'd be glad to see you again before you leave."

"Did you know Olivia Marlowe very well?" he asked, looking out at the rain coming down in sheets.

"She was friendly enough, whenever we ran into each other, but no, I wasn't likely to know her well. She didn't go about much. I was that surprised when they told me she wrote poetry, but then she was an invalid, wasn't she? With time heavy on her hands. Nicholas was here sometimes in the evening, to visit my father. I always thought he might marry Rachel." A pink flush rose in her cheeks. "I've never known a man quite like him—there was an intensity about him, a—a force." She began to search through the Chinese stand beside the door, and took out an old umbrella. "You can borrow this, if you like. Otherwise, you'll sure to be calling on the doctor with a fever." Then, in a rush, as if she felt she had to finish what she'd begun, she said, "Nicholas tried to protect Olivia from everything. He thought if he was there, with her, he could hold off the pain, he could keep her from the darkness that beset her. He tried so hard, you could see it—*I* could see it, I mean— and I thought, when I heard how he'd died, that he was still afraid for her in death. As if, somehow, he could save her from what came after . . ."

Rutledge splashed through the puddles on his way back to the inn, heedless of where he put his feet or the dampness spreading through his socks. Wet feet had been the ever-present hell of the trenches; it had cost more men than Stephen FitzHugh their toes or part of a foot. You learned somehow to shut it out, until the smell told you that the rot had begun.

Hamish was fuming at the back of his mind, telling him something, and he ignored the voice, his mind on Olivia Marlowe.

If she knew where Richard was buried, then she'd killed him. And if she knew, then it was a place that could be *found*. The boy hadn't been taken by gypsies or thrown into quicksand, he'd been killed and hidden.

"With pansies—for remembrance—"

Had Olivia meant that figuratively? Or literally?

"It doesna' matter. What if she meant pansies to put near him, flowers that wilted and were gone in a day? Who would see them, who would guess what she was about?"

The angel then, *a frailer angel*. Herself? Somewhere that Olivia, with her brace, could reach?

She could ride a pony. That widened the circle. He'd been right to order the constable to search the moors again.

Rutledge turned, crossed over to the nearest shop. In the small window fronting the road there was a collection of ribbons and laces behind a spill of colorful embroidery thread, packets of needles, and an array of handkerchiefs that reminded him of those he'd seen in Olivia's room. As he opened the door, a gust of wind and rain nearly jerked the knob out of his hand.

Startled, a middle-aged woman looked up from a cushion of bobbins and threads and a half-finished lace collar on her lap. "Could I help you, sir?" she asked, trying hastily to get to her feet.

"No, sit down, I'm too wet to come in. I need directions, that's all."

She sank back into her chair, somehow preventing the bobbins from rolling to every point of the compass. Then he saw that like the Belgian nuns he'd come across during the war, she had them pinned in place. "To where?"

"I'm looking for the man who did the gardening at the Hall. Wilkins is his name."

"Oh, you've come the wrong way, sir! He's down towards the river, in a little house you can't miss. There's a stone wall and a garden in front, and beehives out back."

Five minutes later, his shoes squeaking with rain water, Rutledge was knocking on the door of a stone house half hidden under its slate roof.

Wilkins came to answer the summons with his bedroom slippers on his feet. He grinned at Rutledge and said, "I've seen drowned men drier than you! Here, wait till I've fetched some rags."

As Rutledge furled his umbrella, Wilkins disappeared down the dark stone-flagged passage towards the back of the house, and soon returned with a handful of old cloths. Rutledge dried his shoes as best he could, and then followed the old man into his kitchen, where something smelled suspiciously like rabbit stew in the pot simmering on the hearth.

"I knew you'd be along before the day was out. They say you're nosing around the Hall and the village, looking for answers that London wants. About the deaths at the Hall. Aye, I'm not surprised. If you ask me, Inspector Harvey is a fool, and Constable Dawlish too full of himself to know the difference between his nose and his toes! I've got some good ale in that jug over there, fresh from The Three Bells. And if you'll hand it to me, I'll pour you a cup."

Rutledge picked up the heavy stone jug and passed it to him. Wilkins filled two cups and sat down with a sigh of satisfaction.

"I never thought Mr. Brian was killed falling from his horse. He was too good a rider. *Born* on a horse, like as not, and knew what he was about. And you don't ride a valuable animal through sea-wet rocks, not if you've got any sense, with the risk of ruining his legs! It were murder, pure and simple, that happened that day—to man and mount!"

12

Caught off balance, Rutledge stared at the old man. "Did you say this to anyone at the time? When Brian FitzHugh died?"

Wilkins gave him a toothless grin, "Lord, and lose my job on the spot? Which I nearly did anyway, when Miss Rosamund gave up the racing stables. And come to that, what was I to say to her? Or to the police?" He drank his ale, belched with pleasure, and shrugged his shoulders with almost Gallic expressiveness.

"But if you believed it was murder—"

"Aye, it were murder," he said bluntly. "I were there when they raised the alarm, running for all I was worth to see what were wrong and to look to the horse. I'd saddled him for Mr. FitzHugh, I knew which mount he'd taken out!"

"Tell me, then."

"Mr. FitzHugh was lying face down in the sea, blood on his head, and they found blood on one of the rocks just there, where he'd been thrown and then rolled into the surf. But the horse were deeper among the rocks, wild-eyed and shaking. A spur had raked one flank, not the other. I'd never known Mr. FitzHugh to use a spur on his horses, and I'd never known Lucifer to need more than the lightest rein, he were that clever. Read your mind almost! Something happened that put the fear of God into him, and he bolted. But with an empty saddle, if *I* know anything about it!"

"What makes you say that?"

"There were neither horse hair nor blood on Mr. FitzHugh's spurs. And if he'd been throwed, just there, where he would hit his head on the rocks coming down, then roll over, his face into the water, why was there water in his *boots* when I pulled 'em off him, so's they could carry him back to the house?"

"Surely the police asked that same question?"

"Aye, and they answered it, too, that the sea'd come in with the tide, soaking his trousers and his stockings. There were no footprints on the shingle but ours and Master Nicholas', coming up from his boat, no signs of a struggle or trouble of any kind, and the doctor, *he* said Mr. FitzHugh had drowned, before he'd regained his wits from the fall." He finished his ale, then went to stir the stew, squinting in the heat of the fire.

Rutledge bent down, untied his shoes, and looked at his stockings. They were wet with rain. The shoes themselves were pliable with rain water. But when he upended them, water didn't run out. The stockings and the lining had absorbed it. Interesting point, he told himself as he laced them again.

"And no one else raised objections about the horse?"

"Mr. Cormac did. He said his father wouldn't have taken Lucifer among the rocks, not without good reason." Wilkins came back to sit down at the table, refilling his cup and offering more to Rutledge, who shook his head. "We found a bee caught under the girth," he said. "Where it'd stung the horse. And that satisfied the lot of them. But I walked back down there later and had a look around. Before the stir, mind you, Master Nicholas'd drawn his boat up on shore just a few yards away, and turned it over, planning to come back and work on the seams. Well, I looked under it, and I found the print of Mr. Brian's riding boot, next to the print of another shoe, but the tide had half erased that. He were on foot, then, talking to someone. He weren't *alone* down there on the shingle, not the whole time!"

"He might have been there when Nicholas Cheney brought the boat in, and helped drag it above the tide line."

"Then why didn't Master Nicholas say so?"

"All right. Who would have wanted to kill FitzHugh?"

Wilkins sighed. "That were the problem, you see. Not Miss Rosamund—she were *Mrs.* FitzHugh—*she'd* not be likely to send him off. The twins, now, they were little 'uns, and you'd not see them on the strand or near the headland or in the stables without their nanny in tow. Miss Olivia were a cripple. Mr. FitzHugh were Mr. Cormac's own father. None of the servants, that *I* knew of, had any quarrel with him. Mr. FitzHugh had a temper, mind you, but he were fair, and no one held any grudge that I'd heard about. And that left Master Nicholas, whose boat it was. Why would *he* want to harm his stepfather? It made no sense to me. So I held my tongue and waited to see what happened, and when naught did, I kept on holding of it."

Nicholas might have no reason to kill his stepfather, but he might well have covered up for Olivia, if he'd had any fear that she was involved.

With the brace on her leg, *could* she have moved around among the rocks?

He asked that question aloud. Wilkins thought about it. "She weren't one to plead helplessness. I'd see her struggle to do what she wanted to do. Aye, she could get over them rocks, spider fashion, pulling her leg along. Slowlike and careful. But where she had the will, she got her way."

Remembering what Constable Dawlish had said, Rutledge asked, "You put the horse down, didn't you? Was she there, watching?"

"Aye, it were left to me, and a hard job it were. Loved that horse, I did. Mr. Cormac were there, his head buried in the horse's neck and crying. Miss Olivia came with Dawlish, who were only a boy then, and said, 'There's no saving him? Not even if he never races again? Must we put him down?' And I said, 'The smith looked at that foreleg, miss, and he said t'were shattered, there were no way to mend it so's it'd take his weight.' Fleet as he were, I couldn't watch him live out his days a cripple, struggling over every step, though I didn't say that to *her* face, her being a cripple herself!"

He looked into his cup and swished the ale thoughtfully. "She stayed till it were done. Not a bit squeamish, as you'd think in a young lady like her. Afterward, she told Mr. Cormac, if he cared so much for Lucifer, he could help dig the hole to bury him in. And we did it, out on the headland, Mr. Cormac and a few of the lads and me."

Rutledge walked back to the inn as the church clock struck twelve. The rain had turned into a misty drizzle again, and the street was no longer a river under his feet. More people were about, now, men and women, a few of them nodding to him in recognition. Mrs. Trepol, hurrying past, wished him a good day, and in the distance he glimpsed Rachel moving head down towards the woods that separated the village from the Hall. Hamish, rumbling with suppressed irritation, kept Rutledge from concentrating his thoughts on the morning's work. Or was it his own reluctance?

At the inn, Mr. Trask took his umbrella and greeted him with the news that he had a visitor waiting in the parlor. Rutledge went through into a long narrow room with a ceiling so low it seemed to brush his head. In the wave of claustrophobia that followed, he saw only the dark furnishings, the empty grate, and a tall man with white hair who rose from a chair and stood where he was, waiting for Rutledge to speak.

After a moment, he managed to say, "I'm Rutledge. I'm afraid I don't know who you are."

The man looked him over, then said, "Chambers. Thomas Chambers. I represent the Trevelyan family—"

Rutledge had him pegged. This was the lawyer who had courted Rosamund and almost won her. The family solicitor, handling the wills. Regarding him with new interest, he crossed the room to light the lamps on the chimney piece. Their glow, added to the one lamp already burning on the table, pushed back the darkness and the cavelike atmosphere of the room. Breathing more easily, he could concentrate on what Chambers was saying.

"—and I understand that you've come down to reconsider the circumstances of their deaths. I'd like to know why."

Rutledge stood with his back to the cold hearth and said, "Because the Home Office wished to be sure that all was as it should be. Miss Marlowe—as O. A. Manning—is a person of some prominence."

Chambers all but snorted in disbelief. "You may tell the locals that, and they'd be impressed. I'm not."

"Suspicious, are you?" Rutledge asked.

"Of course I'm suspicious when Scotland Yard feels it needs to stick its nose into a death where I'm handling the estate."

"Is there anything wrong with the wills? Any provisions that make you especially nervous?" He was deliberately misunderstanding the man, stripping him of his authority and aggressively taking charge of the meeting. Not out of personal animosity but as a tool.

Chambers stared at him. At the thinness, the gaunt face, the lines that had prematurely aged a much younger man than he'd guessed at in the beginning. And wasn't above a little aggression of his own.

"In the war, were you?"

Rutledge nodded.

"Wounded?"

Rutledge hesitated, then said briefly, "Yes."

"Thought as much! Stephen looked the same way when he came back. Shell of himself. Damned foot killed him in the end, too."

Over Hamish's rude comments about that, Rutledge recaptured the salient.

"What did *you* do in the war?"

"They wouldn't take me," Chambers said in disgust. "Too old, they told me. But I knew that part of France better than they did! My mother's mother was from there. Stupid place to fight infantry battles, for God's sake! No geographical advantage. No high ground. Prolonged deadlock, that's what you'll get, I told them. Enormous loss of life, I told them. No one will come out of it a winner. Americans tipped the balance, of course. And the tank. And still the best they could do was an Armistice!" Chambers realized suddenly that he'd mounted one of his hobby horses, and stopped, watching the advantage slip back to Rutledge. Then he grinned. "Over to you, I think."

Rutledge found himself grinning back. He liked Chambers. He could also see what had attracted Rosamund FitzHugh to the man.

"Who sent for you?" Rutledge asked. "Susannah Hargrove?"

137

"Daniel Hargrove. He was worried, because his wife is in delicate health and this whole business was upsetting her. They tell me now she's likely to bear twins, but that runs in the family, not surprising."

They were still standing, Rutledge by the hearth, Chambers at the far end of the room, a position chosen to make Rutledge come to him, not the reverse. Rutledge said, impatiently, "Sit down, man!" He was aware of the smell of wool again, and with resignation ignored it. Hamish, perversely, did not.

After a moment, Chambers moved forward and took one of the chairs near the fireplace. The room was damp, chill, with an old coldness that seemed to come from the walls, seeping up from the earth that waited to consume the stone when it finally sank under its own weight.

Rutledge took the chair across from him, and said, "Actually, I'm glad you've come, I was considering traveling to Plymouth to find you."

Surprised, Chambers said, "Not about the wills, I think?"

"In a way. I know that Olivia Marlowe made her half brother Stephen FitzHugh her literary executor. But then Stephen died soon after. And I haven't been able to find her papers. Do you have them?"

"No, I understood that Stephen knew what was involved in that bequest and was prepared to deal with the responsibility himself. If Nicholas had survived, he'd have had that duty."

"And if Stephen died?"

"Ah, now that's a very good question. I think Susannah, Mrs. Hargrove. He didn't specify her as literary executor, you understand. His will was made out while Olivia was still alive and it would have been presumptuous to consider that need. But he did leave everything else to her, and the courts will, I think, accept the inclusion of Olivia's papers in his estate."

"Not to Cormac FitzHugh, then?"

Chambers frowned. "No. There was some . . . coolness between the two of them. Cormac and Olivia, I mean. She made it very clear to me at the time she drew up her will that she didn't wish Cormac to be in any way responsible for her affairs. Stephen was still very

138

young then, which is why I'd suggested an older and wiser man to handle the papers."

"What was the cause of this coolness?"

"I never knew quite what it was, but Rosa—" his face flushed, and he quickly changed that to "—Mrs. FitzHugh told me once that even she didn't know the reasons behind it."

"You were well acquainted with Mrs. FitzHugh, I think?"

"Yes." He looked down at his hands, turning a ring on his little finger. "I'd hoped to marry her," he added reluctantly.

"Then she would have told you the reasons, if in fact she had known them? It wasn't a polite lie to an outsider?"

"I think she would have been honest with me," he said slowly. "Except at the end. She was very distressed. I begged her to tell me what was wrong, why she was upset. But she wouldn't say. The doctor called it depression. It wasn't that. Rosamund—Mrs. FitzHugh—was not the kind of woman who either felt sorry for herself or dwelt on the sadness of life. God knows, she'd had enough suffering, heartbreak, but she dealt with it with such courage—"

His voice broke off. Then he said, forcing it back to normal tones, "I never knew why she killed herself. It left me scarred. Not just her death, but the fact that she never turned to me in whatever anguish there was."

Rutledge considered him. The thick white hair, still-black brows, the strong, almost attractive face. The squared shoulders and straight back. A good man to have beside you in the trenches when the next assault came, because you knew you could depend on him not to break . . .

Hamish said, unexpectedly, "But he'd protect her, wouldn't he? He'd not give up her confidences to a stranger come to make trouble!"

Which was very true.

Rutledge changed tactics. "Who was the murderer in that house?"

For once, Chambers was completely off guard, completely vulnerable, his face stripped of the mask that the law and his years had fashioned for it.

139

But Rutledge had been right in his judgment as well. Stunned, speechless for an instant, still Chambers didn't break.

"*Murderer*? Christ, man, what are you talking about?"

"A cold-blooded killer who for reasons we can't fathom, decimated the Trevelyan family with methodical cunning. He—or she—was there, in the household. I've discovered that much. But so far, I can't prove it."

Chambers stared at him, his intelligence slowly reasserting itself as the first shock receded. "I don't believe you! In *Rosamund's* house? No, it's not possible, you've been grasping for straws and looking for an excuse to make your trip down here worthwhile! Looking for *promotion* on the reputations of people who can't defend themselves!"

Rutledge smiled, a cold smile that never reached his eyes. "If that were true, I could cause a great deal of trouble. But in the end, I'd only harm myself. No. Come with me, Mr. Chambers."

He stood up, and without waiting to see if Chambers would follow, he went out into the inn's hallway, fetched his coat from the rack, and was already picking up the borrowed umbrella when Chambers slowly came after him through the parlor door.

"Where are we going?"

"To the Hall," Rutledge told him. "Do you have any objections?"

"I don't—I'd rather not go there!"

"Why?"

"None of your damned business!" Chambers flared into anger as a defense. "I have no responsibility to you or to Scotland Yard. Only to my clients. I have neither obligation nor duty to cooperate with the police in a wild goose chase!"

"If you have a clear conscience, I see no reason why you should refuse to go with me to the Hall. Today or any day."

"No." It was very final.

Rutledge shoved the umbrella back into the tall brass stand and went back into the parlor, tossing his coat across the nearest chair. After a moment, Chambers followed him and shut the door with a pointed slam.

"What do you want of me," he asked, standing there blocking

it. "And what do you want of this investigation? Besides this ridiculous charge of murderers in the Trevelyan household."

"You know something was wrong in that house, don't you? *Rachel* felt it, because—she was particularly susceptible to the moods of the people who lived there." He couldn't bring himself, objectivity or not, to betray Rachel's regard for Nicholas. "And you're vulnerable too. Because you cared deeply for Rosamund and you *know* she wasn't a woman likely to kill herself. Or let's take Nicholas as an example, if you find thinking about Rosamund too painful. Would you have pegged him as a potential suicide? The sort of man who'd quietly choose to die with his half sister rather than face life on his own? A sentimental pact, in the moonlight, on a peaceful Saturday night? Or did Nicholas strike you as a man with a burden he carried with great patience and strength?"

Chambers' expression was closed, the solicitor yielding nothing, loyalty to his clients coming ahead of any personal feelings.

"Damn it, you're too intelligent to put your own responses down to sentimentality, but you feel uncomfortable in the Hall. Let me describe it for you. You walk through the door, and the house isn't benign, it's alive with jarring forces. To some extent, it's a subjective response, I grant you, because of the uneasiness in your own mind. Your intuition tries to point out that there's something very wrong here, but you refuse to listen, you don't want to believe that what you sense could be true. And you won't help *me* to find the answers for the same reasons!"

Rutledge was met with a wall of resistance. But he was beginning to take the measure of it now.

"Even I have felt the emotions in that house! I was moved by O. A. Manning's poetry, I was shocked by the manner of the poet's death, I was personally involved in a way that an ordinary policeman wouldn't have been. And I'm not by nature one to look for moods or—what is it that the crackpots call it?—vibrations? I don't believe in ghosts, either. But Trevelyan Hall is haunted, in a sense that you and I both accept."

Chambers still didn't answer, but his face was paler, strained.

"I survived in those hellholes they called trenches for four years. It seemed like forty—a lifetime. I learned to trust my intuition.

Men who didn't often died. I was lucky to possess it in the first place, and war honed it. I learned that it wasn't a figment of my imagination. Nor was it a replacement for the God I'd lost. Whatever it was, you came to recognize it. An inkling, a warning, a sudden flash of caution, a split-second insight that saved your life. Indisputably real, however unorthodox the means of reaching you. It gave you an edge on death, and you were grateful. Then I lost it for a time, it doesn't matter why. But it hasn't failed me completely, and I can tell you why you're afraid to go back to that house. You know that Rosamund's death haunts you there. You can feed yourself lies down in Plymouth. But not here. Not in the house itself!"

Rutledge could see the clenched jaw. The desperate rejection. In his own head Hamish was clamoring for him to leave the man in peace—

"It was an accidental overdose!"

The words, when they finally came, seemed to be torn from the depths of Chambers'soul.

"No." Rutledge waited, relentless. "Rosamund didn't make such mistakes. She was a strong woman. She was sunshine and light, not despair and darkness. It wasn't suicide, and it wasn't an accidental overdose."

"I refuse to accept murder!"

"Because you believe that murder, if it was done, was your fault. For loving Rosamund. For wanting to marry her. For winning her love. Just as suicide could mean a rejection of your love, murder means someone wanted to prevent another stepfather in the house, another family. Another long wait for whatever it was he—or she— wanted badly enough to kill for."

Hamish was saying in agitation, "Where did this notion come from? You never spoke of it before!"

In the tumult of his own emotions, Rutledge tersely answered the voice aloud. "I didn't know before. But it makes sense now. I see the pattern!"

He did. Olivia had systematically eliminated her family—the twin sister who could pass for her and steal her grandfather's love. The stepfathers she hadn't wanted. The half brother who had stirred up the household and kept it on its ear. The mother who was planning to marry again. But not Nicholas, never Nicholas, who had looked after her. Not until the very end, when he no longer served any purpose—

Hamish was still raising fierce objections. Rutledge ignored them. He was angry and unsettled and—yes—bewildered by the leap his intuition had taken without warning.

Without a motive, he could keep to himself his suspicions about Olivia. He could deny, on the surface, that he believed in them because there was no real evidence except the carefully hidden trophies of the dead. It was possible—it was likely—it was practicable— But still theory. Still his own torment.

Now, it was real. Suddenly, it was *real*—

He had nearly forgotten about Chambers in the dark, low-ceilinged room, standing by the door like a man who'd lost his way and waited for a sign.

The hoarse voice startled him.

"Damn you! You should have died in France!" Chambers said with such bitterness that Rutledge knew he'd won.

It was a hollow victory. It had cost both men very dearly.

Suddenly, exhausted and drained, he felt he was on the edge of a precipice inside himself, the blackness he'd fought so long in the hospital, and once, too short a time ago, in Warwickshire. It seemed to draw him, to beckon like the Sirens, a place of peace and darkness and silence where nothing could ever touch him again.

The doctors had warned him he was still at risk, that it might be too soon to go back to the pressures of the Yard, while his own stability was an uncertain factor—and he'd fought them, inch by inch, to try returning.

And then a line of poetry came running through his head like a bright and deadly thread.

> *If I choose to die,*
> *There is peace in darkness, and no pain.*
> *The grave is safe—*

It was as if Olivia herself urged him to fail, to choose the darkness and leave the past intact. Chambers would never speak of it again. Rutledge was certain of that—

But the very last lines of the same poem came back to him too.

If I choose to live,
Oh, God, it will never be the same . . .
Yet I prevail—

The dilemma of Olivia Marlowe, who could give and who could destroy with equal adroitness.

13

$\mathcal{H}$is voice still shaken, Chambers said, "I need a drink. From the look of you, I've no doubt you could use one too." He turned and opened the parlor door, crossing the hall to the inn's dining room. There he took a table by the window, pulled out the other chair for Rutledge, and sat down heavily. In the watery light, he looked old and tired, but Rutledge knew it was an illusion.

Trask came hurrying across the room to ask them what they'd have, and Chambers ordered whiskey, glancing at Rutledge to see if that met with his approval. "Make it a strong one, and then we'll have our lunch. I can't travel back to Plymouth half sober."

When Trask had gone again, Chambers sighed. "You're a damned hard man, do you know that?"

"I'm stubborn, that's all."

Chambers smiled grimly. "Well, so am I. I loved Rosamund, damn it. I don't want to think I missed the causes of her distress at the end, and I don't want to think that one of her family could be—evil. That's what it would have to be. Not wickedness, you understand. That's entirely different. Do you believe in evil, Inspector, or did you lose that, along with God?"

"I've seen enough evil in my work. I respect its existence."

"Yes, that's probably very true. I don't, as a country solicitor, deal with crime as often as I deal with property and wills and contracts, the ongoing bits and bobs of everyday life. Still, God knows money often brings out the worst in people! But it strikes me—having seen some of the dregs of life myself—that evil is something we don't understand because it's outside the pale of ordinary experience."

"You should tell that to the rector, Smedley. He has strong views in that direction himself."

"Yes, I know him, a good man. But the point I'm making here is that I knew everyone in Mrs. FitzHugh's household, and I sensed no evil there. I couldn't point my finger at any one of them, and say, 'There I have some doubts' or 'I can't feel easy about that one.' Mind you, I'm still not *agreeing* with you on any of this," he added wryly, "but for the sake of argument—"

Yet Rutledge could see that Chambers was already following the path of his own reasoning. "We can eliminate both Stephen and Susannah. They were born after it all began," he said.

"Began? Where?"

"With Anne, Olivia's twin sister. To be more precise, with her death."

"Damn it, she fell out of a *tree!*"

"Or was pushed. And our choices are broader now. Nicholas, Rachel, Olivia. Rosamund. James Cheney and Brian FitzHugh. Cormac. They were all alive at that time. The servants. We can't leave them out of the equation."

"You can omit the adults," Chambers said testily. "They weren't there when it happened. Not even one of the nursery maids."

Ignoring him, Rutledge said, "And next was young Richard."

Chambers' black brows snapped together. Trask came just then with their glasses, and as he walked away again, Chambers said, "All right. He was out on the moors, during a family picnic. Olivia was with—"

He stopped.

Rutledge waited, watching the trained mind work behind the disbelieving eyes. Watching the solicitor vie with the prejudices of the lover.

"No!" he said in a fierce whisper. "No, I will not accept that!

Not Olivia! She was the apple of her grandfather's eye. She was Rosamund's shadow. She was, for God's sake, a remarkably courageous and astute woman, never mind the poetry! She wouldn't have touched that child!"

"But don't you see? That's the key to a successful murderer. When no one is willing to believe he or she could possibly be behind such cruelty."

Chambers shook his head adamantly. "No. If we must put the blame on someone, let it be Cormac. He was no child of Rosamund's, and I know very little about his childhood, which makes it easier to point my finger in that direction. Yes, hypothetically Cormac I will accept! But not Olivia!"

"All right, Cormac, if you will. What did he have to gain, killing Anne? Or young Richard? I can see that killing James Cheney might have made way for Cormac's father to marry the grieving widow, but Cormac was never in line to inherit the house or vast sums of money, and still isn't. I don't know how Susannah Hargrove's will stands, but I should think she leaves her share of the estate to her husband, if it hasn't been sold by the time she dies."

"I can't break my trust and tell you how her affairs stand, but yes, I can be frank about one matter. Susannah doesn't leave her share of the house to Cormac. After all, she's got a family of her own to think of. Or soon will."

"Then why should Cormac kill people and risk being caught? If he's nothing to gain? And without fail the outsider is the first to draw suspicion. There's always the ugly possibility of childhood jealousy, I grant you, but somehow that doesn't fit him, does it? Cormac strikes me as a clearheaded businessman who will take calculated risks in the market, but not in his personal life."

"Well, yes, I must agree there," Chambers replied reluctantly. "There was no call to be jealous. I know for a fact that Rosamund saw to his education, then gave him introductions to prominent men in the City when he came down from Cambridge. Just what she'd have done for her own sons! The rest he's earned on his own considerable merit. Which brings us back to where we started. There's no possible motive I can see for your choice to light on Olivia, either. Even if Richard did go wandering while in her care."

He finished his whiskey and turned to signal Trask, saying to Rutledge over his shoulder, "But let me put this question to you. Suppose you're right about her. Where will prosecuting a dead woman, however evil she might have been, take you? Certainly not into a court of law."

"O. A. Manning is still very much alive," Rutledge responded.

Chambers turned back, staring at him speculatively. "I begin to see," he said quietly.

Chambers left after the meal, with a final comment. "I'll give you a hearing when you've got incontrovertible evidence to show me. Until then, I shall do my best not to give credence to a word you've told me. And my best is very good indeed, let me assure you!"

Luncheon appeared to have restored his balance.

Rutledge went up to his room, overwhelming fatigue dogging his steps as he climbed the narrow stairs.

The reactions he'd gotten from Chambers proved how far the case he could presently lay out would go in a courtroom. He'd sown seeds of doubt in the solicitor's mind, but he hadn't done more than make him think. And a jury is no better than the evidence presented to it. That was a maxim at the Yard.

All right then, where to go next?

The men searching the moors in this wretched weather would have to find more than suspicions . . .

Richard's body and the manner in which it was found could go a long way towards proving murder. But by whom? What if there were no pansies at his feet to link the small body with the poem Olivia had written?

In the afternoon Rutledge set out in a lowering mist to look for the small isolated cottage where the old midwife lived. Trask had reluctantly told him how to find it.

"She's harmless, they say, but she gives me the willies!" he'd confided to Rutledge. "Never know where you stand with her. And those eyes—they lay a man bare, like a fleshing knife, but beyond the bone."

"I'm told she's a good nurse."

"Oh, aye, I grant her that. But what does she steal when you're defenseless?" From the expression on his face Rutledge knew he wasn't thinking of money. Or the brass candlesticks.

Of such fears witch-hunts were born, Rutledge thought as he set out.

Sadie lived in a narrow cranny that branched off the main valley of the Bor, hardly more than a cul-de-sac where her sod-roofed house squatted in the rain like a wet gray toad. A garden had been hacked out of the hillsides and into the narrow strip of flatland on which the house had been built. He could recognize herbs of different kinds—although he only knew the names of half of them—and rows of cabbage and onions and carrots next to straggling lines of flowers beaten down by the heavy rains. A dozen bedraggled chickens scratched in a muddy pen out back.

She must have seen him coming, because the old wooden door inched open before he got there. "Leave the umbrella by the sill, and wipe your feet on yon rag!" she told him sharply. "I want no mud on my floors!"

He did as he was told and was surprised when he finally crossed the threshold and stepped into the low beamed room that served her as both parlor and kitchen. She had whitewashed the walls, and they glowed like butter in the fire that didn't begin to fill a hearth broad enough to hold a pig. But the room was warm, and the bright rag rugs that covered the stone floor kept out the damp. The furniture was old, worn, castoffs that had seen finer days. Bunches of drying herbs and flowers hung in the rafters, giving the room an oddly exotic tang of mixed scents. Baskets, woven of rushes, held a stock of dry wood, and a large black cat—her familiar? he wondered in wry amusement—slept on a cushion by the only window.

Sadie looked him up and down with those bright eyes. "What brings a London policeman out in a West Country rain to talk to an old woman?" Her mind seemed clear enough today, he thought, listening for the querulousness that seemed to come with confusion, when she began drifting out of reach.

"I'm trying to piece together information about the family at the Hall. You know that," Rutledge answered mildly. "I thought you might remember some other things that would be useful."

149

"Like?"

"Like, where are the servants who used to work there?"

"Scattered. Gone to other houses, or retired. Or dead."

"Do you remember their names?"

She grinned at him. "At my age?" But he thought she could, if she tried. "Ask Mrs. Trepol. Or the rector."

"Then tell me about Nicholas Cheney."

Suddenly wary, she stared at him.

"Why should I? He's not one I care to speak about."

"I'm trying to understand why he killed himself. Why he chose to die beside Olivia. It seems . . . out of character."

She chuckled. "Ever seen a man gassed in the war?"

"Many times." Their crusted faces and red, blistered mouths, the hoarse gasping as they struggled for air. He shuddered, remembering it.

"Then you don't need me to tell you how the lungs burn, how you can't draw a deep breath because the tubes are raw, and you choke on your own phlegm. He said he dreamt of the scent of violets. And lemons."

"Nicholas wasn't that ill. You know it. And I know it now."

She went over to the window and touched the cat, her face turned away from him. "Don't ask me about Nicholas Cheney. Or the boy Richard. That's why you've come, I can read it in your eyes. And I've listened to the men grumbling on their way to search the moors."

"Do you plant pansies in your garden?" Rutledge asked, reaching to the rafters to touch the upside down heads of strawflowers, brittle between his fingers.

"They don't dry well," she said, straightening up to look at him.

"Do they grow well on the moors?"

"Sometimes they do. Volunteers that the wind blows. Or a bird leaves behind." She was wary still, but not afraid of these questions. He wondered why. "Pansies like the cool of springtime, and a little shade in the afternoon. If that's what you're looking for, find the place where they'd want to grow. Not where someone thought of putting 'em."

Rutledge considered her. The old, stooped body, the worn,

bright eyes, the knowledge and the experiences of a lifetime fading with age, slipping into forgetfulness.

He remembered a chaplain in the war, at a hasty service for a half-dozen soldiers killed in the shelling. Saying, "They'll never grow old—never feel fear and cold, hunger or pain, or the sorrows of lost love or the pity of the young. While they have missed much, these men who won't see their sons in their mothers' arms, or the moon over a summer sea, or the beauty of a rose, they have what we all look for in the end—eternal springtime. It is not their grief but ours that haunts us." Oddly enough, it had helped weary men. But not, he thought, the chaplain.

"Has your life been a happy one?" Rutledge asked her.

Shock spread across her face, then lingered in her eyes. "No one ever asked me that before," she said quietly. "But no. I was never given the choice of happiness. Only of service. I don't know that I wasn't better off, come to that. If you feel happiness, you must also feel grief."

"Did Olivia Marlowe know grief?"

"Miss Livia? She went to funerals like the rest of them, and cried."

"No. Grief for what her life brought her. Not the paralysis. Not the poetry. Not the dead in her family. But grief for what *she* was."

"Aye," the old woman answered finally. "She carried a great burden on her soul. And had no way to put it right. She said to me once, a long time ago, that God had put an affliction upon her, and I asked what that was. She told me, to live with evil and not know how to stop it."

"And did she, by dying, put an end to it?"

Sadie frowned. "I don't know, sir. For her sake, I pray she did. I'd hate to think of her lying in her grave with no hope of peace!"

He turned to go. Then thought of one final question. "Was she the frail angel that watched at Richard's grave?"

But Sadie didn't know what he was talking about. "She were crippled, aye, but never frail. And I'd not call her an angel. She had feelings, like any other woman!"

✻   ✻   ✻

Wet and tired and thoroughly depressed, Rutledge tramped back to the inn and went through to the bar. But time had already been called, and he went instead to his room, where Hamish clamored so insistently in his mind that he couldn't concentrate on the volumes of poetry that rested on the stand by his bed. After a time he put them down again, feeling as if he'd been prying.

Rachel came to the inn for her dinner that night, and he thought it was on purpose, to discover what he'd been up to. For reasons of his own, he was very happy to see her walk through the door.

"I hear that Tom Chambers came to call on you today," she said when he'd asked her to join him at his table.

"I'm surprised that gossip hasn't also told you what we discussed."

She grinned, some of the strain slipping out of her face. "The truth is, Mr. Trask's hearing is failing."

He laughed outright.

Tilting her head, she said, "You're younger when you laugh. I've often wondered what Peter would have been like, if he'd survived his war out in Africa. Stephen seemed to take France in stride—in fact he was quite the daredevil. Not that *he* told us, mind you! But somehow it was as if—as if it was only just another game he was very good at. When his foot went bad and they sent him home barely a month before the Armistice, I expected to find him cheering up half the hospital with his wild spirits. Instead he was desperately depressed. As if he wouldn't have minded dying, but he minded terribly losing his foot. It was the oddest thing."

He knew, but didn't tell her, that often the men who taunted death had a terrible fear of it. And reached out to it in bravery because that was easier than waiting for it to come and fetch them, cowering in some corner. He knew—he'd taken his own wild risks, hoping to put an end to suffering he didn't know how to face.

When he didn't answer, she added, "But it was Thomas Chambers I came to torment you about, wasn't it?"

"Short of fiercely twisting my arm, alarming Mr. Trask, not to mention giving the gossips an earful before morning, how do you propose to do that?" He fell back on teasing her while he considered what he wanted to say to her.

"You don't want to talk about it?" She was disappointed.

"There is little to tell, if you want the truth," he said mildly. "He wanted to know what in blazes I was doing here on his turf—sounded much like Cormac FitzHugh and Dr. Hawkins in that regard—and agreed that if Stephen inherited Olivia's papers, he—Chambers—has no idea what's become of them. And Susannah would be the most likely person to have charge of them now, once they are found."

Rachel considered that. "I wonder what she'll do with them?"

"They have great intrinsic value. I don't know their monetary worth, on the auction block. Oxford would be delighted to have them. Or Cambridge. She was a major poet."

"But a woman. I wonder if she'll be valued so highly, now that everyone knows who O. A. Manning really is. The war poems, for one thing—they seemed so, I don't know, so genuine, a part of *personal* experience. But she never went to France, she was a woman who wore a brace on her leg and hardly ever left Cornwall, much less came face to face with war."

"Does she have to shoulder a rifle and kill to understand war?"

"I don't know," Rachel answered honestly. "I wasn't in France either. I can appreciate the words on the page, but I wasn't *there*."

"You sent a husband off to war. Nicholas went to France. Stephen. You loved all three of them. What did you feel?"

He knew how Jean had felt—she had wanted him back without four years of suffering and guilt and pain coming between them. Unchanged, nothing to remind her that he'd ever gone away from her. The man he was now terrified her. The man he had been was lost somewhere still in France.

She hesitated. "Fear, mainly. I was so afraid. The war dragged on, it seemed as if it would never end. And you tell yourself, 'He can make it a few more days, another month, he can last out this year, there's so little of it left!' But you know, deep down inside, that he can't live forever, that simple arithmetic, the number of shots fired, the number of shells that fall, the number of assaults and snipers—they have to find their targets, sometimes. And it's really a matter of chance—the hazards of war—" She broke off and spread her napkin across her lap, taking pains with it so that he couldn't see her face. He wondered whether she was speaking mostly about Peter or Nicholas. And told himself that he was being unfair to judge her for Peter's sake.

Then she said in a different voice, "That's all that you had to say to Mr. Chambers? Or he to you?"

"What were you expecting him to tell me? That he'd been waiting for me or someone like me, to come down here and open Pandora's Box?"

"No," she said, wistfulness in her face. "I don't know what I expected. Not really."

"Did Olivia like flowers? Pansies, for an example? Did she plant pansies in the gardens at the Hall? Or out on the moors?"

"There've always been drifts of pansies in the borders at the Hall. I don't have any idea who planted them first. But Nicholas was very fond of them, I do know that. As for pansies on the moors," she shook her head, "I don't recall ever finding pansies there. But then I never looked for them."

"I'm having the moors searched again. For Richard's body."

Rachel sighed. "Do you think you'll find it? After all these years?"

"Who knows? I have to look."

"Constable Dawlish must have been very happy about that!"

Rutledge shrugged. "I didn't make an inquiry into his feelings on the subject. I just asked him to set up a search."

She regarded him for a moment, then said, "You're used to having your way, aren't you?"

Surprised, he said, "No. I seldom have my way. But when something has to be done, and the local man can do it better than I can, I expect him to get on with it. He knows who can be spared for the job—"

"While you," she said irritably, "sit in a warm and dry inn!"

"Hardly that. I saw you walking towards the Hall earlier. Why?"

Trask brought a tray with their orders, cutlets for him, a breast of chicken for her, and began to arrange the plates on the table, saving her from having to answer.

By the time the innkeeper had finished and gone away again, she had a pat reply ready for Rutledge. And he had a question of his own ready for her.

There was a pounding on his door in the dark of night, and Rutledge came awake with a start. "Who is it?" he called sharply, after sitting up and clearing his throat. One hand fumbled for his watch.

"Constable Dawlish, sir." There was a certain pitch to his voice, as if he relished dragging the Inspector out of a warm bed at three o'clock. "I think we've found something. Out on the moors."

Rutledge threw back the blankets and reached for his trousers.

14

In a city there's never true darkness in the night. But in a place like Borcombe, where people still used oil lamps and clouds obscured what little starlight there was, the blackness was nearly absolute. Rutledge bumped into the bicycle that one of Dawlish's men had leaned against the wall by the inn door, and swore feelingly.

"You'll make better time with that," Dawlish was saying, "than going in your motorcar. We can take some of the paths. Shortcuts."

Still rubbing his shin, Rutledge nodded, then swung the other leg over the saddle. Side by side the two men pedaled down the wet road, coming to a halt at Dawlish's signal by Doctor Hawkins' surgery. The doctor, rumbling with bad temper, came out leading his own bicycle, then without a word, joined them.

It was a long, wet ride, and Rutledge, who didn't know where he was going, had to follow the shadowy figure of the Constable while Hawkins, still grumbling, brought up the rear. Hamish, of them all, seemed to be most comfortable with the night. The Highlander, keeper of sheep and cattle before turning soldier, had been bred to it.

The moors were several miles away, even by the shortcuts that Dawlish took over fields, across hummocky meadows—once startling a herd of sleeping cows—and through one stand of trees.

The moors were not what Rutledge had expected. Bare, yes. Barren, yes. Rolling, yes. But there were rocks and marshes, rills that tumbled into pools, and scrub growth here and there that rose up like humbled spirits out of the ground. The silence he noticed most. There was a whispering wind that seemed to be saying something just under the range of human hearing, but it didn't displace the quiet. A ghostly white flock of sheep went scurrying off over a hill like disturbed spirits, jostling each other in their haste, and leaving behind a strong aroma of wet wool that mixed with the wind from the sea and the smell of rotting earth like a miasma.

It was nearly two hours before they reached their destination, and Rutledge was never quite sure how the constable had found his way across the featureless expanse. Tracks there were, but they seemed to go where they willed rather than in any discernible direction, to any discernible destination.

A great pile of rocks loomed up, ruins of a colliery, Rutledge thought, peering at it through the darkness. And then the sputtering fire that the men had lit to keep warm if not dry. The rains had stopped, but there was a drizzle in the wind that clung to everything. It was easy to understand why a small boy might die out here of exposure, even in summer.

In the lea of a boulder, where erosion had widened the crevice over the years, there was a pile of bones, pitiful in their smallness. Rutledge could see the whiteness of a longer one behind the others. He dismounted, leaving the bike in the charge of a roughly dressed man who appeared out of nowhere to take it.

"There's no skull," Dawlish was saying to Hawkins. "And no pelvis, as I told you. Only the little bones, and that leg bone yonder. Can you tell anything about it, sir?" Someone was bringing a lantern over to them, its light spilling across their feet, and then their faces.

Hawkins knelt. "You've looked for the skull? Or ribs?"

"Aye, sir, all through the rocks. Nothing."

"Carried off then, by wild dogs," he said, running his fingers over the smaller fragments. Lifting the leg bone, he brought it closer to his face, then adjusted the lantern in the holder's hand so that it fell the way he wished it to. "This was broken. Here." He pointed

158

to a jagged fracture line in the bone. "Died before it began to heal. Caught a foot in the hole by the rock, I'd say, and couldn't get out again." He got up and went to the fire, using that and the lantern to better judge the bone.

After a few minutes he said, "Just as I thought. Sheep carcass. *That's* what you dragged me out here for!"

"There was no knowing for certain, sir. With nothing larger than that one bone to go by," Dawlish said apologetically.

"Next time, bring the damned things in to me."

"No," Rutledge said, countermanding that instruction. "I want to see them in place. Not on a laboratory table. And as soon as they're found."

Hawkins glared at him, went to fetch his bicycle, and Rutledge had to hurry to catch up with him—or stay on the moors with the searchers, as Dawlish was doing.

Halfway back to the village, Rutledge heard Hawkins say, "You're a damned fool. You know that, don't you?"

"I'm a policeman. I do what I have to do. No more, no less."

"You could go back to London and leave us in peace! Half those men out there in the rain will be sick before the week's out, and they'll still have to work the nets or tend their sheep or dig in their fields. The boy's long dead, and God alone knows where he could be. Murdered by gypsies, down one of the mine shafts—"

"I thought those had been searched."

"Yes, of course they have. But a boy that age is small. He could crawl where a man can't go. You could walk by him a thousand times over and never realize it. Predators carry off small bones— birds and animals could have taken his remains anywhere. Dawlish should have explained all that."

"Nevertheless, I'm going to continue. Until I find him."

Silence ruled until they were nearly back in the village again. Rutledge, remembering a case he'd handled before the war, asked, "How long before the flesh rotted off a child's body and you could move the bones? Or crush them beyond recognition, before scattering them?" It was worth considering—a husband had nearly gotten away with murdering his wife, experimenting with temporary burial and a very permanent exhumation.

Turning to look at him, Hawkins nearly skidded in a puddle, then swore again and straightened the wheel in time. "You're mad, d'you know that? Stark, staring mad!"

He turned in at his gate without another word.

Morning dawned fair, though cooler after the rains, as if summer's heat had been washed away. The first task Rutledge set himself was to search the churchyard for flowers growing there.

In his experience, English churchyards, unlike those he'd seen in Europe, were seldom planted with flowers. Along the walls, sometimes, or by the path to the front door of the church. Occasionally by the gates. But not on or around the graves themselves or close to the headstones. The English still preferred their yews as funereal offerings. These had first been set out in churchyards in the days of the long bow, as a source of raw materials, and become a habit. Their shape and somber dark green seemed to suit the mood and the gravity of the place better than a riot of color.

Flowers were more acceptable in tall vases inside the church. Rutledge could remember as a small boy going with his mother to do the altar flowers when it was her turn. He'd sat on the cold stone floor, running his fingers in the deep crevices of the memorial brasses that held place of honor down the aisle, until he knew the shapes by heart. A knight with plumes and sword and handsome spurs. A lady in a conical hat, the sweep of her long, embroidered robes nearly hiding the little dog near the hem. And an elegantly bearded Elizabethan gentleman with padded breeches and coat, looking more like a portly merchant than the adventurer he had been.

He walked slowly through the gravestones in the churchyard, some of them tilted with age and so mossy he could barely make out the words incised on them. Others he recognized at a glance—Trepol and Trask, Wilkins and Penrith, Dawlish and Trelawny. There were Poldarins and a Hawkins, a half-dozen Raleighs, though none later than the seventeen hundreds, and a pair of Drakes.

But no pansies. He walked on, looking at the delicately drawn Celtic cross on one gravestone, the sad lines of verse on another

160

for a small child drowned in the Bor, an open book with a ribbon marking its stone pages, any numbers of "Beloved wife" and "Beloved husband." War dead and plague dead, and a very fine stone angel on a plinth with the legend below it, "In Memory of the Men of the MaryAnne, Lost at Sea in a Storm, October 23, 1847. Eternal Father, Keep Their Souls Safe in Thy Care." And a list of the names, twenty-seven of them.

It was surely Richard's angel, the cool marble cheeks turned slightly so that the serene eyes stared unwaveringly towards the church tower for all eternity. There was both compassion and strength in the body, power in the wings. He could see why it had made an indelible impression on a small boy who passed the statue each Sunday morning on his way to services.

A voice behind him said, "Lovely, isn't it? The village took up a subscription to have it carved in London. The Trevelyans sent an anonymous donation to help make it up to the amount required, in addition to the sum they'd given openly. It was the sort of thing they did."

It was Smedley, dressed in a dark suit of clothes, not the rough corduroys of the gardener. Over the wet grass his shoes had made no sound.

"I saw you here and wondered if you were searching for a place to lay the sheep bones to rest," he went on. But there was a sympathetic gleam in his eyes that took away any sting. "I doubt there's a soul in the village who hasn't heard."

"Yes, well, they never seem to know what I *want* to hear," Rutledge said irritably. "Only what I'm doing."

"You'd be surprised. They seem to think you're on the trail of a murderer. They're wondering—among themselves, not to your face—if that terrible man doing the killings in London might be a Borcombe man. They've gone through the lists of who lived here once, and who moved away. Failing that, someone who'd passed through. It's the only explanation they can come up with for a Scotland Yard inspector wasting his time on two suicides and an accident when half London is in absolute terror thinking the other half is about to cut him to ribbons."

Astonished, Rutledge found himself speechless. Hamish, quick to point out the fact that Rutledge might well be more useful there, was not.

Smedley lifted his shoulders deprecatingly. "The newspaper yesterday morning reported that someone named Bowles was quoted as saying that all available manpower had been diverted to the killings. Do you know him?"

"Yes," Rutledge answered curtly. "The truth is, I was sent down here to keep me out of the picture. Not to run any leads to earth."

"That reassures me," Smedley answered, and there was something in his voice that made Rutledge look more closely at him. "All this fuss over the boy, searching for his grave. His body. Proof that he was in fact dead. I don't know why, I found myself fearful that perhaps he hadn't perished on the moors, that he'd been taken away and somehow turned into a monster."

"You prefer the possibility that someone in his own family might have purposely let him die of exposure?"

"No." There was sadness in his voice. "I prefer that he rest in peace, wherever he may be. Alive. Or dead. I don't want to think of anyone suffering and lost and alone, in need of comfort. Least of all someone I held in my arms and christened. Whose soul is, in a sense, my responsibility. And most certainly not Rosamund's son."

"The murderer in London is very likely mad. What he's doing is the work of a ruined mind. The murderer I'm searching for isn't mad. Whatever reasons he—or she—had for killing, there *was* a reason."

Smedley sighed. "I can give one to you. Envy."

"Envy?" Rutledge repeated. It wasn't necessarily his first choice of sins. And often not a murderer's, either, in his experience.

"Envy is at the root of many small cruelties. Watch children at play, if you don't believe me. It's a natural emotion in them, and they aren't yet civilized enough to suppress it."

A child might kill out of envy . . . "What could Olivia envy?"

"Oh, I daresay many things. A whole leg rather than a shriveled one, for starters."

"And Nicholas?"

The rector tilted his head and looked at the angel's face. "I don't know that Nicholas ever envied anyone. He was a decisive man, in his way. He made his choices and lived with them."

"Then why didn't he leave the Hall, go away to sea, make a life for himself somewhere else?"

"Nicholas had an affinity for the sea, that's true. In another age, he'd have been one of Drake's sea dogs or Nelson's captains—or perhaps one of Hakluyt's geographers. I can see him racing a tea clipper to China and back."

All of which demanded daring and skill and personal courage. Not to mention ruthless leadership. Yet he'd let himself be led into suicide—

Rutledge shook his head. "I'm not any closer to understanding him than I was at the beginning."

"You won't understand Nicholas, trust me there. Have you read the poems?"

After the briefest hesitation, Rutledge said, "No. Not yet."

"Let me give you a word of advice. As a priest."

When Rutledge said nothing, Smedley went on. "Be sure your own ghosts don't infringe on your logical mind—don't rain havoc on Borcombe in search of your own absolution. If you can't finish the puzzle that worries you, be man enough to walk away from it while the rest of us can still get on with our lives. This is a very small village, you see, and we don't have your London sophistication. We shall go on suffering long after you've gone away."

Watching Smedley walk off across the wet grass, Rutledge was prey to a variety of emotions, and Hamish, relishing the turbulence in his mind, was busy taking advantage of it.

"Ye're no' wanted here," he said, "and no' wanted in London as well. I've no' seen anywhere you belong!"

"That has nothing to do with the Trevelyan family," Rutledge replied coldly. "The rector is right. My work and my life are separate."

"Ye're no' keeping Olivia Marlowe from getting under your skin!"

"She's no different from any suspect! Not to me!"

"Except that she's dead," Hamish reminded him. "Is that why

163

ye're no' reading the poems? You read them often enough before, when ye knew she was alive!"

Rutledge swore and headed for the stone walkway that led from the churchyard to the road. His reasons were his own affair, and none of Hamish's.

It was a long and tiring day. He was summoned, twice more, to come to the moors. The first time it was a boy who came to fetch him. The ground he must surely have covered last night seemed very different in the sunlight, brown and green and black and yellow, and not very much like the higher Yorkshire moors he knew so much better. But this too was sour land, that grew grass and reeds in the low-lying damp, and vast stretches of quaking marsh that could become quicksand in the blink of an eye.

The boy cheerfully threaded his way through a maze of paths and chattered on about the war, wanting to know how many Boche Rutledge had personally (and bloodily) killed, and if he'd ever been wounded himself. They'd reached the subject of aircraft, and whether the Inspector had ever been up in one (he was disappointed when Rutledge said no), and how many flaming crashes he'd personally witnessed, when the first lines of searchers came into sight below a knoll.

It took them fifteen minutes to find Dawlish, who was on the far right of the line. The constable was not in good spirits. Inspector Harvey, returned from Plymouth, had been out there very early to demand an explanation for this business. Inspector Harvey had not caught up with his own suspect, and was in no mood for anyone else's wild goose chases.

"Where is Harvey now? I'll speak to him myself."

"As to that, sir, I don't know. There's a problem out on one of the farms, somebody's dog killing sheep, and he had to have a look himself."

"What progress have you made here?"

"More sheep bones and an old dog. They had their heads still, it wasn't difficult to tell what they were. And we found a man, sir, looked like he must have been a vagabond. Dr. Hawkins has been and gone, and he said it was an old corpse, we could bury it later."

"Where?"

"By those rocks there, about a mile away. One of the men sheltered there to light his cigarette, and he saw something white in the earth. We dug it out, bit by bit, first a hand, then the head. Not very deep, you understand, but that's the direction the wind blows, and he'd have been covered over in a season or two."

Rutledge walked across to see the bones, followed by the boy, whose bloodthirsty spirits were fascinated by the line of human remains laid out next to raw earth under one of the towering rock piles that mark the moor. "That a hand, sir? Where's the middle finger, then? What's that? *Pelvis*? Do I have one of 'em too? Who et away that rib, do you think? Why's his jaw over *there*, and his head *here*? D'ye think he was *murdered*, sir? Cor!"

In fact, there was no indication what had killed the man. No holes in the skull, no signs of damage to any of the bones, no obvious indications of stabbing or a bullet clipping a rib or part of the spine. No crushed vertebrae to show a strangling. But the bones were long and well formed. He'd been tall, with no sign of the thickening that comes with heavy work in an underfed childhood or early diseases like rickets that stunted growth. According to Hawkins, the bones had lain in the earth for no more than seven years.

"Were he a soldier, d'ye think? Left to die in the thick of the battle, and then forgotten?" the boy asked hopefully.

Rutledge dug around in the disturbed earth with his pocket knife, looking for remnants of cloth, buttons, coins, or other debris that might have told a clearer tale. If they'd been here, they were gone now.

A man's skeleton, not a child's . . .

All the way back to Borcombe, the boy talked of nothing but the bones, and Rutledge was very glad to give him sixpence and see the last of him by the time they reached the road into the village. He was off then, racing to find his friends and make them envious of his good fortune in viewing the skeleton.

Rutledge ate his lunch alone, the books of poetry beside his plate. He'd tried to approach them in the order in which they'd been published. And he found one short, early poem about the moors. Reading it, he could hear Olivia's response to the emptiness and the mystery of that barren land. "For here the spirit dies," she'd written, "and that is more of hell than I can bear."

And yet it was possible she'd consigned a small child to that same hell.

In the afternoon he went back to see Mrs. Trepol, whose reputation as a gardener was sworn to by three women he'd spoken with in the inn's dining room.

She was working to straighten the storm-battered stalks of flowers, lupine and asters, marigolds and zinnias. Stakes and strips of old rag lay in the small bucket she carried with her, and in the back of the cottage wash hung on the line, blowing like signal flags.

Mrs. Trepol looked up, saw that he intended to come through the gate rather than pause for a few words outside it, and said, "Do you mind if I keep working, sir? These turn their heads to the sun soon enough, if they aren't righted."

"It's about flowers that I came," he told her as she reached for a tall golden head of marigold, its bruised leaves scenting the air.

"Aye, sir? And what flowers would you be wanting to know about?" she asked, over the mallet she was using to pound in a stake.

"Pansies."

"Pansies? A spring flower, mostly. Hardy in the cold, not strong in the sun. Look over there, by the rhododendron."

He did, and saw the straggling green stalks that flopped across the grass, the small faces lifted to stare at him.

"They're twice that size in the spring," she said, reaching for a length of cloth. "But they come back in the autumn, if all's well. That's why I put them in the shadow of the taller bush. A little protection."

"Out on the moor, would they need protection?"

She stopped what she was doing to look at him. "They don't grow often on the moors. Unless someone sows them there. And that makes no sense. A waste of good plants! But you might find a few at the edge of a wood. Gone wild, you see."

Which was an interesting thought.

"Tell me," he said slowly, working it out in his mind as he spoke, "do you know if Stephen FitzHugh ever considered becoming a Catholic? Did the family ever discuss his choice of faith?"

"Not that I know of, sir!" She seemed surprised. "Mr. Brian, now, he was brought up a Catholic, but the children never were. And he went to services with the family regularly, there was no fuss about it that I ever heard. He was a man who wanted to please, not one to set people at odds. But he loved Ireland, and he talked about the country often and often."

"In what way? Was he a supporter of the Irish rebellions?"

"Oh, no, sir, not to my knowledge! Though he used to tease Miss Rosamund that it was a Trevelyan—not her *own* family, mind!—that refused to provide money for the victims of the potato famine, back in last century, so as they could emigrate to Canada or America. He had a bad name in Ireland, that one, and caused a great many deaths. Cruel, he was. I heard Mr. Brian say once that his coldheartedness killed as many people as Cromwell and William of Orange put together."

"Cormac and Stephen never showed any interest in Irish politics? Sympathy for the rebels? For the suffering there?"

"No, sir, Mr. Stephen considered himself an Englishman—he said to me that he was going off to war because it was his duty to the King. And Mr. Stephen was one that always took duty seriously. Mr. Cormac, now, he was in the war too, but I never heard he went to France. Miss Olivia told me he was doing something secret, and I shouldn't ask." She smiled. "I never could picture him as a spy, sir! Sneaking about and telling lies. Mr. Stephen, now, he'd see all that as a game, like hide and seek. He were—more lighthearted. The kind of man who'd shrug it off and not be touched by it. But Mr. Cormac was always one to mind appearances. Not to the manor born, you might say."

Cormac had spent his war breaking codes. Not as exciting as spying. And not as dangerous. But quite as important as shouldering a rifle.

He left her and went to walk through the wood between the village and the Hall, searching along the muddy path for pansies, then looking in small clearings, before giving it up. This was far too close to the village to risk bringing the body of a small boy and burying him. And Olivia hadn't said anything about trees in her poem.

When he was called to the moors the second time, it was a man who came for him, and they trudged in silence to the place where a small cache of clothes had been found. The shreds were small and dirty and rotting with the damp of the earth, but a boy's clothing. Short jacket—you could see how the collar lay, and one side seam. Short trousers—part of the waistband and a pocket, part of one leg. What might have been a shirt and underdrawers, mere threads of white that fell apart at the touch. The good wool of the jacket and trousers was tougher, and had lasted while the linen and the cotton had disintegrated. And someone had wrapped it all quite carefully in heavily oiled cloth, which had protected the fabric for a very long time. He couldn't be sure of the colors. But there was enough of the cloth left to draw conclusions about the shape and general size of the outer garments, as he gingerly spread them out on the grass. Interestingly enough, there were no shoes . . .

"Tregarth found them, sir," Dawlish was saying. "He's walked these moors man and boy for sixty years. Noticed the white stone wasn't natural to the land around here, and was curious, like. He started digging, and what came to light looked odd. He called me and we laid the packet open enough to be sure what was inside, before sending for you."

"Good man!" Rutledge said over his shoulder to the diffident farmer waiting close by. The grizzled head nodded, satisfaction in the sharp, weather-browned face.

Who had buried these articles deep under a bush and covered them with a flat white stone? And why? Or when? There was no way of knowing to whom they'd belonged but it was the first evidence Rutledge had discovered that proved the search mattered. Even Dawlish's doubts were silenced.

Rutledge put the shreds of wool carefully into a brown sack someone offered him, and carried them back to Borcombe with him, ordering the men to comb the vicinity again, until they could swear that there was nothing else to be found. And he promised them beer from The Three Bells with their dinner, if they did their work thoroughly.

He had already arranged to meet Rachel after dinner, while the light was still good, and walk over to the Hall to look for Olivia's papers. It was not all that he had in mind for the evening, but it was an innocuous beginning.

15

$\mathcal{R}$achel was tense as they walked through the door of the Hall. "I miss the flowers," she said, a trace of nervousness in her voice. "The Hall was always full of flowers. You could smell the beeswax polish, the scent of Rosamund's perfume, and the flowers, whenever you walked through the door. Like a welcome. Now the air's—I don't know. Still. Dead . . ."

"You have a right to be here," he said. "Why don't you cut flowers and put them in vases yourself?"

"No. I was bequeathed a share in the Hall. That was the way they wanted it, Olivia and Nicholas. But I have no right here. No place here." Her voice trailed off at the end.

"Let's start with the upper floors and work our way down," he said prosaically, before she could get cold feet altogether. "The attics?"

"This way," she said, shaking off her gloomy spirits and leading him towards the stairs.

They made their way up to the attics, warmed by the sun, spared the wind, and still comfortable. There they began looking through trunks of gowns carefully wrapped in tissue paper, and suits of clothes and coats, moving aside rocking horses and doll's houses, chairs and old bedsteads, cribs and perambulators, canes, odds and ends of lumber, and any number of boxes stored long ago and forgotten, the debris of generations. They found a stuffed fox, ratty with age, glass eyes gleaming in the lamps they'd brought with them, and a wardrobe full of hats that caught Rachel's fancy.

"Look at these! I can't believe it—they must be well over a hundred years old! The braid on these tricorns—I think it's gold bullion! We used to play dress up, sometimes, and Nicholas had such a hat. What's this? Yes, I see, it's a bonnet with a tucked underbrim. Straight out of Jane Austen." It was too small, but she perched it on her head, and made him laugh as she twirled the ribbons. Setting it back in its tissue nest, she turned to the next shelf. "My God! Ostrich plumes and bows, oh, and even a little temple set in among silk trees. Susannah would have adored this one. She was always trying on Rosamund's hats."

It took Rutledge fifteen minutes to distract her, and they moved on, to christening gowns and woolens, old linens and sets of dishes, riding boots and tables of every size, a child's saddle—and nothing that remotely resembled a poet's work.

Dusty and giggling, Rachel led the way to the next attics, which held more of the same, and when she began to cough from the dryness of the air, he suggested a cup of tea.

She agreed, and lamps in hand, they went down to the kitchen to make it. There was no cream, but Rachel found a lemon in the pantry. Then, leaving one lamp in the kitchen, Rutledge took the tray from her and carried it to the sitting room that overlooked the sea. The sun was low now, warming the room with its light, and Rachel went to sit in a chair from which she could watch it set.

It was very domestic, the pot of tea, the quiet of evening, the sense of peace and companionship. The setting he'd arranged, in a room where Rachel must have spent a great deal of her time with Nicholas. A room, unlike the study upstairs, that didn't make her shiver with dread. As she sipped from the cup in her hand, relaxed and off her guard, he said, quietly, "Were you there when Anne fell out of the tree?"

"Yes, I told you that."

"But you told me what you remembered. Time changed what you actually saw as it was happening. What the grown-ups said

172

around you, the questions they asked you, it all influenced you. Would you do something for me? Would you close your eyes and let yourself go back to that afternoon, and see it again?"

She put down her cup, shaking her head. "No, I don't want to go back! To that time or any other! I don't want to play that kind of game!"

"You sent for me," he reminded her. "You must have wanted answers of some kind. So far, I've got very little to show for the time I've spent here. But there's evidence of a sort, and it points to Olivia. Not to Nicholas."

She sat there, torn. He could read it in the tightening of her shoulders. Wanting him to go, wanting him to stay and prove that Nicholas had in fact loved her, though those weren't the words she used even to herself. That his death had nothing to do with what he felt for her. It mattered. In a fashion that went deeper than conscious thought.

"I need to see that day through the eyes of someone who was there."

"Ask Cormac!"

Before, she'd told him that she hadn't thought Cormac was there . . .

"But Cormac was an outsider. You weren't. Cormac was the Irish latecomer, there on sufferance because his father had come with Rosamund's horses. He hadn't played all his life with the family, lived in the nursery with the other children, heard them quarrel and laugh and make up games. He hadn't been part of their growing up, the way you'd been. He saw them as a stranger sees, superficially, the outward façade instead of the inner feelings."

His voice was persuasive, his body very still in the shadows of the room, just out of her line of sight, the warmth of the sun's slanting rays taking away any sense of danger or fear, the quiet absolute, except for the sound of her breathing. And the voice of Hamish, which she couldn't hear.

He'd seen the doctors at the clinic use these same techniques. He'd seen them break through silences that were so deep even the men locked in them couldn't find the key to them. Persuaded by quiet and serenity, and their own sense of need, such men would suddenly speak of events that would send them screaming into horror—and then complete breakdown—and finally, with luck, survival.

It hadn't worked for him. Only drugs had broken down the walls he'd built so high and strong.

Hamish, realizing what he was up to now, roused and thundered at him not to take risks with this woman's mind. "Ye're no' a doctor, you could do grave damage without knowing it!" But Rutledge couldn't see any other way to learn the truth, and forced the voice in his own mind into rumbling, sullen stillness.

"I don't know what there is to tell," Rachel said. "It was an accident."

"Then you've got nothing to be afraid of, have you? Except for grief and the memory of someone you loved long ago."

"I don't know that I loved Anne—" She stopped.

"Why not? She was your cousin."

"She was bossy. Sometimes she made me feel very young, or very stupid. Awkward, somehow. When we played games, I was always the one who had to lose, and then she'd tease me about it."

The cruelty of children. He could hear Smedley's voice saying that.

"She wasn't *mean*. She could be very loving, when she wanted to be. She was just . . . arrogant. Like her grandmother, Nanny told me. Rosamund's mother. But of course *she* was already dead, I never met her. So I couldn't know if it was true or not. Anyway, for a child like me, Anne was very *trying*."

"Whose idea was it to go to the orchard that day?"

"It was hot, we were tired of playing in the gardens, and the house was stuffy, even with the windows open. But in the orchard it was shady, the long grass was cool. In the trees, you felt cooler. I don't know who thought of it first. I remember Nicholas telling Anne that she couldn't climb as high as he could. And Anne had been pestering Olivia about being so slow, walking. Nicholas must have been trying to deflect her impatience."

He could see, from the shadows of her lashes on her cheek, that she'd closed her eyes. Clouds on the horizon began to swallow the

174

sun. It would be dark sooner than he'd thought. Would that matter? Still, he must not hurry . . .

"But that wasn't what you felt then, was it?"

"No, I was hoping she'd climb high enough to fall out—" She sat upright with a jolt. *"No! I couldn't have thought that!* It must have been afterward, when she was climbing, and I was *afraid* she'd fall—"

Yet Rutledge thought she *had* felt that way at the time, and buried it deep. A child's wish, because the bully was beyond her own reach. He waited a moment, then said gently, reassuringly, "I'm sure you wished her no harm."

"No, of course I didn't. In fact I was worried when Nicholas challenged her to climb to the next branches, and then Olivia went up after her, and he tried to prevent her, but she was determined to show she could do it too. I remember he was holding her sashes, trying to help her keep her balance. And then Anne was shouting something from the top of the tree, and Olivia pushed herself higher than she should, and Cormac climbed down from *his* tree and was over there in a flash, saying his papa would thrash him if they got hurt, and he was going to stop this nonsense now. But I saw Nicholas jerk hard on the sashes, trying to pull himself up into the tree or something, and Cormac was crashing about in the branches, and suddenly, Nicholas was ducking, and Anne came tumbling down, bowling Nicholas over, and Cormac was trying to get Olivia down, yelling at her not to put her bad foot just there, he'd hold her arm, and she was screaming at him not to touch her, and Nicholas was crawling over to Anne, and as I slid down my tree, I scraped my leg and it started bleeding, and I got blood all over Anne's dress when I knelt there. And she was still, it was frightening, and I kept asking Nicholas why he'd pulled so hard on the sashes, and he said that Anne had been shoving Olivia, and then Olivia was down, face white as her own handkerchief, something in her eyes that terrified me, and Cormac and I ran for help, he to the stables, which were closer, while I ran to the house and Rosamund—"

She was crying, he could see the tears sliding out from under her lashes. And he himself felt the surge of her pain, the shock, the child who couldn't understand the nightmarish events she'd witnessed. The picture she'd conjured up was sharp, vivid in his mind. Even Hamish was silenced by it.

"Please," she begged huskily. "I don't want to think about it any more!"

"Then tell me about Richard being lost on the moors," he said, after giving both of them a little time to recover. "Were you there when it happened?"

"Yes, I've said it was a family picnic," she retorted irritably. "I don't know why you have to keep harping on the past, raking it up. Stephen wouldn't have allowed it, it was his duty to *protect* Olivia! That's why she left him all her papers."

"Olivia is dead. So is Nicholas. Your memory is all I have," he said again. "Would Stephen have protected her, if he'd known she might have killed his father?"

"Maybe that's why we can't find her papers. Maybe he burned them?" She sighed. "Oh, very well! We went there—to the moors—because it was a day's outing, and children are restless, they need distraction. Uncle James thought we might enjoy looking at the old mines, the tin that'd made Cornwall rich, once upon a time. Rosamund wasn't happy with the idea, she said we could fall down the old shafts. Which wasn't very like her—it was as if she had a premonition—she was usually enthusiastic and fun. But it all went quite *well.* James showed us the mines, and then we talked about where Cornish tin might have traveled, to Egypt or Crete or Phoenicia. He could make whatever he talked about seem so real, not a lesson at all—it was a gift he had. Then we found a sheltered spot to eat our lunch."

He could hear her voice change as she drifted back into the past again, caught up in spite of her reluctance.

"What was Richard wearing?"

"I don't remember—white shirt, long stockings, short trousers, I should think. He did have a jacket too, because he took it off for a time. It was warm in the sun. Rosamund made him put it back on again, when the wind came up. He didn't want to put it on, and fussed about it. Later, we wondered if that's why he'd run off, because he was still in a temper. He was so headstrong, sometimes."

176

She stopped. "Are you sure you want to hear so many little things?"

"Yes. It helps me frame a picture."

She was one of those rare people who could tell a story coherently. Describing clearly the images she saw in her mind, without backtracking and confusing the threads he needed to follow.

"We'd had our picnic, and Rosamund sat down to rest, James had his head in her lap, I remember thinking how comfortable they looked. Cormac had gone to talk to the guide. He was an old man whose sons left for America twenty years before, to work in the mines there. Cormac wanted to know about them, if they'd prospered, if they'd written home about their new life. I was drowsy, and Olivia sat down beside me, to rest her leg a little. But Richard wanted to go back and see the ponies. He begged her to walk with him, because his mother wouldn't let him go alone. I don't know where Nicholas was, he'd wandered off. He did that sometimes, exploring. He always had an unerring sense of direction, no one ever worried about him. Finally Olivia got up and followed Richard, making him promise not to run too fast for her. I was waiting for Nicholas to come back and didn't want to be bothered with Richard, and I've felt very guilty about that ever since . . ."

He let the silence drift, and finally her voice picked up the tale again. "I was nearly asleep when Rosamund said we ought to be starting back. She sent Cormac to look for Nicholas and James to find Olivia and Richard. We walked over to the carriages together and put the baskets away. Rosamund was saying something about a house party she was planning, friends from London. I remember that, because they came for the funeral instead. James' funeral. Then she said, 'I wonder what's keeping them!'"

There was another pause. "Cormac came back alone and said that Nicholas had just seen some of those butterflies you only find out on the moors and didn't want to leave. He took me off with him to persuade him. But Nicholas wasn't by the rocks anymore, and we looked for five or ten minutes, Cormac and I. Then we went back to where Rosamund was waiting, and Nicholas was already there. James came back with Olivia, saying they couldn't find Richard. So Rosamund left Olivia and me in the carriages, while she and James and Cormac and Nicholas went out to search for Richard. But he didn't come back. And they couldn't find him. And Olivia wasn't sure what had happened, except that he'd gone to play with the ponies in plain sight, and she'd thought he was still with them. They sent the coachman to the Hall on one of the carriage horses to collect the grooms and servants while they went back again to look. By nightfall, it was clear we weren't going to find him at all. But James wouldn't hear of calling off the search. He said Richard was just being naughty, hiding from us. Nicholas came back covered in blood and scratches, from a fall, and said he'd located the ponies, and Richard wasn't with them, but there'd been some gypsy boys about. He and Cormac went back to look again. They searched with torches. I remember the long shadows they cast, and how black the men looked in the distance, and then Rosamund sent us home in one of the carriages, Olivia and Nicholas and me. Olivia was crying, there was no comforting her. And when we got to the stables, she had herself strapped to a horse, and went back with the men from the village, to look again. There wasn't a horse for Nicholas, and so he went off on his own. I was told to stay at the house and send out word if any of the searchers found Richard. But of course they never did. Sometime later I remember Cormac, with tears cutting through the dirt on his face, yelling at Nicholas about Richard, wanting to know something, and I always thought that was very strange, since Richard had been with Olivia. But no one was himself, we were all distraught. Nicholas sat with Olivia, when they brought her back ill, talking, always talking to her, but from the door I couldn't hear what he was saying. Uncle James was so exhausted that Dr. Penrith put something in his coffee and it took three men to carry him up to his bed, he was so deeply asleep . . ."

But Rutledge had lost the thread of what she was saying, his thoughts busy elsewhere. When the quiet voice stopped, he said, "Did Olivia and Anne dress as twins, in the same gowns?"

"Sometimes," she answered, surprised at the shift in subject. "Olivia didn't like it. She said she wasn't part of a *pair*, like shoes or gloves. She wasn't in Anne's shadow, she was just herself. That seemed to bother her . . . afterward. We all felt guilty, the way children do, blaming themselves . . ."

"Were they wearing the same dresses the day that Anne fell?"

"I—I don't know. Let me think." She shook her head, "No. Wait! Anne was wearing the gown with bunches of cherries embroidered around the hem and on the sash. Olivia was wearing something blue—forget-me-nots, I think. I remember that my blood and Anne's matched those cherries." The empty cup rattled in its saucer, as her fingers trembled. He got up and poured more tea for her, using the ordinary business of spooning in sugar and taking a slice of lemon to distract her.

"And Nicholas would have known, very well, whose sashes he was holding? Young as he was?"

"Yes, I told you they were Olivia's—"

She stopped. The room was dark now, with only starlight to brighten it, except for the single lamp on the table near the wall. "No," she said slowly, to the darkness and not to him. "The sash ends weren't blue, were they? I thought they were. I'd always been so *sure*. Olivia *told* me they were blue!"

"And it was Nicholas who couldn't be found, when Cormac went out to search for him? On the moors?" He tried to keep his voice level, unemotional. "And he went out alone again, when he'd brought you and Olivia to the Hall?"

"Yes—"

"Was he envious of his brother, the attention he got for being wild? Or were they close? Did they spend much of their time together?"

"I—I think they were too different to be close. Olivia and Nicholas were more alike, really. Quiet by nature, found it easy to amuse themselves. While Richard always needed . . . distractions. He was so exuberant. He took up a lot of Rosamund's time, never wanting a nap, always demanding a game or to be read to, or to be taken to see the horses." She smiled to herself. "Richard and Anne should have been twins. They were so much alike, quite bossy and active. Headstrong. Exhausting, Nanny called them."

"And when James shot himself, where was Nicholas?"

"I don't—he was already in the passage when Cormac wanted

to know what the noise was he'd heard, and Nicholas said it was a shot, and he'd already knocked, and then Cormac and one of the servants broke down the door. But I don't think it was locked after all. I saw Nicholas pushing the bolt back and forth, standing there like a stone. Olivia came then and made him stop, but wouldn't let him into the room, wouldn't let him go to his father. Then Rosamund heard the commotion and ran to see what was wrong, and Cormac went racing to the village for Dr. Penrith, and she stood in the door, white as I'd ever seen anyone's face, but not crying, just shaking as if she'd never stop, and I remember Brian FitzHugh putting his arm around her shoulders, and she shoved him from her, and went on standing there, and Nicholas kept saying, over and over again, 'It was an accident, I know it was an accident!' as if it was dreadfully important to hear the words."

He waited again, letting her take her time, but she said nothing more.

Over the years Rutledge had questioned many witnesses to a crime. Even during the war he'd had to debrief returned prisoners, night scouts, men in the forefront of an assault or an attack. *What weapons did you see, what collar tabs? What's the strength in reserve? Where are the big guns?* It was an art, getting at the truth rather than miring down in the tricks of a man's memory.

The first person on the scene of a gruesome killing in London had told him that she didn't recall much blood, and yet the room to him, hardened as he was, had seemed to be bathed in it. But she had blocked it out, controlling her memory to exclude what had shocked her the most.

Rachel wasn't afraid of blood, she was frightened of betrayal, of the possibility that someone she knew and loved was a stranger.

And yet she'd sent for Scotland Yard, irrevocably calling public attention to her doubts and suspicions.

It was an odd decision for someone like Rachel to make. A washing of hands. A refusal to be a party to accusation, and at the same time, feeling a desperate need for closure.

What had she wanted from him, the objective Inspector from London? What sort of *proof* was she after? What did she know, and how was he going to find it under the layers of protective emotional armor?

And what did it have to do with Nicholas? Nicholas, the quiet one. Always there, always in the background. Had he played an objective role? Or a subjective one? Had he protected Olivia? Or had she protected him?

Was it *knowledge* that Nicholas had carried to the grave? Or guilt?

Hamish was angry with him, telling him he was wrong. But he couldn't stop himself from grasping at this particular straw. It might solve so many problems . . .

"It's your own armor you're after, any excuse you can find to shift the blame! Any name to put in place of the woman who bewitched you with her verse! Ye'll sacrifice *him* for her sake! *Hae ye no conscience, man?*" Hamish raged.

Yet he had to know. If there was a chance, he had to know it.

Finally he asked, "Rachel? What are you afraid of? What are you afraid to remember? Who made Anne fall out of that tree? It wasn't an accident, was it? And who lured Richard away, on the moors? He was only five. How could he have wandered so far on his own? And who put the gun into James Cheney's dead hand? When Brian FitzHugh was down on that beach the day he died, who was he talking to? Someone he trusted enough to turn his back on him— or her."

She sat in stony silence. He went on quietly, "They were murdered. You tell me you don't want to believe it's true, but you *feel* it, deep inside yourself. The truth. Just as I do. And Rosamund very likely died by the same hand. Just because the murderer is also dead doesn't matter. But the truth does. Was it Olivia? Or Nicholas? Who hated—or loved—or envied—enough to commit murder?"

"No one," she cried, turning to face him, her eyes black with despair. "It's nonsense, what you keep trying to say. There's no murderer in this house! *I lived here, I ought to know!*"

"It had to be Olivia or Nicholas. You must choose."

"No! Nicholas never hurt anyone! Nicholas was not the kind of man who'd kill children—or his own father—or his *mother!*"

"Then we're left with Olivia."

"No—I—there is no murderer, I tell you!"

"But there is. And you believed in it strongly enough that you sent for Scotland Yard!"

"No. I had to know why Nicholas wanted to die! I couldn't believe he would want to take his own life, it wasn't right, it wasn't *Nicholas!*"

"But he did. Or else Olivia killed him."

"*No!*"

She was out of her chair, lunging towards him, her face stark with pain, her hands balled into fists, as if she wanted to pound them against him. Rutledge got to his feet, braced.

She stood in front of him, shaking and livid with emotion, but didn't touch him. "Go away! Go back to London, damn you! Leave me in peace!"

"But you sent for Scotland Yard. What did you know, Rachel, that made you think it was murder?"

"No—no! I tell you, no!"

"You thought Nicholas would marry you, didn't you? If Olivia was dead. Instead, he chose to die with her. Or was killed. Or killed *her*, then himself. They're the only possibilities we have."

Her face crumpled, and furious with himself for what he'd done, he reached for her, pulling her into his arms. She buried her face in the front of his coat and cried, her body shaking with the force of her grief. "Tell me what you know," he urged, against her hair, his voice little more than a whisper.

"He wrote to me before he died—Nicholas—" she began brokenly.

Then the door slammed open, and Cormac FitzHugh came into the room, his shadow springing before him across the ceiling, like a great black monster, breaking the spell.

"*What the bloody hell!*" he exclaimed, staring at them in sheer astonishment. "What are you doing—*what's going on here!*"

16

Startled and red-faced, her tears catching in her throat, Rachel broke free from Rutledge's hold and whirled to the night-darkened windows, as far from Cormac as she could move in the little room, drawing silence around her as if it made her invisible.

Rutledge, furiously angry, turned on him instead. The two men glared at each other, shoulders tight, on the balls of their feet, ready to act or to block. They were breathing hard, for an instant the only sound in the room.

"I might ask you the same question!"

"What is this, harassment? Or a rendezvous?"

Their voices clashed, loud and thick with the force of dislike.

Hamish was clamoring. Warning. Rutledge ignored him, his whole attention concentrated on Cormac. For an instant it was touch and go, the policeman struggling to rein in his desire to wipe up the floor with the man in the doorway for interrupting when he did, and the levelheaded entrepreneur fighting the primitive urge to feel fist against flesh. The soldier and the Irishman. But Scotland Yard and the City won.

With difficulty, Cormac managed to say in a near-normal tone, "I saw the light in the kitchen. I came to find out who was in the house. What've you done to Rachel? Why is she crying?"

"The Hall upsets her," Rutledge retorted. "But she came to help me look for something. It was kind of her. Leave her alone."

"Rachel? Has he hurt you?"

She answered softly, without turning around. "I'm all right, Cormac. Just—it's as he said. I—I still haven't—Olivia and Nicholas. And Stephen. I—*if they'd only hurry up and sell this house, I'd be all right!*" she finished despairingly. "I can't go, I can't stay! I beg you just put an *end* to it!"

"I'm—the lawyers are dragging their feet. There're three wills involved," he said slowly, as if she'd blamed him, not Rutledge, for her tears. "But I'll do what I can to speed up the sale." He hadn't looked away from Rutledge, except for a brief glance at Rachel. Now he looked back at her again. "Let me take you home. If the Inspector has any more business here, he can finish it in the morning, damn it!"

"No. I'm all right, Cormac. Truly."

"You aren't. I can see you shaking from here." He crossed the room, ignoring Rutledge, almost daring him to step in the way. Then, gently touching Rachel's shoulder, he turned her towards him and gave her his handkerchief. Rutledge felt himself bristling as she took it gratefully and nodded her thanks, for a moment burying her face in its white folds. With his arm around her shoulders, Cormac led her past Rutledge to the door, but there Rachel stopped and looked at the Londoner with something in her eyes that he couldn't read. Was she asking him to go with them? Or begging him to stay where he was?

When he didn't respond, she turned and let Cormac take her out into the passage. Rutledge picked up the lamp, left the tea things where they were, and went down to the kitchen. Blowing out the lamps, he set them on the kitchen table and walked out to the hall in the cold darkness of the house. To his surprise, Cormac and Rachel were still there, waiting for him, silhouettes without presence.

Cormac held the door key in his gloved hand, impatience marking the line of his body as he watched Rutledge take his time crossing the hall.

Then they were out in the starlit night, the door slamming behind them, the lock turning with a click of finality. Cormac came down the steps to take Rachel's arm, and lead her along the drive. Rutledge, feeling like a left thumb—and knowing that was how Cormac meant for him to feel—followed.

"Will you let me take you back to London tomorrow?" Cormac was saying to Rachel. "Your friends keep asking when you'll come to town again. I promise soon, but it doesn't satisfy anyone. Let's surprise them!"

She had stopped crying, but there were tears still blocking her throat, in spite of all she could do. All the same, Rachel wasn't easily cowed, as Rutledge was learning.

"I—I'm just not ready, Cormac. But thanks for the offer." She glanced across at Rutledge, a shadowy figure to Cormac's left. He could see her pale face turn towards him. There was steel in her voice as she added, "When Scotland Yard goes, I'll go."

"If you're sure that's what you want?" She nodded. "All right. I suppose it never hurts to keep an eye on what's happening. Daniel won't give me any peace; he's insisting that I use my influence in London to get rid of the police. I told him that might cause more problems. But Susannah is in bed right now, doctor's orders, so he may contact the Yard himself."

"Not the baby—is anything wrong?" Rachel asked quickly.

"No, just precautions. But try to tell Daniel that. You'd think he was the one carrying twins, damn it! I've seen foaling horses with more composure."

She laughed huskily, as he'd meant for her to.

"That's better," he told her, squeezing her arm. They reached the shadows of the wood, and Rutledge let them walk ahead, his mind busy.

"I'll go to see her tomorrow," Rachel said. "I'll even take Inspector Rutledge with me. He's made the muddle, let *him* set it to rights again!"

But somehow Rutledge didn't think that was what Cormac wanted.

He could sense the stiffness in the man as they said good night to Rachel at the cottage gate, and watched her walk up the path.

Continuing towards the inn, Cormac said harshly, "I don't understand why you don't pack it in. I don't see what you can hope to achieve here—combing the moors for Richard isn't going to solve any riddles. Or is rumor for once telling the truth? You're here for other reasons?"

"What other reasons might there be?" Rutledge parried.

Cormac sighed. "I don't have any idea." They walked in silence for a dozen yards, listening to the sound of their shoes crunching along the road. Then Cormac went on, his voice weary. "What really happened in that house tonight?"

"It's a police matter," Rutledge said, refusing to be drawn.

"Don't give me that bloody rot!" Cormac fumed. "If you're trying to protect Rachel, I've known for years how she felt about Nicholas. What I couldn't understand for a very long time was why he didn't love her."

"Are you quite sure Olivia is the killer? Anne's killer, and possibly Richard's?" Rutledge asked, hoping to take him off guard.

Cormac stopped in his tracks, peering at Rutledge's face, trying to see his eyes. They were of a height, and a world apart. "What the hell are you talking about?"

"I was just wondering if I ought to put my money on Nicholas, instead."

Cormac swore, inventively and viciously, as they walked on. Even in the darkness Rutledge could see the handsome brows drawn together in an angry frown. "No, of course it wasn't Nicholas! I may be many things, but I'm not a fool. I know what I saw in that apple tree. Nicholas was a pawn."

"She would have protected him. She might well have forced him into killing himself to keep the truth hidden. When she was afraid she couldn't go on controlling him."

"Yes, that's a very fine idea. The only problem is, it doesn't work!"

"Then why didn't Nicholas love Rachel?"

"At first I thought it was because she was *there* so much of his childhood. Like another half sister, familiar and unexciting. Rosamund was very fond of Rachel, treated her like one of her own children, and that's hardly the stuff great romance is made of. Then—later—when Rachel married Peter, I realized that Nicholas was probably protecting her, forcing her by his very indifference to find someone else to love. If he hadn't, I think Olivia might have killed her too."

The voice in the darkness was oddly strained.

"Are you telling me that what Olivia held over Nicholas most of his life—the way she bound him to her—was the threat of harm to Rachel?"

"It was the only way I can think of for Olivia to make Nicholas swallow that laudanum. Unless of course she tricked him. I don't want Rachel to know what I think, I don't want her to carry unnecessary guilt around for the rest of her life. But if you keep digging, that's what's going to happen. You'll solve your case quite neatly, and she'll never have a chance of finding love again. If you've got any compassion at all, send her back to London. Or better still, take her back."

"No."

"It's quite true, what I told Rachel. I've considered going over your head, pulling strings to have the Yard close this case officially. I know enough people in high places, to get it done. And it's what Daniel wants. But even that can cause more grief than good. That's the trouble with this wretched affair, there's no damned solution any way I turn!"

When Rutledge didn't respond, Cormac was goaded into saying more than he'd intended. "I've half a notion to find out why you aren't in London working on this new Ripper—why you've spent a week in Cornwall with nothing but speculation and a good deal of vexatious prying to show for it. I thought we'd been sent a proper investigator, someone who knew his business and was just taking precautions, because of Olivia's sudden fame."

"If you were expecting a rubber stamp," Rutledge said, "you don't have much experience of the Yard."

"No, I wasn't expecting a rubber stamp. Just a man who knew his *job*. I can't quite understand what makes you tick, Inspector. And why the odd persistence in a case that's finished, even if Nicholas and Olivia between them slaughtered half the village!"

"Be patient," Rutledge told him as he held open the inn's door. "And you'll be sure to find out."

It was what his father had often said to him, when he was pestering his parents to know what was inside the birthday wrappings, or under the silver paper on Boxing Day. The way an adult put off a child, and sure to aggravate.

He was delighted to see that it worked perfectly well for a grown man.

Cormac was gone in the morning, whether back to London or to the house, no one seemed to know. In any event, as Rutledge had no need to go back to the Hall straightaway, it didn't matter.

Rachel came, as she'd promised, to take him to call on Susannah. They went in Rutledge's car, the sun bright through the glass and the wind bringing with it first the smell of the sea and then the smell of the land.

"Cormac is right, you *ought* to see her yourself," Rachel said after a long silence. "Susannah, I mean. You're a very hard man. I've never met anyone quite like you. You ought to see the results of your handiwork. It might shame you into respecting the feelings of others!"

As he had seen the results of his handiwork last night, though for reasons of her own she refrained from mentioning that. Rutledge was as aware of the omission as Rachel was.

"I don't see how talking to her is going to deter me," Rutledge said. "And I owe you an apology for last night. I most particularly owe you one for embarrassing you in front of your cousin. It was— awkward. I'm sorry."

Clearing the air. It had to be done.

"And didn't serve any purpose," she reminded him.

"On the contrary," he said, risking a glance at her. "It served a variety of purposes." The roads in this part of Cornwall weren't metalled, just winding lanes for the most part, hardly wide enough for a horse and cart. Puddles from the rains hid deep washouts, while the mud itself was sometimes as slick as black ice. He knew he ought to concentrate on what he was doing. "Rachel, you told me you'd had a letter from Nicholas, before he died."

"Did I?" He gave her another swift glance, and saw that she was frowning. "I don't remember saying that."

188

Or didn't want to. He let it go for the moment.

They were heading inland, away from the sea. The high hedgerows shut off the view, and the deep-cut roads tended to come suddenly out of a curve and into a crossroads, where a heavy dray or a small cart was often and unexpectedly in his way. He nearly missed the turning they were after, but soon found the gates to the Beaton house at the head of a pretty valley.

It was one of those medieval monstrosities the Victorians had loved to build, with half-ruined towers, crenelations, and even a mock Gothic gatehouse. There was so much ivy climbing the walls that when the wind blew, the leaves ruffled and quaked as if the walls themselves were in imminent danger of collapse.

"Gentle God!" Rutledge said, slowing the car to stare.

"Yes, well, I'm told the family knew Disraeli, and admired his novels enormously. They couldn't wait to tear down the old house and replace it with this. If you say *one word*, you'll hurt their feelings! Jenny Beaton is a lovely person. She doesn't deserve to be made unhappy."

"I'm incapable of comment," Rutledge answered weakly.

Mrs. Beaton *was* a lovely person. The house, built on the foundations of a much older structure, had its finer points, for one an exquisite fan ceiling in the great hall that served as a dining room. The craftsman who created it knew how to turn plaster into a work of art. The drawing room, with its coffered ceilings and stained-glass windows, looked as if it had escaped from a stage set. When asked his opinion of it, Rutledge answered, "It's stunning!" Mrs. Beaton was satisfied. Rachel glared at him.

Susannah was lying on a chair with a footstool, a white lacy shawl thrown over her lap, but she looked perfectly healthy to Rutledge.

"I'm sorry to hear you've been ordered to rest. I hope it doesn't mean complications of any kind," he said, taking her hand in greeting.

"No," she said irritably, "just a fussy doctor and an equally fussy husband. I'm perishing from boredom!" She glanced wryly at Jenny Beaton.

"She's a terrible patient," Jenny agreed, smiling warmly at her friend. She was dark and very pretty, with small hands and feet, and Hamish had noticed her before Rutledge had. "We'd toss her out on her ear, if she had anywhere else to go. Sad, isn't it?"

"Daniel's in London, he's running himself thin trying to be in two places at once. But the doctor refuses to let me travel just now," Susannah added, "even by easy stages." She cocked her head and looked at Rutledge. "They say you're searching the moors for Richard."

"Susannah!" Jenny Beaton exclaimed. "Who told you that!"

"I may be pregnant. I'm not deaf! Well, is it true?"

"Yes, it's true," Rutledge told her.

"Why on earth are you interested in a child who died over twenty years ago? Do bodies even *last* that long? I don't see any point in it!"

"I'm interested in what became of him." He paused, then said, "If he's still alive, he's one of the heirs, isn't he? Nicholas' younger brother."

He heard Rachel gasp, across the small inlaid table from him, but he didn't look up at her. It was Susannah's response he was interested in.

"If he's alive, why hasn't he turned up? Even a child of five knows who he is, where he came from. You'd think he'd have found a way home by now. Somehow." Susannah was fidgeting with the fringe on her shawl, more from exasperation, he thought, than nervousness.

"Yes, there's always that possibility. But he hasn't. I'm just being thorough, that's all. Did you ever hear stories of what happened on the moor? As you were growing up?"

"No, it wasn't the sort of thing discussed around children, and by the time I was old enough to be curious about Richard, or Anne, or even my father, Rosamund always managed to change the subject. I remember my father, but of course not the early years, before he married Rosamund."

"He was brought up a Catholic, I'm told. What about you? And Stephen. Or Cormac?"

"We're all Anglican. Well, I suppose Cormac was born a Catholic, but he never practiced, as far as I know. What difference does it make?"

"Does he have close ties in Ireland? Has he ever talked about the rebellions and the uprisings? Michael Collins? The black and tans?"

"He's not interested in politics. Never was, as far as I know. Cormac is typical of the City—he's very good at what he does, he enjoys making money, and he behaves himself. Reputation *is* money, he says."

"He's an attractive man. Wealthy. Socially acceptable. Why hasn't he married? In his position a hostess is almost indispensable."

"Yes, I know, I've acted for him often enough. So has Rachel." She shot a sidelong glance at Rachel. "I always wondered—growing up, watching them together—if there might be something between Cormac and Olivia. The tension between the two of them and the way they very carefully avoided each other. She never married. I thought perhaps he was the reason. I wondered if she was ashamed of her bad leg, and *wouldn't* marry him. But wanted to, very badly."

"You know that's all in your imagination," Rachel said, suddenly restless. She shifted so that her face was out of the light coming through the stained glass in vivid shades of port wine and honey, dappling the walls and the floor and her shoulder. "They never seemed to have much in common, and I was around them for years before you were born."

"Which tells *me*," Susannah said, "that they had a lot in common! Didn't *you* find Cormac attractive? All my school friends were desperately in love with him! Everyone wanted to come down to the Hall for weekends."

Jenny Beaton laughed. "I was fondest of Stephen. I had such a crush on him when I was twelve. Do you remember that?"

"Cormac's very attractive," Rachel answered defensively. "But I never really thought of him in that way—"

"Nicholas didn't like him, and so you didn't!" Susannah retorted.

"Why didn't Nicholas like him?" Rutledge asked before Rachel could answer. Jenny was watching them, her face inquisitive, but he kept his eyes on Susannah and Rachel.

"Nicholas was the oldest son. Until Cormac's father married

Rosamund," Susannah said. "It put his nose out of joint, I think. This newcomer lording it over him. Except that Cormac didn't lord it over anyone."

"That's not true! Nicholas was never jealous. It was something else, something I never did really understand until I asked Rosamund about it once, and she said that Cormac's father replaced Nicholas' father, and sons often found that hard to swallow." She turned quickly, her eyes flying to Rutledge's face. "I'd forgotten that conversation," she said, surprised. "I don't know why it suddenly came to mind. What happened last night must have jarred my memory—"

"What do you mean, *what* happened?" Susannah broke in, sitting up straight, her face sharp with curiosity. "What are you talking about!"

But Rutledge knew what Rachel was thinking, that he had stirred up the past, like a stick spun in muddy water, churning up what lay at the bottom, wanted or not.

"Family relationships," Rutledge answered for her. "We were discussing them. After dinner."

Disappointed Susannah lay back against her cushions again. "Well, Nicholas never took any resentment out on Stephen or me," she said. "And we were the *children* of that marriage! Why blame Cormac? It certainly wasn't *his* doing that Mother chose to marry his father. It probably changed his life far more than Nicholas', when you stop and think about it."

From the mutinous expression on her face, Rutledge could tell that Rachel strongly disagreed. But remembering Susannah's health, she held back the defense that seemed to be burning on the tip of her tongue.

"But I was fond of Nicholas myself," Susannah went on complacently. "He had more patience with us than most boys his age. When Father died, I remember sitting on his knee, terribly frightened about putting Father into that huge, cold vault in the church. I kept telling everyone that he'd want to be out in the light, where he could hear the horses running and the sea coming in and children playing. And Nicholas said, 'That's why he died out on the strand, so he could be free. What we're putting in the vault tomorrow is

192

only a token, a place where Rosamund can put flowers.' Then he took us on a pirate's hunt, looking for Father's gold crucifix to put in the coffin. But we never found it. I don't know whether he did later, or not."

Hamish was already pointing out that it meant nothing, but Rutledge felt the coldness in his bones.

Suddenly tired and out of spirits, Susannah added, "I don't want to think about death and unhappiness. What you're doing in Borcombe is a waste of time. It distresses Daniel, and that always disturbs me. Richard is dead, and so is everyone else, and I don't see why Scotland Yard should care a ha'penny about any of us. Stephen's gone, and you can't bring him back, however hard you try. Nobody murdered him, he just *fell*! And as far as I know, that's still not a crime, is it? So just go away and let us get on with life!"

Jenny Beaton was about to interject a change of subject, but Rutledge was faster.

"Did your brother take Olivia's papers from the house? Those she left him regarding her writing?"

"Stephen took hardly anything. I feel so guilty now about how we all behaved over that. Like—like dustmen quarreling over the bins! You were as bad as the rest of us, Rachel!" she ended accusingly, her face flushing with emotion.

Rachel was on the point of denying it, then closed her mouth firmly.

Mrs. Beaton hastily overrode her anyway, extending an invitation to stay for luncheon, but Rutledge thanked her and claimed pressing business back in Borcombe. He and Rachel left soon afterward.

"A fine diplomat you are!" she accused him, back on the main road. "She's supposed to have rest, *tranquillity*!"

"She seemed perfectly capable of looking after herself. Susannah is a lot stronger than you give her credit for."

"You aren't a doctor—"

"No, and neither are you! Now tell me about Cormac and Nicholas."

"Tell you what? I thought I'd made that plain at the Beatons. They never found common ground. They were envious of each other, Nicholas because Cormac was older, Cormac because Nicholas was Rosamund's son and he wasn't. What's wrong between you and Cormac? Why do you bristle at each other? Explain that, and you'll see why Cormac and Nicholas didn't get along."

Rutledge knew why he and Cormac bristled. They were at opposite ends of the pole. Cormac wanted the family skeletons packed away where they couldn't rattle, and he, Rutledge, was in the process of digging them out and displaying them on the village green. Antagonists. Two men used to having their own way—and each finding the other blocking it.

He found himself wondering suddenly if it was Cormac's City reputation that he was protecting so ardently—or a woman he'd wanted to love but couldn't.

Hamish said, out of the blue, "The heart doesna' care what she is, if he wants her badly enough. But the head doesna' rest easy on the pillow when she's a killer."

Which was true.

He, Rutledge, still wanted Jean, though he knew—he had seen for himself—that she couldn't bear to have him come near her . . .

They were nearly back to the village when Rutledge pulled into a farmer's muddy lane and switched off the engine.

Turning to Rachel, he said, "You told me about a letter last night. Whether you want to remember telling me or not, it's up to you. But it will save all of us a great deal of time and fuss if you simply finish what you started."

"What will you do, if I don't? Make me walk back to Borcombe from here?" she retorted.

"You know I wouldn't do that. Rachel, for God's sake, you may well be concealing evidence."

"No, I'm not!" she said fiercely, turning in her seat to face him. "The letter was to *me*! Not to the police or an inquest full of prying eyes. I don't know how you managed to make me speak of it. If I'd been myself, if you hadn't *tricked* me, I never would have!"

"You told me, the day you sent for Scotland Yard," he said tiredly, ignoring Hamish's accusations and objections. "You made your decision then. And there's nothing you can do now to take it back again."

"I won't let you have my letter!"

"Then tell me what it says."

There was an angry silence between them. And then, in a voice that was so different he didn't realize at first what she was doing, she began to repeat the words from memory.

> "*My Dear,*
>
> "*The time has come for you to move away from the past. Myself. Peter. We've both cared for you, in our different ways. But I'm not the man you think I am—I never was. You must believe that! And Peter is gone. You've grieved for him, and you may grieve for me, but neither of us could have given you the happiness you want. More than anything else, you must remember that we were only pale shadows of what life ought to bring to you, the man who will give you love and children and long years of joy.*
>
> "*I have loved you too dearly to walk away in silence and leave you alone with an empty heart. I have been guilty of many things, but I have never taken your affection for granted. Whatever may be said about me, I have never lied to you. Don't ever let them tell you otherwise!*
>
> "*Yours,*
> *Nicholas.*"

There was a stillness in the car after she'd finished. He made himself look down at his hands, resting on the wheel, and not at her.

"I didn't know, when I got it, that he was going to die. I thought—I thought he was worried for me, Peter's death, my—my own feelings towards him, my hopelessness about that. I did know—for some time—that Olivia was having trouble again, with the paralysis. I suppose I'd told myself that in a few years—five, perhaps—she might—something might happen. The doctors had never held out much hope of—of a long life for her! And if he was free—if I were free—if he wanted to come to me, he could. That for Olivia's sake, all these years he'd lied to himself—lied to me—lied to her. About how he really cared for me. I told myself he'd let me marry Peter because he thought it was for the best. I told myself that he couldn't leave Olivia alone in that house, with no one but the servants to look after her. That he'd stay with her—and I *respected* him for that!—until the end. That—Oh, *damn, damn, damn! I told myself what I wanted to hear.* But he didn't want to go on living, did he? Or he would have!"

There were no tears on her cheeks when he finally looked at her, only a great sadness in her face that touched him deeply.

"And for weeks afterward I asked myself, What hold did she have over him? What was it that was stronger than anything he could have felt for me? Why couldn't she let him live? *What was it that Olivia knew and I didn't?*"

This time there was a fierce anger in her voice, a need that was so ferocious, so passionately real, that she had been driven to act. To send for the Yard.

17

Rutledge didn't know what to say, how to answer her.

Instead he got out and started the car again, and drove silently back to the village. In front of the cottage, as he pulled up the brake, he said, "You weren't prepared for murder, were you?"

"No—I thought—I don't know what I thought." Her voice was still husky. "But I had to know why— And there wasn't anyone else I could speak to. Most certainly not Peter's brother in Whitehall! I told myself that Scotland Yard would be objective and quick, and I'd at least know why Nicholas died. That's all I wanted to hear. And now, now you've dragged in Richard—and Anne—and Rosamund—and I'm so frightened I can't sleep. I don't want to know any more. I'd rather believe that Nicholas didn't love me than discover something awful about him that I couldn't bear to live with!"

"Will you come back to the Hall with me? I want to show you something."

"No, I won't be tricked again."

"This isn't a trick. Let me show you some things I found. Some things I'm not sure I understand. But very . . . worrying. And the reasons why I'm still here. You may be able to explain them away. It would be better for all of us, if you could."

She shook her head, then raised it and looked hard at him. "If I do, will you go away? Back to London and let it be?"

"That depends," he said, "on the truth."

They drove to the Hall, taking the long way around and leaving the car in front of the steps while he led her out to the headland to see the burned stretch of land. The rain had made the grass grow again, and the patch was nearly covered now. But she could still make it out. Barely.

Frowning, she said, "Are you telling me that Stephen burned Olivia's papers here? But why?"

He took an envelope from his pocket and shook the small objects it contained into the palm of his hand. A bit of ribbon, the silver edge of something, the length of leather.

She touched them gently. "My first thought would be love letters, seeing that ribbon. Was it blue, do you think? A woman would choose blue. Olivia liked green, but not that pale shade. It isn't the sort of ribbon you see on a woman's clothing, is it? Or the hair. But a nightgown? Or a very young child's gown? Love letters would be more likely. Olivia's, I'd say." She smiled wryly at him to hide the hurt. "I can't imagine Nicholas being sentimental enough to keep all *my* letters bound in ribbon!"

The corner of silver puzzled her for a time, then suddenly she laughed. "Of *course!* One Christmas, Rosamund gave us all matching frames for photographs. Leather and silver, for traveling. She said we might choose our own photographs, and I had one of Rosamund and Nicholas I put in mine."

"What did Nicholas and Olivia keep in theirs?"

"Nicholas wanted one of his parents. It was in his bedroom, for a time. I don't know what Olivia chose, but she said she wouldn't be traveling much, and might like one of George in India, because he'd done her traveling for her. I remember Rosamund hugging her, pain in her face."

"And the leather?"

"Well, Olivia kept a leather notebook by her bed. There was a strap that closed it, and a small lock. I thought it was a journal. But she said no, it was for thoughts in the night. I didn't understand what she meant, until I discovered she was a poet." She picked it up, turning it in her fingers. "How sad that she burned it. If that's what it was."

"She? Do you think Olivia did this?"

"Who else? Cormac was the first one down here, he might have taken things he didn't want us to find. Personal things. Something to do with his relationship to Olivia. But somehow I don't picture him out on a hillside in the dark, with a fire blazing. The smart thing would have been to carry them back to London and burn them there, where no one would notice."

"Why in the dark? Why do you think this was done at night?"

Rachel shrugged. "It has that kind of feeling. Clandestine?"

Next, he took her into the house and up to Olivia's room. She entered it reluctantly, looking around her as if somehow she'd see the other woman standing silently in the shadows. He opened the closet and began to work. She watched, trusting him in spite of herself to explain when he was ready, but she started when one of the canes fell to the floor with a loud clatter, indicating that she was very tense. He continued to remove boxes from the back of the closet without a word, then pulled out the shelf, and carried it to the window.

Rachel followed him, and bent over him, curiosity aroused, their heads nearly touching as he worked, using his penknife carefully to draw out the strip of wood, then the cotton. Finally, on the windowsill as before lay the row of small gold objects, sparkling in the sun, telling a tale without words.

Rachel gasped, moving them about in turn with her fingertip.

"That's Rosamund's ring. Her father gave it to her when she was very young. And a silver box of wax, so that she could seal all her letters. She wore it on her little finger, sometimes, even when she'd outgrown it. And I remember Anne wearing that locket! She'd let me look at the pictures, if I was quiet in church. Were these Richard's? The cuff buttons? Olivia used to put them in for him, to help Nanny—he couldn't be still for an instant. And that fob's Nicholas', he was so proud of it. James gave him his first watch, and Rosamund gave him the fob. It was a beautiful watch. Stephen let me have it—when—when he was going through Nicholas' room.

The fob had been in the family for ages. I thought perhaps he'd taken that. And that pipe cleaner is James', he carried it everywhere he went. I always thought it was much too handsome to use in a pipe, and he laughed when I told him so. I don't know about the crucifix. Was that the one Susannah mentioned? Brian's? I never saw Cormac wearing one."

"Yes, it has Brian's initials on the back. See?"

He turned it over, and she peered at it for a moment. "They all have initials on them," he told her. "The mark of the owner."

"How very odd. Where did you find these? Surely not inside that board! And where did they come from? Olivia must have had the ring and the locket, but surely not Richard's and James' things. Or Brian's. Cormac might have wanted that crucifix."

"They were hidden in the board, just as I showed you. One fell out—the locket—when I was going through the closet looking for Olivia's papers. After a time I discovered the others."

"But why were they hidden? I don't understand!"

"They're trophies of the dead. I thought that Olivia had collected them from each of her victims. Something they'd treasured and she'd coveted. Now, I don't know." He picked up the board again, and the wood that slotted so perfectly into it. "It was Nicholas who worked in wood. It was his skill that must have made this hiding place. I realize that now. Not Olivia's. And it was Nicholas who led the hunt for the crucifix. Susannah mentioned that. What better place to keep them safe than Olivia's closet? She wouldn't be likely, would she, to go moving shelves around on her own."

There was pain in her eyes. "You can't think—but there's the fob. Why should Nicholas add a trophy of his own, and not one for Olivia, if he was the killer. If he killed her before he took his own life?" Her face begged him to tell her it couldn't be true.

"I don't know what was burned in the fire. But could Olivia have carried things out there, burned them, and come back into the house without Nicholas knowing what she was doing? Especially if it was done at night? Someone made very certain that a number of things were destroyed. Secretly. It would have been easy for him to go out there. At night, while Olivia slept."

"No, not Nicholas!"

"Rachel, Olivia couldn't have gone out there without his knowing."

"She could have! He went into the village, to the church, to visit the rector, to have a meal at the inn, talk to people. She could have done it then."

"All right. But the fire—and the letter—tell me that one of them knew that it was all over. Nicholas couldn't possibly have written to you if Olivia planned all this on her own. If he hadn't known what was about to happen."

She took a deep breath and let it out slowly. "He may—something might have been worrying him—he might have known, without really knowing. You do sometimes! He might have—suspected what she was planning. They understood each other so well."

"And on the moors yesterday," he went on, ignoring her interjection, "they found what looked like a small boy's clothing. Wrapped in oiled cloth, to keep it from rotting too soon. That means someone stripped the boy's body. Took away the clothing that might have made it easier to identify him. That's *planning*, Rachel. Someone planned his disappearance!"

"If you found his clothing, you must have found his bones," she pointed out, desperate now.

"No. I told you, the body had been stripped. If you're going to that trouble, you don't leave the body and the clothing in the same hole. It would make no sense, would it? Next point. I have a witness who says that Brian FitzHugh was talking to someone on the beach just before he died. Can you see Olivia trying to make her way down through those rocks? Wouldn't Brian have gone up to meet her, to save her the effort? Finally, if Nicholas was jealous of Rosamund's remarriage to Brian, he wouldn't be eager to see Thomas Chambers move in to fill FitzHugh's shoes either. And it looked very much as if that could happen. But Chambers lived in Plymouth, not Borcombe. Nicholas couldn't reach him. He *could* stop his mother from taking a new husband. In the grave, she wouldn't betray him again. She was his."

She backed over to the bed, her eyes still on his face, her own very bleak, her mind listening, whatever her heart was denying. She sank down on the edge of the coverlet, and as she did, he caught that same illusive hint of perfume again, and so did she. Straightening hastily, she moved across the room to the desk instead. As far from the fragrance as she could get. "You can't prove it!" Rachel told him defiantly. "You can't prove any of this. And I won't let you ruin Nicholas' memory with speculation and doubt. Olivia was famous. They won't let you tear her down either, wait and see. You'll end up ruining yourself. But I'm going to find out what drives you so hard, and I'm going to stop you, before I've lost my own way, and start believing this filth. *This was a close, happy family! Why do you want to destroy it?*"

"I want the truth," he said tiredly.

"No, you don't," she told him coldly. "You've come out of the war a broken man, I can read that much in your face. You need to prove yourself again. And you think that the dead are easier targets than the living. All right, I don't know what made Olivia want to kill herself. I expect it was suffering that drove her to it. And I don't know why Nicholas wanted to die. But I'd rather go through the rest of my life wondering than lose him entirely. You don't have anything to lose, do you? You've never loved anyone enough to give yourself for them. I must have been mad, asking for Scotland Yard to be sent down here. I believed in justice, and you only believe in revenge!"

She was moving before she'd finished, catching him off balance, and was out the door, slamming it behind her. He could hear her running down the gallery, almost stumbling in blind haste.

He didn't need Hamish's warning. Remembering the stairs, remembering how Stephen had fallen on the worn treads, Rutledge swore and was across the room in four swift strides, going after her.

He overtook her at the top of the steps, catching her arm in a fierce grip, swinging her around to face him.

"I'm not trying to ruin Nicholas! Or Olivia! There's murder here, damn it. You're an intelligent woman, you could see it for yourself if you weren't so bloody wrapped up in your emotions!" he told her, furious with her, furious with himself.

Rachel didn't cry. Where protecting Nicholas was concerned, she was braver than most of the men who wore medals from the war. He hoped that Nicholas was worth it—and feared that he wasn't.

"Don't talk to me about emotions!" she said, her voice like ice. "It's Olivia, isn't it? You don't want *her* to be a killer, you don't want all that poetry to come out of darkness and hate. Those damned poems blind you, and everybody else. Olivia was a witch, she had a withered leg, and yet she was able to take Nicholas down with her into depression and death! She could kill her own sister and her own half brother, and give an overdose of laudanum to her mother, and *still* you want to see her as saint! Her sufferings are just another part of the myth, her writing something you wrestle with because she's a woman and respect because you once thought it was a man's, and women shouldn't write about lying in bed with a lover or standing knee-deep in your own ordure in a trench, or how near we all are to hell! But you wonder, don't you, what kind of lover she'd have been, and where she might have learned the tricks that mattered. Well, ask Cormac. Maybe he'll tell you what she was like!"

Stung, he let her go, dropping his hand from her arm, and she turned, walking down the stairs with her head high and her shoulders straight with anger. Fighting for breath and control even while she still seethed with the fury consuming her.

At the foot of the steps she turned to look back up at him and said, "Now you know how I felt in Olivia's bedroom! I've given you a taste of your own poison, and you found it hard to swallow, didn't you? I don't know if a word of what I've just said is true, and I don't really care. But now you can see for yourself what lies a twisted imagination might come up with. How easily you can twist the truth to debase other people's emotions. I loved Nicholas, and I mourn the man he was. And I won't believe your lies about him. You can think what you like about Olivia. I'm going back to London, if I can find Cormac and ask him to take me. But I promise you this: I'll ruin you if you ruin Nicholas."

"Rachel, listen to me—"

"No. I've already listened to you, and I think it's all hogwash. What you think is your own business. What you do about what

203

you think is very much my business. Consider yourself warned."
She walked to the door.

"Wait!" he commanded, already on his way down the stairs.

"Why? To be insulted again? Or worse still, hurt? I can't think
how you could have been Peter Ashford's friend. He was such a
gentle, good man."

"I'll make a bargain with you."

She laughed. "I don't bargain with the devil."

Ignoring that, he said, "Help me find out the truth. And I swear
to you, if Nicholas is guilty—no, wait, let me finish—if Nicholas
is the one I'm after, I'll walk away from it, go back to London, and
tell the Yard they were wrong, there was nothing further to investigate in any of the three deaths in Borcombe this spring. The past—
the others—can stay buried with him."

Rachel stood with her back to him, the door's handle in her hand,
the door already swinging gently towards her.

"I don't believe you!"

"I swear!" And he would do it. He knew that, deep down inside.

"And if it isn't Nicholas?"

"Then we'll decide what ought to be done. In fairness to the dead.
All of the dead." To O. A. Manning. To the poems that might be
worse than lies.

"I'll think about that. And give you my answer tonight. I'll send
a message to The Three Bells."

The door was open now, and she went through it without looking back, the wind from the sea picking up strands of her hair and
blowing them around her face. She seemed awfully slim and lonely,
very small and very bereft as she moved down the steps and onto
the drive, skirting his car.

Hamish was calling him a fool for swearing to such a bargain.

"The Yard brings in their man, you can't turn your back on your
oath, no' for a slip of a girl that can't see where the wind's
blowing!"

"So you believe me now, do you?" Rutledge silently challenged
Hamish. "You see I'm right."

"I think ye're a damned fool, and a long way from home! What
is there about witchery in a woman that touches you? Your Jean

wasn't that sort, she's no' the kind to spin a man's head or set his soul on the brink. Olivia Marlowe casts a spell out of her grave, and ye're lost!"

"It has nothing to do with Jean. Or Olivia Marlowe," Rutledge countered, watching Rachel's long, clean strides as she walked towards the wood. "And it has naught to do with yon lassie, either!" Hamish retorted.

Rutledge closed the door after Rachel before she reached the shadows of the trees and then took the stairs two at a time, to put away the articles he'd left on Olivia's windowsill. Back into their cotton nests again, for the moment. Until he was ready to bring them out for good. His sixth sense told him he'd won in his bargain with Rachel. He hoped he was right.

As he passed the closed door to Nicholas' room, he said aloud, his voice rough, "You should have lived, you fool, and married her. She'd have made a better wife than any you'll find in the grave."

Hamish chuckled.

Rutledge, irritated, ignored him.

But Hamish was in Rutledge's own mind. And Hamish recognized what Rutledge had just admitted to Nicholas.

That he couldn't be guilty, or he wouldn't have won Rachel's heart.

It was one of the first lessons Rutledge had learned at the Yard. That love seldom had anything to do with murder. Pity, yes. And compassion, sometimes. Even mercy, on occasion. But not love.

And the question in this case was not whether Rachel loved Nicholas, but how Nicholas loved Rachel.

Enough to protect her, as Cormac had suggested, or enough to use her to protect himself. Which had it been? Which way had Nicholas turned?

As Rutledge carefully worked with the little gold trophies, he realized all at once that Nicholas might well have included himself among the dead, before swallowing his laudanum. But not Olivia. That's why there was no trophy for Olivia. She had escaped through her poetry. He had waited too long to kill her—if that's what he'd done, if that was what had actually happened. She'd already found her wings of fire.

18

$\mathcal{R}$utledge drove thoughtfully back to Borcombe, and didn't realize, until he stepped around the men seated on their sun-warmed bench before the inn door, drinking their beer, that he'd missed his lunch.

Hamish pointed out that the dining room had already closed.

Which did nothing to improve Rutledge's mood.

He felt he was ready to start taking statements from his witnesses: Mrs. Trepol and Wilkins the gardener, Rachel and Cormac, Smedley, Dr. Penrith and Dr. Hawkins. Getting it on paper where he could sort it, challenge it, or use it to move forward.

But Borcombe was a tiny place, and everyone knew everyone's business. To speak to people, to ask them for a general picture of the family at the Hall and the events that might—or might not—impinge on matters that concerned him, stirred up talk and rumors. To ask for official statements was tantamount to providing a blueprint for exactly what he was after: old murders, not new ones. Room for Constable Dawlish and his choleric superior to raise hell with London. Bringing Bowles down on him like a cyclone, demanding to know what he meant by stirring up the county, causing problems for the Yard when it already had its hands full. Room too for Cormac to have him recalled summarily, citing harassment of a prominent family, never mind the local police.

And he'd be forced to reveal more than he could, at the moment, defend. Publicly. But he knew he was right. All his experience at the Yard, his own intuition, the facts that he *could* be sure of, pointed to a long, cold-blooded series of killings that had spanned years. Cunningly planned, meticulously carried out, skillfully concealed.

A few more days—

He'd have to wait, damn it! On the statements. It would be foolhardy to push on and wreck everything.

Which merely added to his frustration, and Hamish was there, already taking advantage of it. Rutledge tried to shut him out. The clamor in his head was ferocious, and he forced himself to ignore it.

Very well, then, he promised himself. Wait he would—until he had finally talked to the local man, Inspector Harvey, and seen the way the wind blew there. It could make a difference in his planning, he had to accept that.

Sidestepping someone coming down the stairs as if he owned them, Rutledge settled for mentally laying out his schedule, which of the villagers should give statements first, what approach he was going to take in the questions asked, how he might draw out of each witness exactly what he wanted without arousing rampant speculation, and how fast he could accomplish the lot. There was also the dilemma of what had become of Olivia's papers. He was going to have to find them—

He realized the man on the stairs was staring hard at him, eyes narrowed and angry. Rutledge looked up at him for the first time, and swiftly shelved his own thoughts.

"Rutledge?" the stranger demanded. "Inspector Rutledge?"

"I'm Rutledge, yes."

"Inspector Harvey," the man retorted with equal curtness. "I've come to speak to you."

Swearing silently at the timing of Harvey's unexpected appearance—splitting headaches were not the frame of mind in which to conduct painstaking interviews with choleric Cornishmen—Rutledge led the way to the small parlor, where today sunlight tried fretfully to light the gloom. "We can have privacy here," he said, holding open the door. And advantage to me, on my own ground, he thought to himself. It appeared that he well might have need of it.

Harvey followed, still huffing from the stairs.

He was a bluff man, neither tall nor short, but heavy in build, with a red complexion and thinning dark hair. There was an air of having his own way about him, as if on his own ground he was used to being heeded, and his advice or instructions followed. There couldn't be, Rutledge thought to himself, many police matters in this part of Cornwall which might draw the attention of London. What there was in the way of crime and mischief would be comfortably divided between the police and the local magistrates.

In short, tread carefully.

"I'm glad to meet you finally," Rutledge said, holding out his hand. Harvey looked pointedly at it and walked on into the room, refusing to take it.

"Finally is the key word here, isn't it?" he asked, keeping his voice flat.

"You were in Plymouth when I came. And you've only just returned, I think. Dawlish told me you were somewhere on the moors, talking to a farmer about wild dogs attacking his domestic animals."

"So I was. It doesn't mean I'm blind to what's happening. I don't like strangers meddling on my patch. Not without my keeping an eye on them or having regular reports from them to keep me in the picture. Looks bad when I know less than my constable, and less than London. I don't see what's wrong with our initial investigation into the three deaths in question, and I don't see why you haven't long since come and gone with a clean bill of health on my desk to clear the air in Borcombe."

"As a matter of fact, nothing appears to be wrong with your initial inquiries. I believe that Stephen FitzHugh died as you said he did. In a fall. It's the other deaths that interest me. And I accept them as suicides."

"Just because Miss Marlowe turned out to be famous? Is that's what this is in aid of? Sending a detective inspector all this way? Playing merry hell with my reputation and her family's reputation, all to suit the wigs in London who realized too late they'd missed the opportunity of seeing their names in the *Times* in connection with her death? Or are you in fact looking for a wee success to set off the Yard's regrettable failure to stop this knife-wielding idiot on the loose in London? Oh, yes, I've seen the papers—nobody has a clue! Now the local people tell me you're trying to find a link down here with Master Richard Cheney, the boy lost on the moors. Ridiculous doesn't cover it!"

"That's because what you hear from your own people is not in any way the point of my investigation. But if that's what they'd prefer to think, then I'd prefer to let them."

Harvey all but snorted. "What I'm asking you, man, is to tell *me* what you're after, not what you want the villagers to believe!" Harvey was feeding on his own sense of betrayal, letting it fuel his anger. It was a technique used sometimes by men wanting their own way—make life unpleasant enough for the other party, and he'd be too busy defending himself to attack.

Rutledge considered his own tactics, then said, "Nicholas Cheney had a brother who's been missing since he was five. We presently have no way of knowing if the boy is dead or alive. If alive, he may be an heir. If dead, there's a possibility it wasn't accidental. That he was deliberately murdered."

"By whom, pray? And if the family was concerned about him still being alive after the search was called off and the posters brought in no responses, or later was wanting to know something more about his death, why didn't they come to my predecessor? Or to me?"

"Would you have listened? Or would you have assured them they could safely believe what they'd rather believe, that the boy died of simple exposure? Any new search was bound to lead to the same conclusion."

Harvey bristled. "I don't tell comfortable lies, whatever you're used to in London. And I know how to conduct a search."

"I'm sure you don't tell comfortable lies," Rutledge agreed.

"And given the facts at your disposal, where would you start searching? From what I can see, there was very little evidence of foul play, unless some passing gypsies carried the boy off, or someone wandering on the moors stumbled on him and killed him for reasons of his own. And the officer in charge examined those possibilities very thoroughly at the time Richard went missing. Even when you took over here, you had no reason to suspect more than some sort of tragic accident. What has changed now is the way we're looking at the disappearance, and that in itself may prove to be the key."

"And what is that, pray? He wandered off during a family picnic. And was lost. And is long dead, most likely, because the moors are unforgiving. Why should I have raised false hopes? And as to the present cases, would it have prevented Miss Olivia Marlowe from taking her own life? Or Mr. Nicholas from doing the same? Would it have straightened Mr. Stephen's cracked neck? I think not!" His own neck was red to his collar with the power of his anger.

"No. But it might have righted a very old wrong. It might have revealed secrets that the family itself didn't know the answers to. It might make it clearer to us whose will took precedence, and at what time. Who has the right to sell Trevelyan Hall, and who has none."

"It was my understanding—still is—that Miss Olivia and Mr. Nicholas had nearly identical wills. In that event, I don't quite see legal quibbling over which is which. And I can tell you that Mr. Nicholas was a very straightforward man, very able, concerned about his responsibilities to the church and the village. Fought in the war, did his duty like the gentleman he was—"

Hamish, interrupting, wanted to know what being a gentleman had to do with fighting in France. Rutledge ignored him.

"—and in my opinion had long ago put to rest the question of his brother's death. Never spoke of it to me in the past fifteen years. And never spoke to my predecessor about it either, or it'd have been in the record. Which leaves us with Miss Olivia, and I don't know that I'd put much past *her*!"

It was so different from any other comments he'd heard about Olivia that Rutledge was surprised.

Harvey smiled with sour satisfaction. "We're not all clods here in the wilds of Cornwall, whatever London may have led you to believe."

"No one has suggested that you might be," Rutledge said, moving with great care now. "Tell me what reasons you have to back up your opinion."

"Read her books, man! My wife is a decent woman, she'd never so much as feel or think what Miss Marlowe thought fit to put down baldly in print! It's unwomanly and disturbing. A mind capable of such immodesty is in my estimation capable of the worst in human degradation."

He'd spoken with such venom that Rutledge found himself wondering what Olivia had done to raise Harvey's hackles. He thought he knew. She'd been Miss Marlowe of the Hall, quiet and unassuming, someone he could patronize, the cripple who was content to be seldom seen and not often heard. A tidy round peg in her tidy round hole, like Mrs. Harvey. And then the truth about O. A. Manning had come out, and Harvey had been made to look or feel a fool for misjudging her. That would be unforgivable, and he'd judge her with a vengeance now. Rutledge quelled the urge to rise to Olivia's defense, his own temper held on a tight rein.

Harvey had already moved on to his next grievance. "Now tell me what this new evidence you spoke of might be. Those rags they found out on the moors? You'll never prove they belonged to the boy. Could have been put there any time in the years before or since. Don't they teach you your business in London?"

"Quite well," Rutledge said through his teeth. "And I intend to continue going about it until I'm satisfied."

Harvey was furious, but something about the other man's voice, the steel in it, the natural air of command that came with years in France, made him stop short and reexamine his opponent. His first impression had been of an ill, weary man with no stamina for the course. Someone who could be bullied and sent back to London with his tail between his legs. Stake your ground, wield your temper like a club, and he'd soon apologize and be off.

Instead he'd come up against hard core, and more experience than he'd expected. Harvey tried to think if he'd heard the name Rut-

212

ledge before in connection with any of the major cases the Yard had handled. It rattled him more that he couldn't. Knowing what Rutledge might be capable of gave him more range to push. Not knowing left him in pitch dark on a steep cliff.

Rutledge, meanwhile, was making his own assessment. Of a man who did his job thoroughly and properly, but lacked imagination to do it cleverly. That was going to matter a great deal.

After a swift, appraising silence, both men moved to chairs and sat down, as if the confrontation was finished and the conference begun.

As a form of peace offering, Rutledge said, "Apart from your natural disinclination to see a case opened again for no sound reason—and I understand that, I'd dislike it myself—were you quite serious when you said that Miss Marlowe was capable of anything? Any degradation. Would you for instance include murder in that list?"

And then Harvey surprised him a second time by vacillating. "Yes and no."

"If you discount her poetry, and her reputation there, what gave you the feeling that she was different?" Or was it all hindsight, the willingness to believe that Olivia hadn't hoodwinked him completely . . .

Mulling it over, Harvey said, "It was not something I could put my finger on, mind you. It was more her interest in the subject of crime that made me uneasy. People, most especially women, don't think to ask the questions she asked, unless there's worry in the mind, or fear. Or even depravity. Now in a pub talking to a man about my work, I'll be asked a hundred questions, from how I know I've got the right miscreant to whether I've watched a hanging. That's different, it's curiosity, the same as he'd ask an undertaker or even a glassblower about his trade. Idle conversation. You can tell the man knows naught about it, and you could give him lies and he'd be just as satisfied."

Rutledge nodded. The farmers and tradesmen and lorry drivers he'd fought with had often found it odd to be in the same trench as a policeman. As if he viewed all mankind with innate suspicion. Expecting the worst.

"So it was different when Miss Olivia asked me what made a man take another man's life. What goaded him, whether he was evil by birth and nature or only caught up in a web of happenstance he couldn't fight his way clear of. Whether murdering ran in families or wasn't inheritable." He paused. Rutledge realized that Harvey had kept this conversation buried deep inside himself for a very long time. And was only reluctantly revealing it now. Because he was a fair man, whatever he lacked in cleverness. "Whether a murderer could truly repent and change. And her as fair and innocent looking as the day she were born! I didn't know about the poetry, not then, but I can tell you it gave me the willies, because she was that intense I knew it wasn't idle talk, meeting the new man in charge and making polite noises about his job. She wanted—she wanted something *more*. And I couldn't have told you on peril of my life what it was."

"Knowing about murder isn't the same as killing. A victim's family may understand it better than the murderer himself." If Nicholas had been the killer, Olivia would have felt it deep in her very bones.

"Aye, that's true. But once I read some of her verse, now, I knew it was inside that woman, and not something she'd happened to think of, meeting me on the road, like. That last book has one poem in it that kept me sleepless of nights for nearly a week. The sheer cruelty of it. I don't recollect what it's called, but I'm not likely to forget how it started:

> '*Murderer I am, of little things, small griefs,*
> *Treasures of the heart.*
> *Of bodies and of souls I have taken*
> *All that is there to give,*
> *Life's blood, the spirit's wealth.*
> *And these secrets I keep locked away,*
> *For my own joy and your pain.*'

"Not what Mrs. Browning might write, or even that Rossetti woman."

"No," Rutledge said quietly, considering possible treasures of the heart. Those small golden trophies of a death.

"Are you thinking *she* killed that boy? Good God! She was hardly more than a child herself!"

"You said you believed she was capable of murder."

Harvey looked at him, mind working, mind sorting, but not coming up with anything he could put into words.

"Aye, that's true enough, in the heat of the moment I felt it could be so. But it's different when you have a face to put to someone she may've killed . . ." He shook his head. "We don't get many child murderers in these parts. I wasn't that fond of the woman, but it's another matter saying she was one. She was *different*. That was her problem. She was . . . different." There was something in his eyes that pleaded for Rutledge to understand what he was trying to say. That whatever Olivia Marlowe was, by its very extraordinariness she was outside the realm of his comprehension, and therefore suspect, even if he couldn't condemn her for a specific crime. *Capable* of anything.

"When did this discussion with Olivia take place?"

"Oh, long before the war. I'd just arrived in Borcombe. I didn't know her mother, the one they still call Miss Rosamund, that everyone was so fond of, and I knew only that Miss Olivia was one of the family up at the Hall. Her and her brother, and the two younger ones, the twins."

"How did you answer her?"

"I had to tell her the truth as I saw it. That the darkness in the human soul was something I'd never come to understand in my years of policing but I believed it to be beyond healing. That struck her as sad, I could see it in her eyes. And then she said, 'Do families believe you, when you tell them a son—or a daughter—is guilty of murder?' I said, 'they're often the last to believe,' and she nodded as if she understood, and thanked me for my time, and walked away." When Rutledge made no answer, Harvey added, "Not a natural conversation to have with a young woman, would you say?"

He wanted reassurance. He wanted to believe that Olivia and not he himself had been out of line. He didn't want to think that she had had a guilt on her conscience, had turned to the figure of authority in Borcombe, and been rejected because he had somehow failed to understand her. Rutledge wondered if she'd brought this up before, with Harvey's predecessor, or the rector before Smedley. And found no absolution for the burden she carried.

Which meant in turn that Rutledge was not going to confide in Harvey either. Not until he was sure of his ground. It would be wasted breath, and if he, Rutledge, turned out to be wrong, the damage as Rachel had pointed out, and Cormac as well, could be enormous.

And so, in pacification, Rutledge said, "To the end of the week, then. I'll continue the search for the boy, I'll continue my questions, and then if I have no more to go on than I have now, I'll come to you and confer."

"Find him or not, mark my words, the lad is dead."

The innkeeper, Trask, brought a tray and a pot of coffee to Rutledge in his room and made a show of setting the cup within reach, putting out the sugar bowl and small pitcher of milk, refolding the napkin that had covered the thick sandwiches. Affably mentioning Harvey's visit, he showed all the signs of a man prepared to linger and gossip.

For once Rutledge preferred the innkeeper's opinions to the silence of his own thoughts. Or Hamish's.

"A good man, we've had no complaint of him, keeps the peace and is fair-minded. The magistrates seem to think well of him too, from what I hear. Thorough, that's the reputation they give him." Disappointed when Rutledge didn't take the hint and offer his own views on the local constabulary, Trask reminisced for a time about the Trevelyan family, leaving the impression that The Three Bells had been the center of social life for generations of them. Rutledge swallowed that with his first cup of coffee, and a grain of salt.

Then something the innkeeper was saying caught his attention. "And of course her mother was the old nanny there. That's the reason Miss Rachel prefers the cottage to the inn."

"Are you telling me that the Trevelyan *nanny* is still alive?" He

216

felt a surge of wrath that no one—least of all Rachel—had seen fit to tell him that.

"Lord, no, she'd be near *ninety*, wouldn't she! Polworth, her name was, she'd been nanny to Miss Rosamund, then married and had a daughter of her own, Mary, and when Mary was off to school, she went back to the Hall to care for Mr. Stephen and Miss Susannah. Only ever had the one child herself. Mr. Polworth died of the consumption early on. Mary Otley, the daughter is now. Husband was killed out in Africa, place called Mafeking."

"Soldier?"

"God save you, sir, no, he were a missionary. His death took the heart out of Mary, and she came home. Wasn't her cup of tea, so to speak, preaching to the heathen, suffering from dysentery and them big flies, and water not fit to drink—"

"Thank you, Trask," Rutledge said, cutting him off. Trask wasted another few minutes filling his tray with the empty dishes, brushing away crumbs, leaving the pot of coffee, as if hoping for another opening. But he got none and soon took the hint.

Afterward, Rutledge sat there and listened to the birds singing outside his window in the ruined garden, laying his plans carefully.

19

It was nearly four in the afternoon when Rachel left the cottage and crossed the road to the rectory, disappearing into the house when the liverish housekeeper opened the door. Rutledge, lying in wait in the small wood from which he could see the cottage quite clearly, gave her a full minute in case the call was a short one, then strode quickly to the gate that shut the cottage walk off from the village street.

The woman who opened the door to his knock was elderly, but not, he thought, as old as she appeared to be. From the yellow of her eyes, he could see that she'd had malaria more than once, and still paid dearly for her years in Africa. It was not a continent that was kind to European women.

Startled to see him, she said, "Miss Rachel's just gone over to visit Rector." Her voice held a degree of reserve, and no Cornish accent.

"I know. I wanted to speak to you, if I may. Mrs. Otley, is it? I understand that your mother was nanny at the Hall."

She let him in, and the room itself reflected the odd life she'd lived. There was the coziness of chintz, embroidered cushions, and a worn Axminster carpet. A Zulu shield hung cheek by jowl with a crossed pair of long, deadly spears on the wall, next to a print of the King and Queen in a wooden frame, and a hand-lettered certificate stating that Mary Polworth Otley had crossed the Equator on the ship *Ramses*. The chair she pointed out to him wore a fine fringe of pale cream dog hairs. Resigning himself to collecting them on his clothing, Rutledge wondered where the dog was. It came trundling in, a fat puppy that sniffed his trousers and then tried to tear his shoelaces out by the roots. Mrs. Otley, referring to it as Rhodes, shooed it away and sat down, her face solemn.

"What was it you wanted to see me about, sir? If you're here to ask questions about Miss Rachel—"

"No. I was more interested in your mother's work at the Hall. Did she talk about the family very often?"

"To me? No, sir. She adored Miss Rosamund, you could see that, and was very fond of the children at the Hall, but she wasn't one to make comparisons. And she treated their business as theirs, and mine as mine."

Which was certainly to her credit. "Did you play with the Trevelyan children?"

"No, sir, I was far older than any of them. I did lend a hand in the nursery from time to time, when there was sickness or company coming. It helped me, when I was out in Africa teaching little ones."

"Were you there when Anne Marlowe fell out of a tree in the orchard? Or when young Richard was lost on the moors?"

"No, I was away at school. I wanted more than anything to be a governess, and Miss Rosamund was kind enough to take an interest in me. She sent me to Miss Kitchener's Academy in Kent." A rueful smile moved quietly across her face. "Then in my first position as governess, I met Edwin, just back from Africa and a widower. He was a fiery man, full of God and grand ideas. I became the third Mrs. Otley, but this time it was Edwin who was buried in Africa, not his wife. I came home a widow and childless. I worked in a slum school in London for a time, telling myself it was best for me to stay busy in the church. But it wasn't. I hadn't had a calling, you see. Only Edwin's dream, second hand."

He could hear the sense of grief, not for her husband or herself but for the waste of her life on something she hadn't believed in.

And then as if she'd picked up his earlier conclusion, she said,

"Africa's hard on women. That's why I persuaded Miss Rachel not to follow Peter Ashford to Kenya. She was all for going. She'd have been left out there a widow, if she hadn't listened. And—and for many reasons I was right."

He wondered if Mary Otley knew—or guessed—about Rachel's feelings for Nicholas. He asked a few more questions that took him nowhere, then stood to go.

Rhodes, caught napping, leaped to his own feet before he was quite awake and scrambled to the attack. Rutledge sidestepped smoothly, and the little dog skidded to a halt by the chair, taking on its already well-chewed skirts instead.

But Mrs. Otley, looking up at Rutledge and ignoring the dog as if used to mock battles, said, "Of course I was back here in Borcombe when Nicholas nearly died. If that's any help to you, sir. I wouldn't want Miss Rachel to know of it, but she tells me you've an interest in such happenings at the Hall, and I wouldn't want to be remiss in my duty. But if it serves no purpose, I'd as soon have it left a secret. If you wouldn't mind."

"Secret?" Rutledge repeated, as unprepared as Rhodes for the sudden shift in direction.

"Yes, it was kept very quiet at the time. No one wanted it talked about, but I suppose it doesn't do any harm now, if you're interested in the family's history, as they say in the village you are. Though God knows why. They were always perfectly respectable people up at the Hall."

"Tell me." He spoke more sharply than he'd intended.

"There isn't much to tell, actually. He was coming home to the Hall, late one night, Mr. Nicholas. He'd been visiting the rector— this was well before the war, oh, 1907 or thereabouts, and there'd had been rumors at the time about Mr. Nicholas leaving soon to see some of the ships being built up on Clyde Bank, in Scotland. Those liners everyone was talking about, and the prize for the Atlantic crossing speed record. Young Stephen told me he'd overheard Mr. Cormac saying he'd look into finding a place for Mr. Nicholas in one of the fleets, if he was interested. But I don't know if that's true or not, nothing came of it. At any rate, on the way home from Rector's, Mr. Nicholas was stabbed by some drunkard. Too drunk to know what he was about, thank God, because the knife missed Mr. Nicholas' heart and took a long slash out of his ribs instead. Dr. Penrith sewed him up, ordered him to stay in his own bed and not go wandering off to London or Scotland or anywhere else, and that was the end of that. I don't think anyone knew about it except Miss Olivia and the doctor, and of course me, because the poor man dragged himself to my door when he couldn't make it through the wood and up the hill to the Hall."

"And the drunkard?"

"Oh, he was long gone away by the time Miss Olivia took some of the grooms out to hunt for him. She told them only that the man'd been making a nuisance of himself on the drive. I daresay he fled the minute he'd seen what he'd done. Drunk or not, he'd have known there'd be a hue and cry over it."

"And Rachel never knew?"

"She was away, and Miss Olivia said she'd be here in a flash, worrying herself to death, and to no good purpose. I agreed, and never said a word to anyone. Mr. Nicholas ran a fever for a day or two, then began to heal. It wasn't as if Miss Rachel was needed to help nurse him."

"Did Nicholas get a good look at his assailant?"

"He said he was too rattled at the time to take much notice, except that the man was tall and thin and dressed poorly. Which was very unlike him, to my mind. Not one to lose his nerve, Mr. Nicholas. But men are strange sometimes, when it comes to pride. He wouldn't have a fuss made over it. Someone dragged up before the magistrate for the attack, everyone talking—"

Rutledge agreed with her first comment. Nicholas—rattled?

He thought it was much more likely that Nicholas knew exactly who had attacked him, and didn't want to say . . .

And could that explain the gold watch fob in the small collection in Olivia's closet? Had she tried to stop him from leaving her and the Hall?

He asked Mrs. Otley not to mention the matter to Rachel or anyone else for the time being, and left the house before Rhodes had finished trouncing the chair skirt and recollected his shoelaces.

*   *   *

Rutledge went off through the woods, not ready to return to the inn, restless with the complexities of the evidence in front of him, needing the physical exercise to clear away the temptations offered, to absolve Olivia of blame. It was still there, deep inside, although he knew it was wrong, a muddle of emotions from the war, from his loss of Jean, his insecurities, the persistent fear he might still be unready to do his job properly.

Olivia's poetry had been an anchor for many men. Why hadn't the woman herself lived up to the talent she'd been given?

He crossed the lawns of the Hall, noticing in the afternoon light that the house seemed to have changed since he came to Borcombe. Once it had seemed warmly welcoming, then haunted and alive with pain. Now—it was odd, but he could sense it strongly—there was merely emptiness. As if the occupants, man or ghost, had given up on the living and gone away. But it had only been a trick of the light, he told himself, that had once made the house seem to him so vital. And the fineness of the architecture, which led the senses astray.

He made himself remember instead the house that he'd just visited, the Beatons' Victorian deception. A house without a soul, his father would have called it, because it had been built to reflect a passion, not as a thing in and of itself. The ghosts there would be just as fraudulent, wanting to be noticed as part of the decor, wandering in the turrets and along the battlements like figments of the style, not as figments of reality.

He smiled at the fanciful thought.

For a time he stood down by the shore, near the rocks where Brian FitzHugh had died. Watching the sea come in, listening to Hamish reminding him that what you wanted was not to be considered as proper evidence.

"And ye're missing something, man! Ye're wrapped up in your feelings, because that woman made sense of the war for you, and sense of love, and blinded you with her bonny words. Use your head! Ye'll no' find yon murderer in the sea, nor in the answers people gie you. And ye'll no' find it in Rachel Marlowe's memory, mark my words. Ye'll find it in black and white, or gie it all up for good!"

"What about the clothes on the moor?" he asked, as gulls called overhead, blotting out the sound of his voice.

"Someone stripped the lad. That's what it means. And why strip a corpse? To keep him from being identified."

"No, they'd know, God help them, who the boy was. It was done for another reason. Not to prevent identification, but to confuse."

"Confuse! D'ye no' think that the mother of that child would know his flesh? Clothed or bare, rotting or whole, she'd *know*!"

"And if they found the clothes but not the boy—"

"She'd know those as well!"

Rutledge sighed. "True. So why strip the boy? Then bury the clothes in an oiled sack or cloth? Making them last as long as possible, rather than letting them rot. You'd think the sooner they rotted the better, as far as the killer was concerned. All right, who stripped the body? If I had the answer to that, I'd know the whole. And why the poem about the pansies? Pansies for remembrance. I don't think anyone was likely to forget that wretched child!"

Nicholas or Olivia. That was his choice. Break Rachel's heart— or wound his own by taking away that one small thing Olivia's poetry had given him, a little space of comfort in a bloody terrible war.

He skimmed a few stones across the incoming tide, watching them skip and dance. Just as his evidence seemed to skip and dance. From one suspect to the other. And yet he knew, as strongly as he knew where he was standing at this instant, that it was not the two of them. Not working together. It had to be one—or the other. And he knew—God help him—he knew which.

Walking back to the wood, he saw the old woman by the trees, standing there staring up at the house, looking for something in its shadows, needing something it could no longer give. Sadie, whose mind wandered but whose brain understood more than she was telling him. He was convinced of that. Or else, it was something she didn't know that she knew—

She turned to stare at him as he came over the rise of the lawns and turned towards her. He thought at first she was going to leave before he reached her, disappearing so as not to be faced with more seemingly useless questions. But after a twitch of indecision she stayed her ground.

"A fine evening, isn't it?" he asked, trying to test her mental stability, as always. "Who's strolling on the lawns today? Which spirits do you see?"

"I see Miss Rosamund weeping. I see the Gabriel hounds sniffing around the chimneys, their big feet pattering on the roof like hailstones. Sniffing, looking, searching. They'll howl in the night, once they've scented prey. I'll be snug in my own hearth corner when they howl."

The Gabriel hounds. Her favorite theme when her mind was disturbed. He said, "Did you see the hounds when the Light Brigade charged? Did you hear them howling and racing across the field with the guns?"

"I wasn't there, was I? I was back in hospital, waiting for the dying. But I heard them howling. Heathen, they were, those Russians, no better than the Turks. Bloody heathen, with nothing to lose, having no souls."

"No souls? I thought the Turks went to Paradise if they died in battle?"

"Paradise? Pshaw! A place of pools and cool water, with dancing girls no better than they ought to be, and wine to soak the brain in forgetfulness? I don't call that much of a reward for the faithful. Endless whoring and sinfulness, that's what it means. But fit for hounds. They know no better!"

He said, "Who are the hounds of Gabriel here? At Trevelyan Hall?"

"The same as the others," she said, looking away from the Hall to study his face. "Heathen."

"Protestant? Catholic?"

"Neither, and that's the point, now, isn't it? An unbaptized soul, with nothing but evil filling it. Darkness, not light."

Rutledge thought for a long moment. Olivia and Anne were twins. Was Sadie trying to tell him that one of them hadn't been properly baptized? That with two babies screaming bloody murder by the baptismal font, one had been baptized twice and the other not at all?

225

He said, "Was Olivia baptized? Was Anne?"

She looked at him as if he'd run mad. "Do you think Miss Rosamund would allow it otherwise? Of course they were. I was there, I watched the babes handed to the old rector one at a time. There was blue ribbon on Miss Olivia's christening gown, and pale green on Miss Anne's. To be sure 'twas all done properly!"

Green ribbon . . . a christening gown? No, he couldn't quite see that . . .

"Who burned some small personal belongings in a fire, just above the gardens? Beyond the headland, where the blaze couldn't be seen from the village?"

"What fire?"

"Oh, come now!" Inspiration struck. "The rags you wanted, the rags that'd been promised to you by Miss Olivia. Someone used them instead to keep a fire going, because there were a number of things he—or she—wanted to burn well. A leather notebook. A leather picture frame with silver corners. A pile of letters, perhaps. Who was it who wanted such possessions destroyed?"

"It weren't Mr. Cormac!" she said briskly. "Nor Miss Rachel. I'd have known. It could have been Mr. Nicholas. I don't know why he'd go there in the dark to burn them, but I know it might have been him that did it, because of what I saw."

"What did you see?" He kept his voice low, gentle. Curious, but not probing.

"I saw him with pails, going down to the sea to fill them with water. And then he set them up on the headland. Left them there. And walked back into the house with empty hands."

Nicholas.

"Was this the night they died? Olivia and Nicholas?"

"No, 'twas the night before. I was in the wood, looking for roots while the moon was near full. I watched him for a time because my back hurt, and it felt better to straighten it. So I stood there, and wondered what he was about. And then I knew."

"Knew? Knew what?"

"He was putting water out for the hounds to drink. Because he knew they were coming."

He felt a coldness between his shoulders. As if something evil had come up behind him and laid a hand on his back.

"Do the Gabriel hounds have a human face? Have you ever seen it?"

"I told you. Miss Olivia warned me to have naught to do with them!"

"Yes, I understand that. But Miss Olivia is dead. I think the hounds killed her. I think now she'd want you to be the one to tell me his name. Or how he looked. I think it's time to make them pay for the harm they've done."

She shook her head. "You can't make the hounds pay for killing. It's in their nature. It's part of their blood. Like the Turks."

"Was Mr. Nicholas baptized?"

"Aye, at the Hall, because he was sickly at first. Jaundice. And there was a storm coming that promised to be a bad one. Miss Rosamund said she'd not risk him driving in the carriage, nor in the drafty church. Truth to tell, he was better within the week, but she insisted, and the old rector came to the Hall."

Did a baptism in the Hall count for less in her eyes than one in the church? She was leading him round in circles.

But Hamish, Highland bred, understood better what was being said, and rumbled with uneasiness beneath the surface of his mind.

"The face of the hounds. You said you could tell me, now that Miss Olivia is dead." Rutledge added, "Safely dead."

Her eyes were clouding over, and she said querulously, "*You* said it, I didn't."

After a time he left her there, and walked back to the village. On impulse he stopped at the church. The heavy west door was locked, but the smaller one in the porch was not. He lifted the latch and walked inside. There was a chill in the place, the stone cold as death. He stood for a moment looking at the architecture, the style of the arches, the strength of the pillars, the tall nave that bowed before a shorter, older choir. It was a very fine church, but not distinguished. Its proportions made it fall just short of perfection. The carvings, unlike the angel in the churchyard, were heavier, earthier, more formidable and less delicate, like some of those he'd seen in Normandy.

He walked down the central aisle, looking back over his shoulder at the Victorian organ in the loft, then towards the stone altar that was rather handsomely carved, as if it had come from an old monastery. The choir was plain, the stalls of dark oak, and off to its left was an octagonal chapel dedicated to the Trevelyan family dead.

There was a knight in the far shadows, old and worn, and memorials set into the walls for the dead lying in the crypt below. A very beautiful marble sarcophagus, made for two, held the remains of Rosamund Trevelyan's parents. Weeping figures at each corner, veiled and bent, must have been carved to represent earthly mourning. Above the tomb, where the arches entwined in perpendicular harmony, a cherub with a trumpet floated among voluptuous robes. To one side was a smaller tomb carved from what appeared to be a solid block of alabaster, with a delicate tracery of flowers and birds more like a wedding bower than a place of burial. A figure on the top was barely visible in its shroud, the body seeming to melt into the marble earth almost as it touched. But at the head, the shroud was opened to show a woman's features with curling strands of hair escaping to frame them, as if holding back death. It was Rosamund, he realized as he looked down into her face.

There was beauty and strength, dignity and love there. Warmth. A woman who had much to give in her own right, and in the arms of her family. A woman who had lost three husbands and two of her children, but never faltered, a veritable pillar of life even in death.

He touched the cold marble cheek, and almost swore he could feel its own warmth against his hand. But it was an illusion, and he knew it.

On the wall to his left were several family memorials. The one for Stephen, set between his father's and a slender pillar that supported the chapel, was inscribed with his name, dates, the Trevelyan and FitzHugh coats of arms, and his rank and regiment in the war. And in the back, their newness brightening the darkness there, were two blocks of black marble, side by side. Incised in them were, simply, the names and the dates of the dead. Olivia and Nicholas. Plain, for suicides.

For a moment he stood looking at them, wishing he could reach the living people they had been. But it was too late for that, except in Olivia's poetry. Extending his arm, he again laid his palm against the marble, seeing its reflection against the lettering as if in a black mirror. The long fingers, the strong palm. His hand, no one else's.

"Was it you, Olivia? Or Nicholas," he asked aloud.

". . . Nicholas . . ." the echo repeated softly.

"And you are free of guilt."

". . . free of guilt . . ." it replied.

"Who was your lover? Was it Cormac?"

The echo caught the question in his voice as it responded.

". . . Cormac . . . ?"

"And who is the Hound of Gabriel?"

". . . rial . . . ?"

"Do you know? If so, where will I find the answer?"

". . . answer . . ."

"Is it in your papers—or your poetry?"

". . . poetry . . ."

He stepped across the small space to where he could touch Nicholas' memorial, ignoring the forcefulness of Hamish's voice, calling it witchcraft to question the dead, warning him not to meddle in such matters, to leave it be.

"I talk to you. How is that so different!" he retorted in his mind.

After a moment he asked the shining black face of Nicholas' marker, "Were you the killer Olivia protected?"

But in that single step he'd shifted the odd acoustics of the chapel and there was no echo to answer him. Only the sound of his own breathing. As if even in death Nicholas knew how to hold his peace.

20

$\mathcal{B}$ack at the inn Rutledge ate a fast meal in one corner of the dining room, an old book he'd found in the parlor propped in front of him to ward off conversation from either Trask or any other diners. But it was still early, and he had the place to himself. Asking for another pot of coffee and a cup, he went up to his own room to open the books of poetry again.

They seemed to raise more questions than they answered, but he thought it might be his own frame of mind raising doubts, not the lines he read over and over.

The last volume, *Lucifer,* had very little of the lyricism of Keats, and more of the strength of Milton. The writer was coming into maturity, looking at life and death as if they were the same, a coming from darkness and a returning to it, a brief, bright, glorious span that was often marred by man's own incapacity to learn and trust.

He found the poem that had disturbed Inspector Harvey, and read it first. What Harvey hadn't remembered was the title. It was, oddly enough, "The Failure." Rutledge thought about that for a time, then moved on.

The poem about Eve seemed on the surface to answer the question of the tree of knowledge, from which she'd taken the apple.

Eating it had opened her eyes to the realities of life and cost her the Garden of Eden.

But looking at it not as verse, instead as the experience of a young girl faced suddenly and shockingly with the death of a loved one— her own twin—Rutledge saw something else. Something he'd have missed if he hadn't delved so deeply into the history of the Trevelyan family. Eve was Olivia, tasting of the knowledge that evil existed, and struggling to understand it, to find a place for it in her small, comfortable, once-safe childhood world. Losing her own Garden of Eden. Watching helplessly as the serpent twined itself into the branches and plucked the apple. But it was Anne who had fallen, and the last lines proved it to him.

> The apple was one I knew, had loved, and would not wish
> to fall—
> It was myself, my other self, and terrified, my soul denied
> it all.

Denying that murder had taken place? Refusing to believe in it?

But then Anne's death was the first to happen. And they were all children at the time. Whatever Olivia might have seen, whatever she might have understood—or feared—murder was not a reality she was ready for. Cruelty, perhaps, she'd comprehend that, because children are capable of great cruelty. A knowledge of murder would come afterward. Meanwhile, Olivia had lived with silent, terrified grief.

He sat there, forgetting to watch the sunset, forgetting the coffee growing cold in his cup, his mind focused on the finely printed words on the richly watermarked page. Then after a time he moved on again.

Several pages later, when he had nearly convinced himself that the interpretation he'd given to "Eve" was subjective, not objective, he found the next movement in a symphony of pain and grief.

The title was "The Prodigal Son," and it seemed to capture the story of the youngest son who left home, taking his share of his inheritance with him, leaving older brothers to support their aging father. But life had not been kind to him, and he returned a failure, expecting to be a slave in his father's holdings, only to be treated like the lost and golden boy he'd been.

Richard.

It could be no one else. Richard—still alive? No, that was impossible! But still a threat to his brothers, because his body hadn't been found. They would be left to wonder what had become of him. To wonder if he might someday come home in truth.

Rutledge thought about that.

The second murder.

There had been a long and intense search for the boy. No sign of him had been found. Flyers and posters had been sent out, gypsies and tramps questioned, farms fringing the moors turned inside out. He himself, reading over the reports and the final verdict, had believed that the killer had hidden the corpse—no body, no evidence of foul play. But, what if that was all wrong?

What if murder had been made to look like an accident? A drowning, a fall, a boy's game of hide and seek that had tragically pitched him headfirst into a mine shaft? Knocked down and trampled by wild ponies? There were any number of possibilities. Then consider—

Someone else had found the body—not a search party of half a dozen men, but one person. Who might well have known for other reasons—or guessed—who was behind this carefully arranged scene. And who might have decided that Richard's death—irreversible in itself—might still be a threat to his murderer. Gathering up the corpse, carrying it away in the night while the searchers were occupied on the moor, taking it where it might never be discovered, someone had altered the murderer's design. Left a question mark in his mind, a doubt, a worry. And later, near where the body had been lying, the *clothes* had been buried. In case the murderer came back to search on his own for the child that the searchers *ought* to have found . . .

Hamish was busy picking the concept to pieces, but Rutledge ignored him. You couldn't bury Richard in the church or the churchyard. Any digging or movement of stones there would have been suspect. Nor at the Hall. There were gardeners—they would have seen the first signs of a grave large enough to hold a five-year-old. Most of the villagers had gardens too, digging in them every season, turning them over, disturbing the soil. The wood then? No, it was too close to the Hall, within sight and sound of the village as well. The sea? It sometimes failed to give up its secrets, and other times, it brought them back to shore. All right, none of the obvious choices, then. But somewhere safe . . . for the boy as well as the person who'd moved him . . .

Who could be trusted to keep such a dark and horrible secret?

Someone who might not know what it was . . .

Rutledge got up and went to the wardrobe. He'd brought a heavy sweater with him, dark wool—with dark trousers he was nearly invisible in the night. And there was an entrenching tool in the boot of his car. Changing quickly, he shut the door of his room and went downstairs. No one was around, though he could hear voices from the back, by the kitchens. Letting himself out the front door, he went around to his car, found the small shovel, and set off on his macabre errand.

He'd learned, in the war, to move silently in the darkness. Snipers, trip wires, booby traps, mines—every step might bring sudden death. Where you put your feet and how decided whether you came back safely and unseen, or not at all. And so he walked with stealth and care, leaving the village, circling well out of his way, letting the starlight and his own sense of direction guide him. After half an hour he came to the small cottage half-nestled, half-crouched in its narrow valley. There was lamplight at one of the windows, and he stood in the shadows of the hillside, waiting and listening.

Women like Sadie sometimes had a sixth sense. And the cat she kept would hear him if she didn't. The lift of its head, the twitching ears, the eyes narrowed and still—it was as good as any alarm.

After a time, moving with extreme care, the wind blowing towards him to carry both scent and sound away, he searched the gardens.

When he'd asked whether or not she grew pansies, Sadie had answered that they didn't dry well. That was probably true. But he'd taken it to mean that she didn't have any of the plants in her garden. And that had been his mistake.

How much did the old woman know?

Or, perhaps more to the point, *how much had she known?* She hadn't always been senile . . . there might have been a time when she was a willing party to what was happening. But just as it was impossible to turn back the clock, it was nearly impossible to lift the veil in that old and tired brain.

Well, then, make some assumptions. Could Richard have been brought here without in any way involving Sadie?

If the boy had been buried here, could Sadie have been told that a small patch of pansies set apart from her own flowers was a reminder of a brother lost, a private place to grieve? Possible, yes. Likely, no. On the other hand, she might have pretended to believe. And whatever suspicions she might have harbored deep in her unsettled mind, she'd have kept them to herself. It all came down to how much she understood about the killings at the Hall. And whether she knew the face of a murderer.

He made each step with minute attention to the ground, so as not to leave prints in the earth or crushed blossoms in his wake, his eyes roving this way and then that. Not near the cottage, no, and not where the herbs and flowers grew best. Not where heavy rains might wash the bones out, nor where the boy wouldn't be under the eye of his mentally frail and possibly unwitting guardian. And disguised, somehow, the kind of place that wouldn't draw attention to itself or tempt anyone to rearrange it.

And he found it on the hillside, just where a small natural outcropping formed the anchor of an asymmetrical rock garden. It was no more than a few feet wide in any direction, yet large enough for a child's curled body. A spill of unusual white stones brought from somewhere else lay like a small river tucked in among the flowers. Pansies, and some sort of small, narrow leafed things that formed a mat. Plants that would reseed themselves, half tame, half wild, clinging among the stones and holding the earth with their roots.

He squatted there in the darkness, studying the rock garden.

Very simple, not the sort of thing that would catch the eye of a casual observer, a little patch of color above an outcropping that lent itself to this one use only, wild and half-neglected, unimportant and oddly touching.

There was the sound of a door opening, and he froze, keeping his silhouette low and dark against the greater darkness of the hillside.

Sadie stood for a moment, a hunched figure against the lamplight behind her, in the open doorway. Rutledge could feel her eyes on him, although he knew she couldn't possibly see him where he was.

"Who's there?" she called. After a moment, she went on, "Have you come for me?"

His mouth tightened in anger at himself for disturbing her, giving her a fright. It had been the last thing he'd wanted.

"But she has a sixth sense," Hamish reminded him.

"I'm going to bed," she said, when Rutledge didn't answer her. "Come again in the light, if you have honest business here."

He was very close to standing up and identifying himself. But she shut the door again, and in a minute or two more, the lamp was snuffed out.

His legs were stiff from squatting, but he waited for a little longer, then turned his attention back to the garden.

If the body had been hidden here, how much would be found now? The long bones, perhaps, the jaw. Kneeling, feeling the night's damp soaking into his trousers, he lifted a few of the stones very carefully from their bed and touched the soil beneath. His fingers worked down into it, among the plant roots and the friable earth, spreading and probing. There were no tree roots here, on the hillside. If there had been a body in this ground, *some* trace would remain to a trained eye. He mustn't disturb it too much.

It was useless to dig. In the dark. Leaving behind signs of his presence. Wait until later, and let the experts—

His fingers struck something rough and hard. In spite of himself, a coldness swept over him even though common sense told him he couldn't have found bone at this shallow depth. And not the boy's bones.

Someone had been here before him, lifting the rocks in the center just as he'd done, loosening the soil. He should have realized that as soon as he touched the earth—it would have made sense if he'd had his wits about him.

Working carefully, winkling it and using his other hand to clear a little space here, a little there, he very soon had the long slender length of wood out of its hiding place.

A carving. No, something else, the sides were too smooth.

He let his fingers gently feel the thing in his hand. It was not old wood—he knew the texture of that. They'd used and reused whatever lumber came to hand in the trenches, scavenged for boardwalks to keep their feet dry above the filth, for shelter from the rain, for a place out of the hot sun or the cold wind. On the Somme the generals had forbidden even such simple, rough comforts, while the Germans had lived in tunnels they'd efficiently dug deep in the earth. No, this wood was hard and firm and new to the ground it had been buried in. Three sides were smooth as sanding could make them. The fourth had something cut into it. Deeply incised, and at midlength. Like a blind man he worked at the shapes, slowly letting his sense of touch and not his eyes tell him what was there. There was a flow to the shapes, but they were separate. Letters, then.

R, yes, most certainly an R. Then a space before the next. A. Next to that an E, he thought. No, he was wrong. H. And the very last, C.

He thought back to the photographs he'd been given by Rachel Marlowe, and the names on the reverse. Richard Allen Harris Cheney.

Nicholas had left his calling card. And not very long ago . . .

21

$\mathcal{R}$utledge put everything back exactly as he'd found it, brushing the pansy leaves clean of any bits of earth, using his hands to smooth and press the disturbed earth. Then he got to his feet and thought about what he'd done, whether he'd left any task undone. Then he remembered the entrenching tool, and groped for that.

With the same care he'd exercised coming here he made his way out of the valley and back to the inn, returning the tool to its place in the car before going upstairs again to his room. Looking down at his shoes, he grimaced. The caked mud reminded him of the trenches. Taking them off, he set them outside his door for the boot boy.

Washing his hands well, then blotting the worst of the dew out of his trouser knees, he went back to his earlier task. The poems.

It was in some ways quite unnerving to put the pieces of the puzzle together. Like working out the obituaries of people he knew. But Olivia seldom failed him once he learned the technique of what she had tried to do. All the members of her family were here, cleverly disguised by the allegorical themes she'd chosen for each. Sometimes, like "Eve," they were given biblical names, at others wrapped in Cornish legends, or cloaked in bits of well-known history—whatever fit her purpose, but always with such artistry that the mask itself had a life and drama of its own. He marveled again at such talent, and the tragedy of its loss. She had barely reached her prime . . .

Of course she wasn't the first to use poetry as a vehicle for her own designs. Poets—Swift and Wordsworth were the first names he thought of—had employed their pens to mock political figures or make literary allusions to famous events or writers. Some employed satire and a vicious humor to bring down governments or ruin reputations and careers. But to his knowledge this was the first time one had grimly catalogued a murderer's career.

"Bathsheba," the faithful wife whose husband had been placed in the forefront of battle because King David desired her, had become Rosamund. Olivia described her as an unwitting pawn of a cruel and passionate man who wanted her at any price, and took from her the mainstay of her life, the kind and thoughtful husband who had filled her with happiness. James Cheney? Or Brian FitzHugh? Which had been killed because he was Rosamund's husband?

No, Rutledge told himself, from the description it had to be Cheney, the kind and thoughtful man who'd replaced the dashing soldier.

The hidden depths of feeling in the lines, the understanding of love and lust, gave them a soaring beauty that worked at any level, but it was also a devastating portrait of a killer scheming to have what he wanted most, at any price.

He went on, skimming again, looking for something, missing it at first glance, then turning back again to see.

It was a short poem. Two men standing at the water's edge argued over possession of the land that stretched out behind them, rich and fallow in the sun. Anger turned to blows, and one was killed. To that point the lines seemed to follow the death of Brian FitzHugh, and then it took an odd twist as the killer stared down at the bleeding body. "My hand it was that gave you this, Mine that takes it from you!" And the dying man answers, "Was it so— was it yours to give? I'm glad I never knew."

Nicholas? Somehow Rutledge couldn't quite see that parallel.

What could Nicholas have given and taken away again from Brian FitzHugh? He reread the poem, and shook his head. Be patient, man! he told himself. Olivia knew the answer to that—she'd leave it for him somewhere if not here.

Hamish, in the back of his mind, was more or less agreeing with Harvey about women penning such lines. "A tormented soul—" he began.

"Yes. And a damned brave one," Rutledge retorted.

Later there was a reference to a man passing through a wood, finding Death waiting for him there, and facing it with courage and disdain. Death struck, and laughed. The man managed to break away, but felt no sense of victory, only of postponement.

For Death could come again, and it was not what he
    desired . . .
Not yet, with so much of life in his grasp.

So much of life . . . and yet Nicholas had chosen suicide.

Rutledge was tired, his eyes burning, his head spinning from the effort he was making to follow the remarkable thread set out for him. To sort through Olivia's allusions, to find the bedrock of accusation beneath. And yet he felt he was missing something. What was behind what Olivia was trying to tell him? She hadn't written a great body of poetry just as a memorial to her family's suffering. Or just as a record for any astute policeman who might stumble over the evidence she'd documented in it. It was a warning. A very public forum of denunciation, but to what end? She must have said. Somewhere . . .

Then where had he, Rutledge, gone astray? Surely it wasn't just his own stubborn insistence on closure, surely Olivia would have wanted that too. Then why hadn't he seen it? What didn't he know about the Trevelyan family that might have guided him now?

Another poem to Rosamund was moving, a tribute that made his eyes sting with tears as it spoke of her life, her loves, her deep belief that she could find peace for herself and her family.

And the last line left him chilled.

"When he couldn't have her, the hound of Hell destroyed her."

They were all there. Anne, Richard, Rosamund, James, Brian. All of them. Except the last pair to die . . .

He went through the book again, searching. Finding nothing. And then he saw something unexpected. It was in a poem—on the surface—about Rome, and two small children suckled by a wolf. Romulus and Remus, who grew up to found a great city. Only this was not a city, this was a tower of the heart. He's missed it, confused by the legend. Mistakenly taking the wolf literally, as an animal and not as a childhood nightmare of death and fear that drove two people to a strange and tender interdependence.

*I have loved, and he has listened, both have given holy
    grace.
In his eyes I saw my soul, then found my life in his
    embrace . . .*

Unexpected—and enlightening. If it was true, it explained so much.

But it was only half of the final answer. He was sure of it now.

It was well after three o'clock—he'd heard the church clock strike the hours since midnight, and felt time passing like a heavy burden. His mind was worn and his spirits had sunk like a stone, the earlier enthusiasm already attacked by doubt. Writers often used their own experience for inspiration. Was that all she'd done? Had he counted too much on her, wishing his own need into her words?

No, that was all wrong, all wrong. He just hadn't learned to see it in the right way yet. With exhaustion nagging at him, caught in the tumult of his own depression and Hamish's prodding, he'd failed *her*. Not the other way around.

He rubbed his eyes, then got up and washed his face in the cold water from the pitcher. The coffee was even colder, but he forced himself to drink it, and then stretching his shoulders as he'd done a thousand times on night watches in the war, he finally sat back down again. Giving up was defeat. And by God, he wasn't going to face the shaving mirror in the morning with excuses and evasions.

He'd start all over again, if he had to. At the beginning if that's what it took to cudgel his wits into action.

"There're still the papers," Hamish reminded him. "If ye're half the detective ye think ye are, you'd have found them by now."

The finest moment in the final volume was "Lucifer," the centerpiece of the book, a description of the great and glorious prince whose ambition reached too far. To Milton he'd been the archangel who had dared to envy God, finally to be disgraced and hurled, headlong and flaming, into the pit of Hell to reign over the damned.

To Olivia Marlowe, he'd been the dark angel of death.

Rutledge read the lines again, and this time the image created by the words took shape in his mind.

The dark angel. Beyond her power to control, beyond her power to condemn. Beyond her power, nearly, to understand.

But not an *angel*, not an allegory of Death. A *man*.

Clever, unemotional, his own law. Resolute, fearless. Without compassion. And immutable. However long it took, however dangerous it was, however destructive, he got what he desired.

A man who was neither good nor evil, merely unbound by the constraints of humanity or God. A glittering archangel, perhaps, but without a soul. And yet, like Lucifer, filled with envy and the need to possess what to him was omnipotence. Only, his heaven had been earthbound.

A Gabriel Hound, the old woman called him, heathen.

It was a chilling portrait, and it was the most truly devastating study of cold, hard ego, of a core of being without light or grace, that he'd ever seen.

By the time Rutledge had finished the poem the last time, he felt an exaltation in his blood that had nothing to do with poetry or Olivia Marlowe, and everything to do with the great courage of O. A. Manning.

He knew now the name and face of the Gabriel Hound. Proving it was going to be very dangerous. And Rachel would be brought to tears if he succeeded.

22

Rutledge found it hard to sleep, and Hamish, ever vigilant for an opening, was there in his mind, critical, disagreeing, ridiculing, citing all the objections to his arguments.

Pointing out over and over again—

"You havena' found a *why*. You havena' got the reason!"

"I don't need reasons. Leave that to the lawyers—"

"Lawyers are no' policemen, they'll twist the truth until it's lost!"

"All I need is proof, and Olivia gave me that—"

"Proof, is it? A muckle of lines, that's what ye've got! Would ye stand and recite in yon courtroom, while your fine jury nods in their seats and yon judge begs you to get on with it before he declares a mistrial? Och, man, it's no' a *case*, it's professional suicide!"

"What about her papers? You've reminded me of them yourself. You must have thought they were important when you did."

"They're gone, man, face it. Ye havena' found them, and never will."

"Nicholas wouldn't have destroyed those out on the headland, she wouldn't have let him! Cormac might have, if he found them first, before the lawyers and Stephen got there. But somehow I don't think he did find them. I think he's been looking as hard as I have. I can't believe he wants anyone to know the truth about what happened between him and Olivia. Before I'm finished, I'll find those bloody papers!"

"Oh, aye, we're back again to a dead woman's poems! A dead woman's papers! What you need is a live killer. And a confession. A witness to confront him! *And there's no' any hope of finding those.*"

"No," Rutledge retorted bitterly. "But I'm not beaten yet."

He rose at five o'clock, his head feeling stuffed with cotton wool from an hour's heavy sleep at the very end. Shaving with cold water, he dressed and hurried down the back stairs, startling the elderly scullery maid setting out the crocks of butter and putting the new-baked bread into cloths in a basket in the kitchen.

"*Lord, sir!* You gave me such a fright!" she cried, looking up at him and then burning her fingers on a hot loaf of bread, nearly dropping it. "Was it coffee you were wanting, sir? It's not been put on yet."

"Is there someone here who can carry a note over to Mrs. Otley's house for me?"

Her eyebrows flew up. "A note! At *this* hour, sir? Surely not!"

"As soon as may be," he said testily.

"There's the boy taking out the ashes—"

"He'll do." He was already writing several lines on a sheet from his notebook, frowning as he worded it to his satisfaction, then ripping it out to fold and address on the outside. "Bring him here."

She went to fetch the boy, looking at Rutledge over her shoulder as if he'd lost his wits. The sleepy child, no more than nine or ten, took the note, opened his eyes wider at the sight of the sixpence in Rutledge's hand, and paid close heed to his instructions.

Then he was off.

Rutledge followed him out of the kitchen and down the hall, watched him drag open the inn door and set off through the early mists up the hill towards the Otley cottage.

It was ten minutes before he was back, breathless and red-faced, but smiling.

246

"She wasn't that happy with me, sir, for waking her. She said I was to tell you that, and say that I'd earned a *shilling* for the trouble it took to bring Mrs. Otley to the door."

It was highway robbery, but Rutledge handed over a shilling, and the boy went dashing back down the passage towards the kitchens.

Rachel's reply was hardly more than a scrawl. "If you haven't run mad, you soon will. But if this is what it takes to send you back to London, I'll do it."

Grinning, he stuffed the paper into his pocket and went around to the back of the inn where his motorcar was parked in one of the disused sheds.

Within five minutes he was driving up to Mrs. Otley's cottage, the sound of the car loud in the street, and down near the wood someone's dog was barking in savage displeasure at the racket. The dog the rector had warned him of? You could hear the damned thing all over Borcombe!

Rachel came down the cottage steps ten minutes later, dressed in a dark coat and a hat she'd tied down with a scarf.

Rutledge got out and held the door for her. "Are you sure you can drive this automobile?"

She looked at him in disgust. "Of course I can. Probably better than you do, on these roads. I know them, you don't."

"And you'll tell Susannah that if she'll grant this one wish, I'll be leaving for London as soon as I've tied up all the loose ends?"

"Yes, but I still don't see why you need something like this. It's the silliest thing I've ever heard of!"

"You'll understand. Afterward. It will save *days* of work. Trust me."

"I've seen spiders I trust more," she said tartly, and stepped into the driver's seat. "If you cause Susannah any pain, any grief—if she has a miscarriage because of you—"

"She won't. What I'm about to do will give her peace of mind."

"Learning that her half sister was a murderess? Oh, yes, I call that quite soothing for a woman in her condition." She turned and looked at Rutledge, a long, earnest look that seemed to probe beneath his skin and into his very brain.

"Are you sure you know what you're doing? Are you quite sure?" she asked quietly, her face sober and very worried.

He reached out and touched her hand as it rested on the wheel. "I can only tell you that what I'm doing will be for the best. If there was murder done, it ought to be known, and the past put to rest. There ought to be justice, for the dead, if no one else."

"The dead are dead. It's the living I'm worried about now. And—and Nicholas."

"No one can touch Nicholas," he said gently. "Not now. Not ever again. You know that better than I do."

"I won't let you destroy his memory, Inspector Rutledge. I won't let you. If you do try, I'll find a way to put it right. Whatever I have to do, I will do. Believe that."

He felt cold in the early morning breeze, in spite of his coat.

"I can't hurt Nicholas," he said again. "He's dead, Rachel. You have to accept it, and what it means. He left you, he chose to die with Olivia, not to live with you." He could see the flare of pain in her eyes, and ignored it. "That's what he told you in his last letter. He didn't want you."

Her mouth tightened. "I wanted him," she said quite simply. "Now start this damned thing or I'll not go at all, not even for Susannah's sake!"

He shut the door, walked around, and bent down to turn the crank. He could sense her watching, he knew what was in her mind. As the engine roared into life again and he stepped back, the crank in his hand, she looked straight at him over the bonnet of the car. "Leave Cormac out of this," he said, coming around the wing towards her. "Don't send for him. It's between Olivia and Nicholas, you and me. He's not a Trevelyan. Don't send for him, he'll just make matters worse."

"No one could make them worse. Except you."

She took off the brake, let in the gear and the car moved briskly off down the road. She didn't look back. He watched her handle the car around the curve, his mind on her driving, judging whether he'd made the right decision to send her. But there was no one else who could have persuaded Susannah.

248

Hamish, lurking in the shadows, said only, "Play with witch-craft, and you'll burn yourself."

"It isn't witchcraft," Rutledge answered harshly. "It's the only way I can think of to get at the truth!"

There was an echo of the engine from the narrow hedgerows, although the car had long since vanished to sight. Rutledge started to turn back towards the inn, then looked up to find Mary Otley watching him from the doorway of the cottage.

"You haven't put her in harm's way, have you, sir?" she asked.

"No. With any luck, I've put her out of it," he answered, and walked back to the inn for his breakfast.

"The constable's still at his breakfast, sir," Mrs. Dawlish said, opening her front door to the Inspector from London.

"I'll just come through and have a word with him in the kitchen," he said, gently pushing the door wider. "If you don't mind."

She did, but was too polite to say so, though he could read her face clearly enough.

The constable stood up hastily, napkin still stuck under his chin, as Rutledge came down the passage and turned into the kitchen. It was a large room, with windows on two sides and a door into the back passage at the rear, next to the great polished black stove. A table with the remains of breakfast and an unexpectedly bright bowl of zinnias stood in the very middle of the room. A vast Cornish dresser took up most of one wall, the pantry through a door beyond, and against the other wall the smaller, scraped wood top of the cooking table shone in the light from the east. The curtains at the windows, the pattern on the tablecloth, and the walls themselves were all a summer blue, as if somehow to bring the color of the sea into the house.

"Sir!" he said in alarm.

"It's all right, Dawlish. I've just come to tell you that you can call off the search on the moors. This morning."

The man's face brightened. "Then you've given it up, sir? All this nonsense about the Trevelyan family? You're going back to London?"

"There are some loose ends to tie up. Some statements I'll need, to cover the questions I seem to have raised. You won't mind helping with those?"

"No, sir, not in the least," Dawlish said expansively, willing to do cartwheels if it got rid of the inconvenient man from London and put Inspector Harvey into a pleasanter mood. "Whatever you wish, I'll be happy to help."

Rutledge smiled, but it didn't reach his eyes, and for an instant Dawlish was filled with a new uncertainty. But he brushed it aside as Rutledge said, "I'll be back in two hours with a list of names. I don't want you to tell anyone else who is on that list. Do you understand me? You'll send for these people one at a time, exactly as you're told to do, and you'll have them write their statements for me exactly in the order I'll give you, and in the circumstances I describe. It may seem strange to you, but I think in the end you'll see what I'm driving at. There will be a specific list of questions for each interview. And I want you to ask them exactly as written. Change them in any way, and I'll have it all to do over again. It will only take longer. Do you understand me?"

Dawlish didn't, and Rutledge knew he didn't. But Dawlish nodded, and Rutledge turned to go.

"Two hours. Be here when I come. And don't forget the men on the moors."

"Not bloody likely!" Dawlish answered to himself as Rutledge turned and walked out of the sunny, blue kitchen.

Working fast and steadily, Rutledge made his lists, his mind tied up with the complexity of details, setting them out with precision. He had always been good at organizing his thoughts, at creating a picture of events from start to finish. And this time the facts were there. No gaps, no guesses. No room for doubt. No room for Hamish to creep in and haunt him. But Hamish was there, still debating the wisdom of what lay ahead, a stir in the silence.

Trask came up with a telegram for Rutledge, and he opened it reluctantly, knowing it came from London, knowing it was from Bowles.

It read, "If you aren't doing your job, you're needed here. If there's something happening, I want to know about it."

250

"No answer," Rutledge told Trask, and went back to what he was writing.

Explaining to Bowles would be the same as emptying the Sahara with a teacup. There was not enough time for it. Not today. Tomorrow might be different.

Finally he sat back and looked at the sheets of paper on his desk.

How weak was the evidence?

Damned weak at the moment.

Without statements, without the voices of people and their written words, evidence was always thin.

And yet, it was there. It was *there*. Waiting to be culled.

He felt satisfied.

Rachel had driven straight to the Hall and left the car there before walking back into the village. She came into the inn as Rutledge ran lightly down the stairs, and he knew the instant he saw her face that he'd got what he wanted.

"You'll have to get it out of the car yourself. Susannah says if you damage the frame at all, she'll have you up before the courts. It took two grooms to load it safely."

"Thank you!" he said, smiling, and she felt a deep sense of foreboding as she watched it light his eyes. He seemed to have lost five years over night, a man who had changed so much that she was afraid.

And then the smile was gone, and with it the strangeness. He was himself again, the thin face, the lines. The bone-tiredness. But she thought that that might have been a sleepless night, not the weariness he'd seemed to bring from London with him.

Rachel opened her mouth to say something, then decided against it. "Come on, then," she said instead. "It shouldn't be sitting out there in the sun."

They walked in silence to the house, and Rutledge was grateful for it, for the lack of questions in spite of the doubts that he knew were seething just below the surface in the woman at his side.

She was spirited. She'd have made someone a very good wife. But not for Peter, who had valued his peace. In the long run, Rachel would have needed more than a book-filled house in the country and quiet evenings by the fire discussing Roman ruins. And not for Nicholas. Because the Nicholas she'd seen and loved was a figment, a falsehood built on lies that he couldn't do anything about. The man who cared for Rachel, the man who'd done his best to send her away, was there inside, but for reasons Rachel herself would never willingly grasp.

Rachel's tragedy, he thought, as they came out of the woods and turned up the drive towards the house, was that love had seemed so real and so possible because she had wanted it too much.

Just as he had wanted to believe Jean loved him as deeply as he believed he'd loved her. Jean, who hadn't had very much courage, who turned from him because she couldn't accept any other dream but the shiny, perfect one that had been shattered in 1914. Four years of war hadn't changed her. And it had changed him—their lives—beyond recognition. Had he wanted her so much because he'd thought she could restore what was gone? Or had it really been love? He didn't know any more.

"Which may be an answer of sorts," Hamish reminded him.

In the back of the car, now sitting below the steps at the front door of the Hall, was a large object wrapped in heavy brown paper.

It took him fifteen minutes, with Rachel offering unsolicited advice, to gently dislodge it from its cocoon of surrounding blankets and cushions, then lift it out onto the drive. Between them they got the package up the steps and then, unlocking the door, into the hall and across it to the drawing room.

Another fifteen to find a small ladder and carry it there too. But in the end, stepping back to see the results, he was satisfied.

Rosamund Trevelyan smiled benignly down from her proper place above the hearth, her face turned slightly, her cheek smooth and creamy against the background of light, her eyes full of life and love and hope.

An extraordinary woman, mother of another extraordinary woman. As full of goodness and joy and beauty as the Gabriel hound had been full of darkness and destruction.

23

Rutledge was just returning from the kitchen, where he'd left the ladder, when the bell rang loudly in the emptiness of the house and brought Rachel, frowning, out of the drawing room.

"Who is that?" she demanded.

"Dawlish," he said, and opened the door to the constable, who had Mrs. Trepol at his heels. The elderly housekeeper was staring over his shoulder, her eyes moving nervously from Rachel to the London policeman.

Before Rachel could say anything more, Rutledge closed the fingers of his right hand around her arm to silence her, and nodded to Dawlish. "The drawing room. You'll see the chairs and a table. Use them where they are."

Uneasy and uncertain, Dawlish glanced at Rachel, but Rutledge cut short any query. "See to it, man!" And he led Rachel towards the stairs, his eyes commanding her to wait. Not here. Not now. Her mouth was tight with suspicion and anger, and she moved ahead of him with the stride of a woman biding her time with a vengeance. Behind them, Mrs. Trepol followed Dawlish into the hall, their steps sounding loud and uncertain as they moved towards the drawing room.

Once in the back sitting room overlooking the sea, Rachel

rounded on him in a fury. "What the *hell* do you think you're doing? I won't have it! This is wrong, this is *trickery!* Tell me what's going on, or by God, I'll find the nearest telephone and call London!"

"Look," he said earnestly, "I'm trying to get at the truth. Do you want me to walk away and leave this unfinished? I can't. What I think has been done here—if I'm right, mind you—has to be settled. Now. It can't be put off."

"What you think has been done!" she repeated. "But you haven't told anyone *what you think*, have you? Not me, not the rector, not Inspector Harvey—"

"I have told you. There have been a series of suspicious deaths starting with Anne—"

"Yes, yes! Olivia killed them, you say. Or Nicholas. Dead people who can't answer, can't defend themselves! Well, let me tell you what *I* think! While I was at the Beatons, I made a telephone call. To a friend of Peter's who knew you as well. He tells me that after the Armistice you spent months in a private clinic—a head injury, he said. Quite severe, he said, because you weren't allowed any visitors. Nurses told him that for a time you didn't even know who you were. Everyone was surprised when you returned to the Yard—they didn't think you were well enough, that you'd recovered sufficiently to take on stressful work. He's right, you aren't *capable* of carrying out your duties! That's why you aren't in London, looking for that man—that's why you were sent out to Cornwall, to get you safely out of the way, and why you're searching out old, imaginary murders. *You can't do any better!*"

Shocked by her vehemence, he turned away towards the windows, looking out at the sea, his back to her, his face hidden from her angry eyes.

"You sent for Scotland Yard," he reminded her for a last time. "If I'm mad, if I'm imagining the need for this investigation, then some of the blame must be yours." It was on the tip of his tongue to say more, and he caught himself in time, and added only, "I'm sorry, Rachel. More than you know."

His refusal to defend himself, the odd tone of his voice, brought her up short.

They were a woman's weapon, words. She'd deliberately wielded them to wound, to hurt him, to stop him. She'd telephoned Sandy MacArdle because he was a gossip, and she'd known he was a gossip, and she wanted the worst possible interpretation put on anything Ian Rutledge had done, to use that knowledge herself as savagely as she could.

And suddenly, she felt sick, ashamed. "Oh, Nicholas," she cried to herself with weary grief, "why did I have to love you so much!"

Rutledge still had his back to her, the set of his shoulders betraying his own pain, waiting for her to go on.

She found she couldn't.

"Why did you want the portrait?" she asked quietly, after a time.

He was watching the sea, but his eyes were blind to its beauty. Only the pain within him seemed real. And to his credit, he told her the truth.

"Because I can't close this investigation without taking statements from half the people in Borcombe. But you see, if I do that in the normal fashion, by the end of the day I'll have taken down whatever embroideries they've devised between them to shield themselves and Rosamund's family from scandal, and then we'll never get at the truth. Because they all know *bits* of that truth, Rachel, whether they realize it or not. And I need to bring it out cleanly, bare and unvarnished. It occurred to me that sitting in that formal drawing room where each of them will feel desperately ill at ease, and watched by the one woman they all revered both in life and in death, I won't get lies. I'll have facts. And before anyone in Borcombe has quite understood where what they're telling Constable Dawlish might be leading, the whole picture of murder and deception will be down in black and white. They can't turn around then and deny it. They can't pretend that they were misled or misinterpreted the questions. They'll have to accept it themselves. And come to terms with it, however they can. But that's the grievous cost of murder. We all pay it, along with the victims."

"What a very cruel thing to do." Her voice was harsh with disbelief, her brief episode of sympathy washed away. *He deserved to be savaged!*

He turned to face her again, his eyes sad. "It probably is cruel.

I'd thought long and hard about that myself. I didn't know what else to do. I could have told Harvey and these people what it is I'm after, but I don't think they'd have believed me any more than you have. And the wall they've all drawn around the Trevelyan family would only go higher."

"All this for a dead woman! For *Olivia!*"

"No, not for Olivia. For two small children who never lived to grow up. For James Cheney who died in despair, and Brian FitzHugh who trusted the wrong person, to his cost, and for Rosamund, who was driven to taking her own life to make it all stop. For Olivia, who gave up a quite incredible gift because something far more precious was threatened. And for Nicholas, who had spent a lifetime in her service, because he believed he failed her. For all I know, Stephen's death was a part of it all. He was searching for something just before his fall, and I think I now may know what it was. If he hadn't been late, if he hadn't been in such a damned hurry, he might not have gone headfirst down those stairs. He was, in a sense, a victim too."

"How very morally upright of you, to set the record straight. And will we have a wax effigy of Olivia in the dock, when you present your evidence to the jury?"

"No," he said tiredly. "We'll have a living person."

She stared at him, her mouth moving soundlessly, as if the words were there, but her voice had failed her.

24

There was a pounding at the front door, the sound traveling up the stairs like thunder, and Rutledge brushed past Rachel without a word, going out of the door and closing it behind him before crossing the hall to find Inspector Harvey waiting impatiently outside. Rather than ushering him into the house, Rutledge went out to stand in the bright sunlight beside him.

"I'm told my constable is here. That you ordered him to call off the search on the moors this morning. And that you've got him taking statements from witnesses in the Trevelyan Hall *drawing room*, rather than his office."

"Yes, I left a message for you, explaining. I'm returning to London—"

"So you said! And what use, pray, are these statements you've gone to such lengths to obtain?"

"To clear the record. It's what you wanted, isn't it?"

Not mollified at all, Harvey retorted, "Indeed. But I shouldn't have thought that interviewing the good citizens of Borcombe would serve any better purpose now than it did at the time of the suicides."

"You're absolutely right," Rutledge agreed, watching gulls wheeling over the shoreline. He chose his words with great care.

He needed Harvey's support, but not his suspicions. "They probably can't shed any further light on the deaths of Miss Marlowe and Nicholas Cheney. What I'm hoping they might do is give me sufficient understanding of Miss Marlowe's state of mind over the last few years. Family affairs were worrying her—at least I have reason to believe that may be true. It could explain why, in spite of her literary success, she felt she couldn't face living. Would you mind very much giving Dawlish an account of your discussion with her, about what makes a murderer?"

"I'd feel a fool! That was a private conversation between you and me, what I told you!"

"So it was. But if Miss Marlowe's mind was already dwelling on such matters when you came here as a police officer, such evidence might provide additional weight. I feel she carried . . . a sense of guilt, for want of a better word, about the misfortunes in her family. I found some confirmation of that in her poetry as well. Gifted imaginations are often sensitive and very impressionable. They sometimes see what we overlook."

Harvey looked searchingly at him.

"Are you having me on?" he demanded.

Rutledge's eyes came back from the sea to Harvey's face. Something in them made the other man wary. "I've never been more serious. Olivia Marlowe believed that there was a murderer loose in her family. She believed she knew the identity of the killer, and that she had proof of a sort. Of a sort, mind you. Not the kind of proof you and I might use to ask for an arrest warrant, perhaps, or that a good barrister couldn't make laughable in a courtroom. But she believed it. And she tried to document it as carefully as she could."

"That's—that's preposterous!" Harvey blustered, his neck brick red and the color rising fast. "I've never heard a more ridiculous fiction in all my years as a policeman! This is my country, I'd have known if there was murder done here. My predecessor would have known!"

"Precisely why," Rutledge responded, "I need these statements. I see no point in taking unsubstantiated rumors back to London. In my opinion we should set Olivia Marlowe's fears to rest once and for all. She was famous, and there will be biographers. They shouldn't be left to draw conclusions that might reflect badly on the police." He shrugged. "What may come of it is the truth. I can't think of anything fairer than that."

"That damned woman was a bother when she was alive, and worse now that she's dead," Harvey fumed, thinking over what Rutledge had said. And from the sound of it, Olivia Marlowe wasn't going to stay *quietly* dead. He hadn't reckoned on biographers trampling about his turf and prying into village business. Asking questions, raising doubts, stirring up people. He'd thought that was finished when the reporters had come to find out about O. A. Manning. The specter of an endless parade of troublemakers still to arrive was decidedly unsettling at best.

Rutledge watched the slow, careful progress of Harvey's mind as he considered the situation facing him. And then came to his decision.

Harvey had been told the truth. Not all of it, but the cold, hard kernel of truth that was the center of what Rutledge was doing. The rest would come when the facts were down on paper and irrefutable. When the warrant was required.

"Yes, well, I can understand what you're saying, that there'll be no peace for any of us. If the Home Office wanted this case reopened, we've already had the first round. Some newspaperman may get wind of it next, God forgive us, and we'll be on the front pages! And the academics will be the worst of the lot, reading whatever they damned well please into her verse, and turning Borcombe upside down to show they're right." He sighed. "Oh, very well. Do what you have to do. Just make what haste you can."

Harvey turned and walked off down the drive. Rutledge felt the tension in his shoulders begin to loosen and absently rubbed the back of his neck.

There was something more he wanted to do in the house, but Rachel was still there, and it was more important to avoid her now. The other matter could wait.

The day wore on, a long straggle of people coming to the house, the rector among them, giving their statements to Dawlish and then leaving again, strangely subdued. For a time Rutledge watched them from the headland, and he saw too that Harvey made his appearance in due course, then left shaking his head. Rutledge wondered whether Dawlish had told him more than he should have about the questions asked—and answers received. Reporting to his superior, that's how he'd have viewed it. Rutledge hoped he had not. Harvey's stubborn, straight mind might just make the right leap. Good policemen, clever or not, had a sense about some things. It didn't take imagination to learn from experience. The problem was, where would Harvey turn if he learned the truth? How would he use it? Hasty decisions had a way of wrecking a clean, tight investigation. And Harvey wanted to be seen as running his own territory, not following the lead of strangers from London.

By dinnertime Rutledge had collected the statements from the weary constable eager to get home to his wife. Then he went up the stairs two at a time, and carefully collected the small gold articles from Olivia's closet. For a moment he held them in the palm of his hand, where they shone with soft beauty, as if innocent of blood and death.

As they were, in themselves, he thought sadly.

Downstairs he took one last long look at Rosamund's portrait, silently apologizing for what he'd caused to be done in her drawing room that day. She stared back at him in silence, a faraway look in her eyes.

He walked back towards the village alone, his mind busy.

Sadie hadn't come, Dawlish reported, though Dr. Penrith, walking slowly on his daughter's arm, had arrived at the Hall at the time set for him. And Wilkins, and Mary Otley. Later someone would have to interview Susannah and her husband, and Tom Chambers, the solicitor. Rutledge himself had questioned Dawlish at the end of the day, writing down his answers without looking up at the man's accusing eyes.

The constable was an intelligent man, he could think through what he had spent the long day doing. But how far had he gotten in putting the pieces of the puzzle together? Far enough to wonder, Rutledge thought, but not quite far enough to know the whole . . .

Passing through the woods, Rutledge considered the problem of Sadie. Did she know what a sworn statement was?

He would have to go to her, then, and hope her mind was clear.

As he passed the Otley cottage he could see someone standing in the shadow by the door. Rachel, watching him. He could feel her eyes, the intensity of emotions, the uncertainty. But she stayed where she was, and he wondered what was going through her mind. What she would do now. Or if she would wait. Women often thought along different lines. Where a man saw duty, women were more concerned with emotions, feelings. He'd learned early on that a policeman ignored such differences at his peril.

Rutledge was just beside the Trepol gate when the housekeeper stepped out her door and called to him.

"Inspector Rutledge?"

He opened the gate and went up the walk where he would be out of earshot of Rachel. If Mrs. Trepol had questions about the statement she'd given, it was better not to broadcast them.

When he reached her, she acknowledged him with a nod and then said, "You'll be wanting me to clean up after all those feet tracking dirt into the hall and the drawing room?"

"It would be kind of you," he said. "Yes, thank you."

"Miss Rosamund would never have allowed it," she said, resigned to what she must have considered little short of desecration. One did not invite half the village in to sit in a fine chair under the best portrait in the house, not in the age in which Mrs. Trepol or Rosamund Trevelyan had grown up and learned their respective places in Borcombe.

"I know," he told her, "but sometimes the law must do what has to be done, and worry about the fitness of it afterward. I think she would have been glad to be a party to settling her family's affairs."

"Is that what you're doing, sir?" Mrs. Trepol asked earnestly.

"It's what I'm trying to do. To explain the deaths of Olivia Marlowe and Nicholas Cheney. To set it right."

She nodded, as if she understood.

"Thank you, sir," she said quietly. "I'd not like to think of them in pain and grief over what they did. A sad end to two lives, that was. I could never feel quite right about it, and I couldn't see the purpose. We have to live the lives we've been given, there's naught else for it. God doesn't give us a choice. That's what the church says. Suffering teaches in its own way."

"Yes, sometimes," he said, knowing how close he himself had come more than once to ending his own suffering.

She nodded again, and looked around her for her cat. Rutledge turned and started up the walk again.

Mrs. Trepol said, tentatively, "Sir?"

"Yes?" He only half turned back towards her, wanting to go on to the inn and read the statements.

"If you're finished with us, well, sir, I was wondering if maybe you'd know what was best to do with them boxes Mr. Stephen gave me to hold for him. I kept expecting Mr. Chambers to come and fetch them, after Mr. Stephen died, but he hasn't. Maybe he doesn't want them any more, now that Mr. Stephen is dead? Just some old things, he told me, some treasures he wanted to keep for himself, memories of the family, he said. Nothing but a boy's foolishness, he said, but he didn't want them left behind in the empty house and he wasn't ready to take them up to London with him, no room in the car with all those things Miss Susannah and the others wanted to carry away."

Rutledge turned and looked at her in the late evening light, at the plain, earnest face that waited for him to do what was best.

"I thought of mentioning it to Miss Rachel, but they're Mr. Stephen's things, and I haven't seen Miss Susannah by herself, only with Mr. Daniel there, and I didn't know—I thought perhaps that wasn't what Mr. Stephen would want. He'd said I was to keep the boxes for *him*, you see. Just for him, as a favor. And he was always a hard one to say no to, so I thought I'd just ask and you might tell me what was best. They're not my things—I wouldn't want to do anything wrong."

He couldn't turn to see if Rachel was still in her doorway. He couldn't be sure she wouldn't see him carrying boxes away.

Instead, he scooped up the cat that was coming through the open gate, and said, quietly, "Show me."

Mrs. Trepol went indoors, and Rutledge, still carrying the cat, followed her. In a closet set in the hall between her bedroom and the kitchen there was a stack of boxes, three of them. To the other side two coats, a rack of gardening boots, and a line of old umbrellas crowded the narrow space.

Rutledge had already put down the squirming cat, and he stood there staring for a moment at the boxes. Then he lifted down the first of the three and opened it carefully. Mrs. Trepol turned away, as if afraid she might be trespassing if she looked at the contents.

He felt no such compunction.

The first box held Olivia's notebooks of verse, annotated and revised, her record of creative thought, the process of making words do her bidding. He regarded the neat rows thoughtfully, not reading any of them but paying silent homage to them as his fingers gently touched their spines. The second box held contracts, letters, and bank records. He was amazed at how well good verse paid. The third was a collection of many things, photographs, a genealogy of the Trevelyan family, personal letters, childhood scribbling that gradually foretold the growth of a formidable talent, and a number of books with her name in lovely script on the flyleaves.

Rutledge, trying to hide his disappointment and quell Hamish's fierce litany of "I told you so!" prodded the contents again, as if expecting them to produce, by magic, the answers he wanted. Mrs. Trepol had gone into the kitchen to feed her cat, and he squatted on the wide floorboards, refusing to give up.

It wasn't until then that he noticed that some of the contents, stacked as if in a file drawer, were higher than the others. Lifting them out gently, he found a slim journal under this batch, and took it out in its turn.

The hand was strong and clear, the writing of a woman who had used a pen most of her life and was at home with words.

Not a journal, a letter to her half brother. He skimmed it swiftly.

Dear Stephen,

There are some things you must know, and I shall not be here to tell them to you. I'm sorry about that, to leave you with these revelations when you are grieving for us. But I must arm you for what's to come. I have done my best to protect you and Susannah. For one thing, I have left the house in such a way that it must be sold, and you've been aware for years that that was my wish as well as Nicholas'. For another, I have kept you in ignorance as long as I dared, and drawn the lightning myself all these years. By dying, I have set him free at last. And you will be safe now. You have nothing he wants. I have promised him that. But who can know what the future holds? Circumstances change, and I cannot foresee every possibility. The time may come when what I am writing down here is all you have. Whether you believe me or not, I pray you'll trust me and for your own sake, keep the confidence I am sharing with you. Vengeance will only bring you and Susannah down into the pit. And my death will have been for nothing!

Let me tell you, then, about the murderer who has lived with us for all of your life and most of mine . . .

25

$\mathcal{R}$utledge stopped there and closed the journal, returning it to its resting place. Hamish for once was silenced, his voice if not his presence shut down in the face of truth. Rutledge felt his heart racing, his mind torn between triumph and depression. Triumphant that there was something more than lines of verse on which to base his case, and depressed that Olivia Marlowe had had to sacrifice herself to keep her younger half brother and sister alive. Had that been what drove her to suicide? A threat against Stephen: *his life or yours?*

Was that the bargain struck with Lucifer? Or only a part of it?

Mrs. Trepol stuck her head around the kitchen door and said, "Will you be taking them with you, sir? Mr. Stephen's things?"

Rutledge got to his feet and began to stack the boxes into the closet again.

"Go on keeping them safe for now," he told Mrs. Trepol. "Let them stay where they are. I'll come for them myself before I leave. Sooner, if I can. And I wouldn't bother either Miss Rachel or Miss Susannah about them now. They've got enough on their minds, I don't want to worry them about Mr. Stephen at the moment."

She thanked him gravely and followed him to her door, closing it after him.

Hamish, never silenced for very long, had found his voice again. "I'll hear no crowing, now or later! Ye didn't find them, did you? They had to come to you, out of nowhere, and you can't take any of the credit for that!"

"I don't want credit," Rutledge said, walking down the path and closing the gate behind him, still torn between taking the boxes with him and leaving them where they were. He turned towards the inn once more, only part of his mind taking in the emptiness of the street, the quietness—no noisy children, no neighbors gossiping over garden walls, no young couples strolling hand in hand through the evening light. He'd seen it before, the way villages drew inward in a time of crisis. "I'm starting with the statements. After that, I'll have Harvey collect that letter. Once I've organized all my own information clearly in black and white, he'll be able to see how the letter corroborates it. And if he can see it, London will have to do the same."

"And what about Stephen FitzHugh? Did he find yon letter? Was that why he left the boxes here?"

"He must have read it," Rutledge said tiredly. "He was her executor because she trusted him. That may have been her only mistake. I believe Stephen had changed after the war. Rachel said much the same thing, that he wasn't the same man when he came home. My God, how few of us are!" There was bitterness in his voice, hearing again Rachel's diatribe, and feeling no triumph for what he'd accomplished this day, only doubt over his methods. Beside him the tip of the church tower was touched by the slanting brightness, like a beacon. It gave him no comfort.

Hamish clicked his tongue in disagreement.

"Damn it, look at the facts, then! He decided on a memorial— that was the word Rachel used—instead of selling the house. That went against Olivia's express wishes, and yet he hid the boxes where no one could find them and stumble on the truth. I think Stephen looked at his choices and felt he could turn the Hall into a museum by blackmailing the killer into allowing it. That was arrogance, not courage."

A fisherman, coming up from the strand, caught sight of Rutledge walking towards him and made a point of crossing the street to the far side, to avoid passing him. Yes, the village had drawn its conclusions . . .

"You can't know what was in his mind!"

"No. But I know he left the boxes with Mrs. Trepol. He didn't put them in the car to take to London. He didn't leave them in the house where someone else might have come across them. He didn't give them to the solicitor, Chambers. He put them in the care of a woman who would follow his instructions exactly, and he knew that."

"Aye, but Stephen FitzHugh fell down the stairs. It was an accident, and you said as much yourself."

"I still believe that."

Rutledge had reached the inn, pushing open the door. It was dark and silent, except for lights at the end of the kitchen passage. He carried the statements to his room and locked them in his suitcase along with the small bits of gold before finding Trask and asking that some dinner be sent upstairs. For once the landlord had nothing to say when he brought up the tray. It was as if the village was shunning him.

Later Rutledge walked through the gloaming towards Sadie's cottage. The setting sun still struck the headland with a rich golden light, but in the narrow valleys it was already that soft blue dusk that stole color from the land and left it almost in limbo between day and night.

Sadie was in her garden, weeding a row of carrots. She straightened her back as he came down the path towards her and stared at him in silence.

He felt a sense of guilt, as if it was written in his face that he'd been there the night before, digging among the pansies. But he knew it was impossible for her to be sure—to have seen anything, heard anything.

"She doesna' need to hear or see," Hamish reminded him. "She has the gift."

"Good evening," Rutledge began, keeping his voice neutral. "I've come to ask you why you didn't walk across to the Hall to talk to Constable Dawlish. He waited, hoping to speak to you."

267

"Let him wait," she said. "I've naught to say to him."

"To me then. Will you speak to me?"

"I've told you before—"

"That you want no part of the Gabriel Hound! I know. I won't ask you about him, not directly. But I hope you can tell me more about Olivia. How she managed to keep such secrets, young as she was. How she grew into the woman she was, without breaking under the strain. And then this spring, why she chose to take her own life. If she expected to bring him down with her, or if she'd given up. I need Olivia's help, and she's dead. But she trusted you. Will you let her speak through you? I'm ready to bring this killer into a courtroom, and I need all the secrets now. Except his name. I know that. Finally."

She cocked her head to one side and examined him. "I'd not be in your shoes, then. There's no mercy in him."

"That's why I must finish this tonight." His voice was gentle now.

"Did you come in the night? Last night?"

"Yes. I came. I found Richard. There are pansies at his feet."

Something in her face crumpled. But she said nothing.

"She couldn't stop the hounds," he said. "She couldn't bring him to justice. But she did tried to leave the evidence, one way or another. In hope. Don't let it be wasted! Let me see that justice is done for her."

Sadie pulled her black shawl closer about her thin shoulders. Weighing him. Judging him. "He's run free all these years. He'll slip any leash put on him. And come back here."

"No one comes back from the gallows." He searched for something else to convince her. "And the dead can sleep in peace, then."

"I'd like that," she answered after a time. "Before I die, I'd like to be certain *sure* of that."

He thought she was still going to refuse. He thought, watching the play of emotions on her lined, tired face, the telltale eyes, that he was going to lose her.

But she straightened her back again and started to walk towards the cottage door. "Come inside, and I'll make tea. And answer your questions."

Sadie was the only person connected with the family that Olivia hadn't written about in her poems. He'd noticed that omission last night, and now he understood it. He'd been right to look behind the façade.

He followed the old woman through the low doorway and took out his notebook. She gestured for him to sit, and the cat on the window ledge stared at him through slitted eyes as he took the chair Sadie indicated. In silence she put the kettle on, got out cups and the tin of tea.

He waited, giving her space and time.

When the small teapot was set on the table and she began to pour, he asked his first question. She handed him his cup before she answered.

And in the next hour, he was very glad after all that she hadn't come to the Hall to be interviewed by Constable Dawlish.

Her voice was shaking when she started. A thin, frail thread of sound that worried him, made him careful neither to overwhelm nor overtire her. He could see, too, when it became a catharsis, like confession before a priest. A deep and emotional release that welled up slowly, and yet brought with it waves of intense feelings. She wasn't retelling an old story, she was quite literally reliving old and very bitter griefs. Buried so long they were part of bone and sinew, and a sense of failure. She was—he'd been told it early on—by nature and profession a healer.

"No, we none of us suspected Anne had been killed," she replied slowly to his first question. "But Miss Olivia, she fretted herself near to death over it, and Mr. Adrian—her grandfather, that was—said it was because they were one flesh, Anne and Olivia. But it was deeper than that. The child had nightmares and sometimes I'd be called in to sit beside the bed, a lamp in the corner with a shawl thrown over it, to hold her hand. Mr. Nicholas was only a wee thing, but he'd stand at the door and watch his sister with those deep dark eyes of his, and it was as if he knew what she was suffering. But Miss Olivia, she never spoke of what was in her heart. Not even to her mother. After a time she was better, and yet not the same ever again. She'd sit with a book in her lap, and not know

269

a word on the page. She'd be standing by the window, looking out, and never see what was beyond the glass. I'd tended wounded soldiers in my time. This was a wounded child."

"When did she first mention the Gabriel Hound to you? Or was it you who told her?"

"One day she found a book in her grandfather's library, and read about them. 'Twas an old story, and she wanted to know if I'd heard of it, and of course I had. She wanted to know then if I'd believed in it, and I said, 'Child, I've seen the Turks, I don't need to fear any hounds!' And she answered me with that straight look of hers. 'I've heard them. The night Anne died.' It was all she said, and after that, I found myself lying awake of nights, listening too. Because you took Miss Olivia's flights of fancy serious. She was a *knowing* one."

"Then why didn't she speak to her mother? Or Adrian Trevelyan? Surely they'd have believed her."

"I asked her once. She said, 'I was warned.' And she wouldn't budge from that."

He felt the cold on the back of his neck, as if something had touched him where the hackles rise. Small wonder Olivia had lived in her own world for so very long. She had been frightened into it, and it had become her sanctuary.

Sadie's eyes brimmed with pain. He hastily changed directions.

"Tell me about Richard's death."

She looked at him over her cup before taking a long swallow. "You know about that. It's the burying you want to hear."

Surprised, he said, "You knew what she'd done?"

"Not then. Not when it happened, no. But once I found her crying over that little garden she'd wanted to make on the hillside, and when I smoothed her hair and told her her little brother was with God and happy, she turned to me and said in a voice that curdled my blood, 'God doesn't know where he *is*! I should have let them bury him in the vault with the others, but I thought—I thought it might make Mother happier if he *wasn't* found. If there was hope alive. I thought—I thought the one who'd killed him would be terrified he'd come back and point a finger, and it would make him confess, and I was *wrong*!' I can hear her, clear as I hear

270

you, and it wrung my heart, I tell you! It was later I got the whole story from her, but by then Mr. James had shot himself, and it was better to leave Miss Rosamund with some hope, however small it was. So we did."

Rutledge looked up from his notes. He doubted that anyone else in the village would have taken that step with Olivia. It was a measure of Sadie's understanding of a fragile child. "Did Nicholas know?" he asked.

"Nicholas knew everything," she replied, "and held his tongue because Miss Olivia couldn't prove a word of it then. He was afraid the blame'd turn on her, you see. That they'd say she must've killed the boy herself, because she'd hid him, and was now trying to blame someone else. It was a terrible fix to be in. I thought it would be the death of them both. But Miss Olivia was strong! And he gave her all the courage he had, more than many a man possesses. I never saw such courage in a lad. These were children, mind you, carrying a secret too heavy for them. It made them older than their years. But they thought it had *stopped*, you see! When Miss Rosamund married Mr. FitzHugh. Mr. Cormac and Mr. Nicholas, they went away to school as it was set out they should, a governess was found for Miss Olivia, the twins were born, and the house was happy again. For ten year or more."

"Because *he* had to be patient. To wait until he himself was ready."

"Aye," she told him sadly. "The worst, in a way, was to come. Mr. Brian was thrown by his horse, they said. Nicholas was there on the strand, speaking to him not half an hour before. Miss Rosamund wasn't in the Hall, she was out in the gardens somewhere. Mr. Nicholas went to find her and that was when Mr. Brian died. But not before Mr. Brian had told Mr. Nicholas that Mr. Cormac, he wanted to change his name to Trevelyan, and would he, Mr. Nicholas, speak to Rosamund about it. Mr. Nicholas asked why Mr. Brian shouldn't ask her himself, and Mr. Brian said, 'It's not my place. I'm not a Trevelyan, and Mr. Cormac isn't a FitzHugh.' Mr. Nicholas, he didn't understand what Mr. Brian meant, but Mr. Brian just shook his head and said, 'No, I love your mother very

271

deep, and I'll not ask favors of her! Let her do it out of her heart, not for my sake or Cormac's.' "

"Did Nicholas ever mention that conversation to his mother?"

"Lord, no! Before he'd found her, they set up a shout about Mr. Brian being bad hurt, and Mr. Nicholas, he looked like a ghost walking and never spoke of it to a soul except Olivia, and that was only after the funeral. I was the one laid out Mr. Brian, when they brought him up the stairs and put him in the bedroom beyond the landing. Looking for a clean shirt, so's to make him presentable for Miss Rosamund, I found a letter ready to mail in his drawer, stuck deep under them. It was to Mr. Chambers, and it set out, starkly, the circumstances of Mr. Cormac's birth. But when I spoke of it to Miss Olivia and we went to look for it, it was gone. Mr. Chambers, he never got it."

"You read it? When you found it?"

She got up and went to the door to let the cat out into the night. He caught the breath of the sea and knew that the wind had changed direction. "Have you never lived in a house with servants? They aren't deaf as posts and blind as bats. It was buried amongst his shirts, sir, not in his desk. I'd never have *touched* the papers in his desk, but it fell out on the floor and the sheet of paper went this way, the envelope that. I picked 'em up and read the one before putting it in the other and setting it where it belonged, in the desk. And it was gone from there the next day."

"You're certain Mrs. FitzHugh herself hadn't take it?"

"Well, as to that, sir, we couldn't very well ask, could we, now! But later, when she was restless and uneasy in her mind, wandering the house all hours of the night, trying for sleep and not finding it, I wondered. Mr. Adrian, her father, hadn't wanted her to marry Mr. Brian, and she knew it, but Mr. Brian was a kind man, he made her laugh and he had no eye for her money. The house'd gone to Miss Olivia, but the money was still Miss Rosamund's. Mr. Brian gave no thought to it. He was happy if she was, and he gave her the twins, and Miss Rosamund adored them. It wasn't a bad marriage to my way of thinking. Then Mr. Chambers, he started coming around when the period of mourning was finished, and Miss Rosamund, she looked for a time to be herself again, roses in her cheeks and that special way she had of tilting her head as if listening to something sweet in the air, whenever she was happy."

Sadie, standing at the open door, shut it as the cat came back inside, and went to the hearth to stand. She was tired, her face deeply lined. But Rutledge thought he couldn't have stopped her now if he'd tried.

"That was in June. By September she was dead, and they said it was by her own hand. But Lord, sir, I knew how much of the laudanum she'd took! I was the one that had to beg her each night to swallow *half* a draught to ease the despair she'd felt all through that last month. But she'd shake her head and say, 'No, Sadie, I need my wits about me!' 'You'll have no wits left, if ye don't rest!' I told her plain out, but she said 'There's something I must do, and I'm not sure exactly how to set about it. I'm not going to marry Mr. Chambers. Or anyone else. I've got my children to live for, and that's the most important part of my life now.' There was no changing her mind, she was that strong."

"She'd decided against marrying Thomas Chambers? Had she actually told him that?"

"Oh, lord, yes, but he was there every weekend, come to call and dine with her. I heard her say to him once, 'I've killed them all. George and James and Brian. I can't bear to see you die, and I won't, I tell you!' And he said, 'That's nonsense, my love, you're letting grief turn your thoughts.' She just looked at him, her face sad. 'I'm bad luck, Tom, I'd rather stay single than wear widow's weeds ever again."

"What made her think she had killed them?" He was fascinated, pretending to drink his tea and over the rim of his cup watching the old face in the lamp's light, trying to read the eyes.

"Ah, but did she? I wondered about that for the longest time. Miss Olivia, *she* said it was deeper than that, she thought Mr. Cormac, he was in love with Miss Rosamund. But there was no speaking of it, not to Miss Rosamund. She'd smile and say her spirits were fine, she'd just decided that marriage was not worth the grieving afterward."

"Then how did she come to die?"

"That were odd, sir. One day she said to Miss Olivia, 'I think

I'll ask Tom to come for the weekend. I need to speak to him. Legal matters, and perhaps after that's done, we may find it possible to talk about other things.' I was on the stairs, helping Mr. Cormac and Mr. Nicholas move a chest down from the attics that Mr. Cormac wanted to take back to his London rooms. You could hear their voices as you came down, talking in the drawing room. Then Miss Rosamund, she came out, she looked up at me, and her face turned that bleak I wanted to weep. I didn't know what'd unsettled her, but it was there in her eyes. Cold as death. It was Miss Olivia who found the note she left, and burned it in the grate."

"A *note*? I was never told that there was a note found when Rosamund died!" Rutledge said, appalled.

Sadie sat down, heavily and with great effort, then asked him to fetch her homemade wine, from the small cupboard by the dry sink. When she'd finished half the glass and got her breath with more comfort, she said, "No. Miss Olivia, she burned it, like I said. It was written in a scrawl you'd hardly recognize, and hidden under the pillow. Just a name. And a warning. 'Twas all Miss Olivia needed. She went whiter than she was and bent over her mother's body in such grief I couldn't bear it. So I walked out of the room and went to fetch Mr. Nicholas. The note was never spoken of again. I didn't need to be told. I'd heard the hounds myself since poor little Richard was taken. I knew who'd put the overdose in Miss Rosamund's water. Not her, not that woman so full of life and love—she'd not have gone to her God with self-murder on her hands!" It was spoken with a vehemence that brought an angry flush to Sadie's cheeks. In a stronger voice she added, "The twins, they were still too young to know anything about such things, only that their mother'd taken ill in the night and overdosed herself. Mr. Chambers, he was heartbroken. You'd have thought he was the grieving widower, not the family's lawyer. It was the Gabriel hounds that whispered in her ear, bending over her as she dropped into that last sleep, and she'd known, she'd *known* where the danger was!"

"The danger to herself?"

"Oh, aye, that, and the danger to Miss Olivia. Because the truth of the matter was, you see, Mr. Cormac'd set his cap next for Miss

Olivia. If he couldn't become a Trevelyan in one way, he'd do it another. And Miss Rosamund, she wouldn't marry him. Nor after begging *her*, how could he ask for Miss Olivia, without it all coming out? She'd have told Mr. Chambers too when he came, sure as God gave her the breath. It was what she'd decided, after all the worry and the sleepnessness. He was in a bind, and the easy answer was to remove the light of that house. Miss Rosamund, she'd used every excuse to put Mr. Chambers off, and he hadn't run, he still wanted her with all his heart. He'd have done whatever she asked. He'd have questioned Olivia, too, and she might have told him at long last what was on her soul. But when Miss Rosamund died, Mr. Chambers was so sunk in his own pain that there was no way of reaching out to him. Miss Olivia buried her mother and told the world that grief had overwhelmed her in the night. Mr. Smedley, he loved that family, and he wouldn't hear of suicide. Nor Dr. Penrith. He said her hands had been shaking, she'd been in a muddle from no sleep, and it was easy for her to make such a tragic mistake—dosing herself rather than waking one of the servants from their rest. She was that thoughtful, people believed it was true. And her killer counted on that to go scot-free! Who was there to cry murder? Miss Olivia? Who burned that paper?"

"If it was murder—"

She looked at him pityingly. "I've laid out more than half this village in my time, dead of accidents, dead of sickness, dead of broken hearts—it's common enough, dying. Aye, sometimes murder's been done too, but Dr. Penrith was a good man, he could find that needle in the haystack. And we all knew each other well enough to guess whose hand had done it: the husband, the lover, the jealous neighbor. But it was different at the Hall. There was none there who didn't love Miss Rosamund dearly, and Miss Olivia knew they'd fight against her, unwilling to believe any such tale as she could spin. He was careful, and very clever. *There was no proof!* But that was when Miss Olivia and Mr. Nicholas took Mr. Brian's children out of their will. No house, and the money tied tight in trust. However long and loud the hound might bay, it wouldn't be for their blood. But he came for her, anyway, in the end. Because of the poems. Because he has the money now to do as he pleases.

Because she knew what she knew, and it was time for him to marry. There's a new provision in the deed of that house that if Cormac FitzHugh ever chooses to live in the Hall, he must never marry. Mr. Chambers, he thought it was because Miss Olivia loved Mr. Cormac and didn't want him to bring another bride there. But she said it was her house, she'd do as she liked with it, and nobody could stop her. Which was true enough. And Mr. Cormac, he's never married. But he'll live in the Hall, and I hope, with all my heart, that the hounds come for him there, in the dark, when there's no help to be had!"

She began to weep, tears running down her white, withered face in ugly runnels, as if there had never been places for them to fall before, and now they couldn't find a way.

Rutledge found himself breathing hard, his body tight with black and wordless rage. He gave her his handkerchief and she took it, fumbling in the blindness of the tears. She touched her face with a dignity that was heart wrenching, because these were not tears for herself. She still hadn't cried for herself.

276

26

After a long silence, Rutledge asked, "Why did Olivia choose to die? And why did Nicholas die with her?"

Sadie shook her head. "If she wanted you to know that, she'd of told you. In her poetry. Somehow."

And, God help him, she had.

Huskily Rutledge said, "More to the point, did she tell you?"

"She didn't have to. I may be old and tired and useless, but there was more to me, once, and a heart to match it. I knew without the telling!"

"Was Cormac ever in love with Olivia?"

"He was deathly afraid of her, if I'm a judge. It was the only thing he ever showed fear of, and that fear was nigh on to superstitious! Miss Olivia said he didn't believe in God, but that he believed with whatever heart he had, her death would surely be his death."

For the first time in a very long hour, Hamish stirred and spoke as clearly as if he'd sat there at the table with them from the start. Or because of the tension that held him like a vise, had Rutledge himself formed the words aloud? Somehow he was never, afterward, sure.

"She's wrong there, it was no' her death that brought him down, but Nicholas Cheney's. And yon lassie not understanding it, and sending for the Yard."

Sadie looked up at him, her eyes no longer clear and sharp. "Aye, it's true enough," she answered. "It was Mr. Nicholas dying. But how could *he* have left Mr. Nicholas alive? He'd have come for Mr. Cormac with his bare hands the instant anything happened to Miss Olivia. However carefully it were done. That's all that saved Mr. Cormac for twenty years, Miss Olivia not wanting to see Mr. Nicholas hanged! No, they had to die together. That was the only chance Mr. Cormac had in this world."

Rutledge had written down her words, and afterward, when he'd made more tea and coaxed her out of weariness and the peace of forgetfulness, with his help she read them over and with a shaking hand, signed at the bottom of the last page.

Now, *now* he could walk into a courtroom with all the evidence any barrister might need. Except for what Stephen hadn't trusted to Olivia's boxes. The FitzHugh family history.

It was late when Rutledge walked through the woods, trying to cope with the emotions that still consumed him, listening to his own footsteps on the path, the soles of his shoes grinding on the gritty flint and earth like the mills of the gods. Slowly but surely— But he didn't want slowly, he wanted a reckoning now, bloody and final and with vengeance driving it.

And Hamish, ferociously wrestling for control, was losing.

As he rounded the last bend in the trees, there were lights ahead of him. And behind the bright windows, the heavy thunderheads of a storm building. Flashes of reddish gold lightning laced the clouds, dancing among them as the roll of distant sound like guns firing out to sea reached him. Rutledge felt a cleaving tightness in his stomach.

"Before the battle, aye," Hamish remembered with him, "always the guns. But in God's name, you're not in France now, not *tonight*! That's a storm coming in fast, and yon house has nae claim on you now. Nor the man in it! Your work's done. This is no' your fight, man!"

Pausing in the shelter of the darkness, he turned his eyes back to the house. There were lamps in several rooms. The drawing room. The study where Olivia and Nicholas had died. An upstairs bedroom that had been Rosamund's . . .

An invitation, then. Of a kind. "I'm here. I know what you've done this day. Come and face me yourself, if you dare!"

Hamish said, "Not when ye're sae angry! Not with the darkness on ye! It's not worth dying for, just to see how he'll take his defeat!"

"I'm not dying in there. And neither is he, if I can help it. He's laid down the challenge. I won't walk away from it. Olivia didn't." But he knew very well it was the heat in his own blood speaking.

Hamish retorted, "This isna' the law, it's vengeance! And it's for her—all for that bluidy *woman*!"

He didn't answer, his mind already busy, calculating, weighing—

There was a scent of pipe tobacco on the breeze that ruffled the leaves over his head. Faint but real. Then the sound of feet walking closer.

Rutledge turned his head. Behind him on the path the rector's voice came out of the darkness, low and passionate.

"The people of Borcombe are simple, but they aren't stupid. They've talked to each other, and put most of the story together by now. So have I. And I've spent my day trying to undo the harm you've done here. You've shaken their faith, and in the end they'll blame themselves for all those deaths. They'll shoulder the burden for twenty-five years of wickedness, for not recognizing or stopping it."

Rutledge said, "I've seen it happen before in murder cases. '*I could have prevented it.*' But not this time. Not with this killer. Tell them that."

"If I understood *why* . . ."

Rutledge turned his attention back to the headland. Gauging the storm and what was waiting in the house. The lamps were still burning.

"The bedrock of my faith is redemption. That everyone can be saved, because deep down there's some goodness to search out and nurture," Smedley said tiredly. "I want to help."

"No. There's no goodness to find here. Go back to the village and leave this to me. Here, take this with you." He handed Smedley the statement he'd taken from the old woman. "Keep it safe for me."

"What is it?"

"Just give it to Harvey. It's finished. Or it will be, in a little while."

"*That's* what frightens me. Finished how? Olivia wouldn't have wanted it to end in violence. As a man of God, I can try to reach out, to offer the church's solace and forgiveness."

Rutledge, on edge and wishing the rector back in his church, said savagely, "I'll make it plain. This man has killed for the sake of killing. Whatever he may tell you, whatever reasons he may offer, whatever logic he can bring to bear for his defense, he killed because it suited his purpose! And because the opportunity was there. And the power of shaping his own fate with his own hands he found exhilarating. Whatever went wrong in him, it isn't going to be exorcised by the church. Or by you."

"No! There is good in every human being. I believe it devoutly!"

"Then go down on your knees before the altar and pray for guidance. I need it! Or, if you want to be useful, find Inspector Harvey and tell him I require a warrant. But send Constable Dawlish around to the beach by boat. Just in case he tries to leave in that direction."

"By boat? There's a storm coming."

"I know. Hurry, man! There isn't much time."

Rutledge was already walking away as he spoke. Smedley stayed in the enclosed darkness of the trees as the Londoner came to the end of the path and started up the drive, not concealing his presence, not slowing his pace.

Hamish said roughly, "All right then, ye'll be fighting his darkness and your own, but ye're a clever man, and ye canna' show weakness, it's what he'll watch for. Let the words roll off his tongue and your back."

But Rutledge didn't hear.

Slowly, one by one, the lamps were extinguished, plunging the house into darkness. All but one he could see in the drawing room, with its faint glimmer in the hall's tall windows.

The thunder made him flinch again, his nerves raw, his senses already at fever pitch.

Lightning flickered, and through the windows of the room where Olivia had died, it seemed to dance fleetingly, as if there was a living presence there.

At the steps, Rutledge hesitated, but the door didn't open, and he took out the key he still kept in his pocket.

The shaft of light falling from the drawing room door like a spear was very bright after the darkness outside, making him blink, and he hesitated, aware of what might come out of the hall's shadows at him. Then he turned towards the drawing room, his footsteps brashly loud in the stillness.

There was an airlessness too in the house that seemed to suffocate him, in spite of the high ceilings and the open door behind him.

He could smell the trenches again, feel the earth shaking under his feet as the barrage began. The sappers were still deep underground. He wasn't sure they'd make it out in time—they'd be buried alive in moving earth, as he'd been, breath shut off by tons of soil rising high into the night sky and then collapsing in on them—on him—shutting out everything, sight, hearing, air—

Hamish stirred, uneasily calling out to him.

Rutledge forced himself back into the present, making himself concentrate on the light, not the dark.

On the threshold of the drawing room, he stopped again. There was a decanter and two glasses on the small table by the hearth, beneath Rosamund's portrait. One of the glasses was half full. The other empty.

As if waiting for him . . . they'd both been right, he and Hamish . . .

Leashing his anger with an iron will, he crossed the silent room and stood looking at the portrait for a time, his eyes seeing it, his ears listening to the sounds of the house. It seemed to be electric with tension.

And then Cormac FitzHugh was standing in the doorway.

"She belongs here, doesn't she? I was sorry that Susannah insisted on taking her away."

As if Rutledge was a guest, and Cormac, the host, was making idle conversation before dinner. Rutledge turned to see the man's face, and felt a coldness in his blood.

There was nothing there of anger or tension or a desire to kill. If anything, Cormac's expression was pleasant, welcoming. But the brilliant blue eyes were fire.

Answering him, Rutledge said, "Yes. She's the spirit of the house."

Cormac smiled at him. "That's a very Irish way of putting it."

"Is it?"

Cormac came to the table and picked up his drink, then gestured with the glass. "Won't you join me?"

Rutledge said nothing, and Cormac went on easily, "There's no laudanum in it. Will you join the search for this new Ripper?"

"He isn't my business. Never was. But Olivia Marlowe is."

"Ah." He lifted the glass again, gesturing this time to the portrait. "You didn't know her as I did. Olivia was only a pale shadow of Rosamund."

"She had a remarkable talent. Olivia."

"Her poetry? But talent is transient. Fame is transient. We are all going to die some day, more's the pity. It seems man has learned to do everything except live forever. When we achieve earthly immortality, I suppose we'll finally have the power of God."

"I'm not sure I'd want that. Immortality. To live forever would be—tiresome. Eternal youth, that might be more useful."

Cormac laughed, the handsome face lighting from within. "Would you choose now, or before 1914?"

"Before. I have no fond memories of the war."

"No, I don't think you have. I've read your medical reports—I still have connections in London with the people I worked with during the war. And most things are available for money. A very intriguing file. I'm amazed you survived. But you've nothing to fear from me. I don't plan to expose you."

No, Rutledge thought. You'd much rather kill me.

He said aloud, "It doesn't matter. I never expected to keep my secrets forever. If they come out, I'll find something else to do with my life." But he knew how great a lie that was . . .

"Or end it?" Cormac asked softly, responding to the silent thought.

"You can pray for that. Will you be here when I leave?"

"It depends on what you've come to find." For the first time something echoed in the quiet voice.

After a moment Rutledge said, "Why should I make it easy for you?" and walked past Cormac, back into the hall. To his surprise, Cormac actually let him go. But he could feel the man's eyes still watching him, and he knew it wasn't over.

He crossed the hall, taking the stairs two at a time while Hamish reminded him that Stephen had fallen here, the words tumbling like the man had done, over and down and crashing into the floor below. Yet only Rutledge could hear them. At the top of the steps in the gallery, he made his decision, then took up the small lamp from the table where it had been set, waiting, nearly lost in the surrounding blackness.

Down the passage to the left, not the right, past the closed doors of bedrooms, the darkness here astir with feelings Rutledge couldn't name as the lamplight made a circle of orange light around him. The oil was hot beneath the glass, warming his hand. He thought of Olivia, and of Nicholas. Did one ever come back from the dead? It was an interesting question. He hoped it would be some time before he discovered the answer to it.

The silence in Stephen's room was palpable. In the lamplight the furnishings seemed stark and somehow dauntingly empty, heavily shadowed.

He paused in the doorway for a moment, listening to the sound of his own breathing and Hamish's trepidation.

"Leave now!" the soft Scottish voice repeated over and over. "*Now!*"

But Rutledge crossed to the bed and knelt, his hands moving along the struts that held the springs in place. Fingers careful, sensing their way over the strips of dusty wood.

His nails struck the book's binding, his fingers stretched and closed around it, drawing it out with infinite circumspection.

Then it was in his grasp.

He stood, and in the silence there was now a humming of tension, like the distant baying of hounds. The hairs on the back of his neck lifted in a primeval reaction. Hamish, hissing malevolently, heard it too.

There was very little time.

He opened the slim book. Thumbed through the pages once, then again. Found the family genealogy that had been written carefully here, ever since a century-dead FitzHugh had held this prayer book in his hand at confirmation. Long ago in Ireland. In another time and another world . . .

The sound was louder, the tension something that made his body tighten with anticipation. It was like waiting for the Huns to come over the top, and yet—different. The first rumble of nearby thunder shook the house, and his pulses leaped, as if the first shells had landed.

"Hurry!" Hamish urged him.

With one swift movement he drew his pocketknife, opened it, and gently slit the handwritten pages at the binding so that they fell out in his hands.

He checked once more as the footsteps rang out on the bare wood, coming closer, boldly stalking down the passage towards him.

Yes. He'd gotten them all. The records of a family—and a single line at the end: "Cormac FitzHugh. Mother unknown. Father unknown. Taken from a ditch along the road to Kilarney. FitzHugh by courtesy, not adoption." And the date. The Gabriel Hound, unblessed—and cursed. Without a name or blood of his own.

Lifting out the book on Irish horses from the others Stephen had kept on the table by the window, Rutledge slipped the pages inside, then returned the heavy volume to its place and the closed knife to his pocket.

Was it his imagination or did the echoes seem to double, triple the number of footfalls? As if there were hordes in the passage, crowding it, elbowing each other, cutting off all space and air.

Sudden panic seemed to choke him. He fought it down, refusing to give in to it. *But he was trapped here.* Damn it, he wasn't in France, this was Cornwall!

He was facing the open doorway, the little prayer book in his left hand, his balance even, ready for whatever was coming for him.

And then once more Cormac FitzHugh came out of the darkness and into the light. He was in his shirtsleeves, now. His eyes went directly to the book Rutledge held.

"I wasn't sure my father had kept it. After turning Anglican for Rosamund. Stephen swore *he* had it," he said. "But he wouldn't tell me where he'd put it before he died. I thought it was probably a lie, but I had to keep searching. Thank you for sparing me further trouble over it."

"He must have found it—and hidden it—that same morning. Did you kill him?"

"The fall would have, I think. But I gave him a more merciful end. He couldn't move. Whether it was true paralysis or temporary, I can't tell you. I twisted his neck until it snapped, then shouted for Susannah and Rachel. Give me the prayer book now, if you please."

"Interesting reading," Rutledge said, thumbing the pages lightly. "Apparently you're illegitimate. Not the stigma it once was, of course, but you have lived a public lie for many years, haven't you? Stepson to the Trevelyans. Even these days, the news wouldn't sit very well in London business circles, would it, where a gentleman's word is his bond? Especially not if it came from Stephen Trevelyan, in banking himself. His doubts, dropped in the right quarters, could have ruined you." He flipped the book closed. "Did you ever learn who your real parents were?"

"No. FitzHugh found me abandoned along a country road. Half starved, filthy, and sickly. And he took pity on me. But you're absolutely right about London, especially since the Troubles and that 1916 uprising in Dublin. England saw it as an unforgivable stab in the back, in the middle of war. Being Irish just now is the same as being a traitor. A bastard Irishman—an upstart and a nobody—Stephen swore he'd use that to ruin me in the City if I didn't help turn Trevelyan Hall into a mausoleum. *Rosamund's house!* The Hall is all I ever truly desired in this world. Even the money I've earned was only a bridge to owning it. And I wanted to come here by right, not with my tail between my legs!"

Before Rutledge could read anything more than light amusement in the man's eyes, he'd moved, swift as lightning, without conscious preparation, like a snake striking without warning.

Rutledge, expecting it, dodged, but not quite fast enough. His head, jerked back by Cormac's stiff forearm, hit the wall with a loud crack, and as light flashed behind his eyes, Cormac moved in to follow up with a blow that had the full force of his shoulder behind it.

Rutledge felt his knees buckle and his senses reel under the impact. He was nearly unconscious, Hamish fiercely yelling at him to hold on, when the third and final blow brought down a pall of blackness.

27

He awoke to black nothingness, lashed out in the primeval fear of blindness, and realized suddenly that the lamp had been taken away and he was alone. A flash of lightning told him that he was in Stephen's room, where Cormac had left him. He moved gingerly, and everything worked.

Shaking his head to clear it, Rutledge felt a wave of dizziness that threatened to send him back to his knees. Using the table's edge to pull himself to his feet, he leaned on his hands for precious seconds, willing himself into full control of his senses again. The amazing thing, he told himself, dazed still, was that he was alive.

Rutledge stumbled across the room and in the next flash of light, saw his way through the door. Thunder rattled the windows behind him.

The passage was black but there was still a lamp in the drawing room to guide him down the stairs. He ran across the hall and looked through its door.

The portrait was there, but Cormac had gone.

Where had the man hidden his car? Or had he came by boat, as Rutledge had anticipated. It was the most silent, the most secretive means of coming and going unseen. But was it still there? The boat?

Swearing as the rising wind caught the big door when he opened it, Rutledge went out into the night, down the steps, towards the strand. Ahead of him was Cormac, moving through the darkness. Which meant that he, Rutledge, couldn't have been unconscious very long.

Rutledge called out to him, shouting his name.

Cormac turned and lifted an arm mockingly.

"He wants you to come after him! That's why he didna' finish it in the house!" Hamish exclaimed. "Will you no' stop and think, man!"

Rutledge said nothing, his eyes straining to follow the figure ahead of him. But Cormac was no longer taking the path to the beach; he'd veered off towards the headland, picking up his pace. Swearing again, Rutledge plowed on, the wind tearing at his face and his coat, pushing him sideways. His head seemed to split open with the pounding pace he'd set, but he clenched his teeth and ignored it.

At the headland, where it curved to its highest point, Cormac turned. In the lightning, his pale hair blowing in the wind, his shirt white against the black clouds beyond, he seemed to glow with malevolence.

"Lucifer—!" Hamish warned.

Rutledge saved his breath and ran on until he was within a few yards of the other man.

"The way it will look," Cormac yelled, "you broke under the strain tonight. Unable to sleep, disoriented, you came out here to the headland to watch the storm, and in a wild moment of self-doubt, you went over the edge. Thunder brought back the guns, and guilt, and all the nightmares."

"Did you kill Olivia? Or did she choose her own death?"

"Ah, Olivia. She mesmerizes you as Rosamund mesmerized me. I meant what I told her the weekend before. That I wouldn't hesitate to tell London that she and Nicholas were lovers. The *Lucifer* poems created quite a stir. And I had the feeling another collection was coming out. That she hadn't finished with me. I wasn't sure I could ruin O. A. Manning, but I knew how to kill Olivia Marlowe."

"How did she answer you?"

288

"She laughed in my face and said that she might welcome the darkness, if it brought me harm. And promised to burn any new poems. She's been a sword in my flesh since I was twelve. We've been bound together like lovers, by the bonds of a mutual fear. But the tide's turning and I have to go." Then he said very distinctly, "They were not quite dead when I slipped into the house that night. I think she must have known I was there—"

The wind was snatching his words away, but Rutledge heard them and hated the man with a ferocity that was deep and cold.

Cormac, for a second time in his life, miscalculated.

This time Rutledge moved first, with such speed and anger behind it that he caught Cormac off guard and sent them both reeling back, then before either man could brake their momentum, over the edge of the cliff.

It wasn't a sheer drop. It was rock eroded by wind and weather. It was clumpy grass and earth, punctuated by straggling shrubs and heaved outcroppings. A long and rough slope that took its toll on bone and flesh as they tumbled down towards the fringe of boulders where the surf crashed whitely. The noise rose to meet them, so mixed with the thunder that there was only an endless, deafening roar.

As Rutledge's shoulder hit the slope, he grunted with the force of it, then forgot it as Cormac's body slammed into his, nearly winding them both. They grappled for a hold as they rolled and slid, yelling, cursing, pure fury fueling flailing knees and fists. Rutledge tasted blood and salt on his lips and felt a warm wetness just under his ribs, where something had ripped through the skin. Cormac's flesh was also taking a beating, but he was ignoring it with the single-mindedness of a lifetime.

Rutledge fought with the cunning and strength of the battlefield, the ruthless, unforgiving training of hand-to-hand combat. He found himself wishing fervently for a bayonet, a rifle butt, a weapon of any kind. He could feel if not hear the sucking in of breath, the grunts from the savage effort Cormac made to match him hold for hold, blow for blow. There was grit in Rutledge's teeth, one eye was half closed, and his left elbow felt numb as they came suddenly to the end of the long, ragged slope and pitched with savage momentum into the cold, wild water, shocking both of them.

In his grasp Cormac went limp.

Rutledge heaved himself up through the rough sea and pulled the other man with him.

"You aren't dead—I won't—let you die!" he shouted, gasping for air, but Cormac made no response as his face came out of the water. "Damn it—you'll hang yet!"

There was a dark smear across Cormac's forehead where he'd struck rock under the water, laying open the skin. It was bleeding ferociously.

Now Rutledge was fighting the great rocks and the surf rolling in haphazardly before the wind, and the storm seemed to be tearing at the headland above, downdrafts sending a sandpaper of grit and dirt against his face.

He clenched his teeth with the effort, feeling his body tightening then tiring in the cold water, feeling the pull of the current and the edges of the rocks and the weight of the other body he was dragging after him.

Hamish was screaming at him, and he ignored it, concentration centered on keeping Cormac's head above water even when his own sank and he seemed to swallow half the sea, unable to breathe, feeling himself choke and sputter. And start to fail. From somewhere in the whirling darkness he heard Hamish calling his name, forbidding him to die.

"Not now—not yet—by God, I won't let you go this easily!"

Or was that what he was telling Cormac, over and over in his mind?

Panting and coughing, he broke the surface again, and brought Cormac with him. The other man's weight seemed lighter now, as if he'd come to his senses again, yet he made no effort to swim or struggle.

Every muscle seemed stretched beyond its limit, but Rutledge kept one hand locked in the collar of Cormac's shirt and with the other fended off the rocks as his feet and legs pushed and pulled and dragged them against the pull of the water, in the direction of the strand. The numbed elbow sometimes gave way and they both crashed into rocks were washed high on the inpouring of heavy surf, and then were slammed back into the headland, but Rutledge refused to give up, sheer will keeping the two of them afloat. Water was everywhere, there seemed to be no end of it. He dug with his heels, bobbed, bumped, thundered into sharp edges, felt the bruising and lacerations on his back, and still held on.

I didn't survive the damned war to die in a Cornish sea! he swore to himself, again and again. I'll live to see this bastard hang!

So absorbed was he in the ordeal of surviving, he wasn't even aware that his feet had struck the shingle of the beach where it met the rocks. It caught him ill-prepared for the next surging wave.

The tide was flooding in and he was swept forward with such force that he lost his grip on Cormac. They both were dragged up the shelf, the water and the sand unmerciful to their faces and hands, then the salt burning fiercely where the flesh had been scoured open.

He lay there, digging in with his fingers and toes as the water worked to suck him out again, the tide pulling with an energy he'd long since lost. Then it was past him, and he fought now for breath, trying to stop the shuddering of his lungs and the pounding of his heart.

Beside him he heard Cormac breathe as well, roughly at first, then a long, deep draught of air. And then the man was on his knees, something in his hand, raising it high above his head and bringing it down with all the strength he'd hoarded while he let Rutledge struggle to save them both.

Hamish shouted as Rutledge rolled, and the stone came thudding down without sound, ploughing deep into the wet sand, unstoppable with the renewed power of Cormac's whole body behind it.

Enough, damn it, was *enough*!

Rutledge swung his foot and caught Cormac in the groin. He'd lost one shoe, but the toe of the other came into the soft flesh with the might of fury driving it, and Cormac screamed in a high-pitched howl of pain that could be heard above the sound of the water and the screech of the wind, rising in a gurgling, choking cry that was cut short as he doubled over in anguish, sobbing and spluttering as the next wave came in.

The cold water, Rutledge thought with fierce satisfaction, breathing hard with the effort he'd had to make, had turned out to be an ally after all . . .

Reducing Olivia's *Lucifer* to the human plane of mortal suffering.

He lay there on his back on the wet shingle, rain pouring down over his face, and felt the scrapes and bruises and aches begin to come alive. His elbow throbbed with an intensity that made him wonder if it was broken or only cracked. Under his ribs there was another sensation, of fire and ice, where something sharp had gone in, and his head was still splitting with pain. Every muscle burned with exhaustion. He wanted only to sleep.

After a long, suffering silence Cormac said, in one shuddering breath, "I knew—when I first saw you that—you were different—mettle."

"Why did you kill them?"

"You're the policeman," he said after a time. "You tell me."

There was silence again.

Then an odd passion filled Cormac's cracked voice. "The first day—the first day I came here—the Hall held me fast. There was a warmth about it—I don't know. But—Anne laughed at me, when she heard me tell a groom I'd give anything to live in such a place. I wanted to choke it back in her throat, that laughter! Instead I had to walk away and pretend I didn't care. When she fell—when I pulled at her sash to make her fall out of the tree—and she died on the grass in front of me, I realized I'd just found a way to have everything I wanted—if I was careful, and patient. After that, after that they were none of them safe."

"What about the man on the moors? Did you kill him too?" Rutledge asked, suddenly remembering.

"The tramp. There was a chance—they never found Richard, you see—I thought he'd come back one day—yes." He was still doubled over, hugging his body, his face grimacing as the waves of pain subsided in their own good time.

From somewhere in the distance they could hear voices calling.

Cormac lifted his head in the darkness, and stared at Rutledge.

"You had better kill me now. If you don't, I'll ruin you in the courtroom. They'll blame you—before I'm done—"

292

For a split second, there was an overwhelming temptation to take him at his word. Rutledge clamped down on it, the policeman in him routing the soldier who'd swiftly calculated the odds, and he heard Hamish growl when the policeman won. In satisfaction? Or regret. He was too spent to care.

"Or will they be glad to convict the Irish bastard whose deception took in half the City?" Rutledge answered, and got slowly, achingly to his feet. He reached down a hand, and then thought better of it, grabbing the back of Cormac's collar instead and dragging him to his knees.

Cormac managed to stand, half bent over, then suddenly found the strength of will to stand straight, eye to eye with Rutledge.

Lucifer had been stopped but not vanquished. Not yet.

Down the strand Constable Dawlish appeared in the heavy rain, peering towards them and shouting, "I think they're over here!"

Inspector Harvey, with Smedley at his back and Rachel coming up at the run, something in her arms—blankets, he thought as she stumbled and slipped down the path from the lawns.

Cormac swung to face them and smiled as Harvey clapped handcuffs over his wet wrists. Watching, Rutledge unconsciously braced himself. It *would* be an appalling trial. The tragedy—as always, in Rutledge's eyes—was that the murderer could never be charged with the havoc he'd brought to other people's lives, only with the deaths laid at his door. Smedley was right, it wasn't over for the villagers of Borcombe. Not for Rachel and Susannah. Not even for Olivia and Nicholas and Rosamund . . .

"And you. They'll be after breaking you on the stand," Hamish warned.

"They can *try*," he answered, silently.

Rachel, looking up at him, said in a low, strained voice as she gripped his arm with wet, icy fingers. "I have to know. Was it me that Nicholas loved, *or was it Olivia?*" The words seemed to be torn from her, as if they had never been allowed to surface from the darkness of her dread. Until now.

Rutledge shook his head. And consciously told a lie, out of infinite compassion. "He didn't want her to die alone," he said. "It took courage to make such a choice. Forgive him for it."

She bowed her head and began to cry.

When they'd taken Cormac away, and Rachel, her face set and pale, had followed Smedley back towards the village, Rutledge was left on the headland alone. Pulling one of the blankets she'd brought tighter against the cold air that had followed the storm, he limped across to where the black patch of burned grass had once been, even its shadowed outline filled in with green now, the ashes long since washed away.

He knew what had perished here in the fire Nicholas had built. Why Olivia and Nicholas chose that moonlit night of beauty in which to end it.

A love they couldn't have.

After a time . . . "I envy you both," he said softly in the night, lifting his head to look up at the room where they had died.

As he turned towards Borcombe, the wind followed, but Rutledge wasn't aware of it. He stopped at the end of the drive and looked once more at the house below the headland. It stood there dark and silent, man-made and vulnerable, yet somehow invested with a grace all its own.

And he knew, without knowing how, that Olivia was finally at peace.

But that he would be possessed, for a very long time, by the woman she had been.